Romantic Suspense

Danger. Passion. Drama.

Targeted With A Colton
Beth Cornelison

A Spy's Secret
Rachel Astor

MILLS & BOON

Beth Cornelison is acknowledged as the author of this work
TARGETED WITH A COLTON
© 2024 by Harlequin Enterprises ULC
Philippine Copyright 2024
Australian Copyright 2024
New Zealand Copyright 2024

First Published 2024
First Australian Paperback Edition 2024
ISBN 978 1 038 91772 0

A SPY'S SECRET
© 2024 by Rachel Astor
Philippine Copyright 2024
Australian Copyright 2024
New Zealand Copyright 2024

First Published 2024
First Australian Paperback Edition 2024
ISBN 978 1 038 91772 0

MIX
Paper | Supporting
responsible forestry
FSC
www.fsc.org   FSC® C001695

Published by
Harlequin Mills & Boon
An imprint of Harlequin Enterprises (Australia) Pty Limited
(ABN 47 001 180 918), a subsidiary of HarperCollins
Publishers Australia Pty Limited
(ABN 36 009 913 517)
Level 19, 201 Elizabeth Street
SYDNEY NSW 2000 AUSTRALIA

Cover art used by arrangement with Harlequin Books S.A.. All rights reserved.

Printed and bound in Australia by McPherson's Printing Group

Targeted With A Colton

Beth Cornelison

MILLS & BOON

Beth Cornelison began working in public relations before pursuing her love of writing romance. She has won numerous honours for her work, including a nomination for the RWA RITA® Award for *The Christmas Stranger*. She enjoys featuring her cats (or friends' pets) in her stories and always has another book in the pipeline! She currently lives in Louisiana with her husband, one son and three spoiled cats. Contact her via her website, bethcornelison.com.

Visit the Author Profile page
at millsandboon.com.au for more titles.

Dear Reader,

Working on a Coltons continuity with the many talented authors and editors of Harlequin Romantic Suspense is always an honour and a pleasure. *Targeted with a Colton* was no exception. I enjoyed creating Harlow and Wade, two heartbroken and struggling characters, and seeing them find each other and love again. Happily-ever-afters are why I write romance. This book also offered the special opportunity to write about PTSD companion animals and the great service they provide to our veterans. I love including animals in my stories!

I hope you enjoy this trip to Owl Creek, Idaho, as the Coltons continue to search for answers about and justice for the Ever After cult.

Happy reading,

Beth Cornelison

DEDICATION

For Kasey—mental health professional extraordinaire and sweet friend. Thank you for answering my questions!

Prologue

One year ago

First Sergeant Wade Colton stood behind the young Marine private, watching as the other man worked through the steps of setting a charge, learning the proper techniques for using munitions. The sun beat down on the back of Wade's neck, and he used his hand to wipe sweat from his brow. Private Sanders was perspiring, too, Wade noticed. Beads of moisture were popping up on the younger soldier's top lip. The private's hands were shaking as he moved through his training.

"Private Sanders, a word?" Wade said, motioning for the private to come closer to speak to him.

Private Sanders approached, then stood stiffly before Wade, his chin raised. "Sir?"

"Is there a problem, Private? You seem rather nervous."

"No problem, sir. I can do it."

"Because before you're allowed to work with live munitions, you'll have to get your jitters under control. Shaky hands and volatile explosives are not a good combination." Wade added a half smile, hoping to ease the private's tension with a degree of humor. "Wouldn't you agree?"

The other trainees who were gathered in a circle around Wade and Sanders chuckled.

Private Sanders twitched a grin. "I agree, sir."

"Okay then. Take a breath, still your hands and try again," Wade said, hearing a truck engine and the squeak of brakes behind him. He turned to see who was arriving and snapped to attention as his superior officer climbed out of the front seat. "Sergeant Major Briggs," Wade said, saluting.

Briggs strode forward, returning a salute. "How is the training going, Colton?"

"Very well, sir."

"Good," Briggs replied, "because I received word this morning that Colonel Meyers will be visiting the base today and wants to observe your training after lunch."

Now it was Wade's turn to feel a spurt of jitters. Though he knew his team was ready, having any officer observing always put his men on edge. Which gave Wade qualms. Nodding his understanding, he said, "We'll be ready, sir."

Briggs asked a few more housekeeping questions before returning to the truck where his driver waited. "Look for the colonel around fourteen hundred."

Behind him he could hear the murmur of his men. A few guffaws. Whispers.

Wade had only turned a half circle back toward his men when he was hit by a blast of heat and energy that knocked him backward. Searing pain blazed over his right side, his face. His ears rang. His men yelling. Fire. Smoke. Burning flesh.

His vision dimmed.

The materials were supposed to be inert, he thought numbly. Then darkness swallowed him.

Chapter 1

Owl Creek, Idaho,
May—a year later

"Welcome to another edition of *Harlow Helps*," the beautiful brunette woman on Wade Colton's laptop screen chirped. "In honor of May being Mental Health Awareness Month, I'm doing these live events with my friends to answer a few questions and highlight the importance of mental health and mental health professionals." Harlow Jones smiled at her audience through the screen. Wade's attention was drawn to her dark brown bedroom eyes—eyes that Wade remembered with heartbreaking clarity shining with tears as they stared at him in disbelief.

His heart clenched seeing Harlow's face again, and he almost left the Facebook Live event then and there. But a powerful yearning and possibly self-destructive curiosity made him stay with the broadcast.

"...and have a few laughs along the way. While mental health issues are no laughing matter," Harlow said, "it is also true that laughter is medicinal, and keeping a sense of humor is always helpful."

Keeping a sense of humor? Wade furrowed his brow, an action that tugged at his new scars. He tried to remember the last time he'd really laughed. The day of the accident flashed in his mind's eye. Joking around with the recruits. A teasing exchange with Sanders before—

He squeezed his eyes shut as the sights, sounds and smells of the tragic explosion replayed vividly for him. He gasped and shuddered as he tried to shake off the memory, but wave after wave of adrenaline sent tremors to his core, a cold sweat to his brow and nausea to his gut.

"Hello, caller! What is your name and where are you calling from?" Harlow's bright voice cut through his derailed and terrifying thoughts.

"Uh, it's Cindy. You asked me to call so you didn't have dead air, remember? You know where I live," the new female voice said.

Harlow pulled a face and made slashing motions at her throat. "Ah, ixnay the commentary. We're live on the air, *Cindy.* How can Harlow help you live a better life?"

Wade took a breath and, out of habit, raised a hand to pinch the bridge of his nose. When his fingers encountered the eye patch that now covered the damage to his permanently blinded right eye, he muttered a curse word under his breath. He hated his eye patch. It felt like an affectation. A costume. A flashing billboard sign that screamed "damaged" to the world. But the injury the explosion had caused to his eye was more unsightly than the patch, and he'd vetoed the suggestion of a prosthetic eye, so he sighed in resignation to his new accessory.

"Yeah, um, I've been hearing voices lately, and I'm worried what that might mean," the caller told Harlow.

Harlow arranged her face in a thoughtful moue. "Voices? What are they saying to you?"

"Strange but oddly comforting things. First I hear crying, which is pretty freaky. Then I hear a woman saying, 'Ahh, it's okay. I'm here. Who's a good girl?' and the crying stops."

Harlow arched an eyebrow. "Cindy, do you have a radio of some sort on in your house?"

Wade groaned, already seeing where this silliness was going.

"Yes. I drive a taxi and have my dispatch radio here at the house."

"I see. And do you know if one of your neighbors recently had a baby?" Harlow asked with a half grin.

"Oh, uh, yeah. My downstairs neighbor had a baby two months ago. Why?" Cindy's voice cracked with a chuckle as she gave her obviously staged response.

"Don't worry, Cindy. You're fine. I think you're hearing your neighbor's baby monitor through the dispatch radio."

"Oh, right!" Cindy said as they both chuckled over the lame act.

"Hearing baby monitors is not a sign of mental illness," Harlow said, sobering a bit, "but if you or a loved one is hearing unexplained voices or sounds, it is important to get the help of a trained psychiatrist for further evaluation. Today, many once unexplained or misinterpreted mental health conditions are better understood, and help is available from a variety of resources."

Wade rose from the wooden table that bore even more scars than he now had on his own chest, shoulder and face and shuffled to the refrigerator to get a beer. Twisting off the cap, he took a long pull and glanced at Harlow's face on his laptop. Why was he torturing himself this way? Harlow was gone. Part of his past. His family, doctors and friends were all telling him to focus on the future, to accept his new normal and forgive mistakes of days gone by.

"Letting Harlow go is a mistake, man," his big brother Fletcher had said years ago. "One you'll regret."

"What choice do I have? She wants no part of my life in the Marines. I leave for training Friday. She put me in a position to choose her or my dream of the Marines."

"You're burning bridges you may want a year or two from now. That's all I'm saying." Fletcher clapped him on the shoulder and gave him a dark look. "You will regret losing Harlow."

"Hello, caller! What's your name and where are you calling from?" Harlow's voice pulled him out of his melancholy reverie.

Fletcher had been right, of course. But Wade hadn't needed a year or two to regret breaking up with his high school sweetheart. He'd regretted losing Harlow before the harsh words severing ties with her had even left his mouth. He'd missed her, longed for her and hated his choice every day since telling her that he didn't love her when he announced he was leaving Owl Creek for his new career in the Marines. Now he was back in Idaho, in his small hometown, and Harlow was the one who had left for bigger, brighter things. Los Angeles, according to Hannah, who'd kept up with Harlow's life and career moves through Facebook. Hannah had been the one to tell Wade about Harlow's *Harlow Helps* Facebook presence and her new live broadcasts to promote mental health awareness. Wade had pretended not to be interested. Pretended he was over Harlow. Pretended he wasn't desperate for any morsel of guidance or help navigating his own mental health crisis. Because he'd gotten really good at denying he had a mental health crisis, to others and to himself. All he needed, he told himself, was fresh Owl Creek air, quiet and solitude to decompress. In time, his memories and his scars, glaring reminders of *that day*, would both heal and fade.

With another sip of beer, Wade put his hand on the laptop lid, prepared to slam it closed. Harlow's face and voice were not helping him feel better. They only reminded him of loss. Pain. Hollowness inside him.

"I need your help, Harlow. I have nowhere else to turn," the trembling voice of her new caller said.

Wade hesitated, removing his hand from the laptop when he saw the subtly startled look on Harlow's face. She blinked once, her mouth twitching slightly. He knew her well enough to realize something significant was amiss. Harlow had been caught off guard and was confused. Concerned. And trying to hide it.

"Yes, caller. I'm here to help." Only someone who knew Harlow as intimately as he did would have recognized the tension in her voice. "Can I have your name and where you're calling from?"

"I, uh… Janet. I'm in my car. I—I want to die. I c-can't—" A sob stifled the caller's words.

Wade dropped heavily into the kitchen chair, his heart pounding as he imagined Harlow's was, given the way the color had leached from her face. He studied her body language, seeing the moment she lifted her chin the slightest amount and firming her shoulders with resolve. The color returned to her face along with an expression of honest compassion and concern.

"Janet, I know things look bad right now, but we can work through whatever is wrong together if you'll trust me. Will you let me help?"

A broken hum of agreement answered Harlow.

Wade leaned toward the computer as if he could bolster Harlow, as if drawing nearer to her would give her the courage, strength and wisdom to handle this distraught caller.

"I think you want to find a way through this bad time. Isn't that why you called? You want to live, and you want me to help guide you through whatever's happened, whatever has left you feeling hopeless. Am I right?"

"I…" Janet sniffled and was silent for several tense seconds before saying, "I guess. I'm just…so lost. So alone."

"You are not alone, Janet. I'm here, and I will not leave this call until you are ready. I'm one hundred percent with you now and any time you want to call me."

"Okay," Janet squeaked.

Wade held his breath. He couldn't imagine what must be going through Harlow's mind right now. The pressure to get things right. The worry for the hurting woman. The panic knowing this whole thing was playing out live through her Facebook page.

Wade narrowed his gaze on Harlow's face and modified the last assumption he'd made. Harlow's intensity and attention were razor sharp. The set of her brow, the slight tilt of her head, the keen focus of her eyes on some fixed point off-screen. She was fully locked in on Janet's plight, the live broadcast and other viewers forgotten.

Harlow had had that same intensity and fervor during sex. Wade's blood heated just remembering. When she committed to something she was all in. Which was why he'd had to be so harsh, so clear about breaking things off with her. So decisively, painfully final when he left Owl Creek for the Marines at nineteen.

"Now, Janet, you said you are in your car. Are you driving or are you parked somewhere?"

"Parked."

"And where are you parked?" Harlow asked.

"In my garage."

"Is your engine on?"

Wade leaned even closer, his hand fisting as the silence stretched.

"Janet, are you there? Is your engine running?"

"Yes. I just want to go to sleep and never wake up again."

Heart sinking, Wade dragged a hand over the "good" side of his face. The unscarred left side. Unshaven stubble scraped his palm. He could remember feeling the same despondency in the earliest days in the military hospital when he learned he'd lost an eye. Lost a fellow Marine. Lost his career. Those black moments could really suck at your soul and drag you down. He still fought the pull of those moments at random times. Unexpected triggers. Days when the doubt demons seemed to hound him harder.

"Don't do it," he whispered to Janet. To himself?

When he turned his attention back to Harlow's voice, she was cajoling Janet to turn off the engine, step outside for fresh air. The sounds and responses Janet gave indicated she had complied. Wade released the breath from his lungs. *Well done, Harlow. Well done.*

He sipped his beer again and listened with rapt wonder as Harlow eased the conversation skillfully through the maze of tragedy and grief that surrounded Janet. Her tone was compassionate, earnest. Her focus was steady and her advice sage.

"Life can feel so overwhelming when you have such big things to deal with in your life. But, Janet, be kind to yourself. You didn't make these things happen, and no one expects you to snap back from such hardship and loss overnight."

Wade clenched his back teeth as ripples of recognition washed through him. His doctors had said much the same to him.

"Give yourself the grace to take each moment, each breath, each step as it comes. Do one tiny thing, even if that is just getting out of bed, and give yourself credit for making that step. Celebrate that step. Tell yourself that you did a good thing with that step. It counts. It matters. You matter."

Wade's cell phone rang, and caller ID showed it was Hannah. He considered ignoring it, but in the past months, ignored calls had been interpreted as flashing red beacons to his family, who all seemed to feel the need to walk on eggshells around him.

He swiped to answer the phone, anticipating the reason for the call, and saying, "I'm fine."

"Are you? Really? I swear I had no idea the broadcast would take such a serious turn. I was worried you might think…" Hannah didn't finish saying what she'd thought.

"I guess I shouldn't have even mentioned Harlow's show to you at all. I'm sorry."

"Don't apologize. I'm a big boy, and I can decide for myself whether I want to look in on my ex-girlfriend's live show or not."

"Then work toward taking a shower. Then toward getting dressed," Harlow was saying to Janet.

"Is that Uncle Wade?" a tiny voice said in the background at Hannah's house. "Can I talk to him?"

"Have you brushed your teeth?" Hannah said, her voice muffled as if having placed her hand over the phone. "Okay, but just for a minute. You have school in the morning."

Wade rolled the cursor on his laptop to pause Harlow's live broadcast as his five-year-old niece came on the line.

"Hi, Uncle Wade! Guess what?"

"Hi, Lucy Goose," he replied, his chest filling with a welcome warmth as he pictured his niece's bright smile. "I can't guess. You tell me what."

"My best friend, Bella—well, I guess she's not my *best* best friend. Ginger is my *best* best friend. I guess Bella is my next best friend. At school. Hilary is my next best friend in the neighborhood. We both like the same TV shows, and Mommy says having things in common and shared int— Um, shared—"

"Interests?" he prompted.

"Yeah! Shared interests is part of making friends."

"She's right."

"Anyhoooo," Lucy intoned, imitating the expression she'd doubtlessly heard the adults in her life use.

Wade bit back a chuckle over the five-year-old's precociousness. God, he loved this little girl and the innocent joy she brought to his life.

"So… Bella—wait for it!"

Wade smiled brighter. "Waiting…"

"Got. A. Puppy!" Lucy's squeal of excitement was so long, loud, high-pitched, he had to pull the phone away from his ear.

"Wow! A puppy? That's pretty cool. Have you met the puppy yet?"

"Yes! It's so soft and squirmy, and it licked all over my face! She hasn't named it yet, but I think she should name it Yippers cause when it barks it goes, 'Yip yip yip!'"

Wade chuckled as his niece imitated the puppy bark, then heard his sister telling Lucy her time was up and she had to go to bed.

"Awww," Lucy whined. "But I haven't even told him about the end-of-school program."

Wade cast his gaze to the frozen computer screen, where Harlow's face had been caught in a worried frown. A beat of impatience, a need to get back to Harlow's conversation with Janet, rippled through him. As much as he adored Lucy and her sweet lift to his spirits, he couldn't help wondering how Harlow was managing the suicidal caller.

"Mommy says I have to go. Bye, Uncle Wade. Mu-ah!"

"Mu-ah," he said in return, imitating the sound of blowing a kiss. "Sweet dreams, Lucy Goose."

Hannah came back on the line. "I have to put Lucy to bed now, but…you're sure you're okay?"

He sighed and repeated the line he'd said to his family a thousand or more times in the last several months. "I'm fine."

"Okay. I'll call you later. Bye, Wade."

"Bye, sis." He disconnected the call and started the live broadcast playing again. The video playback skipped forward, catching up to what was currently airing.

"Look up at the stars," Harlow was telling Janet. "Fill your lungs with air. Allow yourself to notice little things that can help you root yourself and feel a bit of control over this moment in time. We're not going to think about tomorrow or an hour from now. Just here and this moment in time."

"Okay."

"What can you hear?"

"Crickets. Tree frogs. The wind in the leaves."

"Good. What do you smell? Fresh air? Gosh, I don't know how fresh the air is where you live. Here in LA, fresh air is relative." Harlow gave a gentle smile for her quip. "Where do you live, Janet?"

"Omaha."

"Oh, the Midwest. I visited Omaha once. Beautiful place," Harlow said.

He continued listening and marveling as Harlow continued to calm Janet. Eventually she got her caller to reveal her home address in a private message to Harlow. When Harlow's eyes flickered briefly to something in her lap, Wade could guess what that something was, what Harlow was doing. It was the same thing he'd be doing—calling emergency services in Omaha.

"Smooth," Wade said with a nod. He raised his beer in salute to Harlow. She had handled every aspect of the obviously unexpected crisis call with aplomb and composure.

When it was clear that emergency services had found

Janet, Harlow made sure that Janet was referred to local counselors and promised to follow up with her in the coming days.

Taking a deep breath and feeling rather like he'd run a marathon, Wade finally leaned back in his chair and tried to shake the tension from his limbs. He couldn't even imagine the relief and emotional fatigue Harlow must be feeling.

Harlow rubbed her eyes and, as if suddenly remembering that her computer camera had just captured and broadcast live the exchange with Janet, she rallied and address the audience. "Friends, that was obviously not what we had planned for tonight. Ideally, I would not have conducted such a personal emergency so publicly, but I didn't want to risk losing my connection with Janet even for a second." She swallowed hard and exhaled. "Emergencies don't give us a chance to plan or schedule—" she raked fingers through her thick dark brown hair, clearly deciding what needed to be said "—which is why it's so important to constantly be addressing your mental health, paying attention to what's happening with your family and friends, taking measures to promote mental wellness just as you take steps to protect your physical health."

Wade picked at the label on his beer bottle. *Emergencies don't give us a chance to plan or schedule.* That was an understatement. His own recent disaster had altered his life in a fraction of a second. A stray spark. A faulty blasting cap.

Harlow was staring straight into camera now, her eyes so piercing not even Kevlar could have protected him from their impact on his heart. "This is exactly the point of highlighting mental health in May. Your mental health is every bit as important as your physical health and cannot be ignored. There is no shame in asking for help if you are struggling."

Wade grunted. He'd heard that line, too, several times since waking up in the hospital a year ago. But that advice was antithetical to his Marine training in so many ways. Needing such personal help was not something a member of the Marines Special Forces unit could easily admit. He'd been trained to be self-sufficient in the direst of circumstances, to endure the most difficult environmental conditions, perform the most dangerous and difficult military operations, and shove his personal comfort, wants and desires aside. The mission came first. Suck it up and do the job. *Oo-rah!*

"So until next week, this is Harlow Jones with *Harlow Helps.*"

Wade squeezed the beer bottle, not wanting the live feed to end. He wanted to sit there all night and stare at Harlow's beautiful face, wallow in the dulcet tones of her voice and remember how, with her, he'd once felt complete.

But instead, he listened as she said, "Be kind to yourself and others, and join me next time as we continue to talk about how to protect your mental health." Then with a wave to the audience, she ended the live feed.

Wade closed the laptop, drained his beer and released a sigh. Had it been a mistake to watch Harlow's live broadcast? He'd told himself he wanted the closure of seeing her and knowing she was doing okay. That she'd moved on and was fine.

Instead, he'd reopened the hole in his soul that had never healed when they split up. He'd only reinforced for himself how alone he felt and in so many aspects, how far away from him she was.

In Los Angeles, Harlow's phone was blowing up— texts, calls and Facebook messages. She answered a call from her friend Yolanda, who had been the *planned* guest for the broadcast, with a softball question about the importance of exercise for mental well-being.

"Wow," Yolanda said. "Just...wow."

"Yeah." Putting Yolanda on speakerphone, Harlow moved from her desk chair to lie supine on the floor and stretch her back and arms. Her black cat, Luna, took that as an invitation to walk on Harlow's chest and curl up on her stomach for a nap.

"You were amazing. I mean, I'm sorry I didn't get my call in before she rang in, but...big picture, that was fate, I think. You saved her!"

Harlow didn't want to go down that thought path. As soon as she'd realized what was happening, she'd shifted into counselor mode, shut everything else out, and just... followed her instincts and training. "Alexa, remind me to follow up with Janet tomorrow," she said to her Echo device. She rubbed Luna's head and let the rumble of her cat's purr soothe her. She took a few slow breaths, steadying her nerves.

"Holy cow, Harlow! There are *already* like two hundred comments on your Harlow Helps page. Most are support and encouragement for Janet, but a lot are commending you for how you handled the situation." Yolanda chuckled with awe in her tone. "This is amazing. You need to follow up."

"I intend to. I mean, I know I referred her to a counseling group in Omaha, but I don't want her to think I've abandoned her, that I don't care." Harlow closed her eyes, pointing and flexing her toes to stretch her calves.

"Well, that's good, too. I wouldn't expect otherwise from you. You're nothing if not conscientious and caring. What I meant was this could be the start of something big. What a launch pad for your platform!"

Wrapping an arm around Luna, Harlow sat up, frowning at her phone. "Hang on. You're not suggesting I exploit Janet's call, her pain, for commercial gain, are you? Because that would be...too reprehensible for—"

"No! Of course not! I just mean...if you want to reach more people with your show, help more people, increase the exposure of your message..."

Yolanda fell silent, letting Harlow fill in the blanks. "Well, of course I want to reach as many people as I can. The whole point of using social media is to try to reach a larger audience. More people reached means more lives helped. In theory."

"Well, you certainly have a great start tonight," Yolanda said. "You saved Janet's life. And you have... geez, five hundred comments now and two hundred shares already."

Disturbed from her attempt to cuddle, Luna sauntered off, tail high, and Harlow rolled her shoulders. She'd been so tense, so tightly wound during her conversation with Janet, and her muscles were still in knots.

"Say, you know who could help you make the most of this momentum? My friend Nadine. She's in public relations and is great with maximizing social media exposure. Want me to put her in touch with you?"

Harlow laughed tiredly. "Yolanda, jeepers! My brain

is still numb from talking with Janet, and you're already planning my next career moves?"

"Strike while the iron is hot, my grandma used to say," Yolanda replied without an ounce of remorse in her tone. "I'm texting you her number now. You'll love her. She's the best."

"Thanks, but if I decide to hire a PR consultant—big *if*, that seems way premature—I'd probably call a friend of mine from Idaho. Vivian's got her own company, and I like to support small businesses."

"Okay. Your choice. But if you change your mind about—Oops, gotta go. I hear the baby waking up. Love ya, girl! And congrats again. You were great tonight!"

"Thanks, I—" But Yolanda was gone. The buzzes and pings of incoming messages and texts continued, and she lifted her phone to mute it. She'd answer the barrage of attention tomorrow. Right now, she needed a hot bubble bath and a chance to decompress.

Her brain replayed her conversation with Janet, and she examined every bit of advice and word of comfort she'd given the distressed woman, hoping she'd struck the right tone, said the most appropriate things, done everything she could.

And for the first time in several months, her thoughts traveled back eleven years and north a thousand miles to Owl Creek, Idaho, to a night when the scent of pine had filled the air and a warm spring breeze had ruffled her hair. The night Wade Colton had broken her heart and left her standing alone in her backyard, believing her life was over.

"I understand, Janet," she whispered as she turned on the bathtub taps and dumped in a generous dollop of lavender-scented bubble bath. "But you can survive it. I did."

But as she had many times before, Harlow renewed her pledge to herself to never give her heart to anyone so blindly and fully. She never wanted to risk that depth of heartache again.

Chapter 2

"So, I've confirmed the interview with the local magazine in Boise," Vivian Maylor, Harlow's high school friend and current PR consultant, said. "They want it to be a 'local girl's rise to success' kind of article."

"Except I'm not from Boise. I'm from all over. The closest I ever came to Boise was Owl Creek, and you know I only moved there when I was in junior high. Does four years in a town make it your hometown?" Harlow asked, giving Vivian a wry grin.

On her laptop screen, via Zoom, Vivian waved off Harlow's concern. "Details, details. It's great exposure. I'm working on similar articles with a magazine in Boston and one in Savannah. You're going to be a household name when I'm finished, Harlow."

Harlow shifted uncomfortably in her chair. A household name? Was that what she wanted? Fame and national recognition had never been her goal when she hired Vivian to help boost her social media presence, and thereby increase her audience for the *Harlow Helps* live Facebook broadcasts.

Back in May, her emergency counseling session with Janet had gone viral. Taking Yolanda's advice, Harlow had seized on the attention to grow her audience, expand her online counseling program and reach more people in the name of mental health awareness. Sure, the attention of advertisers and increase in her income had been a boon, but it had never been her motivation.

Harlow sighed, reflecting on the past few months' whirlwind of business opportunities, growing exposure— and personal turmoil. Amid the excitement of her growing counseling program, Harlow's mother had died unexpectedly.

Grieving her mother, just two years after losing her father to cancer, had sapped much of Harlow's energy, but had also been a good reason to address grief and share her own experience with self-care after loss during her live broadcasts. The topic had struck a chord with a huge audience, especially when she highlighted how grief over pets, job losses and broken relationships were just as real and important to address as the sorrow following the death of a friend or family member.

Knowing how many people she was reaching, hearing from dozens of grateful listeners daily and learning how her program was making a difference both validated and inspired Harlow to keep going. She wanted to keep expanding her program, keep building her platform.

But only seven months into the exponential social media expansion, Harlow was already getting uncomfortable with the limelight. As her media presence grew and she attracted advertisers who wanted to share her high profile, critics lambasted her for selling out. Guilt had hit Harlow hard when those accusations were made.

She'd never wanted to use her platform for anything but good. Promoting mental health services available in most communities, highlighting healthy practices and debunking myths that harm or hinder people with mental health issues had been her only agenda. That she was now making a good living with the Facebook Live programming and had advertisers and representatives from Spotify proposing a podcast deal were secondary benefits to Harlow.

"Speaking of households," Harlow said, rubbing her temple where a headache was building, "I still haven't done anything with my parents' place. Between the holidays and all the promotional stuff you have me doing, I haven't found five minutes to call a real estate agent to inquire about listing the Owl Creek house."

When Luna jumped up on the desk and walked across Harlow's keyboard, demanding attention, Harlow lifted her down with a chuckle. "Not now, Luna."

"Are you saying it's my fault you're procrastinating?" Vivian asked with a sassy lift of her eyebrow. "You know you can do your job from anywhere with a Wi-Fi connection, right?"

Luna jumped back up, and Harlow pursed her lips in a frustrated scowl. "Yeah, yeah."

"If you're putting off cleaning out your parents' home, that's on you."

"You're right, of course." Harlow bobbed her head in concession, scratching her cat behind the ears. "But it's more than a lack of motivation. I'm so mentally drained at the end of a day hearing about other people's problems that I don't have the bandwidth left to take care of my own." That, and she hadn't found the nerve to return to Owl Creek in person. Too many memories lived there.

But Los Angeles had begun to feel uncomfortable in recent weeks, too. Along with the popularity of *Harlow Helps*, her growing fan base also meant she'd gained some online trolls. And a stalker.

As best she could determine from the cryptic Facebook messages she'd started receiving, someone had taken exception to something she'd said in one of her live broadcasts. She'd initially engaged the man she knew only as Chris72584, in case he was open to mental health advice, offering help to the obviously distressed individual. Harlow had left lines of communication open, offering replies such as "How can I help you?" or "I'm here to listen. Tell me what is upsetting you."

But the angry replies were cold and had become threatening. "What gives you the right to judge me?" and "You're what's upsetting me. You've ruined my life," and then, "Want to help the world? Die. I wish I could kill you."

At that point, she'd stopped communicating with Chris72584. She'd blocked him as his threats grew more disturbing.

"Don't ignore me."

"I will find you."

"I'm coming for you."

"Sounds like the counselor needs to take her own advice and take a mental health break," Vivian said, drawing her out of her thoughts. "What do you say? A weekend on the beach? A quick trip to Mexico for margaritas and sun? I'll come with you!" Vivian added the last with a singsongy tone and an unabashed grin.

Harlow chuckled. "I'm sure you would. But no Mexico for me."

"Spoilsport. I was looking for an excuse to put this freezing Idaho weather in my rearview mirror for a few days."

"Sorry," Harlow replied. "I actually like winter weather. I miss cold days curled up by the fireplace and making snow ice cream and…"

Harlow let her sentence trail off as she glanced at her phone and read the notification of an incoming text. The message from an unfamiliar number simply read, "Boo, bitch!"

Acid curled through her stomach.

"Harlow? You okay? You look like you've seen a ghost."

"I, um…" She blinked, trying to clear her head, settle her gut. But then another text came through. A picture of her condo, her car parked on the driveway, and Luna visible, sitting in the open kitchen window.

I found you. Be scared.

A shudder raced through Harlow as she snatched her hand away from her phone as if it were a snake that could bite her. She *was* scared.

"Harlow?" Vivian's tone sharpened with concern. "What's wrong?"

"I—I think I'm going to take that break after all. And, uh, close up my parents' house. Getting that albatross off my mind will help my stress factor considerably."

"You're coming to Owl Creek?"

She hated the idea of returning to the place where her heart had been broken. But old ghosts were a safer bet than dealing with a potentially dangerous stalker—

who'd somehow gotten her private cell phone number. Harlow's mouth dried.

"Y-yes," she said, hearing the tremble in her tone. "Could you pick me up at the Boise airport tomorrow?"

"Of course," Vivian said, chuckling lightly. "Tomorrow, huh? Once you make up your mind, you don't mess around! What time should I be there?"

"I'll let you know. I'm going to look up flights now."

"Can I ask what spurred this sudden change of heart?" Vivian became more serious, leaning toward her camera as if wanting to grasp Harlow's hand or trying to make a deeper connection despite the impersonal Zoom call. "Something spooked you just now. I can see it in your face. What happened?"

Harlow forced a stiff grin. "I just took your advice to stop procrastinating. No time like the present." *That, and the fact that my stalker has just upped the ante by a factor of ten.*

Her house, her life, Los Angeles, no longer felt safe. She would call the police as soon as she disconnected with Vivian. Tomorrow, she'd hop on a plane to the only place she'd ever truly felt at home. Owl Creek was haunted because of Wade Colton, but she could hide in the safe haven of her parents' home until the authorities caught the person who was so maliciously closing in on her.

Even as she set her plan to flee to Idaho, another text came in from the same unfamiliar number. Her breath stuck in her throat as she read the new message. It was as if the stalker had read her mind.

You can run, but you can't hide.

Chapter 3

Vivian pulled in the driveway of the ranch-style house that had been Harlow's first real home. After years of moving from one city to another as her father changed Army bases like he changed his socks, her family had finally settled down in Owl Creek. Her father's military retirement and the roots the family had planted in the small Idaho town had given Harlow a sense of permanence when she needed it most. Having reliable friends, a sense of security and the promise of consistency during her high school years had been a welcome relief.

"Looks just the way I remember it," Vivian said.

"If in need of a little TLC," Harlow countered, noticing a loose shutter on a front window and the faded paint on the trim. "It's like the house knows it's vacant and droops a little in loneliness."

From her travel carrier, Luna gave an impatient yowl.

"Poor girl." Harlow turned to poke her fingers in the carrier and scratch Luna's head. "She's been cooped up in this thing all day, other than the quick breaks for litter box and food at LAX and the Boise airports. Come on, girl. Let's go inside and get you set up in Grandma's house."

A twinge of grief plucked Harlow's heart as soon as the words were out. Her mother and father would never meet their real grandchildren, assuming she ever had any kids. That prospect was starting to look dim, considering her bleak love life of late.

Ticktock, said her biological clock, and Harlow firmly shoved those thoughts aside. Before she entertained any thoughts of romance and attracting the attention of a potential spouse, she had to rid herself of the unwanted and rather scary attention of her stalker. Harlow shouldered open the door of Vivian's car and yelped at the cold bite of the Idaho winter.

"Problem?" Vivian asked as she opened her car's trunk to get Harlow's suitcases.

"Only that I've apparently gotten spoiled by the mild California weather. I'd forgotten how cold it can get here." With Luna's carrier in one hand, Harlow hoisted her computer bag and the handle of her largest rolling suitcase and headed for the front door.

Vivian followed, rolling a smaller bag and carrying the tote bag with Luna's supplies. "I know you came up here to get your mom's house cleaned out and market-ready, but I'd love to put our heads together while you're here and brainstorm some promo ideas for this spring. Strike while the iron is hot, you know?"

"Um, sure. We'll do that."

"And lunch?" Vivian waited while Harlow keyed open the door and carried Luna inside. "Or maybe dinner and drinks with some of the old gang? Hannah and

Lizzy are still in the area. Have you talked to either of them lately?"

Harlow turned on the lights in the foyer and living room and gave her mother's house an encompassing glance. She'd last been here for a quick in-and-out weekend for her mother's funeral back in the fall. The gloom of the gray winter day did little to brighten the homecoming. She unzipped Luna's carrier and stroked the cat's fur as her cat poked her head out with a suspicious sniff.

"No, I haven't talked to anyone," Harlow said, finally answering Vivian's question. "I didn't really keep up with many people after high school. Most of my closest friends were part of the Colton family, and after Wade and I broke up, I just couldn't…"

Vivian's expression lit with recognition before she winced. "Wade. Right. I can see how that might be awkward."

Excruciating, more like. Even the mention of him now sliced through her like barbed wire tangled around her soul.

Harlow rallied herself, pasting on a smile. "But I really shouldn't let bygones stand in the way of friendships. Right? I mean, that's what I'd tell a client. Don't let fear of the past stand in the way of important relationships."

"Amen!" Vivian said with a laugh. "So… I'll set something up and be in touch." She squatted and held her hand out for Luna, who was timidly creeping out of her carrier to check out her new surroundings. "Um… speaking of Wade…"

Throat tightening, Harlow said, "Were we?"

Vivian tipped her head to glance up at Harlow while stroking Luna's back and tail. "You know he's Nate's half brother, right? Robert Colton was living a double life with two families, including a son and daughter he didn't tell anyone in Owl Creek about."

"Seriously?" Harlow blinked hard, trying not to gape as she digested this news. Wade's father had a second secret family? Wade had half siblings he'd never known about? Clearly, she had missed a bit of drama in the years while she was away. She schooled her face and said, "No, I hadn't heard that. That's...wow!"

"Will it be a problem for you, seeing as how Nate and I are involved?"

Harlow scoffed. "Why should it be? You're my PR agent and friend. If your friendship with Wade's cousin Lizzy doesn't bother me, why should your relationship with Nate?"

Vivian gave her a silent scrutiny before nodding. "Okay. Just checking. I know this is an emotional enough trip for you without piling on because of my connections." She twisted her mouth, and her eyebrows dipped. "What do you think you'll say to Wade if you see him while you're here?"

Harlow's pulse jumped. "Why would I see him? He's in North Carolina or somewhere with the Marines, right?" Harlow saw something flicker across Vivian's face, and her insides grew cold. "Isn't he?"

"Um...no. He left the Marines a while back. He's been in Owl Creek ever since. He lives in a small rental cabin by Blackbird Lake and works for his uncle on the Colton Ranch now."

Harlow felt her knees tremble, and she moved quickly to a chair in the living room before she could slump onto the floor.

*"Why can't you stay here and be a ranch hand or po-
liceman or an accountant for your dad or something?
Why do you have to be a Marine?"* young Harlow sobbed,
her voice tight with anger and hurt.

*"Because that's not who I am. I'd never be satisfied
being a rancher or accountant. You should know that
about me. We've talked about this before!"* Wade's eyes
blazed with determination, chipping away another piece
of Harlow's breaking heart.

"Harlow? Are you all right?" Vivian hurried into the
living room and knelt by the wingback chair. "I thought
you knew."

She shook her head. "No. But then I've intentionally
avoided any news or reminders of Wade since we broke
up." She met Vivian's worried look. "You're sure? He's
here? He's…ranching?"

Vivian nodded. "According to Lizzy. I haven't run
into him myself, but I hear he's been lying low since he
got back in town. He works the ranch, then goes straight
home."

Harlow drew and released a breath, gathering her
composure. She gave her friend a wry grin. "Well, thanks
for the…warning."

So Wade had changed his mind about ranching, about
living in Owl Creek…

What else had changed for Wade? And why did the
answer matter so much to her?

The sun was just cresting the ridge of distant mountains as Wade arrived at Colton Ranch. He took a moment to appreciate the peaceful sunrise, and once he'd
parked his pickup near the front door of his Uncle Buck's

barn-style home, he glanced around the ranch yard. He spotted extra vehicles near the horse stable and some unusual activity in the paddock. He hesitated a moment before heading up the gravel path to knock on Buck's door. He squinted, trying to determine if one of the people in the paddock was his uncle, but the figures seemed too petite and slim. Women?

He didn't see as well as he used to out of his "good eye," though as scar tissue healed and swelling receded, his vision was getting better, like the doctor had promised. He knew he needed to get a contact for his left eye, but in the past eighteen months, he'd had his fill of doctors and appointments and physical therapy. He just wanted to be left alone. No more doctors poking and prodding, and no more relatives and friends hovering like spy drones, watching his every move, expecting him to…do what? Have a meltdown? Grow horns to go with his new scarring? Find him abusing painkillers? Wade grunted at that possibility. He took pride in the fact that he'd purposely avoided narcotic pain medicines after leaving the hospital. He'd endured the excruciating pain of his healing wounds and physical therapy, specifically to avoid dependence on any drug. If he was hurting, if he lost sleep from the searing pain some days, he considered it a small price to pay to be alive. Private Sanders hadn't been as lucky.

The sound of laughter, male and female, sounded from behind Buck's front door. The woman's voice sounded *very* familiar. Very…familial. Wade weighed his options. Let his mother have her secrets or—

The front door opened, and his mother and Buck both

pulled up short, their faces reflecting surprise at finding Wade on the front step and...was that guilt?

"Wade, uh...hello, darling."

Buck jerked a stiff nod of greeting. "Mornin', Wade."

Jenny Colton stepped over to her son for a hug and looked him up and down. "Why are... I mean, is everything all right? Are you okay?"

Wade gave his mother a quick squeeze, then stepped back, furrowing his brow. "I'm fine. I just had a question for Buck before I started work today."

"Oh. Right." Jenny's hand fluttered up to twist her stud earring. "I'm only here because I, uh, brought Buck some cinnamon bread I'd baked." She aimed a nervous finger over her shoulder to the kitchen and flashed a weak smile.

Wade nodded once. "You don't have to explain yourself to me."

"Of course not," Jenny said with a tight laugh. "I just... Well, I should go. Bye, darling."

"Bye," Wade and Buck answered at the same time, eliciting another nervous laugh from Jenny and putting an uncustomary flush in his uncle's cheeks. Wade chose to dismiss the obvious explanation for both his mother's presence at his uncle's house at this hour of the morning and the awkward vibe he was getting from the older couple. He had no interest in family drama or intrigue if he could avoid it.

His mother patted his arm and, tipping her head to a concerned angle, gave him another worried scrutiny. "You're sure everything is all right? You've been keeping to yourself a lot lately."

Wade gritted his back teeth, hunching his shoulders

against the cold when a stiff winter wind buffeted him. "I'm fine, Mom."

Jenny looked unconvinced but hiked her purse strap onto her shoulder and moved past him before giving another awkward laugh. "Silly me. I parked in the back." She sidled past Wade again and shrugged as she passed Buck. "I'll call later. Okay?"

Buck folded his arms over his chest and mumbled, "Yeah. Bye." Then facing Wade, he shifted his feet before leveling a narrow-eyed gaze on his nephew. "You had a question?"

"Uh-huh. I was wondering if you'd heard anything back from the mechanic on the four-wheeler? I can take my truck to pick it up from the shop, if it's fixed."

"Oh, uh, no. Not yet." Buck exhaled heavily and dropped his hands to his sides. "Waiting on a part. Could be Friday before it's ready."

"Okay." Wade turned to leave. "Unless you have something of higher priority for me, I'll take Cactus Jack out to check fences."

"Sure. Ruby said she'd drop by this afternoon to give another round of vaccinations to the cows from the upper pasture," Buck said, meaning Wade's younger sister, a veterinarian. "You could give her and Malcolm a hand with that later."

"No problem."

Wade started to walk away when Buck said, "Wade? I think you should know…"

Facing his uncle, he shook his head. "Like I told Mom, I don't need an explanation."

"That's not…" Buck scowled. "I was only going give you a warning. Nate is here."

Nate. The half brother he only recently learned about. The half brother who had been excluded from their father's will.

"Is there a problem?" Wade asked.

Buck shook his head. "Naw. At least I don't think so. He's here with Lizzy…and Vivian."

"Oh. Right." Wade mentally connected the dots. Buck's daughter Lizzy was best friends with Vivian Maylor—whom Nate was now dating. "Makes sense." He gave a wry grunt at the tangle of linked relationships. He'd forgotten during his ten years in the Marines how close and interconnected the people of Owl Creek were. *Small towns…*

That explained the extra cars and people at the paddock, anyway. Wade lifted a hand to wave as he walked back to his truck. "Thanks for the heads-up, but I have no beef with Nate or his sister."

Half siblings. The legacy of his late father's double life. Wade groaned and cranked the truck's engine. He'd come back to Owl Creek for peace and solitude. A place to hibernate and lick his wounds until he figured out what he was going to do with the rest of his life. What he'd found in the last several months was an increasingly complicated web of family secrets and lies. His siblings and cousins had been caught in an unrelenting series of dangerous events and dramatic conflicts that made his life with the Marines seem like a vacation.

Big families always had some drama, Wade acknowledged, and the Coltons had known their share through the years. But the past several months had seemed especially thick with life-changing moments and new relationships.

As long as I don't get drawn into the spiderweb, Wade thought. Solitude and quiet was all he wanted until he could get his life back on track. What defined *back on track*, he couldn't say. He only knew he still saw no direction for his life beyond the next day of ranching, surviving each restless, nightmare-populated night and watching the glacial healing of his scarred body each morning in his mirror.

When he reached the stable, he parked his truck and stuck his keys in the cup holder in case someone needed to move the vehicle while he was out in the pastures. He ambled toward the dimly lit stable, and the warmth of the overhead heaters washed over him as he stepped into the alley. He glanced toward the sound of voices coming from a stall at the back, next to the stall where Cactus Jack was housed. He exhaled heavily. He didn't exactly avoid other people, but he hated the pitying looks and obvious questions that paraded over the faces of new acquaintants when they saw his eye patch and facial scars. The awkwardness of introductions was tedious and tiresome, even all these months after returning to Owl Creek. While he'd met everyone in the stable before, he didn't know Nate well and hadn't spent much time around Vivian since high school.

Mustering his best public expression, the polite one he'd employed in recent months that said, "I'm fine. No problem here. Just minding my own business," he marched down the hay-strewn alley toward Cactus Jack's stall. He'd almost reached the small cluster of visitors to the ranch when a female laugh wafted out from behind the wall of Sunflower's stall.

He stopped in his tracks. A chill shot through him,

making his limbs tingle with recognition and...was it anticipation or dread?

Harlow? Surely he was wrong. Harlow had no reason to be here. Maybe he was just imagining—

But then the group moved out of Sunflower's stall, and the foursome—Lizzy, Nate, Vivian...and, yes, Harlow—drew up short, apparently startled to see him.

"Oh, Wade, hi!" Lizzy said cheerfully. "I was just showing these guys around a little. Vivian and Nate wanted to meet the new horses, and since Harlow was in town, Vivian invited her to come along."

Wade forced himself to make eye contact briefly with Vivian and Nate as he jerked quick nods of greeting and muttered, "Yeah. Hi." Then his gaze returned to Harlow and stuck.

She stared back at him, clearly just as stunned to have run into him as vice versa. His tingle of dread morphed into a full-fledged jangle of self-conscious expectation. Harlow hadn't seen his injuries before now. If she'd heard about his accident, it hadn't been from him. He wasn't sure who from Owl Creek, which of his siblings or cousins, she'd kept in touch with. He hadn't wanted to know, hadn't wanted to be tempted to ask, *What do you hear from Harlow?*

He waited, holding his breath as he watched for the crinkle of her forehead or tightening of her mouth that reflected the dismay, the repulsion, the morbid curiosity, the sympathy he got from others when they first encountered his new look. The awkward glance away that said, *I'm not staring,* but also, *I don't know how to process the change in your appearance.*

He refused to be the first to look away, as if daring

her to acknowledge the light ripple of scars that pocked half of his face. He drew his shoulders back, assuming a posture of confidence he had to dig deep to project. Let her grimace in pity. Let her frown and drop her gaze in discomfort. He could take it, he told himself. Everyone else in the family had been visibly distressed over his injuries and still treated him with deference. Why not Harlow, too?

But Harlow's expression said none of those things. All he saw in her dark eyes was the bittersweet shock of encountering the man who'd so cruelly broken her heart eleven years ago. She blinked and quickly shed the momentary surprise as she said, "Hello, Wade."

Harlow flashed him a smile that bore only the slightest tremble of nerves and nostalgia.

He swallowed hard and wrenched a terse, "Harlow," from his throat.

A soft gasp caught his attention, and Lizzy said quietly, "Oh my God. I forgot that you two dated! I—"

Vivian cleared her throat and said quickly. "It's nice to see you, Wade. Harlow and I were just making plans for lunch. You should join us."

Harlow sent Vivian a quick, silencing look.

Jamming his hands in his back pockets, Wade shifted his weight to his heels. "No. Thanks. I'm sure Harlow would rather I *didn't* join you."

Harlow tipped her head slightly and arched one sculpted eyebrow toward the edge of her knit hat. "Don't speak for me."

Wade inhaled slowly and flipped up a palm. "Am I wrong? Haven't you spent the last decade avoiding me?"

Her eyes widened, and he realized how cold his tone

had been. Before he could apologize, she returned, in a more magnanimous voice than he'd used, "I could say the same of you."

Nate tugged Vivian's arm and hitched his head toward the front of the stable. "Viv, why don't we give them a moment alone? Huh?"

Lizzy and Nate were already edging away, and Vivian glanced at Harlow with a wrinkle of query on her brow. "Okay?"

Harlow flashed a smile at her friend. "Yeah, I'll be with you in a minute."

"Actually," Wade said, aiming a thumb toward Cactus Jack's stall, "I need to get to work."

"Work?" Harlow blinked and cocked her head slightly. "That's right. Vivian mentioned that you work here at the ranch."

Wade shrugged one shoulder. "For now."

The furrow of confusion on the bridge of her nose deepened. "But…what happened to the Marines? I thought you intended the military to be your life's work."

He didn't answer right away. He narrowed a gaze on her that asked, *Seriously?*

But her expression held no irony or duplicity that he could detect. He chuffed a sarcastic laugh and aimed a finger at his face. "This happened." He waved a hand indicating the right side of his chest and upper arm. "There's more of the same under here. Don't tell me your contacts here in Owl Creek didn't tell you about my career-ending accident."

Now her face fell with sympathy. "Career-ending? Oh, Wade. I am sorry. I know how much the Marines meant to you."

You have no idea, he wanted to say. *My service cost me the most important person in my world, and I've never forgotten that.*

Instead, he gave another shrug and mumbled, "Yeah. Well, stuff happens and...you deal with it."

She shifted her feet, and the inquisitive look on her face said she was going to drill him for more details, so he cut her off with his own question. "What are you doing here? In Owl Creek, I mean. I thought you lived in LA." He mentally kicked himself as soon as the words left his mouth. Did he want her to know he'd looked her up on Facebook, had listened to her show, had checked to see where life had taken her since he'd let her get away?

"I do live in LA," she said. "But I'm considering a change of scenery." She flapped a dismissive hand before he could ask for follow-up details. "Long story. I won't bore you. The short version of why I'm in Owl Creek is, my parents have both died, and it was time I dealt with cleaning out and selling their old house."

Wade took a turn sending a sympathetic frown to her. "I hadn't heard. I'm sorry."

Her smile of acknowledgment held a hint of regret and grief. "Thanks. I miss them but...stuff happens and you deal with it. Right?"

He couldn't help the wry grin that cracked his face when she tossed his words back at him. He could see the spark of deeper emotion in her eyes that said that she wasn't as glib or resigned to her loss as she pretended.

He balled his hands at his sides. He knew all about faking acceptance and well-being, showing the world the face he knew they wanted to see. The urge to reach for her, to hug her and offer her comfort kicked him in the gut, but he shoved it down. Consoling Harlow, holding her, wasn't an option anymore.

She tucked stray wisps of her chocolate-brown hair behind her ear, then tugged her knit hat back in place. "Truth is, I thought I could spend a long weekend getting the house in shape to sell, but it's proving a far bigger job than I'd imagined."

"How so?"

"Well, my mom had apparently put off some important maintenance on the house. I'll have to get some repairs made before it can be listed. And I'm finding a butt-load more junk in the attic and closets than I'd expected, stuff I'll need to sort before I toss anything."

Unsure what to say, Wade just gave a grunt of understanding.

"It seems my mom was something of a pack rat...or maybe the right phrase is super sentimental. She saved everything."

A strained silence fell between them. Harlow chafed her hands, red from the cold, before tucking them under her armpits to warm them. "Anyway, it's a big job, so I'll be busy with that for the foreseeable future."

In his stall, Cactus Jack nickered, drawing Wade's attention. He hitched his head toward the gelding. "Listen, I...should get going. Lots to do today."

"Oh. Right." Harlow motioned to the stall with both hands. "Didn't mean to keep you."

He shrugged. "You didn't. I just..." *Good God. Why was this so damn hard? So awkward? You used to tell her everything. You used to spend hours sharing your hopes and dreams...your body with her.*

Used to. Past tense. He'd forfeited the privilege of Harlow's confidence and companionship.

She raised a hand as she shuffled past him, flashing a half smile. "Well, good to see you, Wade."

He nodded and mumbled, "Yeah. You, too."

As he turned to open Cactus Jack's stall, Harlow said, "Wade." He turned back to her.

She met his gaze levelly, her expression sincere. "I mean it. It was good to see you. I'd...kinda dreaded running into you, honestly. But... I'm glad we did. I don't hold any grudges against you...just so you know."

He drew his shoulders back, startled by her admission. "You don't?"

"It's in the past, right?" She lifted a corner of her mouth, her dark eyes twinkling with humor as she added, "Stuff happens and you deal with it, huh?"

He gave a short laugh. "That's what I hear." He took a cleansing breath to loosen the tight grip on his chest. "It was good to see you, too, Harlow. Really."

"Thanks." She cleared her throat. "Bye, Wade." Her smile brightened, and after a few backward steps, she spun around and jogged down the stable alley.

"Harlow," he called after her, not knowing what prompted him and not pausing to analyze what he was doing. When she stopped and turned around, he said, "I could give you a hand at your mother's house, if you want."

Chapter 4

Harlow and Vivian spent some time later that morning buying all the cleaning supplies, trash bags and storage boxes Harlow would need to get started sorting through her mother's house, then headed to meet Lizzy at Tap Out Brewery for lunch.

As Vivian drove them through the streets of downtown, Harlow noted all the changes, the growth, the revival that had kept the small town vibrant and relevant. Some of the shops catered to the tourists who visited town year-round thanks to nearby ski slopes for winter fun and Blackbird Lake for warm-weather boating, camping and water sports.

Once Vivian parked and fed coins in the meter, they hustled into the brewery that smelled of spicy barbecue, handmade pizzas and yeasty beers. The lunch crowd was buzzing, and televisions spaced around the bar and dining room silently played sports channels from around the world.

"Wow. Popular place," Harlow said, scanning the full tables for an empty booth.

"Lizzy said this was one of the best places for lunch. Clearly most of the town agrees!" Vivian smiled as she craned her neck to search the crowd. "Oh, there she is." With a tug on Harlow's coat sleeve, she started into the busy dining room to join Lizzy.

Harlow followed, noticing Lizzy was with two other women. Both were blonde. Both had their backs to her.

Both were Coltons. Even without seeing their faces, Harlow knew.

Her feet stopped as if frozen to the floor. Did she want to have lunch with Wade's family? How could she pretend—

And then the darker-haired blonde stood to greet Vivian and turned toward Harlow. Familiar green eyes latched on Harlow's and widened. Harlow's heart thudded a rhythm, half anxious, half joyful.

Hannah Colton—Wade's sister and Harlow's best friend for four years of high school. Later, she couldn't say who made the first move, but the next thing Harlow knew, she and Hannah had rushed to each other and embraced, laughing and crying at the same time.

"Oh my gosh! Harlow, I had no idea you were in town!" Hannah said, while Harlow could only repeat over and over, "I'm sorry. So sorry. I've missed you so much!"

Hannah levered back, meeting Harlow's gaze with a tearful, confused expression. "You're sorry? For what?"

Harlow dropped her chin, humiliated and ashamed of her treatment of her friend after high school. "I ghosted you. I cut you out of my life for no reason other than my own self-protection. It was cold and selfish of me, and I'm so sorry."

"You mean…it wasn't my fault?" Hannah's brow dipped, and her grasp on Harlow's arms tightened. "I thought I'd said or done something to make you mad. I thought—"

Fresh guilt stabbed Harlow's heart. "No! Oh, Hannah, no! Now I'm doubly sorry. All you ever did was... be Wade's sister. You were just a too-painful reminder of what I'd lost in him. I was afraid of all the ways a continued relationship with you would keep the wounds he'd caused open and raw. But I... Hannah, I was wrong to walk away from our friendship!"

Hannah drew her back into a hug and said, "You're forgiven. I'm just so glad to know I didn't do something terrible to hurt you."

Harlow backed out of the embrace, stepping aside as a server with a loaded tray sidled past them. "No. Not you. Never you. Wade's the one who—" Harlow shook her head. "Never mind all that. I'm just...so glad to see you!"

"Same. Please, join us. We have so much to catch up on!" Beaming and wiping happy tears, Hannah led Harlow the last few steps to the table where Lizzy and Vivian sat with another of Wade's sisters, Ruby.

Ruby's face brightened as Harlow took a seat at the table. "Well, if it isn't Harlow Jones! Is this the *H* squared reunion tour?"

Vivian tipped her head. "*H* squared?"

"Harlow and Hannah. These two were like this in high school," Ruby said, holding up two crossed fingers.

"When Harlow wasn't like this—" Lizzy touched her index fingers together and made kissing sounds "—with Wade, that is."

A prickle of embarrassment heated Harlow's cheeks as Lizzy and Ruby laughed. Hannah shot Harlow a worried glance that Harlow waved off despite the sting at her core for the bittersweet memories.

Ruby sobered first. "Oops. Did we step in it? I'm re-membering now that things ended kinda badly between you." She winced. "Sorry."

Harlow put on a brave face. "Ancient history. Life moves on."

Lizzy handed Harlow a menu. "I'm sure seeing him this morning was…awkward. I swear I didn't know he'd be in the stable that early in the morning. He's not usu-ally around until later. I've never seen him out in the pastures or in a pen working with Dad before eight."

Harlow forced a grin as the shock of having seen Wade at the Colton stable earlier reverberated through her again. Being at the Colton Ranch again for the first time in so many years had been hard, had opened the door to so many memories she'd closed away.

The color in Ruby's cheeks faded. "You saw him? Then…you know about…his accident."

Harlow's gut clenched, and she jerked a nod. "I do now."

After his appearance in the stable, his eye patch, his facial scars, his uncharacteristically somber mood were the next bombshells. She prayed she'd hidden her sur-prise at seeing him, seeing his injuries, well enough. Knowing that he was working at the ranch, a career he'd rejected in his pursuit of his Marine commission, had been perhaps the most painful revelation for her. He'd sacrificed their relationship for his dream of the Ma-rines, and now his dream was dead. The price they'd both paid had been for nothing.

Laying the menu aside, Harlow flattened her hands on the cool tabletop. "When did it happen?"

The sisters glanced at each other, obviously searching their memories.

"He moved back to Owl Creek about a year, thirteen months ago," Ruby said, and Hannah nodded confirmation. "Before that he spent several weeks in the burn unit at the military hospital."

"So like seventeen or eighteen months ago," Hannah said.

Harlow didn't want to spend the lunch talking about Wade, but she needed one more question answered before she moved the conversation in a new direction. "And is he...will he be okay?"

The pregnant pause that followed her question and the exchange of concerned looks among the other women told Harlow plenty. Wade was still hurting, somehow, someway.

"Physically, he's healing well, I believe," Ruby said.

"That is, considering he lost his right eye and had burns on twenty percent of his body," Lizzy added.

Vivian made a sound in her throat of sympathy and dismay, and Harlow's chest tightened. She'd heard that the treatment of burns was one of the most painful things a person could endure. Her soul ached for Wade, and she shied from the notion of his suffering. She couldn't bear to think of it.

"But..." Lizzy added ruefully, bringing Harlow's attention back to the conversation, "he's changed."

Harlow cut a glance to Hannah for confirmation. Or maybe hoping she'd deny her cousin's assertion.

Swallowing hard, Harlow asked, "Changed...how?"

Hannah's face brightened then. "That's right! You're a professional counselor! I've heard your show, Harlow. You're awesome! Maybe you could talk to Wade and help him find his path."

Around the table, the other Coltons seemed to warm to the idea and nodded their agreement.

Harlow held up a hand and shook her head firmly. "Whoa. Slow down. I'm only in town for a few days to get my mom's house ready to put on the market. Besides, considering our history...well, it wouldn't be right for me to try to counsel him or—" She let her sentence drop off, seeing Hannah's face fall. "Of course, I'll do what I can to help him while I'm here, but my plan was to avoid him as much as possible. Things between us were civil this morning, but it's still raw, and picking at those scabs doesn't serve either of us."

Harlow could tell Hannah wanted to push the topic further, so she jumped in with her own question. "Ruby, what's happening in your life these days?"

Fortunately, the Colton women took the hint and let the topic of Wade drop. The conversation shifted to Ruby's new baby, her veterinary practice and engagement to Sebastian Cross, the owner of Crosswinds Training, a K-9 search-and-rescue training facility. Harlow could easily see how fulfilled and happy Ruby was from the glow on her face as she showed pictures of her baby and talked about Sebastian and Crosswinds. Lizzy had had much the same joy in her voice and expression this morning when they'd talked at the ranch about her new love, Ajay Wright.

Turning to Hannah, Harlow hoped to learn her best friend from high school had found the same happiness. Instead, Hannah's eyes held a degree of forlorn longing.

"Hannah?" Harlow said, touching her friends arm lightly. "What is it?"

Hannah shook her head, rallying and fixed a smile on her face. "It's nothing." Pulling out her phone, she woke the screen and angled it for Harlow to see the picture of a cherub-faced little girl with light brown pigtails and an endearing smile. "This is the love of my life. Lucy. She's five going on thirty."

Harlow clapped a hand to her chest as happy tears filled her eyes. "She's precious, Hannah!" When Harlow glanced up at her friend, the pure maternal love and pride radiated from Hannah like spring sunshine. Harlow noticed no mention was made of Lucy's father, so she took the hint and let that pass.

"Between Lucy and my catering business, I stay plenty busy." Hannah took her phone back and gazed at her daughter's image a moment before stashing the phone in her purse again.

"Catering?" Harlow prompted, and Hannah detailed the business she ran and her satisfaction with the job. Still no mention was made of a husband or hint given regarding Lucy's father. Harlow tucked her curiosity away. If Hannah wanted to tell her that story later, she would. Today was about celebrating a reunion with old friends and shoving old hurts aside.

But as their server brought out their meals, Harlow felt her phone buzz in her pocket, and she dragged it out to check the text. She read the message from the real estate agent she'd contacted and made a note of the proposed meeting time. Before she put the phone away, she noticed she had a Facebook message as well. Heart in her throat, she opened the message. When she read the words on the screen, she froze.

You cannot hide from me.

The attached picture was from inside her Los Angeles condo.

Icy fear sluiced through her veins. If her stalker had found and broken into her LA house, she'd been right to leave town.

"Harlow, are you all right?" Ruby asked. "Your expression looks like you're being chased by a demon."

She forced a grin to appease her friend. "I… I'm fine."

But Harlow was afraid Ruby's quip was far too close to the truth.

Chapter 5

When the doorbell rang the next morning, Harlow struggled to her feet amid a pile of clothes she was sorting on her mother's bedroom floor and scurried to answer the summons. "Coming!"

Knowing she'd arrived to a house with an empty refrigerator and pantry, her mother's neighbors had brought by a steady stream of casseroles and desserts. Harlow was moved by the outpouring of kindness from her mother's friends, neighbors she barely remembered from when she'd lived in the neighborhood with her parents. One neighbor had even taken it upon himself to keep the yard in shape without being asked, not wanting the street view of the home to shout, "Vacant!"

When Harlow peered cautiously through the peephole to see who was there—she hadn't forgotten that some creep was still sending threats via her social media—she was startled to find Wade waiting on her mother's porch instead of another food-bearing acquaintance. Surprise rippled through her, along with a jolt of something more...sensual. She yanked open the door and gaped at him. "Um, hi."

Wade had been fit as a high school senior thanks to his

work on the family ranch and participation in a variety of team sports at school. But the Marines and time had transformed him into a solidly built and incredibly appealing man. No fleece-lined ranch coat could hide the wide set of his shoulders or the way his blue jeans hugged his muscled thighs and tight derriere. The new eye patch he wore, rather than detracting from his appearance, gave him a roguish, sexy aspect that stirred a tickle in her belly. She was imagining the pirate-centered role-play his new look inspired when she realized she was staring. She shook herself out of her daze and asked, "What are you doing here?"

Spying Luna at her feet, trying to sneak outside, she blocked the cat with her leg and gently nudged her back.

When she raised her gaze again, Wade was studying her, his gaze wary. "You did say you wanted my help with the house." He spread his hands. "So here I am. But if you've changed your mind..."

"No," she blurted as she grabbed his arm and tugged him inside from the frigid weather. "I just... I guess I'm surprised to see you this early in the day. Don't you have ranch work to do?"

She closed the door behind him, before Luna could escape, and held out her hand. "I'll take your coat."

As he shucked off his gloves and stuck them in a pocket of his coat, he pulled a different, smaller pair of gloves from his other pocket. "Here. These are for you."

She took the proffered gloves made of a buttery soft leather and lined with cottony fleece. "Wade, these are beautiful." She sent him a curious glance. "What... why—?"

"Because I noticed you didn't have gloves when you

were at the ranch the other day. You may not need gloves in LA, but you certainly will in Owl Creek."

Warmth spread through her. This was the sort of thoughtfulness that had first endeared her to Wade. But now, all these years later, she couldn't afford to fall for him again. He'd made his choice after high school, made clear she wasn't what he wanted. She'd be a fool to forget that and leave herself open to the kind of pain he'd inflicted when he'd left for his military career.

She pushed them back toward him. "Thank you, but... I can't accept them."

He folded her hands around them, encapsulating her fingers with his. "Yes, you can. They come with no strings attached."

She met his gaze and opened her mouth to refuse again, but something pained and pleading, as if this were a test of where they stood, a gesture of apology, the offer of a truce, filled his face. He also bore a faint ripple of scars on his cheek that she hadn't noticed in the dimmer light of the stable yesterday. As much as she wanted to ask about whatever obviously serious incident had caused the injuries and ended his military career, she swallowed the questions. If and when he wanted to tell her, he would.

She gave him a crooked smile. "All right. I accept. Thank you." Without pausing to reconsider, she rose on her toes to kiss his cheek. "I love them."

Dang...he smells good—crisp and fresh like the outdoors.

He peeled off his ranch coat, and she hung it on the hooks by the door, next to hers. Squatting, he held his hand out for Luna to sniff. "I thought your mother was allergic to cats. When did she get this one?"

"She didn't. That's Luna. She's mine."

"She's cute. But why didn't you just have a neighbor feed her while you were up here?" He angled a curious look up at her while Luna rubbed on his leg.

Because I'm not sure when I'm going back to LA— if I'm going back. She swallowed the honest answer, knowing it would only raise questions she wasn't prepared to answer, and hedged with, "Because I wasn't sure how long I'd be here, and... I didn't want to impose on a neighbor."

She twisted her mouth knowing how lame that answer sounded, mentally tagging on, *and because if the house in LA isn't safe for me, it could have been dangerous for Luna, too.*

Who knew what kind of cruel person her stalker was, and well...she wanted her feline buddy with her, darn it!

After tucking her new gloves in the pocket of her parka, she led Wade to the bedroom where she was sorting clothes. "So this is what I'm into today. I'm putting the outdated or ratty stuff over there to throw out, and the nicer things go over here to be donated."

Wade stopped in the doorway and stared at the pile of women's clothing on the bed. "Seriously? You think I have any notion what is considered out of date in women's clothing? I'm happy to be used for manual labor, but if you're counting on my opinion regarding what to toss..." He angled his head in a way that said, "bad idea."

Harlow looked at the clothes, then back to Wade. "You're right. This will keep. Let's tackle one of the closets. You can help reach the top shelves for me."

Stepping over a box of shoes, Harlow headed for the kitchen. "Can I ask a question?"

He visibly tensed and gave her a guarded look. "I guess."

"If you're helping at the Colton Ranch nowadays, how is it you have time to help me sort through frying pans and thirty-year-old Tupperware?" She opened one of the floor-to-ceiling kitchen cabinets and waved a hand to the clutter with flourish.

Wade's good eye widened in dismay, and he dragged a hand down his cheek. "Wow. That's a lot of frying pans and Tupperware."

"Yeah. It seems my mom did a little hoarding in her later years." She braced her hands on her hips as she considered the job in front of them. "So…are you going to answer my question?"

"I asked Uncle Buck for a few days off. He told me to take all the time I wanted. Winter is usually slower than other months around the ranch." His mouth tightened. "Thing is, I don't think he really needed my help on the ranch from the start. I'm pretty sure he just gave me a job out of…pity."

"Pity? Why would he pity you?" she asked, pulling a stack of mixing bowls from the middle shelf and moving them to the kitchen trestle table. As soon as she created the space on the shelf, Luna jumped up in the cabinet to explore the newly emptied space.

"Really? Isn't that obvious?" His dark brown eyebrows knit in consternation.

"Well, I can assume you mean because you had no job after your discharge from the Marines." She lifted Luna out of cabinet and set her on the floor. "Or maybe even because of the circumstances of your discharge, but I don't like relying on assumptions. It leaves too much room for error and miscommunication."

He grunted and reached for a stack of serving platters of various sizes. Setting them next to the mixing bowls, he sighed. "You're in the ballpark. Let's just say I was in need of something to occupy my time, and he offered a solution I was too—" he hesitated, twisting his mouth and twitching one hand as if choosing the right word "—too desperate to refuse."

Harlow frowned at him. "Desperate? That's an extreme word."

He shrugged.

"Do you mean desperate like...financially? Didn't you get any severance or disability or something from the Marines?"

He chewed his bottom lip for a moment, then said darkly, "Let's just say Buck thought I needed a reason to get out of bed in the morning, and he provided one."

A shimmer of disquiet crept through Harlow. Had Wade gone through a deep depression after his discharge? He wouldn't be the first person to struggle mentally after a life-altering accident that ended their career. She wet her lips and studied his grim expression. "And... did you need a reason to get out of bed?"

He shot her a look, the blue fire in his good eye speaking of an inner disquiet. But his mouth remained tightly clenched. Clearing his throat, he removed a dusty stand mixer from a higher shelf and moved it to the table. "So all of this stuff needs to be emptied from the cabinet?"

Oo-kay. So he didn't want to talk about his discharge,

the accident or the days following. She got the message, and she would respect his boundaries.

Probably just as well that she didn't hear his story. She didn't need to get drawn into the strife that Wade had endured or get emotionally tangled in the tragedy that had led him back to Owl Creek. She had her own problems to deal with. A house full of junk, memories and personal treasures to sort. A career that was growing as fast as she could keep up. And, more importantly, a menacing troll, who, though previously blocked, had recently created a new online profile and resumed posting threats to her business Facebook page.

Harlow shuddered and tried to play off her shiver as a response to his query regarding the cluttered cabinet. Averting her gaze from his, she stared at the shelves of kitchen detritus. "Yep. All of it has to go."

She removed the cat from the emptied shelf again, then pulled down another stack of pots and moved them to the table for sorting. Until she found a way to get rid of her stalker, the best she could do was bury herself in cleaning her mother's house—and protect herself from the kind of entanglements with Wade that would break her heart all over again.

Having finished the main kitchen cabinet and deciding to donate all of the pots, pans and small appliances to a charity that helped people in need set up a household, Harlow opted to move next to a hall closet with high shelves. If Wade should decide he'd had enough of the tedious task of cleaning out someone else's home, or if he simply balked for another reason—she couldn't rule out him simply walking away like he had eleven years ago—she wanted to take advantage of his six-foot-one height while she could. Climbing on chairs or ladders was dangerous enough without doing it while alone.

She pulled open the doors of the linen closet, but instead of sheets or towels, her mother had crammed the shelves with boxes of…stuff. Random bits of a life that apparently had no other logical storage place.

A low rumble emanated from Wade's throat when she stood back to show him their next job, and she couldn't help but chuckle. "I know, right? Have I mentioned how much I appreciate your assistance with this?"

"Mmm," he hummed by way of acknowledgment. "Where do you want to start?"

"Top down?" She aimed a finger at the boxes on the highest shelf. "That way, if you decide to run screaming from the house in surrender, at least we'll have gotten the hardest-to-reach part done." She sent him a teasing grin, but his returned scowl reflected no amusement.

"Marines don't run screaming in surrender. From anything."

The blue of his uncovered eye held a bright heat.

"Except their high school girlfriends," she returned before she could bite back the caustic retort.

His chin hiked up, and his mouth firmed. "Harlow…"

She shook her head and waved him off. "No…"

His nostrils flared as he drew a deep breath. "I did ask you to come with me."

Tension coiled in her gut. "And I told you why an unsettled, transient military life was all wrong for me. I needed stability, a home, roots."

He glanced away, his expression stony.

"Tell me something, Wade. How many times did you

move, transfer to new bases, not even counting deployment, in the years you served?"

Instead of answering her question, he said, "Are we really going to relitigate this?"

Harlow let her shoulders drop, then, running her fingers through her hair, she sighed in resignation. "No. I'm sorry. My comment was uncalled for. Let's...forget it."

Forget it? She scoffed to herself at the absurdity of her suggestion. First, because there was no way she'd forget anything about Wade or their breakup as long as she lived. And second, what mental health counselor of repute would advise a client to sweep a conflict under the rug to be ignored? Talk about unhealthy...

They were both silent for several taut seconds, avoiding eye contact.

Luna appeared from the kitchen and wove between her legs, meowing for attention.

Wade broke the stalemate. "Seems to me if we're both going to be in Owl Creek, we might need to talk enough to reach some sort of understanding. Leaving things unresolved is a bit like having loose ends of a live wire lying around."

He was right, damn it. And she was supposed to be the one with the cool head, dispensing practical wisdom and hard truths in palatable doses. "Touché. Better to defuse the situation than have it blow up in our faces later. But for the record, I'm not staying in Owl Creek. It's not my home anymore."

When she glanced at him, expecting a nod of consent or understanding, she encountered something far different. His complexion was ashen, his gaze fixed in near space, his square jaw as full of tension as she'd ever seen. She replayed what she'd just said, wondering what he could have been reacting to.

She wasn't staying in Owl Creek. Could that have been such a surprise or disappointment?

"Wade?" She touched his arm lightly, and he flinched, jerked his attention to her, blinking rapidly. "Did you think I was moving back here? All this effort, this cleaning—" she motioned around her to the boxes she'd been packing and sorting "—is so I can sell this house."

He scrubbed a hand over his face and flexed his hand, shaking tension from it. "Can we just get back to work?"

Turning away from her, he stepped to the open closet and reached for a box on the highest shelf. In his haste, the box tipped, and a cascade of photographs tumbled to the floor. Luna spooked and ran into the back bedroom. Wade grumbled a bad word as he stepped out of the scattered pictures and set the now-half-empty box on the floor a few feet away.

Harlow knelt to begin collecting the photos, taking a moment to glance at the memories captured on paper. Nostalgia washed through her, along with a fresh scrape of grief as she studied the smiling faces of her parents, her grandparents, her favorite aunt. Snapshots of her childhood, the numerous houses where they'd lived, school friends she only vaguely remembered—there'd been so many, each for such a brief time before her family packed up and moved again like circus performers or vagabonds. Fledgling bonds broken, again and again.

She tapped a handful into a neat stack and reached for more as Wade squatted beside her. He scooped up the pictures with efficient swipes, ignoring the images. And why not? He wouldn't feel the pull to linger over her family's captured moments. The faces and places wouldn't stir in his heart the way they did for her. Not his family, not his memories.

That's why when he did pause, lingering over a photo, longer than the others, her curiosity was piqued. "Whatcha got?"

She leaned closer to peer over his shoulder and, seeing the young couple in the picture he held, she froze. Prom night his senior year. She'd looked resplendent in a garnet dress that matched the red tie and cummerbund he'd worn and the red rose corsage on her wrist. The night they'd stayed out until 5:00 a.m. The night she slept with him the first time. Her body quaked with echoes of the sensual night. He'd made her first experience so wonderful, been so careful, so patient, so thorough as he loved her. He'd awakened feelings, sensations she'd never imagined possible.

She must have made some noise, because he glanced over his shoulder and met her gaze. After a beat, he asked, "Keep or toss out?"

More than the photo, he seemed to be asking if he should hold on to his recollections of that night or discard them on the trash heap of lost dreams.

"Just put all the pictures back in that box. I'll probably have most of them scanned later to save electronically."

He did as she asked, but his movements seemed stiffer to her, jerky. The prom photo had goosed the elephant in the room, adding to the hum of unspoken tension between them.

Sitting back on her heels, she gathered her courage to lance the wound and ease some of the pain between them. She'd like to think she could be friends with Wade going forward, and his presence there helping her seemed to indicate he wanted to put hard feelings behind them.

"It was a good night," she said quietly.

"Hmm?"

"Prom night. I have no regrets about anything that happened that night."

He angled his head toward her, his jaw tightening. "What's your point?"

She gave a startled chuckle. "Just making conversation. And maybe…trying to defuse a little of the tension in the air." A flicker of some sharp emotion flashed over his face when she said this. "What?"

He turned away and continued finger-raking the fallen photos and dumping them into the box.

"I came to work, not talk."

"Is there a reason we can't do both?" Harlow gathered a few pictures around her knees but kept a keen gaze on him.

"There is, if the topic of our conversation is going to be rehashing ancient history. The past is gone, and talking about it does no good. Nothing can change the mistakes we make. We just have to learn to live with the consequences."

He threw the photos in the box with more force than needed, a clear indicator of his agitation. A voice in her head whispered that she should back off, let the issue drop. But something haunted filled his expression that cried out to her, made her heart ache. "We can't change the past, but we can find closure. Forgiveness. Healing."

"So I'm one of your patients now? I don't remember asking for a counseling session." His tone was curt as he shoved himself to his feet and snatched another box from a high shelf.

Harlow sighed and raised a hand in resignation. She didn't want to antagonize him, and pushing someone who wasn't in a frame of mind to listen was counter-productive. "All right. We don't have to talk about any-thing you don't want to."

Once she'd climbed to her feet, she moved the box of gathered photos to the living room to sort later as she watched television. When she returned to the hall, Wade was dragging down a large box labeled "Harlow college." She hurried forward, knowing that box would be heavy, and reached for it. "I've got it."

He handed the old cardboard box to her, but as soon as she took it, the side tore, and thick textbooks and a dusty desk lamp crashed to the hardwood floor with a resounding *boom*.

Wade jerked as if shot. Tackled her. His cry of alarm sent a chill to her bones.

He landed on her hard enough to knock the breath from her, and she gasped for air as he pressed her to the floor, his entire body shaking.

"Wade?" she rasped, still struggling to find her voice. "What—?"

She managed to angle her head enough to see the stark terror and bloodless complexion of his face. His unpatched eye stared straight ahead, clearly not seeing what was before him, but some other time and place.

Harlow had studied PTSD in all its forms as she worked toward her counseling degree. But she'd only been in the presence of someone in the throes of a panic attack a handful of times. Wade was having just such a post-trauma panic attack, she was certain.

She wiggled a hand free and stroked his back lightly. "Wade, it's okay. You're safe."

After calling his name a couple more times, her voice finally cut through whatever had terrorized him. His gaze locked on hers before blinking as if trying to recall where he was.

At which point *she* became all the more aware of where he was. Namely, on top of her. The weight of his body, pressing her against the hard floor, conjured images all too recently dusted off. Prom night. Wade's nakedness entwined with hers.

An unbidden wave of desire shimmied through her. Her heart thumped louder in her ears, and her breath caught. "Wade—"

He lurched to his feet, his expression shifting instantly from terror and confusion to something more like horror. Or was it anger? Frustration? His body tensing, he staggered back a step or two, glaring at her. With a shuddering exhale, he stormed past her and slammed through the front door.

Chapter 6

Wade gritted his teeth and plowed fingers through his hair as he worked to quiet the echoes of the explosion that reverberated in his memory. Bad enough that he was still jumpy as hell, every loud noise taking him back to the day of the accident, but he hated—*hated*—that Harlow had seen him experience a flashback. He stalked across the yard, the frozen grass crunching under his boots, and let the icy air wash over him and shock him fully back to the present. He stared up at the bare limbs of the nearest tree, intentionally registering it. Something he could see…a dormant white poplar. He exhaled slowly, tuning his ears to the subtle sounds around him. Somewhere down the road an engine, diesel by the sound of it, rumbled. He inhaled again, noting the scents in the air. Something he could smell…pine. And woodsmoke from the neighbor's chimney.

He heard the front door open, interrupting his inventory of his senses, the exercise he'd been given by the Marine psychologist before his discharge to help root him and calm him when the flashbacks happened. He didn't have to turn to know Harlow was walking up behind him. Didn't have to hear her footsteps in the frosty lawn to sense her presence. Even before his Marine Corps Special Forces training had taught him to be hyperaware of his surroundings, he'd had a sixth sense when it came to Harlow.

Without looking up, he'd always known when she'd entered a room. He'd been able to read her thoughts, predict her moods. Anticipate her phone calls. He'd felt her to his marrow as if she were an extension of himself. Leaving for the Marines without her had felt like an amputation, a missing part of him for which he still experienced ghost pains.

"I brought your coat," she said now. "I figured you'd be freezing out here without it."

He glanced over his left shoulder. "I'm fine."

She scoffed. "You're shivering. Take the coat."

He unclenched his fists long enough to take the coat she held out to him. As he slid his arms into the fleece-lined sleeves, he gave her a measuring scrutiny. "Are you hurt? I shouldn't have knocked you down like that."

She shrugged one shoulder. "I'll live. Question is, are you okay?"

He ground his back teeth together, resenting the question he'd heard a gazillion times in the last eighteen months. *"I'm fine."*

Her dark eyebrow sketched up, and he realized belatedly how sour his tone had been. He forcibly shoved down his irritation and shook his head. "Damn it… I'm sorry. I'm just…sick to death of answering that question. People won't give me space. Peace…"

"People are worried about you," she said, her voice as quiet as the icy breeze stirring the lodgepole pines across the street.

"*People* don't need to be worried. They need to leave me alone. I just need...time."

"Hmm," she hummed, a sound that neither agreed nor contradicted.

He furrowed his brow. "What does *hmm* mean?"

She blinked as the first few flakes of a gentle snowfall landed on her eyelashes. "It means... I'm listening. I want to hear what you have to say."

"There's nothing to say. Especially not to you." He turned away, debating whether to get in his truck and drive away. *Run away, you mean.* Silencing the judgmental voice in his head, he stalked toward the front door, determined to end the discussion of his mental health there. But of course, Harlow pursued him...and the conversation.

"Why especially not me? What does that mean?" She jogged a few steps to keep pace with his long strides.

"That should be obvious." He stomped up the steps to the front door. "We have history. Even if I did want to talk to someone—which I *don't*—why would I open myself up to someone responsible for the greatest pain and regrets in my life?"

She stopped walking, and after opening the door, he glanced back at her.

Shadows filled her face. Her coffee-brown eyes reflected a hurt he'd seen in his own mirror for years. "Regrets? What kind of regrets?"

He sighed. "Harlow, don't. I didn't come over here to talk about me or my accident or our history. I only wanted to offer my help with what you'd said was a big, taxing job. I just wanted to be useful."

He expression shifted. "Do you not feel useful at the Colton Ranch?"

I haven't felt useful in eighteen months, he wanted to say. Instead, he cleared his throat and swallowed the bitter taste of frustration.

Hitching a thumb toward the open door, he gave her a level look. "Do you want my help or don't you?"

Harlow returned to the hall closet, following in Wade's stiff-backed wake. She was accustomed to prickly patients, clients who were wary of her peeking behind their mask to see their tender and hurting core.

Wade's panic attack, the visible wounds on his face and throat, only hinted at a greater turmoil roiling beneath the surface. She'd intentionally *not* asked him about the accident that had led to his medical discharge when she'd seen him yesterday at the ranch. If and when he wanted to talk about it, he would, and she would listen. But she wouldn't pry. In truth, she didn't want to open any emotionally fraught doors with Wade that would scrape raw the wounds she kept wrapped and tucked away where the past couldn't hurt her. But neither could she ignore his obvious pain and distress.

Wade was collecting the textbooks that lay strewn across the floor. He read aloud a couple of the titles as he stacked them next to the torn box. "*Introduction to Chemistry. British Literature from Dunne to Burns. Early American History.* These are all yours?"

She recognized his distraction technique. Anything that could pass as conversation and avoid a return to the topic of his breakdown. "All mine and going to the used bookstore tomorrow, so grab anything you want to keep for yourself."

"Pass. I've already got boxes in storage waiting for me

to decide my next move," he mumbled, then in a quieter darker tone. "I don't need to add anyone else's clutter to my life."

"A simple no would have sufficed." She crouched to add *Advanced Psychology Theory* to the stack.

"Fine. Then, no."

She studied the stony set of his jaw and caught the subtle tremor that lingered in his hands. "So you're not staying permanently in Owl Creek?"

"What?" He angled a curious look at her.

"You said you have things in storage until you decide your next move. That kinda implies you are thinking you'll move out of town at some point."

He frowned. "No, it means I don't know what is next, and the cottage I'm renting by the lake is small, came furnished, and doesn't have room for all my stuff."

"Oh. All right. How long do you think you'll stay in Owl Creek before you make a choice about your future?" She collected the desk lamp from the floor, noticing the light bulb had broken when the box fell. She stood to find a broom to sweep up the broken glass.

He slapped a hand down hard on the stack of books, growling, *"I don't know!"*

"Whoa," she said, lifting a hand in concession. "Forget I asked. I didn't mean to upset you."

"Look," he said, his lip pulling in a sneer, "I know you fancy yourself some kind of miracle-working, celebrity counselor—"

"What!" she said, stunned by his bitter tone and condescension.

He raised a hand to forestall her argument. "I've heard your show. I even heard *the* show that launched your celebrity status, but I'm not in the market for a talk show therapist."

She chuffed a humorless laugh. "Wow." She shook her head, not sure what to address first. His bitterness? The fact that he'd listened to her show? His obvious attempts to push her away with his hurtful comments?

Finally, taking a slow breath to recover her composure, she said, "How about a friend? Are you in the market for a friend? I kinda thought you were, seeing as how you were kind enough to come help me today. And the gloves..."

Wade's face scrunched as if he were in physical pain. "Harlow... I—" He hesitated, then, huffing out a sigh, he said, "Since my accident, everybody I know has had advice for me. My family. My friends. The doctors. Get some rest. Stay busy. Give it time. See a shrink. Talk it out. Put it behind you." His hand clenched into a fist. "I'm just so sick of it all. I want..."

When he didn't finish the thought, she prompted softly, "What do you want, Wade?"

He gave her a forlorn look, then pushed to his feet and headed for the door. He paused at the end of the hall. "I wish I knew."

The front door closed quietly behind him, and Harlow's heart squeezed in his absence.

Harlow was still eating breakfast when she heard a knock at her front door the next morning. Pulse jumping, she rose to answer the summons and, finding Wade on the porch, gave him a wary look.

He spread his hands, and his expression filled with regret. "Shall we give this another shot, if I promise not to be such a jerk today?"

She chuckled. "So you admit you acted like a jerk?"

"I've been guilty of that a lot lately, I'm afraid."

She opened her mouth to asked, *And why is that?* But Wade didn't want her to be his counselor, didn't need more probing questions. So she swallowed the query and said, "If that's supposed to be an apology, it needs work. Saying *I'm sorry* is simpler and to the point." She flashed a teasing grin and earned a twitch of his mouth and eye roll in return.

"I'm sorry." He stepped inside, out of the blustery weather, and unbuttoned his coat. "Can we agree not to mention our past or my future plans, though?"

"No past, no future." She pulled her lips into a moue as she pretended to be considering his request. "So... only the present?"

He snorted his amusement. "Something like that."

She waved him into the kitchen. "Care for some coffee? I was just finishing breakfast."

He accepted and pulled out one of the kitchen chairs. "I apologize for my comment yesterday about your internet show. I did listen and...you are good. You were... amazing with the suicidal woman."

She smiled at him and nodded her thanks. "Honestly? I was scared stiff. So afraid of screwing up and losing her." She shuddered, then lifted the coffee carafe from the machine. "But when you help someone get through a crisis, it is so fulfilling. So...worth it."

He wrapped his hands around the mug she gave him, steadying the cup as she poured. "And now your show's popularity has skyrocketed. Congratulations. Would it sound condescending if I said I'm proud of you?"

Startled by his praise, she sloshed some of the hot brew

onto his scarred hand. She gasped and grabbed for paper towels. "I'm so sorry. Did I burn you? Do you want ice?"

He lifted his hand to his mouth and sucked the coffee drips off with a sound a lot like a kiss. Her gaze lingered on his mouth, the pucker of his lips and sweep of his tongue as he licked the brew from his fingers. He took the paper towels from her and wiped his hand dry. "I'm good. I've survived worse." Then, as if realizing what he'd said, he lifted his gaze to hers, adding, "Obviously."

She bit the inside of her cheek, swallowing the reply on her tongue. He didn't want her questions...or her sympathy. So she gave a nod and let it pass. *Patience.*

"I planned to clean out the bathrooms today," she said as she returned the coffeepot to the brewer. "How are you with a mop and scrub brush?"

He lifted one eyebrow, and she laughed.

"All right, all right." She waved a hand of surrender. "We'll tackle the attic instead. Mothballs here we come!"

Several hours later, Harlow straightened from the box she'd been hunched over and stretched the kinks in her back. "I'm ready for a break. Can I interest you in a sandwich or reheated casserole for lunch?"

Wade stood from the plastic crate he'd been using as a stool, and when he straightened to his full height, he bumped his head on one of the slanted ceiling beams. Rubbing his skull, he mumbled, "Ouch," then, "Is it lunchtime already?"

She lifted her cell phone to check the time. "It's past lunchtime. It's almost two."

Harlow noticed she had a new text waiting and automatically swiped to open it. A pit of cold filled her belly when she read the message.

I will make you suffer like I have.

She gasped and dropped the phone as if it had scalded her. She raised a shaky hand to her thundering heart and sat down on the closest box.

"Harlow? What's wrong?" Stooping slightly to avoid knocking his head again, Wade approached her. He squatted to pick up her phone and glanced at the screen. Frowned. "What's this? Who sent that?"

She shook her head. "I don't know."

He knelt in front of her and narrowed a keen gaze on her. "You don't know or you don't want to tell me?"

She raised her head and swallowed the sour taste at the back of her throat. "I don't know who he is. He uses the screen name Chris72584."

"You've had threats like this before, from this same man?"

She nodded stiffly.

His jaw tightened, and a shadow filled his good eye. "Why didn't you say something before now? How often does he send threats like this?"

She wrenched her phone from his hand and sighed. "I didn't want to worry anyone. I've reported him to the LAPD already. And I blocked his number, but he finds ways to get around the blocks and—" She furrowed her brow.

The hard set of his mouth said he didn't like that response, and he repeated in a firmer tone, "How often does he send threats like this?"

"One or two a day for the last couple weeks. Always with new numbers. It's like playing whack-a-mole. Block one number and he gets another."

Wade bit out a curse word. "Why is he threatening you? What's his beef?"

She pushed past him, headed for the attic steps. "I can handle it, Wade. You don't need to get involved."

He followed her down the narrow stairs from the attic and into the kitchen. "I'm just worried for your safety."

Her shoulders drooped. "Yeah, well…me, too. That's… kinda why I came to Owl Creek this week. I wanted to put some distance between myself and LA."

"So this guy lives in LA?" Wade maneuvered himself in front of her, his positioning demanding her attention and answers.

Harlow rubbed her eyes. "I don't know that. But he knew where I lived and implied he was coming after me. I…panicked and fled town that night." She glanced up at him, frowning. "I know. I'm a coward. But I live alone, and the cops couldn't promise more than extra drive-bys on my street."

"You're not a coward. You're smart to get away."

He brushed the back of his hand along her cheek, and the shivers that chased down her back had nothing to do with fear.

"Can I do anything?" he asked, his voice warm.

Hold me, she wanted to say, but instead she shook her head. "I'm here now, essentially in hiding until the police track him down. I think I'm safe here. I mean… Owl Creek is about as off the beaten path as you can get, right?" She forced a laugh. "But once my mother's house is ready for market, I'll be moving on. I might not go back to LA, but I'll find somewhere else to lie low until the stalker is found."

Wade lifted a corner of his mouth, but his stare remained direct and concerned. "If you need anything, if you get even a hint of anything unusual, I'm a phone call away."

"Thank you, but... I'll be fine." She exhaled a cleansing breath, determined to put the stalker out of her mind. "Now...about lunch..."

Wade shook his head. "Can't. I'm afraid I have to go. My family has a meeting with our lawyer to discuss my father's will with our newly found half siblings."

"Nate and Sarah," Harlow said, and he sent her a startled look.

"How'd you know?"

"Vivian told me. She's dating Nate. They're pretty serious, too. Like really serious. In love."

Wade's nostrils flared, and he grunted. "Good for them."

She chortled. "Really, Wade? You may be down on love, but can't you be happy for Vivian and Nate? Or is it that you have bad feelings toward the half brother you just learned about?"

He raised a palm in self-defense. "I'm not down on love at all! Most of my siblings have found themselves in new relationships in the past several months. I'm happy for them. And as far as Nate goes..." Wade shrugged a shoulder. "I hold no ill will toward him or Sarah. What our father did, the circumstances of their conception, is not their fault. I have no reason to hold a grudge. In fact, that's kinda what this meeting is about." He checked his phone. "Which I'm going to be late for if I don't go now."

Harlow followed him toward the front door, a shiver chasing down her spine at the thought of being alone in the big quiet house.

You can run but you can't hide.
I will make you suffer like I have.

"Hang on a sec." She pulled out her own phone and called Vivian. After a brief discussion, she faced Wade. "Vivian is going to come with Nate to the meeting at the lawyer's office, and we are going to huddle up somewhere and discuss *Harlow Helps* while your family does your thing. Mind if I ride with you?"

The eyebrow over his good cerulean eye lifted. His expression said he understood, even agreed with, her reason for not wanting to stay home alone, but he had the good grace not to make an issue of it. "Sure. Let me move a few things off my front seat."

They grabbed their coats by the front door, and Harlow locked up the house. She stood by the passenger door of his truck while he shifted fast-food trash, a pair of work gloves and a coil of rope behind the seats. After brushing off some crumbs, he waved a hand to the empty seat. "All yours."

She eyed his trash and shook her head. "I thought Marines were supposed to be neat and tidy."

He glowered as he slid behind the steering wheel. "I'm not a Marine anymore."

"What! What happened to 'once a Marine, always a Marine'?"

He stared vacantly out the windshield for a moment before cranking the engine. "There are parts of my military experience I'm trying to put behind me. Deep down, I'm still a Marine, I guess. But…" He didn't finish his sentence, and she could see the warring emotions on his face. As he backed from her parents' driveway, he added, "I made my bed this morning, all tucked tight and smooth as glass. Does that count?"

She pictured Wade smoothing the wrinkles from his sheets and plumping his pillow, which led to a much different image of him rumpling his sheets...with her. A swirl of something warm and gooey puddled in her belly like a sweet dessert. Mercy! She didn't need to go down that mental path. Where your thoughts go, actions follow, and she would not, could not tangle herself up with Wade. Literally or figuratively.

"That counts," she replied finally, hearing the unwanted husky quality in her voice.

The look he gave her said he did as well.

Twenty minutes later, Wade and his siblings gathered around the conference table in Henry Deacon's downtown office, copies of their father's will before each of them. Along with drafts of the proposal they were making to change the distribution of Robert Colton's estate.

"And you're sure this is legal? I really don't want to find myself in court over this," Wade's younger sister Hannah asked.

Deacon, the family's lawyer, spread his hands. "Your father's will is valid and will be executed as is. Equal shares of his estate will go to each of his six children with his legal wife, Jenny Colton. What each of you choose to do with your share of the inheritance is strictly your business and separate from the execution of Robert's will. These papers I drew up—" he tapped the new document, of which Wade and each of his siblings had a copy "—simply spells out the terms of the private arrangement Chase discussed with me. If it meets your approval, we'll ask Nate and Sarah to join us, and we'll go over the terms together."

Wade squinted at the document, unwilling to tell anyone he had trouble at times with his "good" eye. He needed to see an optometrist for glasses or a contact for his left eye, he knew, but kept putting it off. He was sick to death of doctors and doctors' offices and dealing with the lingering effects of the explosion. How was he supposed to move on when he saw the physical reminders every time he looked in the mirror?

But Chase must have seen his struggle, because he leaned over to whisper, "Do you want me to ask Deacon to print a new copy in a bigger font for you? Or I could—"

"I'm fine," Wade said tightly. "But if I did need a special copy, I can ask for it myself."

Chase raised a hand in concession. "Okay, just checking."

With effort, Wade made out the important lines of the document, all the more determined to make do with the fine print in light of Chase's deference.

Everything seemed in line with what he and his siblings had discussed prior to the meeting, so he said, "It all looks good to me. I say bring them in."

"I agree with Wade," Ruby said. "It's perfect. It's fair. Let's do this."

Henry Deacon hit the intercom button on the phone at his end of the conference table. "Ms. Shaw, will you please bring Nate and Sarah Colton up to the conference room? We're ready for them."

Chapter 7

Harlow looked up when the receptionist's phone buzzed. She'd had her head bowed over the printout of media data Vivian had brought her, studying the rising numbers that reflected her show's viral popularity. She wished she could feel good about the growing audience, but the swimming numbers before her reminded her of the dark side of celebrity. Specifically, her stalker.

The text she'd received this morning shook her to her core. How had the guy gotten her private cell phone number?

She watched as the receptionist rose from her desk and motioned to Nate and his sister. "They're ready for you."

Nate bent at the waist to drop a kiss on Vivian's lips. "Wish us luck."

"You don't need luck," Vivian returned, smiling.

Sarah hooked her arm through her brother's. "Come on. Don't make me walk in alone."

When the brother and sister had disappeared down the corridor with the lawyer's receptionist, Harlow returned her attention to the data sheets. "So you think Facebook ads targeting the Southwest region will boost our audience there?"

"That and a few appearances on local news shows. I've had requests for interviews from Phoenix and Dallas TV stations and have a call out to a radio station in Santa Fe."

"Will I have to go in person or can I call in? Do the interviews remotely?" Harlow asked.

Vivian blinked. "Well, in person is best. You saw how your listenership spiked in the Boston market after your live appearance at the public health fair."

Harlow nodded and pressed a hand to the seesawing in her gut. In-person appearance was best for her ratings, but what about her safety? Even tucked away in Owl Creek, she felt as if the stalker was breathing down her neck.

Vivian cocked her head to one side and narrowed her eyes. "What's going on, Harlow? You were fine with the media tour and interviews before. Why do they bother you now?"

Harlow exhaled through her lips, making an exasperated sound with her lips. "I didn't say anything before, because I didn't want to worry anyone, but…well, Wade saw one of the texts this morning, so I guess the cat's out of the bag."

Vivian's expression darkened. "What cat?"

Wade studied the brother and sister sitting across the table from him and realized he was looking for signs of his father's genes in them. Did Sarah have his green eyes? Nate, their father's chin? Was that lift of his brow a gesture Nate had learned from Robert?

"As you are both aware," Mr. Deacon was saying,

"Robert's will divided his estate and holdings among his six—"

"Sir, if I may interrupt," Sarah said, and squared her shoulders. "I think I...*we*," she amended with a glance to her brother, "can cut through a lot of unnecessary business. We're aware our father didn't leave us anything. And we're fine with that. We don't need a payday, and the last thing we want to do is cause a problem in the family. Having been kept in the dark about our father's other children, we consider the discovery of our six half siblings to be a windfall."

"Ten half siblings, when you count our mother's children with Buck Colton," Nate said.

Hannah smiled warmly. "We feel the same way. Which is why we've asked you here."

Chase cleared his throat. "We've discussed the terms of our father's will amongst ourselves—" he motioned to his five full siblings "—and we are in agreement that it isn't fair."

"I can't imagine why Dad would have left you out! That's just...cruel!" Ruby added.

"Regardless," Nate said, raising a hand to halt the murmurs of agreement from Fletcher, Wade and Hannah. "That was his choice, and what's done is done. We don't blame you or hold any grudges. We don't want to start our new relationship with you by bickering over money."

"Good," Chase said, and tapped the document in front of him with his index finger. "That makes it easy. All you need to do is sign off on this new division of property we six have agreed on, and we can move on in harmony."

Sarah's frown voiced her skepticism. "New division of property?"

Nate picked up the paper Wade slid across the table to him. "The pertinent lines are about halfway down the page. Start reading where it says that the entirety of Robert Colton's estate will be equally divided and distributed to his *eight* offspring."

Sarah gasped. "Eight?"

Ruby beamed as she squeezed Sarah's arm. "That's right. We want the two of you to receive your fair share. We want all of Robert's children to get a share of his holdings and inheritance."

Hannah spread her hands as if stating something obvious. "It's the right thing to do."

"But we didn't ask you to—" Nate's voice cracked, and he tried again, "We'd never presume to—"

"We know." Wade waved off Nate's obvious doubts. "Which makes it all the easier to know we made the right choice."

"Your concern for putting family relationships ahead of the money," Ruby said, "demonstrates to us that our trust and choices are well-placed."

Sarah covered her mouth with a trembling hand. "I—I don't know what to say!"

Nate barked a laugh. "I do! Thank you. This is…incredible!"

Surging from her seat, Sarah wrapped her arms around Ruby, laughing though her tears. Then she came to stand beside Wade and opened her arms. "Can I hug you, big brother?"

Wade blinked and rose from his chair slowly. He couldn't remember the last time a member of his family had hugged him. *Really* hugged him. When he'd come home from the hospital, his burns and raw wounds made hugging painful for him, and his family had avoided the gesture. In the months since, his siblings—even his mother—had treated him like fragile glass. Gentle touches, soft pats, a handshake. But no firm hugs like the one Sarah wrapped him in now. He released a shuddering sigh, privately thanking her for the gift of the embrace. He'd never voice the truth, not wanting to show even a hint of neediness, but he'd missed human touch and connection.

If only Harlow were the one to hug him, hold him, touch him…

The huskiness in her voice this morning hinted that she still thought about the physical relationship, the passion they'd once had.

He released Sarah and stepped back, shoving thoughts of Harlow aside. She'd been clear enough that she wasn't staying in Owl Creek, hadn't forgotten how he hurt her and wanted nothing to do with him. Like the accident had closed the door on his military career, his past actions had closed the door with Harlow, and that was a burden he'd have to learn to live with.

"What aren't you telling me?" Vivian asked, meeting Harlow's eyes squarely.

Wiping the sudden anxious perspiration from her palms on the legs of her jeans, Harlow said, "A listener has taken exception to the advice I gave in one of my shows. I don't know who it is or what he found offensive, but he's been persistent in letting me know he's upset. I only know him by his username, Chris72584."

Vivian covered Harlow's hand with her own. "When you say he took exception…?"

Harlow shivered, and Vivian squeezed her fingers tighter.

"He's sending me threatening messages. He's managed to get my cell phone number and...based on recent Facebook messages, he's been to my house in LA. He's sending threats about making me pay for something, and I'm afraid he's tracking me. He might even know I left Los Angeles."

"In other words, he's stalking you!" Vivian said, her tone sharp with a cocktail of dismay, anger and concern.

Harlow nodded. "I don't want to cower or let him hold my life hostage, but until I know more, until I feel like this Chris person isn't a threat, I can't see myself traveling to any in-person interviews or presentations. I'm sorry."

"Don't apologize! Your safety is what matters. Have you reported him to Facebook? You can block him, you know."

"Yes, and I have. But then he gets a new account, and it starts over."

Shadows crossed Vivian's face as she mulled this news. "I hate to say it, but it might be best to shut down your social media accounts until this guy is caught."

Harlow shook her head. "That's the platform I use for my show! Besides, if I change platforms, he'd just follow me to the new one. But how many of my current listeners would follow me?"

"I see your point, but if this guy is dangerous..." Vivian sighed, chewed her bottom lip. "I did tell you Nate is a detective with the Boise police, didn't I? I can talk to him, see what connections he has in LA and here in Owl Creek to set up protection for you and—"

The banging of the office's front door yanked them both from their conversation with a jolt. Harlow clapped a hand over her racing heart. "Geez. This whole business has left me jumpy as heck."

"Understandably," Vivian said as they both turned to see a woman with chin-length, pale blond hair storm up to the receptionist's desk.

"Where are they?" the blonde demanded.

"Pardon me?" Deacon's receptionist asked.

The woman, who visibly vibrated with rage, aimed a finger of her frail hand at the receptionist. "Don't play stupid. You know who I mean! Where are Robert Colton's children?"

Vivian and Harlow exchanged a startled and wary glance. The woman seemed vaguely familiar to Harlow, and she struggled to place the woman's attractive, if sourly pinched, face.

"I'm sorry, ma'am, but Mr. Deacon and the Coltons are in a private meeting."

"Not without me, they're not!" The woman spun from the front desk and whisked past Vivian and Harlow in a cloud of hostility and cloying perfume.

Though the woman's appearance had changed in the last eleven years, her identity came to Harlow just a fraction of a second before Vivian gasped, "Oh my God! I think that's Nate's mother!"

Harlow swallowed hard as she bobbed a nod of agreement. "And Wade's aunt, Jessie."

Chapter 8

Wade stuck his hand out for Nate to shake. "I hope this can be the beginning of a good relationship going forward. There's no reason we shouldn't all get along, stay in touch."

"I agree. And thank you again for including us in our dad's inheritance. That's—"

The door to the conference room was flung open so hard, it crashed against the wall.

Wade jerked his head toward the sudden bang, his nerves jumping.

His aunt Jessie strode into the room and took in the gathering with narrowed eyes and a black scowl. In a shrill voice, she shouted, "What's going on here? Why was I not included in this meeting?"

Nate faced his mother. "Because it doesn't involve you."

"Doesn't involve me?" she shrieked. Jessie cast her gaze around the room, from face to face. "This is about Robert's will, isn't it?"

"I'm sorry, sir," Deacon's breathless receptionist said, trotting into the room behind Jessie. "I tried to stop her."

"It's all right. I'll handle this." The lawyer moved around the long table toward Jessie. "Mrs. Colton, I have to ask you to leave now."

When Mr. Deacon reached for Jessie's arm, she snatched it away. "Don't touch me! I'm not going anywhere. I demand to know what this meeting is about! If it concerns Robert's will, then it concerns me."

"I don't see how," Deacon said. "You were not named in his will."

Jessie's face grew red. "That has to be a mistake! I know he wouldn't cut me out that way! I deserve my share!"

Sarah approached Jessie, raising a conciliatory hand. "Mom, please don't make a scene. Father had every right—"

"Don't make a scene? Young lady, I have not even begun to make the scene I intend, if I don't get what I deserve!"

"What you deserve?" Wade asked, stunned by his aunt's hubris.

When she turned to face him, she flinched, actually wincing when she saw his scarred face. The reaction shouldn't have hurt, but somehow it did. Her cringe was a reminder of how people saw him now—someone damaged, someone difficult to look at. He gritted his back teeth and held her glare, determined not show anyone how her reaction to him stung.

"Well..." Jessie said, "I'd heard you were caught in an explosion. Left the Marines."

"What of it?" he asked.

She gave a dismissive sniff. "Nothing. Just a bit surprised to see you here. I'd heard you were living as a virtual hermit by the lake."

"Mom!" Sarah said in a low warning tone. "Stop it. You need to leave."

Facing the rest of the room again, Jessie lifted her chin and beneath her heavy winter coat, she drew her shoulders back. "No. I'm not going anywhere until I get what I came for. Either the lot of you cough up my share of the inheritance, or I will see you in court!"

"Court?" Wade's youngest sister, Frannie, cried in dismay. "Why?"

"Because I will contest the abomination that left me out in the cold. I should have inherited *at least* half of his estate! I bore that man two children. I kept his bed warm and kept his dirty secret, his second family, under wraps for years! It is a disgrace that I was excluded from his will." She waved a frail finger at Deacon. "A disgrace and an injustice!"

Henry Deacon, keeping his composure, moved to stand directly in front of Jessie. "Regardless of your beliefs about what you feel owed, the fact is Robert's will was legal and has been executed. According to the terms of that last will and testament, you do not receive anything and therefore have no business here. I must ask again that you leave peacefully."

"And if I don't?"

Fletcher stepped forward. "Then in my authority with the Owl Creek police I will escort you off the premises. Your cooperation or lack thereof will determine whether I take you out to the sidewalk or to the police station."

"Are you threatening me, Fletcher?" Jessie asked with a pinched mouth.

"I'm advising you of your choices," Fletcher replied calmly.

Her mouth pressed in a line of fury, Jessie glared at Fletcher, then at the rest of the family gathered around the conference table. "I will have Robert's money. I deserve my share, and I will get it." Her tone grew darker and trembled with what seemed to Wade to be an almost rabid passion and disturbing intensity. "I have special weapons available to me that I *will* use to get what I have coming." She aimed a finger at the ceiling. "God himself is on my side. I do his work and have his army behind me. Beside me. I will bring down you high-and-mighty Coltons, and I will get my just share! I swear it."

With that, Jessie turned on her heel and stamped out.

Wade and his siblings sat in stunned silence for several seconds before Wade said, "What in the hell was that all about? God is on her side? Special weapons available?"

"Is she talking about the Ever After Church?" Sarah asked.

"You know about her involvement with those crackpots then?" Fletcher asked.

Nate nodded. "Yeah. She's in deep."

"Off the deep end, more like," Frannie said. "She's completely under Markus Acker's sway. And Mom has said for some time she doesn't believe Jessie's involvement with the Ever After Church has anything to do with real religious conversion. It's a money grab. This—" she waved a hand to where Jessie had been standing "—whatever it was she just spewed kinda supports that theory."

Ruby chewed her bottom lip then, dividing a look between Jessie's children and Fletcher, she asked, "Do you think she's dangerous? Could she really cause us trouble?"

"Legally she hasn't a leg to stand on," Deacon said. "The will and your agreement signed today are airtight.

Your father's final wishes were clear and aboveboard, and your arrangement with Nate and Sarah has been signed and will be filed by the time the courthouse closes today."

"Seems to me the people at Ever After have done a number on her," Wade said.

Nate nodded. "She's clearly not in her right mind. I'd seen changes in her before this, but I've never seen her quite so riled up and talking nonsense."

"Whether we consider her comments today real threats or not, I'd say it's worth keeping a close eye on her and her dealings with the Ever After Church," Hannah said.

"Agreed." Chase rose from his seat and cast a gaze around the table at his siblings. "We should stay in close contact with each other, especially concerning anything that seem fishy in the coming weeks. We already have far too many reasons to be wary of Acker and his so-called church. If he has his hooks in Jessie, we need to add her to our watch list."

Wade nodded his agreement. "Will do."

A soft knock sounded on the conference room door, and Vivian poked her head in. "Everything okay in here?"

Wade's attention shifted to spot Harlow entering behind her PR rep and scanning the room until her gaze locked with his.

Nate crossed the room to enfold Vivian in his arms. "Besides my angry mother dropping in unexpectedly to make ludicrous demands and threats?" He kissed Vivian's forehead. "Everything is great. My newly discovered family has made a most generous gesture."

"Not the least of which being welcoming us into their fold," Sarah said, smiling warmly at Ruby and Hannah.

The women hugged, and Fletcher and Chase added their welcomes and shook Nate's hand.

"Are you finished with your business then?" Harlow asked, motioning to the buzz of activity. "We didn't mean to break up your meeting. We only came to say we were headed out for coffee."

"I'm finished. Can I take you for that cup of coffee? I have something I want to discuss with you. Frannie's bookstore is just down the street, and she serves the best coffee in Owl Creek."

Hearing her name, Frannie glanced over and beamed. "Why thank you, Wade. But if you're angling for free food, I'll have to have a word with the owner."

"I'm not angling for any special treatment," Wade said, an edge to his voice even though he knew his sister was teasing. Frannie's jest cut too close to the irritating habit his family had of tiptoeing around him and treating him with kid gloves.

Harlow gave him a puzzled look. "Uh...sure. That sounds good. But..."

He saw where she was going and added quickly, "Not a date. I've asked Chase and his fiancée Sloan to join us. Sloan has a company called SecuritKey that might be able to help us track down the guy who's been stalking you."

"Help *us* track him down?" Harlow said, her head tipping to one side. "Wade, I appreciate your concern—and I'm definitely interested in talking to Sloan and Chase—but my stalker is my problem. Not yours."

He stiffened, scowling at her. "So I'm not allowed to help? Did you really think I could learn someone is threatening a friend of mine, and I'd turn my back on the situation?" He firmed his mouth as a new thought occurred to him. "Or is it you don't think I'm capable of helping any longer?" He held out his scarred right hand and turned it for her to see, as if showing exhibit A in a courtroom.

Harlow sighed. "Don't put words in my mouth. I haven't given you any reason to believe I think any less of your abilities since your accident."

Chase stepped up and divided a look between them. "I don't want to interrupt, but Sloan says she's at Book Mark It and has snagged us a corner table. Shall we go?"

Harlow nodded. "Yes. I'm ready." She turned and left the conference room with Chase, while Wade let her words soak in.

As he trailed after them, headed out of the office, he reflected on the past couple of days—from his first un-expected meeting with Harlow at the stable through their conversations while packing her mother's house. She was right. While she hadn't pretended he hadn't been injured—which honestly was just as annoying as his family's kid-glove act—neither had she treated him as if his scars or his eye patch made any difference in who he was or how she viewed him. He'd even caught her looking at him with the sort of heat in her gaze that she had in high school. The lingering, hungry stares that had distracted him in physics class and sparked numerous afternoon make-out sessions on the banks of Owl Creek.

He followed Harlow and his brother outside and clutched the lapels of his ranch coat closed against the icy January wind as they all trooped out of the lawyer's office building. He took a couple of quick, long strides to catch up with Harlow and Chase and focused on what his oldest brother was saying.

"Well, the town hasn't changed that much since you left. Small business owners have managed to keep corporate America from storming in and taking over, but some of the shops in the downtown area have changed hands. Book Mark It, Frannie's shop, is in the building where Fincher's Farming Supply used to be."

"That wine shop is new." She pointed across the street to the shop called the Cellar and slowed her pace. "Weekly tastings?" she said reading the sign in the front window. "Intriguing."

"Yeah. Sloan and I went a couple weeks ago, and she loved it." Chase waved a finger toward Wade. "You should have this guy take you before you leave town again."

"Oh, uh, yeah," Harlow hedged, casting an awkward look toward Wade. "Maybe."

Without commenting on his brother's matchmaking, Wade hustled to the front door of Book Mark It and held it for Harlow. The mellow aroma of books and coffee flowed from the store, and Harlow stopped to inhale deeply. "Oh, Lordy, if there's a better smell in the world, I don't know what it is."

I do, Wade thought as he nearly collided with Harlow. *You.* When he inhaled, his focus was on the notes of something floral that wafted around Harlow as she peeled off her coat and hat, then shook her hair into place. Wade gritted his back teeth, shoving down the surge of desire that poured through him. If he wanted to keep Harlow safe from her stalker, he'd have to spend more time with her. And if he wanted to stay sane while protecting her, he had to find a way to tamp his still-powerful hunger for her.

Yeah, good luck with that.

Chase escorted them to the corner table, where a woman with long dark hair that curled around her face in soft clouds rose to give Chase a kiss. "Sloan, this is Wade's former girlfriend, Harlow Jones. Harlow, my fiancée, Sloan."

Harlow shook the other woman's hand, and Sloan's face lit with recognition. "Hang on. Are you the same Harlow Jones that has the internet advice show?" She snapped her fingers as she fumbled, then blurted, "*Harlow Helps*!"

Harlow grinned. "Guilty. In fact, the show is indirectly related to what Wade thought you might advise me on."

"Now I'm even more intrigued," Sloan said with a charming smile that put Harlow instantly at ease.

"Before we start," Wade said, peeling off his coat and tossing it on a spare chair, "can I get you a coffee, Harlow?"

She nodded, the chill of the walk over still burrowed to her bones. "Definitely. I've been told it's the best around."

Wade tugged up a corner of his mouth. "Three creamers and a hint of sugar?"

She gave him a wide-eyed look. "You remember?"

He dismissed the knowledge with a shrug. "We drank enough coffee together in high school to float a boat. I'd have to be pretty lame to forget your order."

He could be nonchalant about it if he wanted, but Harlow found it moving that Wade had remembered a detail about her others might consider too trivial to hold on to. She shucked off her gloves—the ones he had given her earlier that week—and watched him stride up to the counter. What did it say that she remembered his regular order was black coffee with a sprinkle of cinnamon?

Chase met Sloan's gaze. "Your usual?"

"Please." The affection in Sloan's eyes as she looked up at Chase tugged at Harlow's heart. Seeing how many of Wade's siblings and cousins had found loving relationships in recent months was heartening. After all the shared high school classes, lazy days at Blackbird Lake, family barbecues at Colton Ranch, Harlow was happy to know her friends, members of Wade's family, were finding happiness.

A warm sense of comfort and familiarity washed through her, chasing away the lingering chill of the January day. Harlow sighed as she settled back in her chair and glanced around at the cozy bookstore Frannie ran. A half circle of comfy chairs created a homey reading spot in front of a stone fireplace, and a handwritten chalk notice on a blackboard over the coffee bar advertised a weekly story time for children. Harlow loved every book, mug and wicker basket in the store. The bookstore, the renewed businesses of Owl Creek, the warmth of her old friends and new acquaintances, tugged at her soul. She could all too easily fall back into her old routines, the patterns and people of her life in Owl Creek.

Including Wade.

A different sort of heat rippled through her as she studied his profile in the light from the front window. He wore a thick layer of stubble on his cheeks, which only added to his roguish appeal. She was clearly still attracted to him and his thoughtfulness. The easy way he seemed to plug back into her life as if nothing had happened eleven years ago—

But something did happen eleven years ago. Something painful and harsh and devastating to her young heart. She needed to not forget that. Forgive, maybe. But forgetting would be setting herself up for another heartache.

"Harlow?"

She shook out of her wayward thoughts and blinked as she turned to Sloan. "I'm sorry. What were you saying?"

"I asked how long you were going to be in Owl Creek," Sloan said chuckling. "Where were you just now?" Sloan's attention shifted to the coffee counter where Chase and Wade were talking in low voices as they waited for the barista to finish the drinks. "Hmm. Never mind. I can guess."

Harlow opened her mouth to deny Sloan's implication, then closed it again with a soft click of her teeth. "It just feels strange being back in Owl Creek. It's almost like picking up where things left off after high school. Except…things *have* changed."

The men returned with the coffees, and as he took his seat, Wade opened the discussion. "So I called you—" he divided a glance between his brother and Sloan "—because Harlow has acquired a stalker."

Chapter 9

Chase and Sloan both sent Harlow wide-eyed looks of alarm.

"I thought you might be able to help," Wade said, "both with some levels of added security and also some computer knowledge. It'd be great if we could track down this guy through his server or IP address. Maybe his cell phone?"

Sloan wrapped both of her hands around her mug and frowned. "Back up a bit. Fill me in on when this all started, how this creep has contacted you, what he's said and so forth."

With a nod, Harlow explained how Chris72584 had first contacted her through the comments on her Facebook Live post, then directly messaged her, progressing from irritation and displeasure with the advice she'd given to implied threats.

"When he messaged me a picture of my own house he seems to have lifted from Google Earth, I got spooked and decided to leave town." She shuddered as the sense of violation tripped through her again.

"Have you reported all this to the police?" Sloan asked, scribbling notes on a small notepad.

Harlow nodded. "I did. In LA, after the picture of my

house was sent to me. They took my statement, but the officer who responded to my call didn't sound especially optimistic about finding the guy. He said they get hundreds, even thousands, of online bullying and stalking reports every year and have far too few people to work all the cases."

Wade grunted in a way that said he was displeased with the LAPD's response. "Well, you're not in LA now. We'll talk to Fletcher and get the local guys on it. The department may be small, but Fletcher and his fellow officers will take your case, your safety, seriously."

Chase nodded his agreement.

"If I'm honest, I came to Owl Creek not just to close out my parents' house and get it ready to sell, but because I thought I'd be safer here until this creep either gives up and leaves me alone or the California police find him."

"Not a bad idea. When was the last time you heard from the guy?" Sloan asked.

"Today... Maybe."

Chased pulled a frown. "Maybe?"

When Harlow hesitated, an anxious stir in her gut, Wade said, "This morning she got a disturbing text from an unknown number. While we have no proof it is the same guy, the message read much like the online threats from this Chris72—whatever—person."

Sloan raised both of her delicate eyebrows and tipped her head as she looked at Harlow. "He texted your private phone?"

Harlow exhaled through pursed lips. "Yeah."

Extending her hand, Sloan asked, "May I see it?"

Harlow fished in her handbag until she found her cell

phone and handed it to Sloan. Bending her head over the device, Sloan swiped and tapped through a number of screens, studied the text, then groaned. "Yeah. Not good."

Harlow reached for her phone, but Sloan drew the cell away. "Harlow, do you want my best advice? My help keeping you safe?"

"That's why we're here," Wade said, his expression all business.

Sloan waited for Harlow's nod, then reached in her own handbag and took out a small tool kit. She set to work, prying the back cover off Harlow's phone and removing both the battery and a small piece of plastic. "Your SD card. Chase, honey, will you ask at the counter if they have a small plastic ziplock bag?"

Harlow gaped at her dismantled phone. "But… I need my phone."

Sloan shot her a commiserating look. "I understand. Really. And I'm not suggesting you destroy any of the parts just yet. But I do suggest you buy a burner and be very selective who you give the new number to."

"A burner? Where do I get one of those?"

"Not in Owl Creek," Chase said, returning with a small bag that he offered Sloan for the parts of Harlow's phone. "Closest store likely to sell burner phones would be in Conners."

"That presents a small problem, then. I don't have a car. I flew here from LA and Vivian picked me up at the Boise airport." She split a questioning look between Chase and Wade. "Does anyone in Owl Creek drive for Uber or Lyft?"

Wade's brow dipped in consternation. "You don't

need Uber, Harlow. I'll take you to Conners. We can go this afternoon."

Her pulse jumped at the thought of an afternoon expedition with Wade.

"Um," Chase interrupted, "I thought the doctor had restricted your driving until your left eye heals completely."

Harlow choked on the sip of coffee she was drinking. "What?" She sent Wade a sharp look. "But…you drove us into town today! And you've been driving over to my mom's house!"

Chase scowled. "Wade? Is that true?"

Wade's jaw flexed and tightened, a sure sign he was grinding his back teeth. "That was months ago. My eye has healed considerably since then."

"How much is considerably? Has the doctor signed off on your driving?" Chase asked.

Wade didn't answer, turned his head. Which was answer enough.

Chase growled. "Wade…"

Wade's jaw tightened. "I'm doing well enough. I don't need a doctor to tell me when I can or can't drive. Besides, I know the roads in town like the back of my hand."

His brother grunted. "Don't be stubborn, Wade. You want to kill someone driving with impaired vision?"

Harlow saw the color drain from Wade's face, the tension that turned his countenance to stone. The pain that flashed in Wade's unpatched eye sent a clawing reciprocal ache through her.

Harlow shifted her attention to Chase. Did Wade's brother see what she saw?

Extending an upturned palm, Chase gave Wade a sympathetic gaze. "Give me your keys, bro. Just like I won't let anyone I love drive drunk, I can't in good conscience let you behind the wheel until your eye's healed or I know you're wearing a contact."

Wade's breath came quick and shallow, his nostrils flared, and a combination of hurt and anger simmered from him like steam.

Harlow cleared her throat and suggested in a gentle tone, "Wade, what if I drove us to Conners in your truck?"

Wade's head, his attention, turned toward Harlow, and after a beat, she saw his jaw relax a little, his hard-edged glare soften. His breathing slowed enough for him to take a deep lungful of air and release it with a sigh of resignation. He leaned on his hip enough to dig his keys out of his jeans pocket and drop them on the table by Harlow's hand. "Looks like you're Uber now."

Clearing her throat, Sloan took a laptop from a satchel on the floor beside her. She scooted her coffee aside and opened the computer on the table. "Tell me more about your stalker's communication with you through Facebook. Did you delete his comments? Block him from posting?"

"Yes and yes. Blocking him only angered him, and he set up a new account and came at me again."

"You're sure it's the same guy with a new account?" Sloan asked.

"He made sure I knew it was him. And don't suggest I get off Facebook because that is how I make my living, how I reach my audience. Even if I shift to another platform, I'd have to tell my Facebook followers where to find me, so I don't lose my current audience."

"Which would mean the creep would know where to

find your show, too," Wade said with a defeated sound-ing sigh.

"Exactly." Harlow took a sip of her coffee as she mulled over the situation. "I've already put the show on a brief hiatus, presetting show reruns to air for the next couple weeks while I'm here. I don't want to lose listeners over this."

Sloan pulled her hair back from her face with both hands and secured the unruly curls with a stretchy cloth band. Then unfolding a stylish pair of glasses that she slipped onto her nose, she started swiping and typing on her laptop. "My security company can definitely dig into this for you. We'll need your written permission to ac-cess some of your account information, passwords and so forth, but we may be able to track down at least the lo-cation of the stalker's computer through his IP address."

"That's a start, but what about her personal safety while she's here in Idaho?" Wade asked.

Harlow sent Wade a startled look. "You think he's tracked me here? That he'd actually travel here to hurt me?"

"You really want to trust that he won't?" Wade re-plied.

"It's a possibility we need to consider." Sloan looked at Harlow over the top of her glasses. "Does your par-ents' house have a security system? Cameras outside?"

Harlow shook her head. "This is Owl Creek. When I was in high school, my parents didn't even lock their doors on the nights I went out. I never had to carry a house key."

"Times have changed, even in Owl Creek," Wade said, his gaze full of concern.

"We've had a spate of crime around here lately. Violent attacks, break-ins and murders."

"Fletcher has been busy working cases of all sorts lately," Chase said. "Our cousin Lizzy was even kidnapped."

Harlow gaped, her stomach performing flip-flops. "Lizzy? My goodness. I had lunch with her this week and she never mentioned it."

"She's not the only one in the family who's had a run-in with a dangerous element lately, either," Chase said.

"Good grief! Vivian told me about what happened to her, but I had no idea it was part of a crime spree."

"There's a new church just outside of town," Sloan said, "and we have reason to believe they are involved with all sorts of illegal stuff."

"The Ever After Church I've been hearing about? The one Jessie is tangled up with?" she asked.

"Cult is a better descriptor," Chase said, "and yes. That's the one. We even think the cult could be behind our father's murder."

Harlow jolted. "What? You think Robert was *murdered*?"

Wade nodded. "We have reason to believe so. Yes."

"But *why*? Who would want to kill your father?" She goggled at the notion, remembering Wade's father as a kind and gracious man—secret family aside.

"Good question. Right now, our lead suspect is Marcus Acker, the founder and leader of Ever After."

"Um…" Harlow blinked hard and fumbled to process the onslaught of tragic and disturbing things she was learning. "What… I mean, that's—"

"A conversation for another time," Wade said.

Harlow snorted derisively. "Not much of a selling point for my parents' house. I can see the listing now. *High crime rate in neighborhood.* That'll drive the selling price up. Not."

"What *will* be a selling point is a good security system," Sloan said with a crooked grin. "And SecuritKey can fix you up. I can get someone out there tomorrow if that works for you."

Harlow's head spun as she processed what she was hearing. "I, uh…" She'd always felt so safe in her parents' home, in Owl Creek, but on the heels of the stalker's text on her private phone this morning, the revelations of local crimes rattled her. She imagined herself sleeping in the dark house tonight, only a cat for company, and a shiver raced down her spine. She didn't consider herself the sort to scare easily, seeing danger lurking around every corner. But neither was she foolish enough to take unnecessary risks. "I suppose it would be prudent."

"Good," Sloan said, tapping her laptop keys as she said, "I'm clearing my schedule, so we can take care of that first thing in the morning."

Harlow glanced at Wade, who bobbed his chin in approval. "I can be there to help."

"I don't need—" Harlow started, but when determination fired in Wade's gaze, she dropped her protest. She might not believe she needed his help, but what did it really hurt to humor him? If it gave him a sense of purpose, eased his mind, satisfied a need he had to be useful, so be it.

"Meanwhile, this afternoon, I will call the LAPD and see what progress they have made and get with Fletcher to see what the local police might be able to do for extra protection for you," Sloan said.

Harlow nodded. "Thanks."

"And I'll get my best hackers to track down anything they can find online about—" she consulted the hand-written notes she'd made earlier "—Chris72584. Those numbers after his name could be a birth date or anniversary or part of an address. Most people are not especially creative when creating usernames or passwords. In order to help them remember account information, most people use something personal...which helps my hackers fill in a lot of blanks and track the right information."

Harlow thought about her own passwords and cringed internally. She was as guilty as the next guy of taking such shortcuts.

Sloan closed her laptop and gave Harlow a reassuring smile. "Don't worry. My team is good. I have every confidence we'll root this guy out and get rid of him for you." She finished her coffee and stuffed her dirty napkin inside the cup. "If there's nothing else, I'll get started on this and have my security people at your house at... is 8:00 a.m. too early?"

Harlow rose from the table, collecting her own trash. "Eight is fine. Thank you for your help." She included Chase in her glance. "Truly." Facing Wade, she said, "I guess if we're going to Conners for a burner phone, now's as good a time as any."

Wade nodded, collected both of their empty cups and returned them to the dirty dish rack by the coffee bar. Harlow slid into her coat, and after thanking Chase and Sloan again, pulled Wade's keys from her pocket and accompanied him to his truck.

Despite the bare trees and gray tones of winter, the drive to Conners was beautiful to Harlow. The majesty of the snow-capped mountains and crystal beauty of the lake and streams along the route spoke to Harlow's soul. Like a siren's song calling her home, the natural landscape reminded her of hours spent on Blackbird Lake in the summer and hiking the mountain trails amid the rich fall colors. In a few months, the green shoots of spring would pop up and wildflowers in a rainbow of hues would brighten the fields. Many things in Owl Creek had changed, but the ageless rhythms of the river and hills offered a constant that she craved while so much in her life now was uncertain.

"I missed this," she said, gesturing to the scenery out the truck's windshield. "Having lived so many places growing up, I can say without question that Idaho is my favorite place on earth."

Wade was silent for a moment, his expression contemplative, before he said, "Mine, too."

"That's saying something. I'm guessing you got to see a lot of the world during your time in the Marines." She cast him a side glance in time to see him frown. "What?"

"Can we talk about something else?"

"Something besides your travels with the Marines?"

"Something besides the Marines."

"Oh." She focused her attention on the road. "Sure." She fished for something to break the silence. "Sloan seems nice. How did Chase meet her? I mean, last I'd heard Chase was married."

Wade grunted and shook his head. "He's divorced now. Obviously." He waved a hand in dismissal. "Long story. Sloan's from… Chicago, I think. That's where

SecuritKey has its main office. But a few months ago, Chase noticed some funny business with Colton Properties and hired Sloan to help him root out the problem. To put it in a nutshell, she came to Owl Creek, they hit it off, and now they are planning a future together."

"And did they find the problem at Colton Properties?"

Wade grimaced. "Yeah, an employee was embezzling money. But after Sloan figured that out, she started digging into the Ever After Church and Markus Acker. It looks like there are a lot of shady things going on with that church."

Harlow gaped at him. "Good grief! This Acker guy is everywhere and into everything!"

"We've noticed," Wade said dryly.

"If they can connect Acker to so many crimes, why isn't he behind bars? Why is the church still operating outside town? Can't they be closed down or...or... *something*?"

"Believe me, Fletcher is working with a number of people and other agencies, trying to find the piece of the puzzle that will make something stick. But the guy is slippery. He uses other people to do his dirty work and buries his connections deep, so that there are multiple layers of deniability between him and the chaos he's causing."

Harlow shivered. "Geez, what happened to the safe and quiet little town Owl Creek used to be?" She gripped the steering wheel tighter and knit her brow. "Maybe I was wrong thinking I'd be safe here until my stalker is caught."

Wade shifted on the seat, angling his body toward her. "Are you saying you want to leave Owl Creek?"

"No, I—" She sighed. "I mean I still have to get my

parents' home ready for market. But honestly, I could do that anytime. The dead of winter wouldn't have been my first pick of times to be back in Idaho, but..."

"But?"

She turned up a palm. "But... I don't know. The text this morning, this news about a dangerous man stirring up problems in town...it's all got me spooked. I thought if I lay low up here that I'd be safer—"

"You are safer," he interrupted, his blue eye focused on her with an intensity that penetrated to her marrow, "because I will keep you safe."

"Wade, you don't have to be—"

"And toward that end..." He squared his shoulders and hardened his expression in a way that said he'd hear no arguments from her. "Let's go over what we know about your stalker, your shows and see what we can figure out."

She angled a withering look at him. "Don't you think I've done that?"

"Not with me. Maybe I'll think of something you took for granted."

"Wade..."

"Humor me. We have another half hour in the car."

Harlow groaned but nodded. She pinched the bridge of her nose as she conjured the events of the past couple months to review again with Wade. "I've told all this to the police in LA."

"But I have a vested interest and all day to work on it. Go." He waggled a finger, urging her to start talking.

"Fine." She rolled her head side to side to stretch her neck as she explained, "I got the first message from him in the comment section of one of my Facebook Live broadcasts."

"Which one? Do you still have the broadcast and comments archived where I can look at them later?"

"Uh, yeah. Well. Not the original comment from him. I deleted it after I reported him to Facebook."

She heard his sigh and said, "Yeah, I know. Not the best move, but I just hated having his vitriol polluting my mental health page."

He grunted and waved a hand for her to continue. "But then more comments came in, and I left them for the police to see and trace. After I blocked him from commenting on the show's posts, he started direct messaging me on my personal account."

"And what was the topic of the show he commented on? What was his beef?"

"That particular show was about the need for caregivers to take care of themselves, how mental and physical exhaustion can affect the people responsible for caring for elderly parents or sick family members or small children."

"Huh." Wade's brow furrowed as he considered the information.

"Right? I mean, what is offensive about wanting people to give themselves rest and seek support from others when they feel overwhelmed?"

"And the comment said…?"

Harlow's gut clenched remembering the cruel words. "It said, 'Your *expletive* advice is a crock of…*another expletive*.'" She cut a side glance at Wade. "'It's all your fault. Her blood is on your hands. I'll see you in hell.'"

The creases of concern lining his face deepened. "Whose blood is on your hands? Any indication of the guy's relationship to the 'her' that presumably died if you have blood on your hands?"

She lifted a shoulder. "Your guess is as good as mine. He never said. Because of the content of that show, I was working on the assumption of a loved one, maybe a sick child or elderly parent. Maybe that child or parent was left in someone else's care while the primary caregiver took the respite I recommended, and maybe something tragic happened while the primary caregiver was gone. Maybe the stalker is the caregiver, and maybe he needs to find someone to blame or—"

Wade snorted. "That's a lot of maybes."

She scowled. "Maybes are all I have, Wade!"

He raised a hand conceding the point. "Your scenario is possible, but—" he twisted his mouth as he thought "—if a third party were involved—the babysitter or hired nurse or neighbor who stepped in to help but allowed the child or patient or whomever to die—why not make that person the focus of his rage and blame?"

She shrugged again. "I got nothin'." After a beat, she added, "The thing is, I have people call in to the show who are suicidal, people who are dealing with abusive relationships, people fighting addictions of all kinds, people who are struggling with fears and anxieties and… gosh. So many of life's hardest problems. Any one of the callers' cases could have taken a bad turn, whether they took my advice or not. This Chris guy who's taken exception to something I did or said could be anyone. The father of a teen who died of an overdose. The husband of a woman suffering from crippling anxiety who killed herself. I just—" She heard the pitch of her voice rising and stopped, took a slow breath and exhaled slowly. She braked as they arrived at a crossroad, and she waited for the traffic to clear. In a calmer tone, she said, "I just don't know, Wade. It could be anyone."

He reached for her hand, lifting it from the steering wheel and pressing it between his. She could feel the light ripple of scarring, the rough scrape of ranching calluses and the warmth of affection as he held her hand sandwiched between his. His touch soothed her, steadied her.

"We'll figure it out, Harlow. I promise. We'll figure it out together. Until this creep is caught, I'm all in."

Chapter 10

All in...

A shudder rolled through Harlow as conflicting emotions swirled inside her. She was both relieved and comforted by the idea of having Wade's support, but also a tad resentful that it took her being in personal danger to hear those words from him. Where had his *all in* been after high school when her world had centered on him? When her heart had been invested, he'd ignored her needs, turned his back on all they had and cut her from his life like a cancer.

When the car behind them honked with impatience, he released her hand, and she shoved down the ache of lost love. Again. How many times would she have to battle back the painful memories before losing Wade no longer hurt so much?

She pulled out on the crossroad to Conners and swallowed against the lump in her throat. As long as she was in Owl Creek and regularly crossing paths with Wade, the past would be hovering, following her like a shadow she couldn't outrun. All the more reason to work quickly on her parents' house and move on to...wherever she decided her next refuge would be. Seattle? Portland? Heck, maybe she'd flee across the country to Boston. Or visit Sydney. It was summer in Australia now, after all. She could escape the winter cold, her stalker and Wade all at once.

Escape. The word roiled in her gut. Wasn't that just a nice way of saying she was running from her troubles? How many times had she told clients that strategy never worked? Problems, conflicts and hard truths needed to be faced and addressed before real healing could take place.

"Let's try this place," Wade said, drawing her out of her ruminations. He pointed out the passenger window to a large supercenter department store.

Within an hour they'd purchased and activated the burner phone for Harlow and had bought a few groceries they each needed.

They were almost back to Owl Creek when Wade said, "How do I access your archived shows? I think I'll do a marathon listen tonight and see if anything pops out for me."

"I can send you a link, but… I've been through them all twice and sent them to the LA police."

"With all due respect, you're too close to the show. I may be able to pick up on something you missed. And the cops?" He shook his head with a twist of his lips. "They're swamped. I can't imagine the backlog of cases the LAPD has."

She cast a glance to him from the driver's seat. "Fine. If that's really how you want to spend your evening…"

"Can't think of a better use of my time than making sure you're safe."

"Then I'll send you what you need once I get home and can boot up my laptop."

"Good." He paused, a worried look crossing his face. "Except...use your new phone to send info, okay?"

"But it's saved on my laptop."

The muscle in his chiseled jaw tightened. "And you've used your laptop since arriving in Owl Creek?"

A chill raced through her as it clicked. "You think my stalker might be able to track me because I used my laptop since coming to Owl Creek?"

He dragged a hand over his jaw as he exhaled. "I guess that depends on how tech-savvy the guy is. He's already found a way to skirt your blocks on Facebook, so he's no dummy. And in the same way the police department and Sloan's computer experts are trying to track your stalker's individual computer fingerprint and IP address, your stalker could be tracking you. Even if you go to an internet café, if you're using your laptop, you're leaving a data trail that can be followed."

Harlow's heart sank. "So I have to get a new laptop, too? I mean, I will if that's what I have to do to shake this guy but...geez!"

Wade shook his head. "You can probably hold off on that for now. Just don't get online, turn off your Wi-Fi connection, and...well, you can come to my place and use my computer any time. And we'll download the files of your show onto a thumb drive for me to take home."

She nodded. Groaned. Then turning to Wade, she said, "If I haven't said it before now...thank you. I appreciate all your help."

Later that night, after stopping by Harlow's to drop her off and download her program files, Wade plugged the flash drive into his desktop and called up the files on his desktop. While the files loaded, he grabbed a beer from the fridge and a box of crackers from the pantry. He leaned over the computer and opened the first file. Harlow's sultry voice filled the air from his speakers, and he carried his snack and drink to his recliner and settled in.

"Hello, my friends! This is Harlow Jones back with a new episode of *Harlow Helps*."

Wade took a pull of his beer and dug his hand in the box of cheesy crackers.

"I'm a licensed mental health counselor, and I'm here to heal the world and promote mental wellness, one person at a time."

Wade arched an eyebrow. *Speaking of cheesy...*

"But Harlow, you may be saying, there are billions of people in the world. If you reach just one person at a time, you'll never finish in one lifetime!" Harlow's melodic laughter flowed from his computer and tripped down Wade's spine. "You'd be right. But one life can touch another one, then another, in a chain of healing and love that spreads like ripples on the water."

Wade snorted. Harlow was being rather trite and sappy, but he wasn't listening to grade the presentation or her showmanship. His only interest was content. His job was to focus on who may have called in or what Harlow might have said to enrage Chris72584.

The first episode played out without him finding anything of note. The focus of her advice centered on helping a woman deal with her anxiety and trouble sleeping. Next was a woman with a shopping addiction. The next episode turned to grief, a woman who had lost both her spouse and cherished pet within a month and was struggling.

"Grief has no timetable and no set prescription for dealing with it, Helen," Harlow told the woman in a gentle tone. "Don't let society or friends or media tell you how you should react. Your emotions are genuine and important, and no one can tell you how you *should* feel. Don't be afraid to grieve, either. Allow yourself to walk through the emotions, because suppressed feelings only fester and become a bigger problem down the road."

Wade's hand tightened on his bottle of beer. Harlow's advice, meant for the caller, struck a nerve. Were his nightmares, his lingering trouble dealing with the munitions accident a symptom of him suppressing his grief and guilt? His doctors at the military hospital had tried to talk to him about the explosion, but he'd refused. How could he open up about something so raw and painful? The horror of that day was hard enough to get through when it happened without reliving it—with an audience to witness his most private battle, no less.

The next episode tracked along a similar vein. Harlow guided a man with depression and thoughts of suicide over a broken relationship through an emotional exchange in which Harlow acknowledged the man's pain without making any judgments. She listened to the man's story and gave him sympathy and support without sounding condescending. By the end of the show, she'd convinced the man to talk to a professional counselor with whom Harlow had promised to put the caller in touch.

The next episode was from a woman whose husband became violent when he drank. Wade cringed internally at the all-too-common story of violence against women by men who'd sworn to love and protect them. Guys like this woman's husband made Wade's blood boil.

As his fury and dismay on behalf of the caller grew, Wade rose from his chair and hurried to the computer desk. He took out a notepad and pen, and after consulting his monitor, he jotted down the episode number for future reference before starting that episode over. He also wrote down the woman's name, Susan, even though she said it wasn't her real name. But perhaps there was a kernel of truth in the pseudonym. A mother, a sibling, a middle name.

With keenly focused attention, he listened for clues about the woman as she described the abuse she lived with. Knowing Harlow as well as he did, he could hear the tremble in her voice that betrayed her own alarm for the woman's safety and the pressure she put on herself to get this case right. The yearning to reach through the internet and snatch the woman from the dangerous situation and tuck her safely away from harm. He recognized it, too, because he felt the same way. But even with the slight tremor, Harlow still projected a compassion and assurance, authority and urgency.

"I know the idea of leaving him is scary," Harlow said. "I know he's tried to convince you that you could never make it without him. Maybe he's threatened to do more harm if you leave. All of that is terrifying. I agree. But I also know you cannot change him. You must protect yourself, or he will continue to hurt you and control you."

Wade battled his frustration as the woman hedged, expressing her doubts and reluctance, all of which Harlow countered ably with patience, grace, strength and encouragement.

"Susan, you trusted me enough to call tonight and tell me your story. That took tremendous courage. Will you trust me enough when we get offline to give me your real name and location? Will you allow me to contact people who can help you?"

"I—I—" Susan sighed and in a tiny voice said, "Okay."

Wade exhaled for the first time in several long tense seconds. The episode ended, and Wade returned to his recliner, feeling emotionally drained, and took another swallow of beer.

She's good, Wade thought as he realized the tightrope Harlow had walked so skillfully.

In the next episode, she spoke to a woman having on-going arguments with her boyfriend over finances. He was all the more attuned now to how Harlow dealt with each caller, her comments and questions, her compassion and tactful honesty, all pointing to just how well Harlow was listening, how much she truly cared.

But then she'd been a good listener in high school. They'd talked for hours when they had dated, parked in his car by the shore of Blackbird Lake or sitting on her bedroom floor. His family issues, her teenage squabbles with her mother, high school angst and jealousies and rivalries were all hashed out between them, openly, honestly. And he'd shared his dreams of serving in the Marines, a goal he'd shared with his best friend, Sebastian Cross. That memory caused irritation to chew at his gut. Harlow had heard Wade say how much the Marines meant to him, knew how long the dream had shaped him. How could she not understand his reasons for leaving Owl Creek when he did? And why couldn't she have supported him in that dream?

Wade huffed his frustration. Why was he rehashing their breakup *again* after all these years? He finished his beer and lunged out of the recliner, tossing the bottle in the recycling bin with a bit too much gusto. The bottle broke with a jarring clatter. He gripped the edge of the kitchen counter, letting the mild zap of adrenaline and edginess settle.

From his computer, Harlow's voice continued. "Sometimes it's hard to see your own part in disagreements. Relationships take compromise and a willingness to admit mistakes. Listening goes both ways. If you want your boyfriend to hear you express your needs and unhappiness, then be ready to truly hear what he is saying as well."

Wade stared hard at the countertop, letting Harlow's words wash over him. Had he listened to Harlow when they'd argued that fateful night after her graduation? What had she said about Owl Creek being her home? About not wanting to give up what she'd finally found?

The current *Harlow Helps* episode ended, and another started with her chipper, cheesy introduction. A parent looking for help with a rebellious teen. Wade scrubbed a hand on his cheek. He was supposed to be listening for clues that might identify or point toward Harlow's stalker, not wallowing in his own issues and memories of the past.

He took out another beer, paused, then returned it to the refrigerator. Tonight, he wouldn't use alcohol to anesthetize his pain and help put him to sleep. Tonight, he'd keep his mind sharp, analyzing Harlow's broadcasts, using his focus to help him keep his promise to Harlow.

He would do what it took to keep her safe, and that included putting her need for answers above his own problems. Taking out a can of soda instead, he popped the top and returned to the recliner to continue his listening marathon. Somewhere, hidden in the hours of Harlow's sage and caring advice and her callers' issues with dysfunction, heartache and pain, lay the seed of discontent that had taken root for her stalker. Somehow Wade had to find that seed before Harlow's stalker found her.

Chapter 11

As Sloan had promised they would, an installation team from SecuritKey arrived early the next morning. By the time Wade showed up, looking rather drowsy and rumpled, Harlow had shown the installation team where the circuit breakers were and been briefed on the schematic showing where all the cameras and alarms would be placed throughout the house and yard.

"Coffee," was all Wade said as she held the front door for him to come in from the icy cold. "Now."

Harlow closed the door and gave him the stink eye. "And good morning to you, too, Mr. Sunshine."

Looking chastened, he inhaled deeply and said, "Coffee, now…please?"

Harlow chuckled and headed to the kitchen. "Better, but keep working on it."

"I promise to give you all the sugary greetings you want after I have caffeine coursing through my veins." He walked straight to the cabinet where her mugs were kept and helped himself to one. Harlow filled his cup, and he groaned his pleasure as he drank deeply.

The sexy rumble from his throat reminded her all too clearly of the sultry sighs and impassioned moans they'd both made during their sexual encounters in high school. Grabbing the back of a kitchen chair when her knees buckled, she forced the erotic thoughts aside and cleared her throat. "Couldn't sleep last night?"

"Oh, I slept at some point, given that I woke up in my living room chair about ten minutes ago." He drank again, then refilled his cup. "I stayed up listening to your program recordings."

She barked a laugh. "And they put you to sleep? Thanks a lot!"

His good eye glared at her over the rim of his mug. "I didn't say that. The show is good. You're good. But you gave me fortysomething hours of broadcasts to listen to."

He liked her show? Thought she was good? A giddy thrill spun through her. Wade's offhand compliment meant more to her than all the gushing of strangers who followed her Facebook page or her viral status on social media. Wade's approval had always meant more to her than anyone else's. She didn't stop to dwell on that truth.

"And?" she asked, pulling out the chair she'd clutched and sitting in it. "Did you figure anything out?"

"You mean besides the fact that there are a lot of people with problems in this world, and at the end of the day, I wouldn't swap problems with any of them?" He dropped into the chair opposite her and cradled the mug between his hands.

"I think most people would agree with that." She couldn't help but wonder if and when he might share some of his problems, the demons that clearly haunted him. *Don't push. He'll open up when he's ready.* "But did anything jump out at you that might help us identify my stalker?"

"Jump? No. But a thing or two did have me doing a

double take. Relationship issues mean there's another person involved, and it was typically the woman that called in. The man in the relationship could have felt you were taking the woman's side and formed a grudge."

Harlow considered that. "But I try so hard not to take sides. I specifically say relationships are the responsibility of *both* partners."

He flipped up his palm. "I'm just saying, a partner who took umbrage at something you told their spouse could hold a grudge." He drew a notepad from his pocket and folded back the top page as his gaze darkened. "Speaking of bad relationships, this lady—" he tapped the notebook "—from episode twelve, called herself Susan—"

Harlow's gut flipped. She knew exactly the episode he meant. Even if the case hadn't burned itself in her memory the night Susan had called, Harlow had been grimly reminded when she got reports back from her contacts in Houston whom she'd called to get the woman to safety.

She nodded, choking back the surge of bile in her throat, even as Wade said, "A domestic abuse situation."

"I remember her." Harlow took a cleansing breath as she met Wade's gaze. "It's not her husband, if that's what you're thinking."

"How can you know that?" he asked, then shifting on his chair his expression grew wary. "What happened with Susan?"

"She left him—her husband, I mean—and went to the safe house the women's shelter offered." She took a moment to gather herself before adding, "But a few weeks later, she went back to him."

Wade sucked in a sharp breath of dismay, mumbled a bad word under his breath. "You're sure?"

She nodded. "The contact I made in Houston let me know when I called to check on Sh—um, Susan."

Wade lifted his hand from his mug, dismissing her slip. "She used an alias. I figured as much. So what happened when she went back?"

"An argument. A neighbor called the police. There was a standoff with her husband, and when he appeared at the door wielding a weapon, threatening both Susan and the police officers, he was shot and died at the hospital."

Wade's jaw hardened, and dread filled his face. "And Susan?"

Harlow's brow crumpled with sadness. "She blamed herself and overdosed on drugs a week later." She swallowed hard, forcing down the knot of regret and disappointment that strangled her. "So it's not Susan's husband. He's…dead."

Wade was silent, his good eye full of pain and shock and frustration. She got up and took the coffee carafe from the brewer, refilled his mug and her own, then stared out the back window where the installation team was surveying the eaves around the back porch.

"How do you do it?" Wade finally said, his voice hoarse.

"Pardon?" She faced him, taking in his haggard expression.

"How do you stay sane when you hear one horror story after another from your clients? How do you get up each morning knowing your day is going to be filled with listening to people complain and hearing life stories full of pain and tragedy and cruelty? How does it not break you?"

This was far from what she'd expected to hear from

Wade, and Harlow took a moment to not only absorb her shock, but also formulate an answer that wasn't glib or untrue. She valued honesty in others and would only give Wade the same. "Some days, I wonder the same thing. There is a great deal of stress involved in counseling, but I do it, because I want to help my clients. I keep at it, because I feel I'm making a difference. To say I love what I do isn't quite the truth. It's fulfilling, and I treasure the moments when I share a breakthrough with a client or see the transformation of a hurting soul."

Wade nodded, his expression pensive. "It just seems like you'd get overwhelmed after a while. I mean I just listened to your shows for a few hours last night and my head's reeling."

Harlow sipped her coffee, then said, "There is definitely a lot of self-care required. I have to de-stress at the end of the day and find ways to compartmentalize my work and my private life. Counselors, in general, do suffer a high rate of burnout, just like other professionals with intensely emotional or stressful jobs."

He seemed to be considering her answer. "And how do you de-stress? How do you handle the job so you don't go bonkers?"

She met his gaze, noted the twitch of muscles in his tight jaw and sensed he was asking for advice as much as for interest in her life. "I watch cheesy sitcoms in the evening. Laughter is as good a medicine as the cliché claims. Or I might take a walk at the beach. Or have a hot bath, read escapist fiction or occasionally drink a glass of wine." She paused, feeling compelled as a professional to add, "Not that alcohol should be considered an answer to problems or a way to medicate personal pain. Everything in moderation, right?"

He angled his head, his mouth twitching wryly at the corner. "Of course."

"I start every morning with prayer and meditation," she continued, "and I make time in my schedule every week to hang out with my friends. Social connections are key to good mental health."

His brow lowered now, and the tension returned to his jaw.

"Talking about things," she said, determined to make her point, "even just mundane life stuff, helps me feel supported, connected, loved."

She watched his reaction, knowing from his sisters that Wade had been far too disconnected since leaving the Marines. Though he said nothing in reply, his averted gaze, grim set to his mouth and furrowed brow spoke volumes.

He led a loner lifestyle, even when working at the ranch, preferring time in the pastures checking fences or rounding up strays to sharing duties with other hands. For someone who had been so outgoing and full of life in high school, always ready with a joke and surrounded by friends and family, this change in Wade's routine and persona were troubling to Harlow.

"You've been talking to my family, haven't you?" he said, his attention fixed on a spot across the room.

She didn't pretend not to know what he meant. "They're worried about you. The changes in your personality. They love you, Wade, and just want to help."

"Can they change the past?"

"Of course not. But they—"

"Then there's nothing they can do for me." He stood abruptly and carried his mug to the coffeepot, where he dumped more of the hot liquid in so fast it sloshed over the rim. He cursed under his breath and sucked coffee from his fingers.

"Wade," she said quietly after a moment in which the silence seemed to vibrate with emotion. "I know that it's hard to talk about things that are painful and—"

"Don't," he interrupted, his gaze fixed out the window over the sink.

"You can talk to me." She had to say it, had to at least try to reach him.

He turned, his unpatched blue eye blazing. "Don't patronize me."

She blinked and shook her head. "I'm not! I care about you, Wade. I want to help, if you'll let me. I can see the pain you're carrying and, like your family, I hate seeing you hurt."

"I'm fine," he said tersely, the balling of his hands and clenching of his teeth contradicting his assertion. "I didn't come here today to get psychoanalyzed. I came to help *you* find the creep who's threatening you. To protect you."

She lifted her chin. "Why? Why would you do that for me?"

Her question clearly startled him. "What do you mean, why? You've been threatened by a stalker. I'm not going to stand by and let some guy with an unreasonable grudge hurt you."

Keeping her face placid, she repeated, "Why do you want to do that?"

He clearly caught her drift and gave her a disgruntled

sigh. "It's not the same thing. Your life is in danger, and I'm trained with weapons and defense skills that can keep you safe."

"And your mental health is in danger, and I'm trained with the tools and skills to keep you safe."

He snorted and drained the contents of his mug rather than answer her. After thunking the coffee cup in the sink, he strode to the kitchen door, pausing only long enough to say, "I'm going to check on the progress of the camera installation."

Harlow sighed. She was used to having to break down walls of resistance. The first step, admitting one had problems, meant making yourself vulnerable. Asking for help was often the hardest step for her clients. Wade had had eighteen months to build and strengthen the walls he'd erected, believing the fortifications would shut out his pain rather than trap him alone with it. Breaking down those walls would take time. Patience. Determination. For the sake of the man she'd once loved with her whole heart, she would not give up on Wade.

Chapter 12

Harlow and Wade spent the day working on her parents' house, and he quizzed her further on the *Harlow Helps* episodes he'd listened to. Had she followed up on Joey? Had she heard anything out of the ordinary in Victor's call? What happened when she talked offline to Sharon? Harlow answered all of his questions, but still no one stood out.

What had been obvious was that Harlow still made his body hum and stirred a restless need in him. He hadn't been with a woman in a couple years, and being around Harlow was feeding the sexual tension coiled inside him. Watching her bend over or reach for upper shelves, inhaling her scent, brushing against her as they collaborated on cleaning and sorting, was a slow torture. He wanted her so badly, but how could he make a move when he had nothing to offer her but a tumble in the sheets?

By 6:00 p.m., the cameras and the door and window alarms had been installed, and Sloan had trained Harlow on their use. Sloan checked with her tech people, but they had no good leads on the stalker either.

Wade should have felt better about Harlow's safety, but the idea that some unknown *someone*, some unknown *somewhere* was gunning for Harlow left him off-balance in a way even his accident hadn't.

At least with the explosion, his injury and his guilt over Sanders's death, he knew who the enemy was. He had a specific something where he could direct his anger, focus his attention and start putting broken pieces back together. He had none of that with Harlow's stalker. The obscurity left him with a sense of helplessness that gnawed at his gut. He was a Marine, damn it! He didn't do helpless. He had to find a way to protect Harlow regardless of the circumstances.

Wade watched from the front window as Sloan's taillights disappeared down the neighborhood street. After the shrill sound of drills and rumble of workmen's voices filling the air all day, the Joneses' house seemed oddly quiet now. He listened for the snick of the front door lock as Harlow returned from seeing Sloan off, and when her feet tapped on the foyer floor, he turned to meet her gaze as she entered the living room.

"It's getting late. I don't want to keep you if—"

"No." He lifted one shoulder. "I'm in no rush. Nothing waiting at home for me other than canned soup and whatever's airing on ESPN."

She crossed the floor to him and angled her head as she eyed him, grinning wryly. "If you're trying to wrangle a dinner invitation with that canned soup line…"

He chuckled lightly. "No wrangling. Just speaking the truth."

"Hmm. Still, I do have the rest of that lasagna Mrs. Norris brought over."

"True."

"And most of Mrs. Vanderbilt's lemon pound cake…

which will do my thighs no favors if I eat the whole thing myself."

"I'd be remiss if I let any harm come to your thighs," he quipped back, but growing more serious he added, "Or any other part of you."

Her head came up, and she gave him a skeptical look.

He shoved aside the niggle of doubt and said, "I should stay here tonight."

She chortled as she squared her shoulders. "Oh really? I invited you for dinner, not a sleepover."

"Just the same, security system or not, I don't feel right about you being here alone tonight. Not while that guy is still out there, still a threat."

She took a beat, a breath, shifted her weight. "Wade, this is why I didn't say anything about the stalker earlier. I don't want to be a burden, to inconvenience anyone or cause undue worry. If you hadn't seen that text, I might never have told you."

"Then I'm glad I saw it. You need someone watching your back."

"And you're volunteering?"

He flipped up a hand as if that should be obvious. "I am."

She sent him a dubious frown. "Do you really think you're the best person for that job?"

He stiffened at the unspoken reasons behind her doubts. His voice tight, he said, "Despite appearances, I'm perfectly capable of defending you from an assailant."

"I didn't mean—"

"My vision isn't as bad as Chase implied yesterday," he continued over her, "and my body has healed enough that I'm physically capable of anything I could do before." Feeling peevish and still jittery with the sexual energy that had been firing in him all day, he took fiendish pleasure in stepping so close to her their bodies touched. In a husky tone, he added, "Anything."

He heard the sexy catch in her breath, telling him she got the message loud and clear. But what would she do with the information?

As if in answer to his private question, she took a measured step back from him. "Not a good idea, Wade."

He battled down the stab of hurt her refusal caused but kept his tone even as he replied, "What's not a good idea? My spending the night or what might happen between us if I did?"

She raised a shaky hand to push her hair behind her ear, and she sounded flustered when she said, "Either. Both. I—Wade, I'd be lying if I said I wasn't still attracted to you, but..." She turned and put more distance between them. "Surely you can understand why anything physical between us could only open old wounds."

Before he could acknowledge or deny her assertion, she forged on. "And for similar reasons, I have to believe that you becoming any further involved in my problem with the stalker is unwise. We don't need to be getting entangled again. It can only end badly. My safety is not your problem."

For several moments, he only stared at her, digesting her determination to push him away. Since returning to Owl Creek after the munitions accident, he'd been the one keeping his distance from people. He'd sworn to others and himself that he wanted to be left alone, to brood, to think, to sort out the turmoil in his life, in his mind. The irony didn't escape him that when he found someone he wanted close, she kept him at arm's length. Not that he blamed her. He couldn't give her the kind of soul-to-soul intimacy she'd want from a sexual relationship. They'd already tried that, and it had failed painfully.

Despite her assertion that the creep who kept sending increasingly dark messages and harassing her wasn't his problem, wasn't his battle to fight, he wouldn't— *couldn't*—let this situation go. He already had Sanders's blood on his hands. He refused to add Harlow's due to negligence or dereliction.

Finally, he cleared his throat and firmed his jaw. "I'm making it my problem, because I believe the situation with this stalker is more serious than you're willing to admit." She flinched, and he raised a hand to calm her. "I'm not saying that to scare you or weasel my way into your life. But to my mind, anyone sick enough, determined enough to find ways around all the roadblocks you've already thrown up, is someone dangerous enough to follow through with hurting you. I choose not to stand aside and let this creep have that chance."

The next morning, Harlow stumbled out of her bedroom and found Wade already awake and doing some kind of stretching or strengthening exercises on her living room floor. "Morning, early bird."

He glanced up, pausing from his regimen long enough to acknowledge her with a nod and quirk of his lips that might be called a grin if she was loose with the definition. "Morning." He continued his workout. "I just have a little more stretching to do. I had to stretch to keep the scars from contracting as they healed, and I've kept up the routine just because…"

"I see. Can I fix you some breakfast? Or coffee?"

"Already had coffee. Hannah woke me at the butt-crack of dawn, calling and wondering where I was."

"Why would she think you were anywhere other than at home?"

He shoved to his feet, still stretching his arms and shoulders. Harlow caught her breath, savoring the sight of all those glorious muscles rippling and flexing. Clearly his ranch work had kept him in good shape since coming home.

"Because she went by my place last night kinda late, and I wasn't home," he said, dragging her attention away from her lusting, "which for me was unusual. And while she didn't panic last night, when I still didn't answer her knock early this morning, she got worried."

"How early?" Harlow said, pulling her new phone out of her pocket to check the time. "I didn't sleep that late, did I?" The screen read 7:32. Luna rubbed against her calf and meowed that it was well past breakfast time.

"She had a morning catering job. Breakfast for a business conference somewhere out of town. I didn't catch the details." He grunted as he shook his head. "If I'd known my family was going to be checking up on me, I'd have told someone I was staying with you. I swear, they've been like helicopter parents hovering over me since I got back last year. I can't even sneeze without someone in my family assuming I need around-the-clock care and monitoring."

"Had you sneezed around Hannah?" Harlow asked with a lopsided grin. "Is that why she was stopping by your house so early?"

"No, she wanted me to know Lucy had lost a tooth

and was eager to show me. When I didn't answer the door, she thought Jessie had done something to hurt me, or Acker had come after me for some reason."

Now a warmth filled his face. "Anyway, Lucy wants me to help her price her tooth, so she can leave a bill for the tooth fairy." He gave a soft grunt that might have been a chuckle. "God that little girl's something else. Already quite the negotiator."

Harlow smiled and bent to lift Luna into her arms. "Can't wait to meet this aspiring businesswoman."

"So come with me this afternoon. We're meeting at Book Mark It at four. Hannah is taking Lucy to the story time and cocoa hour after school." Wade strolled closer, stopping to scratch Luna's head.

This close to him, she could smell the crisp scent of soap and see the dampness in his hair that indicated he'd already showered. She *had* been sacked out if she hadn't heard the shower running.

She was usually a light sleeper. But then, lack of sleep while worrying about her stalker had been building. Between accumulated fatigue and the assurance and security she'd felt knowing Wade was close, Harlow had gotten the comfortable night's rest she needed.

Wade made her feel safe. A tangle of relief and regret swelled inside her as she acknowledged the truth.

"Surely you can take a short break from working on the house to get coffee with Hannah and me," Wade said, before heading into the kitchen.

Luna jumped from Harlow's arms and followed Wade, her meow insisting she be fed.

Harlow shook herself out of her distracted thoughts and padded into the next room. "I'd love to meet Lucy and have another chance to visit with Hannah." Harlow pulled the used coffee filter out of the machine and carried it to the trash. "If you'll start a fresh pot of joe, I'll get Miss Meow her breakfast. You sure I wouldn't be intruding if I go this afternoon?"

He nodded, and as he filled the carafe at the sink, he said, "You're more than welcome. In fact, I'd prefer you come instead of me leaving you here alone."

She rolled her eyes. "I'm sure I'd be fine. Isn't that what the new security system is about?"

"Just the same..."

"Just the same... I'd appreciate the chance to go. All too soon, I'll be done cleaning out the house and moving on. I want to spend as much time with old friends as I can before then." From the corner of her eye, she saw Wade pause, his hands stilling as he measured coffee into the filter. His jaw tightened, and his brow furrowed before he exhaled and continued his task. "You okay?"

He sent her a flat look and grumbled, "Why wouldn't I be?"

She shrugged and let the matter drop. Somehow she'd poked a bear. But how specifically? She could imagine he got tired of people asking if he was okay. His sensitivity to his siblings' delicate treatment of him was obvious. Rather than press the matter, she changed the subject. "I thought I'd tackle the basement today." Harlow filled Luna's bowl with dry food and refreshed her water. "My dad had a lot of fishing equipment and baseball memorabilia stored down there. Feel free to claim anything you want for yourself. The rest of it is getting donated to charity or getting trashed."

He jerked a nod as he turned the coffee maker back

on, and it hissed as it heated up. As he opened the cabinet to the right and took down a box of cereal, Harlow was struck by a powerful sense of déjà vu, which was crazy because she'd certainly never woken up with Wade in her house and made breakfast with him.

Yet in high school, she'd pictured this sort of scene— an average day, a life with Wade, mornings as his wife— so often. Perhaps all she was feeling was a longing. The circumstances of her life were not what she'd ever dreamed for them, but had her private fantasies been enough to manifest this moment? She knew plenty of practitioners who believed in visualization as a tool for achieving change.

Wade nudged her, and he gave her a funny look. "Hey, I need to get the milk."

Harlow's cheeks heated as she stepped back from blocking the refrigerator door. He'd caught her day-dreaming again, lost in bittersweet memories and heart-breaking wishes that could never be.

"I've been thinking about your shows and what might have triggered the stalker," he said as he sat down with the cereal and milk.

Harlow moaned. "Could we, just for today, not talk about that?"

"But we need to find the guy."

Her shoulders drooped. "I know that better than any-one, but Sloan is working on it, Fletcher is aware of him, and the LAPD has a report. Just for a day or two, I don't want to dwell on the stalker. I finally got a good night's sleep last night, and I want to savor the semi-calm in my soul."

He twisted his mouth. Nodded. "Okay. But I'm still

going to call Sloan later and run ideas by her, see what she's found."

Harlow chuckled. "It's been less than two days. Give her time to work!"

He put his spoon down and reached for her hand. "I admit I'm impatient. But every minute the cops don't come up with anything is a minute you're still in danger. That's not something I can ignore."

"Your being with me is plenty. I got my first good night's sleep in weeks because I knew you were close and looking out for my protection. You don't have to solve the case for the police, too."

"But I want—"

"I know. And I thank you. But the best thing you can do today for my peace of mind is distract me."

He exhaled and squeezed her hand. "Okay. But tonight, I'll be listening to more of your broadcasts. I won't rest until I know you are safe."

A warmth spread through her as she squeezed his fingers back, a sense that went deeper than gratitude and momentary relief from the constant buzz of anxiety over the disturbing texts.

That odd sense, what Harlow could only call *rightness*, stayed with her throughout the morning as they worked side by side. Sharing the tedious sorting together felt good. Making lunch together felt natural. The easy patter of their conversation felt familiar. What's more, she sensed that Wade was growing more comfortable around her. He seemed…happier. Less guarded. His body language was more relaxed. And while the old and easy rapport between them seemed to be returning, the familiarity was also increasingly poignant for Harlow. The more she and Wade got along and found their old pattern and chemistry, the harder it would be when she had to leave town. The house would be cleaned out in a few more days, and she'd have no good excuse to stay put. For her safety's sake, she felt compelled to keep moving, change cities, stay a step or two ahead of her stalker.

At three forty-five, the alarm Wade had set on his phone buzzed, and he shoved the box he'd been sorting out of the way. "We need to head out if we're going to meet up with Hannah and Goose."

"Goose?"

He shrugged. "That's what I call Lucy. Lucy Goose."

Just the fact that the tough Marine had a sweet nickname for his young niece gave Harlow a warm feeling in her belly. Wade would have been such a good father. No, not past tense. He would still be a great father. Knowing they wouldn't be her children sent a sharp pain slicing through her. The ache was an all-too-clear reminder why she'd avoided Owl Creek in recent years, why spending so much time with Wade was dangerous to her heart. She pasted on a fake smile for Wade and said, "Let me get my purse, and I'll be ready to go."

Wade glanced across the front seat of his truck to Harlow, realizing she had dust on her cheek from one of the old boxes they'd sorted that morning. Something warm and tender tugged in his chest.

All too soon, I'll be done cleaning out the house and moving on.

Her comment that morning, tossed out so casually, had rocked something deep in his core. The irony. The truth he'd hated accepting. Harlow was not staying in town. Before, he'd been the one bailing on Harlow and Owl Creek. And now the tables were turned.

She was just passing through his life, a flash of nostalgia that hurt too much to examine closely. Maybe this time with her was supposed to be about closure. Forgiveness. Finally shutting the door on what they'd had together.

He might pretend to the world that he'd moved on after making the hard call to end his relationship with Harlow years ago, but he hadn't been able to erase her from his heart. For the first time in far too long, he'd been hopeful he could repair some of the damage he'd done at age nineteen. He could admit now that he'd made mistakes back then. But when she'd been so opposed to the idea of a life in the military with him, had begged him to follow a different route, he'd believed he was making the right choice.

Wasn't it better, kinder to make a clean break than string her along through murky years of a dying long-distance relationship? Hadn't he, in helping on the ranch with wounded animals, always heard a clean cut, even an amputation, healed faster and was more humane than a wound left to fester?

Apparently, his heart had not gotten that message. Harlow had never left his thoughts, his desires, his dreams of the future. And now, knowing some creep was threatening her made him see red.

After they parked, a couple blocks down from the bookstore, he and Harlow walked down the sidewalk, side by side, and yet, in so many ways, miles apart. They stopped now and again for Harlow to stare in a storefront window at the shop's wares or take in the struc-

tural changes to renovated buildings she remembered
as other things during high school. "I can't get over how
much has changed, how much the town has grown and
updated since I left."

"You never came back for holidays with your parents
or summer visits?" Hannah had told him as much, but
he found it hard to believe. If she'd loved Owl Creek,
had called it her home, why…?

"Not really. They came to see me in LA mostly, or we
went to Lake Tahoe together for vacation, or if I did need
to come to town for some reason, like Dad's funeral and
later Mom's, I stayed close to home and was in and out
pretty quickly." She angled her gaze up at him. "Too many
ghosts, you know?"

His heart kicked. Yeah, he knew. Considering he had
avoided Owl Creek and kept to Colton Ranch or his parents' house when he came home from the Marines, he
had little room to judge her. Yet considering her vehe-
mence on the night they broke up that she couldn't give
up the home she'd found in Owl Creek to follow him in
a military career, the news surprised him.

When they reached Book Mark It, he held the door
for Harlow and another woman, who gave him the side-
eye as they entered. Trying to ignore the woman's curious look, he inhaled the inviting aromas of fresh coffee,
woodsmoke and new books as the door swung shut behind him.

Just inside the door, the stout woman stopped to
glance around the shop, scowling, then quipped to Harlow, "A fireplace in a store full of paperback books?
Bold choice or asking for disaster?"

Wade tried to place the grumpy lady, wondering if

her curious look was because she remembered him, re-membered how he *used* to look, but he didn't recognize her. However, his family had said many out-of-towners now populated the area, thanks to the growing tourism for the winter skiing in the mountains and summer water sports on Blackbird Lake.

"I think the fireplace is charming and cozy," Harlow said, wiggling out of her coat. "Perfect for story time on a cold afternoon."

The woman gave Harlow a condescending look, then headed to the counter to order.

Wade took Harlow's coat from her. "I'll hang that up."

"Uncle Wade!" Lucy shouted as she and Hannah entered, letting another cold blast of air inside. "You made it!"

"Of course I made it. I understand you lost a tooth and need some advice from me?" He bent to pull his niece into a hug that lifted the girl's feet from the floor. "Show me this new hole in your mouth."

Lucy opened wide, sticking a finger in her mouth to point. "Wight hehw."

Hannah had met Harlow halfway across the floor and folded her in a hug. "Let's get a table over there, near the story time circle."

Wade carried Lucy with him as he moved to the table where the ladies had seated themselves, telling Lucy, "So here's what I think," he said, loud enough for Hannah to hear. "Each time you lose a tooth, it becomes more and more valuable to the tooth fairy, because it means you have fewer left to lose. It's the scarcity principle in economics."

Lucy's eyes widened. "Huh?"

"It means, your tooth should get…hmm, ten bucks from the tooth fairy, minimum."

Hannah made a choked noise and raised a glare to her brother.

"Ten dollars?" Lucy said with an excited squeal. She wiggled down from his arms and rushed to her mother. "Did you hear that? Uncle Wade say I should ask the tooth fairy for ten dollars! That's enough to get a Junie B. Jones book!"

Hannah gave her daughter a forced smile. "Yes. It is." Then with a glance to the rug in front of the fireplace, she added, "Looks like story time is starting. Better grab a seat."

Wade reached in his pocket as he claimed a chair next to Harlow and slipped his sister a ten-dollar bill. "Don't worry. I've got you covered."

Hannah shook her head, trying to push the money back. "I can cover my daughter's tooth fairy expenses," she said in a low voice, "but we really need to talk about how this family spoils her."

Wade shoved the cash toward Hannah again. "If she's spending it on books, I don't consider her spoiled. Just smart."

"I agree," Harlow said.

Hannah rolled her eyes as she accepted the money and turned to slip it in her purse.

A sense of satisfaction filled Wade as he sat back in his chair, but the contentedness was short-lived. The prickly feeling of being watched, one he was all too familiar with since his accident, rippled through him. One of the many reasons he chose to stay close to home was the awkward sense of being on display because of his injuries. He felt awkward in public with his eye patch and the pink scars on his hand and the side of his face. He clenched his back teeth and scanned the room.

The woman who'd come into the store with them stared openly. He shifted uncomfortably and scowled. Rather than glance away, he met the woman's stare boldly with his own glare. He didn't care if his actions were rude. He was sick of people staring, sick of being made to feel like a freak because of his injuries. Finally, the woman looked away, took her coffee and left the store.

"Wade? What is it?" Harlow asked, touching his arm.

He shook his head, dismissing the incident. The last thing he wanted to do was bring any more attention to his injuries and the issues he now dealt with all too often. "Nothing."

Harlow's gaze lingered a moment, then turned back to Hannah, who continued with the story she was telling.

"Anyway, I think the lock must be frozen or something," Hannah said, "because I can't get the door open. I called both Fletcher and Chase to see if they can fix it, but neither of them has come by yet. So I had to work with only a fraction of my usual chafing dishes."

"What's stuck?" he asked. "Is it something I can help with?"

Hannah twisted her mouth and wrinkled her nose. "I didn't want to bother you. Chase will probably get to it tomorrow."

Wade sighed. "Get to what?"

His sister licked her lips and hesitated. "The door on the storage shed behind my house is jammed. I can't get inside the shed, and that's where I keep a lot of my extra equipment for catering jobs. I have a big job next weekend and need what's in there. I already had to get creative at my job this morning."

"Why not call me? I'm a lot closer than Chase or Fletcher and have more free time these days."

"I...didn't want to bother you," she said, her grimace saying she knew the excuse was thin.

Shoving down his irritation, he met Hannah's gaze evenly. "I'll have it open by dark tonight."

Hannah opened her mouth, her expression reluctant, when Harlow cut in. "Great! Problem solved! You know, he's been a big help to me packing my parents' house."

His sister blinked. "He has? Oh...good. I didn't know you'd taken leave from the ranch."

He shrugged. "Things were slow because of winter, so I asked for a few days to help Harlow out."

Hannah divided a look between Harlow and Wade. "I see."

"Don't read anything into it. I just needed someone tall and strong to do some reaching and lifting. And, of course, the free labor for all the stuff in between." Harlow gave him a smile and a wink. "So...what's this big catering job you have? And when do I get to try your wares?"

The conversation shifted away from him, and he mentally thanked Harlow for coming to his defense. Like she had so many times in high school, her verbal rescue now showed she still had his back, could sense what he needed and had been there for him. When he caught her gaze a moment later, he mouthed, *thank you*. And she smiled.

The next day, Harlow turned her attention to the rest of the boxes she and Wade had dragged up from the cold, damp basement the previous morning. As they worked, they continued listening to the recorded episodes of *Harlow Helps*, trying to single out the caller who might have been triggered by her advice...and growing more concerned that the answer wasn't in the recorded episodes. Anyone who'd listened could have taken umbrage to what she'd said. Or the stalker could be a random individual who got his kicks terrorizing women. But reviewing the broadcasts seemed to give Wade a sense of purpose and usefulness, so they persisted.

As they sorted the boxes, Harlow was surprised at how much her parents had kept, considering they'd moved time and again with her father's changing military assignments. Boxes full of her childhood toys and books, knickknacks acquired from vacations all over the globe, tools for her father, outdated home decor her mother had kept, more pillows and quilts than they'd ever use, and sports equipment that reflected the variety of locales they'd called home. Boogie boards from their years in Florida, skis from their time in Colorado, the pink basket and bell she'd had on her first bicycle when they lived in Texas, snowshoes from their years in Germany.

She found herself lingering over the memorabilia, letting her mind recall the houses, the schools, the friends, the unique traditions of the far-flung locations. "As much as I hated the transient lifestyle," she said, and Wade glanced up from the stack of magazines he was tying up for recycling, "I certainly got a broad education and exposure to so many cultures."

"Join the Navy and see the world. Wasn't that the recruiting mantra of old?" Wade asked.

"I think I've heard that before. But my dad was in the Army."

Wade lifted a shoulder. "And I was a Marine, but I still got stationed in the Middle East and a brief assignment in Japan."

Harlow chewed her lower lip. "It's just that when you're a kid, trying to make friends, trying to figure out who you are, wanting stability in your life, the constant movement and changing scenery gets old. All I wanted for so many years was just to feel like my family had a place to put down roots. I wanted to keep the same friends for more than two years, wake up in a room that felt familiar and safe, and finally be able to call a place 'home' and know it would stick."

Wade grunted as he sat back on his heels. "And after living in this small, remote town my whole life, I was champing at the bit to get the hell out of Owl Creek."

"Yeah," Harlow said, her tone sad. "The key difference and great divide we hadn't seen coming until too late."

Wade's jaw tightened, and he shoved to his feet, grabbing a few stacks of bundled magazines. "I'll put these in the back room until we're ready to take a load to the recycling drop-off this weekend."

Harlow rose from the living room floor as well and stretched the kinks from her back and shoulders. She glanced around at the sorted piles stacked in all four corners of the room. They'd made significant progress but still had more to do. Would she be here another week?

She laughed at herself for having thought she could do the job over a long weekend. Her parents' whole lives were stored in this house, forty-five years of marriage and numerous moves and rearing Harlow together. She rubbed the spot in her chest where a hollow pang settled, the sting of grief for her parents and the memories she was packing away.

Hearing the rumble of an engine, Harlow glanced up. Situated at the end of a cul-de-sac, her parents' house had little drive-by traffic. Was another neighbor bringing a meal?

A dark blue pickup truck with a US Mail decal on the door was at the mailbox at the street curb. She reached the window in time to see the arm poking from the driver's window close the mailbox and the truck drive away. She furrowed her brow in confusion. She'd notified the post office that her mother was deceased and the house was vacant. All deliveries should have stopped.

"Hey, Wade, I'm running down to the mailbox," she called as she moved to the foyer to put on her coat. "Be back in a second."

Wade appeared from the hall, folding the sleeves of his shirt up his forearms. "What'd you say?"

She aimed a thumb toward the door. "Mailman just put something in my box. I'm going to see what it is."

His dark brow dipped, his face expressing skepticism. "You're sure it was the mailman? Seems kinda late in the day for deliveries."

"That's what the truck door said. I'll be right back."

Wade's mouth opened as if he were going to say something else about her errand, but she slipped out the door and hurried down the front steps. She walked carefully down the driveway, spotting patches of ice, and shivered as a stiff wind buffeted her.

At the bottom of the driveway, she cast a glance down

the street, but the delivery truck was long gone. Moving over to the mailbox, she opened the box and made a mental note that for street appeal, she might need to repaint the—

From the inside the dark mailbox, she heard an angry hiss. And a large snake launched out at her.

Chapter 13

Harlow screamed and jumped back several steps, stumbling and slipping on a patch of ice. She fell on her backside as the snake landed on the pavement, writhing inches from her. Recognizing the snake as a rattler, she screamed again and scuttled crab-style until she could roll to her feet. Turning to look for the viper, she saw the creature slither quickly across the road and into the woods opposite her parents' house. Casting a wary eye back on the mailbox, she found the open end of a plain white pillowcase hanging out of the box, no doubt how the snake had been transported.

She trembled from the inside out, and nausea sawed in her gut.

The pounding of running feet sounded behind her, and she spun to fall into Wade's arms as he rushed to her.

"What happened? Harlow, are you all right?" Wade lifted her hands, which bled from being skinned on the street when she fell.

She shuddered, replaying the blur of motion as the serpent shot out from the mailbox, fangs bared. "S-snake… rattles-s-snake!"

Beneath her embrace, his body tensed. "What?"

Clutching at his shirt, she pointed toward the woods

where the rattler had disappeared. "It slithered off th-that way!"

He shoved her to arm's length so he could examine her. "Did it bite you?"

Shock had so numbed her, she hadn't even considered that. As he gave her an up-and-down appraisal, she took inventory as well. Her hands stung and bled, and her bottom ached from dropping so hard on the pavement. She'd bitten her tongue and tasted the coppery tang of blood in her mouth, but she didn't—

Wade's expression darkened as he focused his attention on her puffy coat. He fingered the fabric next to two small, neat holes, spaced an inch apart near her shoulder. "It got you. Or your coat anyway. Without that puffy coat, we could've been making a trip to the ER."

Knowing how close the strike came to her face, Harlow gasped. "Ohmygod." Casting a wary eye to the woods, she asked, "What do we do? It…it went that way." She pointed across the street, her hand trembling.

"Nothing about the snake," Wade said, drawing her close again and buffing her back with soothing strokes.

Her chin shot up as she angled her gaze to meet his. "Nothing?" She heard the note of near-hysteria in her tone. "I don't want that thing hanging out around the house, waiting to jump at me again when I take out the trash or—"

The low chuckle rumbled from his throat. "Trust me, sweetheart. As little as you want to do with the snake, he wants even less to do with humans. I'm sure that, one, he's long gone, and, two, his first priority right now is finding someplace he can burrow in, curl up and hibernate. Snakes are cold-blooded, and whoever put him in the box clearly woke the poor thing from his winter nap. No wonder it was pissed off."

She stepped closer to his warmth, unable to banish the chill that had seeped to her bones, a cold that had nothing to do with the January weather. She swallowed hard as she considered the truth of his reply. "I guess you're right."

He grunted, clutching her close. "The bigger question is who put it in there. This was clearly a malicious act."

Her mouth dried as the most likely scenario finally dawned on her. "It was…him. He found me."

Wade guided Harlow back inside the house and had her sit at the kitchen table while he fixed her a hot drink and called Fletcher. Harlow's assertion replayed in his head like a bad earworm. *He found me*. He had to agree with her. He could see no other reasonable explanation for someone to put a poisonous snake in her deceased parents' mailbox.

Once he'd summoned his brother so Harlow could file a report and get the local cops started on the case, Wade took his own mug of coffee and sat in the chair beside her.

She stared at the walnut table, her face a mask of horror and tension, her drink cradled between her hands but obviously forgotten. When he gave her shoulder a comforting rub, she twitched as she snapped out of her daze, sloshing the hot tea and angling her gaze up to his.

With a heavy exhale, she gave her head a slight shake and reached for a napkin to mop up the spilled tea. "I'm sorry. Geez, I'm a ball of nerves."

"Don't apologize. More than most people, I can understand being jittery after a scare." He wrapped both hands around his mug, wondering why he'd admitted such a telling detail. But then she'd already witnessed one of his episodes. His aversion to sudden loud noises was no secret to her.

He took a sip of his coffee, and when he cut a side glance at her, he met her searching brown eyes. She covered his wrist with her hand and squeezed. "I suppose so. Any chance you'd tell me the story behind your scare the other day?"

He was spared from answering when the doorbell rang. Harlow stood to answer it, and he pushed his chair back. "Let me go. Just…in case."

Her eyes widened, clearly alarmed by the notion that her stalker could be at her door, as unlikely as it was that the creep would bother to ring the bell. Wade found Fletcher and one of the other patrolmen from the city police department on Harlow's porch, and he let them in.

"She's back here." Wade led them into the kitchen and ignored the obvious question in his brother's gaze about what he was doing at Harlow's house to begin with.

Harlow stood as Fletcher and the uniformed officer, who introduced himself as Brad Kline, entered the kitchen. Fletcher gave Harlow his full attention, becoming all business as Harlow explained what happened, detailed the snake's escape and told him about the empty pillowcase.

Fletcher asked for further description of the dark colored truck with the USPS insignia on the door, but Harlow couldn't remember any more detail. "While it was curious to me that I was getting a delivery, I didn't see it as a threat…at the time. And I only caught a glimpse of the truck as it hurried off, so I didn't get a plate number. I assumed the delivery was real because of the logo on the truck."

Officer Kline rested his hands on his gun belt. "The insignia on the door would be easy enough to obtain. A number of mail carriers in the rural areas around here use their personal vehicles with a magnetized postal logo on the door. The person who left the snake could have stolen the decal from a legit delivery person."

"I'll check with the local post office and see if any of their delivery people drive a dark blue pickup or have reported their car decal missing," Fletcher said. "I know you had a security system installed earlier this week. Do any of your cameras face the street? Would you have any images of the truck that might help?"

Harlow glanced at Wade, then shook her head. "The cameras just monitor the perimeter of the house, the doors and windows."

Fletcher pressed his mouth in a hard line of frustration. "Well, we'll do our best, of course. As we leave, we'll collect the pillowcase as evidence, and I'll have forensics out shortly to dust the mailbox for prints. Beyond that... I can ask the chief to assign extra drive-by patrols for the neighborhood. And I'm always just a phone call away. Wade has my number."

She nodded and a strained smile touched her lips. "Thanks, Fletcher."

Wade's brother turned to him, adding, "Security system or not, it might be wise for you to stay with her tonight, in case the guy comes back."

"Way ahead of you, brother." Wade sent Harlow a level look as she sipped from her mug. "In fact, I plan to have her move to my cabin until this guy is caught."

Chapter 14

Harlow sputtered and choked on her tea. Setting her drink down with a clunk and wiping her mouth with her fingers, she wheezed, "Excuse me?"

"You heard me. Your stalker has shown he's far too determined to track you down and menace you. If he does come back, I don't want you here, security cameras or not. Better that you move to a new location. My cabin is off the beaten path, and I can keep an eye on you."

Harlow blinked and coughed again before she shook her head. "Wade, I appreciate the offer—"

"It's not an offer. It's a fact. You need to relocate." His jaw set with mulish decisiveness.

Fletcher gave a soft chuckle under his breath. "Buddy, you have a lot to learn about relationships with women. No wonder you're still single."

Wade lifted the eyebrow over his good eye. "You disagree with my assessment?"

"No. She'd definitely be safer at your place. But your delivery needs work." With a glance to Officer Kline, Fletcher hitched his head toward the door and started for the foyer. "Come on, Brad. Let's let the lovebirds hash this out for themselves."

"We're not—" Harlow said at the same time Wade said, "It's not like that."

They exchanged an awkward glance, and Harlow rose from the table to see Fletcher to the door. She thanked him again as they left, then returned to the kitchen where Wade was waiting, his expression brooding.

"I don't think we should—" His stern look stopped her before she finished.

She understood that he could keep her safer if she relocated, so she didn't bother finishing her protest. The dangerous intimacy they'd face with her living under his roof was of far less concern in the big picture than the man threatening her with poisonous snakes.

His expression softening, he gripped her shoulders and met her gaze with a gentle look. "Your opinion counts, of course, but I know how fiercely independent and stubborn you can be. I didn't want to haggle over what is obviously the right choice. You heard Fletcher. You'll be safer with me at my cabin."

"Me, stubborn? You're the one who—" She chuckled and bit off her words again. She didn't want to debate with him. Especially when she still had adrenaline coursing through her after the near miss with the rattlesnake. Instead, she stepped closer to him and let him enfold her in his arms. He rested his chin on the top of her head, and she simply let herself inhale the clean scent of him, wishing she could shut down the anxious thoughts parading through her head.

Her stalker had found her. In Owl Creek. At her parents' house. This was no passive, angry listener who just wanted to rant and spook her. He'd researched her, tracked her, found her when she fled Los Angeles. He meant business, and she knew in her bones she hadn't heard the last of the creep.

"What about Luna?" she asked.

He tipped his head as he frowned down at her. "What do you mean?"

"I'm not leaving my cat here alone. Is Luna allowed at your house?"

His mouth opened and shut. He blinked. Clearly he'd never pictured himself with a feline roaming the halls of his bachelor pad. "Uh, sure. Of course. Bring Luna."

With a sigh, she nodded. "All right then. I'll go pack a bag."

An hour later, Harlow had Luna's litter box set up in Wade's utility room, her food and water bowls by the kitchen counter, and her own suitcase and toiletries unpacked in his guest room. With those jobs accomplished, she had no further excuses not to join Wade in his living room, no matter how oddly intimate it felt. She fixed herself a cup of hot tea, then took a seat on the faux leather couch and cast her gaze around the surprisingly stylish decor, which leaned heavily on shades of navy and hunter green and featured a woodsy theme appropriate for a lakeside cabin.

"I like what you've done with the place." She picked up the carved wooden bear tchotchke from the end table next to her and studied it. The bear held a sign that said Welcome to the my den.

Wade grunted. "Thanks, but I rented the place already furnished. Very little of this is mine."

She set the bear down. "Oh. I didn't think the bear was your style. So where are your things?"

"In storage, until I decide my next move." He pressed his mouth in a grim, taut line.

"As in...until your find a house here in Owl Creek or...?" She flipped her hand, inviting him to fill in the blank.

"As in... I don't know what I'm supposed to do next." He sighed heavily, his hands balled, and glanced away. "I never had any other plan besides the Marines. But the explosion changed all that."

His statement was so close to the argument they'd had years ago when they broke up that an unexpected pain slashed through her. She worked to hide her reaction, lifting her mug to sip her tea, not wanting to interrupt Wade when he was finally opening up to her, if only a crack.

When he glanced at her, she met his gaze with an open, encouraging look that asked silently, *Will you tell me about it?*

Wade clamped his back teeth tighter, doggedly fighting the quiver of ill ease that stirred at his core. If he gave his nightmare an inch, he feared he'd never get the beast back under control. He'd spent the past several months reining in the images and sounds of fire and screams and earth-shaking blasts. Blocking out the phantom scent of burned flesh and acrid smoke and choking down the bitter taste of bile and fear. "I know I should talk about it. But... I don't know how."

Harlow turned to face him and angled her head. "I am a professional counselor. I could help."

He frowned. "Is that what I am to you? A case to be analyzed?"

Her brow furrowed, and her tone was firm as she said,

"No. You are far more to me than a client or a PTSD case to be studied." She reached over and squeezed his wrist. "You're...my friend."

Friend. He let the word sit for a moment, a measure of disappointment settling inside him. "Your friend."

"Well, yeah. Isn't that why I'm here at your house? I wouldn't have thought you'd be concerned about my safety if I weren't your friend."

"But...is that all? I kinda thought the last several days had changed things. Am I wrong that you still feel the chemistry between us?"

Her forehead wrinkled, and she drew her hand back as she sighed. "You're not wrong. But... I can't afford to act on that attraction."

Frustration gnawed at him, but he'd be damned if he'd let her know how her rejection stung. He tore his gaze from her to stare across the room at the stuffed trout mounted on his wall. He'd have been better off not having run into her again, not having fanned that hope of rekindling the passion and connection they'd once had.

After a moment of silence, she added, "That doesn't mean I don't care about you or your happiness. And based on what I've seen in the last week, you aren't happy. You only truly smile when you're with Lucy."

"Because she doesn't judge me or treat me like I'm less of who I was before—" He gritted his back teeth, hating the topic of his accident and how his family still treated him.

"No one thinks you're less of who you were."

He frowned skeptically. "Really? Have you not seen the way they hover and defer and look at me with pity?"

"Not pity, Wade. Concern. They love you, and you

have not acted like your old self since you returned. How can you expect them to believe you're okay when you keep to yourself and don't laugh and don't have the same joy for life that you had before?"

He scoffed. "So I'm supposed to pretend a man didn't die on my watch?" Wade heard the sharpness of his tone and immediately regretted it.

She placed a hand on his arm again, and the warmth of the gesture burrowed deep inside him. "No one is asking you to pretend anything, Wade. Pretense is unhealthy and counterproductive. Suppressing genuine hurt and trauma is never the answer."

He fisted his hands and tensed his mouth, knowing she was right but not knowing how to answer. His head throbbed as tension built at his temples.

"When I found that snake in the mailbox and I was shaken and scared, what did you feel? How did you respond?"

Now he jerked his head toward her and scowled. "What? That's—I'd think that was obvious."

His heart raced like it had that afternoon as a fresh wave of panic and cold dread rolled through him.

"Humor me," she pressed. "Why am I here?"

Because I love you, and I'm genuinely scared your stalker will take you from me again.

But all he said was, "Because I was shaken, too, and wanted to help you." And once he'd known she was unharmed, he'd wanted to find the man responsible for trying to hurt her and wreak his vengeance in a most barbaric way.

"So think about how your family felt," she said, her gentle tone in stark contrast to the roil in his gut, "when you were so severely injured in the explosion. Can you imagine how it scared them?"

He didn't have to imagine, because too many times in the past several months, he'd been terrified when murder, kidnapping and other danger had threatened his family. Just thinking now of his father's death, his brother tangling with a serial killer, or his sister being held hostage by a cult member was enough to fill him with an icy horror. He shuddered and struggled for a breath, shoving the bad memories aside.

"And while you're healing physically," Harlow was saying, "you haven't given them a lot of reason to believe you're healing inside." She tapped her chest at her heart. "Cut them some slack for loving you and wanting to help with your PTSD, huh?"

Wade took a beat, needing a moment calm his spinning thoughts and racing pulse before he could respond. Her request wasn't unreasonable. If he was honest, he didn't like the version of himself that had groused and kept his family at bay.

Had he kept Harlow at bay the same way? Was he scared to open himself to her, show her the true depth of his regrets and doubts? Probably.

His only excuse was that Harlow, even before she'd become a mental health counselor, had known him better than anyone. Even better than his own family. She was the one person most likely to see through any pretense he put up, to call his bluff on his attempts to convince his family and friends that he'd moved on from the explosion, that he didn't still wake at night in a cold sweat and shaking from bad dreams and suffocating from guilt and grief.

Realizing he'd still not answered her question, he muttered, "Of course. I know I've been...difficult. I don't mean to be an ass, I just—" He turned up a palm and left the thought unfinished.

With a nod and a half smile, she withdrew her hand and sipped her tea. "Good."

They sat in silence for another moment before he said, "PTSD, huh?" And there it was, the name he'd been trying to ignore but could no longer deny.

"How can you say I have PTSD without even hearing my whole story?" Wade asked.

Harlow lifted a shoulder and flashed a smile. "I know enough. You were in a bad accident. Loud noises rattle you. Your family says you've been withdrawn, moody, hard to reach."

He gave her a startled look. "Who have you talked to?"

"Hannah and Lizzy directly. All of your siblings indirectly. It's in their eyes when they look at you. I saw it in Chase's expression at the bookstore when we met with him and Sloan. And... I see the changes in you for myself."

A moment passed before he said, "Of course I've changed. My whole world's been flipped on its end. After the explosion, I couldn't work—*anywhere*—and in the last few months..." He scrubbed a hand over his short, cropped hair, and the muscles in his jaw flexed as he gritted his back teeth.

When he spoke again, tension darkened his tone. "I've... procrastinated making any decisions. Ranching is okay, but it's not what I want to do with the rest of my life."

Luna, having finished her exploration of her new digs,

strolled into the den and paused by Wade's chair, looking up at him with her whiskers twitching. Wade stuck a
hand down for the cat to sniff, and when she bumped his
fingers, asking for pats, he lifted the cat onto his lap and
stroked Luna's fur. The gesture surprised Harlow, though
she couldn't say why. She'd seen Wade's gentle interaction
with all kinds of animals throughout high school. Ranch
dogs, cattle, horses, chickens, and, yes, the barn cats whose
job it was to keep the mouse population under control.

As she watched him run his hand down Luna's back
again and again, heard her feline companion's rumbling
purr, she imagined a tingle on her own skin, remembered the heady feeling of Wade's hands on her when
they'd made out in high school. To an inexperienced
teenager, her intimacies with Wade had seemed like the
most erotic and exciting thing on earth. And having
shared only a couple sexual liaisons since then, both
sadly disappointing, he was still her high-water mark
of sensual experience.

As a quiver raced through her, she wrapped her arms
around herself and averted her gaze. She was *not* jeal-
ous of her cat! she told herself, though not convincingly.

"What do you want to do with your life?" she asked,
forcing her attention back to the conversation, though
she kept her eyes on the dark window across the room.

"If I knew that, I wouldn't still be herding cattle, fixing fences and vaccinating calves for my uncle."

She nodded once. "Touché."

"It's hard to see myself in any other role than the one
I dreamed of, trained for, spent a third of my life doing."

The sadness in his voice broke her heart and drew
her gaze back to him. Luna hopped down from his lap,

and he dusted cat hair from his hands. Despite his glum admission seconds before, Wade seemed...*different* as she studied him now. She bit her bottom lip as she tried to figure out what she was sensing.

"You were always a good student. You had good grades in everything, especially math and physics. Do either of those fields interest you?" she asked, as she began piecing together the subtle change she'd noted. His hands had unclenched. His jaw was more relaxed. His shoulders less tense.

Petting Luna had relaxed him.

A tickle of an idea started but danced just out of reach.

"Hmm. Maybe. I just don't want to commit to anything while I'm still—" His fingers bounced restlessly on the arm of the recliner where he sat. As if noticing his anxious fidgeting, he grabbed one hand with the other, then stared down at the scar tissue on the back of his right hand.

"Wade," Harlow said softly, "will you tell me about the accident? What happened? What is it about that day that still haunts you the most?"

His brow dipped, but he didn't look at her. He remained silent so long, she began wondering if he hadn't heard her question or was refusing to answer.

But finally, he spoke, his voice a whisper at first, hoarse and choked with emotion. "I was responsible for my men. It's on me. Sanders..." He took a shuddering breath. "Sanders died. Just like that. We were joking together just that morning at breakfast. Then at training, I had him go first, setting the charge. I knew he was inexperienced. Nervous. But I turned my back. Just for just a few minutes. To talk to Sergeant Major Briggs.

Next thing I knew…" Wade squeezed his good eye shut, grimacing. Shaking.

Harlow launched from the couch to kneel in front of him and take his hands in hers. "It's okay, Wade. You're safe. I'm here."

"I can still hear the blast… Feel the shock wave that knocked me back. The flames that—" Instead of finishing the sentence, he loosed a half growl of frustration, half wail of despair.

She rubbed his arms, leaned in to hug him as he rocked back and forth in agitation. Luna, roused by Wade's anguished cry, trotted over as if to ask what was wrong.

And it clicked. The idea that had niggled earlier jelled.

At lunch a few days earlier, Ruby had talked about the dogs she and Sebastian raised at Crosswinds. Most of the dogs were trained for search-and-rescue, but she'd mentioned PTSD companion dogs as well. Luna had calmed Wade earlier. How much more so would a dog trained to recognize PTSD, taught to ease an owner's stress and quiet their fears? She definitely needed to look into this idea and discuss arrangements with Ruby and Sebastian.

When Harlow's awkward angle, hugging Wade while still kneeling by the large chair, made her back hurt, she pulled away, only to have him grip more tightly on her arms. "Harlow…" he rasped.

Wedging herself into the chair with him, she draped her legs over his and looped her arms around his neck. He pressed his face into the curve of her shoulder and released a trembling sigh. As she held him, feeling his tremors ease, he whispered, "Sanders's death on my watch is the second-worst event of my life. My biggest regret is letting you go."

Chapter 15

Harlow stiffened in his arms, and Wade stopped breathing. Why had he said that aloud? He should have pushed it back down, tucked it away under all the other unspoken things, the rest of the black memories and parts of his life too ugly to look at.

Except now he'd not only shared his guilt over Sanders's death, but he'd shared his sorrow over losing her. *Damn it.* He'd not only exposed the source of his nightmares, he'd admitted a truth that left his heart more vulnerable than it had been in a decade. He hadn't dated anyone while in the Marines. Not seriously, anyhow. Dates, sure. Most of them fix-ups by mutual friends. But how could he get involved with any other woman when his soul still belonged to Harlow?

With his jaw clenched and his eye squeezed shut, he wished he could reel the words back in, erase them from her memory as easily as deleting a computer file. He startled a bit—damn his adrenaline-drenched blood—when she stroked a hand along his cheek. Her sigh escaped as a wisp of breath that bathed his face and teased his senses.

"Wade, look at me. Please."

He didn't want to. Hellfire, he didn't want to see pity

or disgust or censure in her eyes. He considered getting up from his chair and closing himself off in his bedroom. Walking away from this conversation before he dug the pit of shame any deeper. But Harlow was on his lap, and when he nudged her, letting her know she should get up, she stayed.

"Wade," she repeated, her grip on his scarred chin firm.

Man, her touch felt good. He hadn't had gentle hands touching him, loving him, in so long. His body thrummed in response as his turmoil faded and a keen awareness of her bottom snuggled in his lap crackled through him. Harlow was on his lap, in his arms, touching him. He'd longed for this, dreamed of this, ached for this for so long. How could he squander this moment? This chance?

"Talk to me. Don't shut me out. Not now."

If talking to her, opening up about the accident, confessing his culpability in Sanders's death, meant he could hold Harlow close for a few more minutes...

He dipped his chin to press his forehead against hers and whispered, "Sanders died because of my distraction, my dereliction. His blood is on my hands."

In his embrace, Harlow stiffened. She lifted her head and said with a groan, "No. Wade, don't put that on yourself."

"I was his commanding officer, in charge of the exercise that day. I knew he was nervous, that he needed extra coaching and encouragement and careful observation, and I...turned my back. I walked away to talk to another officer and—" He paused as another dark thought occurred to him. "Someone had given us live ammunition instead of inert materials to practice with.

I had double-checked the paperwork the night before to be sure I had everything right before the drill that day. But that day I hadn't noticed the screwup. I—"

Fresh waves of well-rehearsed recriminations and shame poured through him, scalding him hotter than the flames that had seared his skin that terrible day.

"No," Harlow said, her tone as hard and unyielding as he'd ever heard it. "Wade, just…stop right now. Stop lashing yourself with these bitter self-indictments."

Her hands framed his face, and she gave him a small shake, saying, "Look. At. Me."

His chest tight, his breath stuck in his throat, he peeked at her, reluctantly. When her thumbs tipped his chin up higher so she could stare more fully into his good eye, his gut flip-flopped. Her dark brown eyes sparked with a passion, a determination and conviction that shook him.

"You did not kill Sanders."

"Maybe I didn't light the fuse, but I was responsible—"

Her grip tightened. "You are *not* to blame for Sanders's death."

He had to swallow several times against the rising bile in his throat before he could counter, "You weren't there. I know you're trying to make me feel better but—"

"Screw feeling better! This isn't about giving you some emotional salve you can spread on when you're feeling guilty."

Her unexpected reply stunned him, silenced him. For a fraction of a second, he allowed himself to feel hurt by her harsh stance.

"I don't want to simply soothe your wounds by applying a comforting balm. I want to help you root out the source of the infection and heal from the inside out.

I want you to be healthy going forward, not just stuck in a routine of applying medicines to ease the pain."

Her eyes, locked on his, penetrated to his soul, and something inside shifted.

Not a balm. Real healing.

He thought of all the times people had said how sorry they were for his accident, how often his well-meaning family had offered to do things for him to make his life easier, had pasted on smiles around him and avoided talking about hard topics they thought would trigger bad memories for him. And he'd cringed internally at the pity and deference and soft treatment. And he'd grown more and more isolated to avoid the pitying, worried looks and kindness that only reminded him how far he'd fallen, how different he was now in their eyes, how much he hated the pretense he put up to alleviate their concerns, as well. They were all playacting, tiptoeing around each other.

And he hated all of it.

But Harlow had stormed into town and hadn't shied from confronting him, wanting answers, offering solutions.

He drew a tremulous breath. "How?" Hearing the rasp in his voice, he cleared his throat. "How do I heal?"

A gentle warmth and compassion filled her face. "You have to let the poison out. Lance the wound and drain the stuff you've been letting fester."

He groaned. "You want me to see a shrink, don't you?"

"Not necessarily."

Again, her answer startled him. But then Harlow's unpredictability had been part of her appeal when they dated. Spontaneous trips, taking picnics on hikes after school, making love in a dressing room at the Boise mall, gifts of no real cash value but huge sentimental significance for no reason except she'd thought he'd like it. Choosing Thai food in Conners instead of their social group's regular pizza after a football game…and her refusal to marry him when he left for the Marines.

That had been the biggest surprise of all. She'd wanted to go to college. Understandable, he supposed. She'd thought they were too young. Maybe, but they could have made it work. And she'd wanted to stay rooted in Owl Creek. Unfathomable. All he'd talked about for months was how he couldn't wait to leave the small town in the dust, see the world, serve his country, pursue bigger, better things for their future together. How could she not support him in that dream?

He noted, now, that she had yet to comment on his admission of his regrets concerning their breakup. He knew she'd heard him. He's seen the color wash from her face, felt the shudder that raced through her. Shoving aside memories of her perfidy on that painful night that they split, he eyed her skeptically. "What do you mean? How else am I supposed to *let the poison out*?"

"There are support groups for veterans with PTSD." When he frowned and opened his mouth to reject the idea, she rushed on to say, "Or…you could talk to Sebastian. I think he'd understand most anything you're feeling. And he's your best friend."

Wade clenched his back teeth. Admit all his failures and fears to his best friend? Maybe. He knew he could trust Sebastian's confidentiality, but…

"Or me," she said, and he blinked as he returned his attention to Harlow. "You've made a good start tonight. And I will listen whenever you need to talk to someone."

She stroked his face tenderly. "We may not be together anymore, but I still care deeply about you. About your happiness."

A bubble of something tenuous swelled in his chest—and then popped as soon as her earlier assertion replayed in his head.

I can't afford to act on that attraction.

He reined his hope, doused the flicker of emotion that sparked whenever he sensed a growing connection with Harlow. She was leaving Owl Creek again. Soon. And she'd told him in so many ways she wouldn't give him her heart again. He'd squandered his chance with her eleven years ago.

"And…" she continued, calling his focus back to what she was saying. Her expression said she was about to drop a radical idea on him. "What would you think about getting a support animal? One of the dogs that Sebastian is training out at Crosswinds?"

He arched one eyebrow. "Most of those dogs are for search-and-rescue."

"True, but not all of them. I hear that Sebastian has started branching out a bit in other specialties."

Sebastian had suggested he get a PTSD-trained companion dog before, but Wade shut him down quickly, not wanting to admit he needed help of any sort. His best friend had offered other kinds of assistance and advice in the past, too. Wade exhaled harshly and scrubbed a hand over his face. Going to Sebastian now with any sort of ask would be…hard. Humbling. Humiliating.

As if reading his mind, Harlow said, "You have to know anything you ask from your family and friends will be greeted with compassion and readiness to help.

I'm sure Sebastian and Ruby would move mountains to get you the perfect dog if you'd agree. Your sister and best friend love you as much as—" she stopped short, her mouth open, before finishing awkwardly "—as much as the rest of your family does. They all want what's best for you. Surely you know that?"

He tried not to dwell on the fact that she'd refused to say she loved him—because he sensed that's what had been on her tongue. Instead, he considered her suggestion of getting a companion dog.

"Earlier, when you were talking about your future, your memories of the explosion, you seemed to find some comfort when Luna got on your lap. Animals are well known to be therapeutic, and if you got one trained to help with PTSD…" She turned over a hand as if to let him fill in the blank.

"I don't know." He chewed the inside of his cheek, and her idea tickled his brain, growing more palatable the longer he considered it. "Maybe."

"Do you have a good reason *not* to?" she asked, then fell silent while he stewed, debated, warmed to the idea.

Finally, he threw up his hands and gave a defeated chuckle. "Okay, okay, I'll get a dog!"

Harlow beamed at him for his decision. Her eyes sparkled with joy and pride and relief.

If he weren't already beginning to believe a companion dog would at least be—well, a good companion, he'd have been satisfied with his choice simply to know, this once, he'd made Harlow happy.

After devastating her with the cruel words he'd tossed at her to make their breakup cleaner, anything he could do to make her smile, any effort it took to give her a moment of happiness, was a small price.

"I'll go call Ruby now," she chirped as she started to wriggle off his lap to retrieve her burner phone.

He stopped her with a hand around her wrist. "No need. If I'm going to do this, then I should take complete ownership. I can call Sebastian myself."

"Absolutely." Harlow gave a firm nod. "You are right." Before turning away to climb off his lap, she leaned in and kissed his cheek, catching the corner of his mouth. A quick kiss. A kiss not unlike ones he'd seen her give other friends' cheeks. But the small peck set his blood ablaze and roused memories of greater intimacies he'd shared with Harlow in the past. Rather than release her wrist, his grip tightened, drawing her up short.

Harlow gave him a querying look, and his heart thumped harder against his ribs. Was he bold enough to act on his impulse? He wanted to taste her lips again, wanted to explore the velvet recesses of her mouth and feel her shimmy with pleasure as she had when they were younger. She must have read his intent in his gaze because her breath caught. When he tugged her closer, her pupils dilated and her fingers curled against his chest. He could hear her breath grow shallow and quick...or was that his own?

As he seized his chance, ducking his head to slant his mouth across hers, he whispered, "My God, I have missed you."

Chapter 16

Harlow greeted his kiss with her own, parting her lips to draw fully, deeply on his.

Sliding his hand into her hair, he cradled the back of her head, massaged the tendons of her neck as he slaked years of longing in their kiss. But all too soon, she pushed against his chest and averted her head.

Harlow sighed sadly as she ducked her chin. "Wade, stop. I'm not—we can't—"

When she wiggled to get up this time, he released her, and she scrambled to her feet, crossed the room. Reaching the kitchen door, she paused, not looking at him. "I've spent the last eleven years trying to get over you, trying to put the pain of our breakup behind me."

He swallowed hard as bitter guilt rose in his throat. "I know I hurt you. I said the harsh things I did thinking it would make it easier for you to hate me, to move on."

She spun now to face him. "Hate you? After what we meant to each other, shared together, how could I ever hate you? I hurt *for* you, because I knew I'd let you down. I was selfish. I wouldn't give up the home I'd found in Owl Creek to make a home with you. You were understandably angry with me. I hurt because I knew I'd lost you, because I knew I'd hurt you."

Wade scoffed wryly. "God, Harlow, I never blamed you. I'm the one who left, who joined the Marines and told you I'd never loved you."

His mind whirled. If she blamed herself, if they both were clearly still attracted to each other, was it possible they could rebuild what they'd thrown away? He scooted to the edge of his recliner, narrowing his gaze on her. "Harlow, if we both have regrets over what happened, if we both have blamed ourselves all these years, do you think we could ever—"

Her hand shot up to silence him. "Wade, no. I know where you're going, but I've told you, I'm not back in Owl Creek to stay. My life has changed. We've both changed." She paused, shaking her head and biting her bottom lip. Then with a deep breath, she said, "When we were together before, we had so many things working for us. We had passion and a foundation of friendship and interests in common, but we still failed to make it work when life happened."

We failed...

Wade gritted his back teeth to bite back the growl of frustration her words stirred in him. She meant *he'd* failed. He'd failed to fight for her, failed to prove his love for her, failed to do everything he should have to make her happy.

"How are we supposed to build something that will work now at a time when your life and mine are both in a state of limbo? With so many factors still unresolved, trying to put the pieces of a broken relationship together now is...not a good idea."

And there it was. Her doubt, her lack of faith in him. Not that he blamed her. He couldn't even see a path forward in his own life. How was she supposed to believe she could depend on him, trust him with her future, when he couldn't even sort out his past?

When he didn't answer her, Harlow glanced away, then headed for the back bedroom. She hesitated only long enough to say, "Thank you for sharing your story with me. I know it was difficult." She cast a quick glance over her shoulder. "But it's an important first step toward rebuilding your life and being happy again."

Bracing his forearms on his thighs, Wade bent his head and thought, *No. You are.*

Harlow stared at the ceiling in Wade's guest bedroom. Her mind was too keyed up, too full of the day's hideous twists, tantalizing moments and heartbreaking revelations to simply turn her thoughts off and find much-needed rest. When she closed her eyes, she saw the fangs of the rattlesnake lunging at her, fiery explosions, Wade lying burned and suffering in a hospital, taunting text messages, and the bleak expression on Wade's face when he'd told her how much he regretted breaking up with her after high school. As much as the physical threat of the snake had shaken her, hearing Wade speak of his grief over losing her, his wish to reunite, was what had left her the most unsettled. And the kiss…

Heaven help her, the kiss had been a mistake. While she was actively trying to quell her misguided longing for Wade, when she'd just finished telling him she couldn't see a way forward for them, why had she let herself be tempted into kissing him back? The last thing she wanted to do was send him mixed messages. He was already tortured by his past and confused about his path forward. Any confusion over her feelings for him could only be unhelpful.

She could have pulled away, told him no. Wade had always honored her choices, respected her no without coercion or guilt. So she could have walked away from the allure of his lips, the heat that had sparked between them. So why hadn't she? And, damn it, now that she knew how strong the pull between them still was, had experienced again the crackle of the electricity that still sizzled with Wade, what did she do with the fire in her blood, the yearning in her soul?

He hadn't pushed when she rebuffed his suggestion that they give their relationship another shot. Wasn't that proof he wasn't fully committed to a reunion? Their life choices were what had pulled them apart before, so how could she risk her heart when he was still uncertain what he wanted for his life going forward?

Had he not pushed back because he saw the truth of her argument? And why was she disappointed he *hadn't* challenged her position? Didn't the past prove that without certainty and a shared commitment, anything else was a recipe for heartache? She knew better than to repeat old mistakes.

She rolled onto her side and punched the pillow, sighing her frustration and choking back the tears that clogged her throat. Luna, who'd been trying to sleep curled at her feet, stood and stretched, casting a baleful glare at Harlow and hopping off the bed.

"I'm sorry, Luna," she whispered, snapping her fingers and clicking her tongue to try to call the feline back to her. She patted the top quilt. "Come on, girl. I promise I—"

She fell silent, hearing an agonized cry from the next

room. Tossing back the covers, she padded in her bare feet to the door of Wade's room. A slice of light from the moon and the outside security light spilled across Wade's face. He scowled, and sweat had beaded on his forehead. His body writhed as if in pain, and he moaned again in his sleep.

She blamed herself for his nightmare. She'd encouraged him to relive his accident, to open the wounds he'd swathed in layers of gauzy denial and distance. She hovered there on the threshold, debating whether to wake him or not. It seemed cruel to let him continue the bad dream. But how would he react to being woken? She couldn't imagine he'd enjoy having his nighttime torture set out before her like exhibit A in an examination of his hurting soul.

She stood watching him, debating and hurting for him long enough that after a few moments, his twisting limbs stilled and his grimace relaxed. Releasing a deep breath, she backed from his door and climbed back in her own bed. Luna followed her and curled on the second pillow of the double bed. Stretching out her hand, she sank her fingers in Luna's warm fur and listened to the mesmerizing sound of her cat's purr.

At some point, she finally drifted to sleep, because the next thing she knew, watery light peeked through the curtains and the scent of fresh coffee brewing greeted her. Luna was nowhere around, but she suspected she knew where her cat had gone. The fuzzface was a sucker for an early breakfast.

Sure enough, when Harlow scuffed in her slippers down the short hall to Wade's kitchen, she found Luna rubbing against Wade's legs and meowing insistently.

"Give me a sec, cat. I have to get a plate or something. You know, the barn cats at Colton Ranch get their own breakfast. Ever thought about hunting mice, Luna?" He popped open a can of cat food and dumped it all on a small plate. Moving to a corner of the kitchen, he placed the dish of the floor and tossed the can in the trash. "Bon appetit."

Turning back toward the counter, Wade finally noticed Harlow. The instant joy that crossed his face when he spotted her warmed her heart. But in the next second, he schooled his expression, sobering to a more sedate smile and nod. "Morning."

"Morning. Thanks for feeding the beast. I know she can be a pest about breakfast."

He shrugged. "No big deal. Getting up early and feeding animals is the story of my life these days. I don't mind." He gave his attention to a bowl of beaten eggs waiting to be cooked. "Hungry?"

She chuckled. "Am I another animal to be fed?"

He shook his head. "I'm not going to answer that."

She squeezed his shoulder. "You always were a smart man."

He twitched a grin. "How'd you sleep?"

"Honestly, I...didn't sleep too much. A lot of tossing and turning until the wee smalls." She cast him a tentative glance. "And you?"

"Good enough, I guess."

No mention of his nightmare, so she let it go. Instead, she moved to the front window to gaze out at the thin layer of snow that had fallen overnight. She relished the sight, having not seen snow since moving to LA. She was surprised to realize she'd missed it.

"I called Sebastian a few minutes ago," he said as he dumped the eggs in a hot pan.

"Oh?" Harlow turned from the window and into the kitchen.

"He has a husky mix that he's been training as a PTSD service dog."

Harlow looked up from the mug she was prepping for her coffee. "Perfect!"

He raised a hand toward her. "But…she's young and still needs more training."

Disappointment plucked at her. Wade needed help now, not months from now. "How long?"

He shrugged. "He wasn't sure. Depends on the dog. And the owner." He exhaled. "I'm going to need to spend time at Crosswinds learning how to work with the dog." He stared into the frying pan as he stirred the eggs. "But I can bring her home today, let her start learning her new environment."

Harlow beamed. "Excellent!"

Harlow helped Wade shop for dog accessories that morning, loading the back of his truck with food, a kennel and a dog bed. Once equipped for his new roommate, she and Wade arrived at Crosswinds after lunch. Sebastian met them just outside the kennel where the dogs currently in training were kept. The place was surprisingly quiet, and Harlow cast her gaze around looking for the dogs. "Where is everyone? And by everyone, I mean all the dogs."

"In class," Sebastian said, guiding her around the corner of the kennel building so she could view a large field where several dogs of various breeds were practicing skills for search-and-rescue. Some were adult dogs, while a few puppies seemed to be receiving basic obedience training. Harlow grinned watching the wiggly and enthusiastic puppies.

"So—" Sebastian shook Wade's hand in greeting "—what made you change your mind about getting a dog?"

"Harlow did," Wade said simply, his expression still skeptical.

Harlow tipped her head as she turned toward Wade. "Changed your mind?"

"Yeah. Sebastian's been nagging me about getting a dog for months," Wade admitted.

Sebastian grunted. "Nagging makes me sound like an old lady. I've been helpfully suggesting that a dog would do you a world of good." He shifted his attention to Harlow. "And stubborn mule that he is, he's refused to hear anything I had to say."

Wade growled under his breath, shoving his hands in his jeans pockets.

"Well, my idea might not have been original, but at least I got him to listen. So where is the dog you picked out for him?" Harlow raised her hands in query.

"Inside." Sebastian hitched his head toward the door of the kennel. "Ruby's just giving her a bath and a last minute once-over to make sure she's shipshape."

Harlow and Wade followed Sebastian inside the kennel building and down the long row of pens to a back room where Ruby was brushing out a white husky.

Hearing them approach, Ruby looked up and smiled brightly. "Look, Betty Jane, it's your new dad."

Betty Jane, who'd been sitting obediently while Ruby

groomed her, rose to all four feet and wagged her tail seeing the trio arrive. Sebastian rubbed Betty Jane's head and received an affectionate nuzzle in return. "Good girl." Glancing to Wade, he motioned him forward. "Come meet her. Let her smell your hand."

Harlow wanted to move closer to ruffle the beautiful dog's thick fur but checked herself. This introduction was about Wade and Betty Jane. She was just along for the ride.

Wade moved toward Betty Jane and let the husky sniff his hand before scratching the dog's cheek and ear. "Hi, Betty Jane." After a few moments of petting the husky's head and looking into Betty Jane's different-colored eyes, Wade quirked a lopsided smile and asked, "So, girl, you wanna go home with me?"

Betty Jane wagged her tail and lifted a paw to Wade's arm.

"I think that's a yes," Harlow said. She waited until Wade had had a minute or two more to greet Betty Jane before she stepped closer and stroked a hand down the dog's soft fur. Betty Jane turned to sniff Harlow, and she held her hand out for the dog's inspection.

"Okay, what do I need to know? How does this service dog thing work?" Wade asked.

"Well, like I told you earlier, Betty Jane is still pretty young and needs a bit more training. She can live with you, but you'll need to bring her in daily for a few hours to work with Della. Best case would be if you were involved in the training. You two need to learn each other." Sebastian wagged a finger from Betty Jane to Wade and back. "Like a squad in the military, you two are a team now, and you have to get to know each other to be able to work seamlessly together, depend on each other, support each other."

Harlow caught Wade's almost imperceptible wince and wondered what part of Sebastian's instructions had landed the sour note.

"I still have to work at the ranch, earn a living. What do I do with her during the day?" Wade asked.

"She'll go with you."

"What?"

"Betty Jane will become your shadow. She'll go everywhere you go." When Wade's expression reflected his surprise at this information, Sebastian chuckled, adding, "What good is a service animal that's not with you when you need their service?"

"I, uh…just…" Wade scratched his cheek, his brow furrowed. "You don't think she'll be in the way at the ranch?"

"Why should she be?" Ruby asked. "The other ranch dogs aren't in the way."

"But…" Sebastian said, and paused to chew his bottom lip as he mulled something. "We should probably take her to the ranch and do some training there as well, so she can get used to the cattle and horses, the smells and general activity of a working ranch. The idea is for her to learn not to be distracted by the kind of things that rile up other dogs. To focus on you."

Betty Jane nudged Wade's hand again with her nose, and Wade gave the husky a good scratching behind the ear. "Partners, huh?" he said, obviously directing the comment to Betty Jane. "I'm in if you are, girl."

Betty Jane's plumed tail swished as she licked Wade's face.

In the purse she had tucked under her arm, Harlow's

new phone rang. She responded as conditioned, opening her purse to fish it out, when a disturbing thought gripped her, and for a moment, she froze.

She'd changed phones. So who had her new cell number?

Chapter 17

Harlow stared into the pocketbook as if the phone were a growling beast instead of a device. Though she tried to play it down, for Wade's sake, she lived in fear of the stalker getting the new phone number and resuming his reign of terror. When she felt Wade watching her, she took a breath for courage, dug the cell phone out and checked the screen.

Relief whooshed through her, seeing a number she recognized. Still shaking from the spike of adrenaline, she answered the call with what she prayed was a steady and cheerful tone. "Hannah? Hi! How are you?" Had she given Hannah her new number? Texted Hannah from her new phone?

"I'm good. Say, Lucy and I stopped by your parents' house earlier and everything was dark and locked up. Have you finished packing it up already?"

Harlow scoffed a laugh. "Far from it. But I'm taking a break for a while to…work on a different project." She paused a beat then asked, "How…did you get this phone number?"

"You called me from that number yesterday. I saved it to my contacts." Hannah sounded confused and wary, then continued, "So...what kind of project? Something for *Harlow Helps*?" Hannah asked.

"More like something *because* of *Harlow Helps*."

"O-kay," Hannah said, her confusion obvious. "Anything I can do to help?"

"Thanks, but no. Wade's helping me out, and in return, I'm helping him with a new project, as well."

"Wade?" Intrigue filled Hannah's tone. "Do tell!"

"I know what you're probably thinking, and it's nothing like that," she said in a hushed tone, turning her back to the others. "We're at Crosswinds, getting Wade a dog."

"What!" Hannah's shocked reply was so loud, Harlow was sure Wade and the others had heard it. "I have so many questions right now," Hannah said, a chuckle in her voice.

Harlow walked away from Wade, Ruby and Sebastian so she could talk to Wade's sister more privately. Did Hannah know about Wade's PTSD? She didn't want to break Wade's confidence, but the fact that Wade was getting a service dog would be evidence enough to his family that he was dealing with the lasting effects of his trauma. "Apparently, Sebastian had been urging him to get a service dog, and I was finally able to convince him it would be helpful. So we're here to take Betty Jane back to Wade's cabin."

Hannah was silent for a moment, and Harlow could imagine her friend processing the news and all its implications. "That's great! A dog will be good company for Wade. And if Betty Jane serves a greater need as well, then that's even better. I'd been so worried about him. He seemed to be...searching. Alone, despite all our offers to help. Chase and Fletcher said to give him space, but..."

Harlow glanced behind her where Sebastian was fitting Betty Jane with a vest that read Service Animal. "So, we kinda got sidetracked. You must have had a reason you stopped by my folks' house."

"I thought you might like to join Lucy and me for lunch. We were going to give you a break from packing boxes and dusty closets."

"Oh, I'm sorry I missed that. Rain check?" Harlow moved back down the center aisle of the kennel toward Wade, who was taking Betty Jane's leash and shaking Sebastian's hand again.

"Of course. I can't tomorrow. I have a catering job out of town, but maybe Thursday?"

"Sounds good." Harlow caught the nod Wade sent her, and she added, "I better run. I think Wade and Betty Jane are ready to head home."

"Hey, before you go, can I have a word with my brother?" Hannah asked.

"Sure." She held the phone out to Wade. "Hannah wants to talk to you."

Furrowing his brow in query, he took the phone and said, "Yes?"

Harlow squatted to give Betty Jane a scratch behind the ear. "Listen, girl, Wade has a cat visiting him. Luna is pretty laid back, so she won't bother you, but I expect the same from you. Okay?"

"A cat shouldn't be a problem. She's been trained not to let other animals distract her from her watch over her person," Sebastian said. Then, giving Harlow an odd look, he asked, "But why is your cat at Wade's house instead of your parents'?"

"I've moved out of my parents' place, at least for a while. Wade thought I'd be safer staying with him."

Sebastian's frown deepened, and his spine straightened. "Safer from what?"

Harlow hesitated, glancing at Ruby and back to Sebastian. She didn't want to alarm them. The two had a new relationship, a new baby, a new start that she didn't want to cast a pall over. She waved a dismissive hand and kept a light tone as she explained, "A listener from my show has been kind of harassing me. Wade's just being protective."

Ruby arched an eyebrow and cast a glance to Wade, who was in conversation with Hannah, but clearly still listening to what Harlow was saying. "Just protective?"

Harlow stood, dusting dog fur from her hands. "I know everyone wants to play matchmaker. While we've addressed our high school breakup and are friends again, we both agree that a romance is not in the picture. It's not practical for either of us. Neither of us plan to stay in Owl Creek, and starting something now just doesn't make sense."

Even as she said the words, denying she wanted more with Wade, her chest ached and a hollow loneliness pulsed inside her. Despite a successful career and new friends in Los Angeles, had she really felt whole since she and Wade split up years ago? She didn't want to admit that he was the missing piece in her soul. How could she risk putting her heart on the line again when so much about their futures was unknown, likely transient?

Ruby twisted her mouth, and her eyes reflected her disappointment. Her reaction didn't surprise Harlow. She knew Ruby only wanted her brother and friend to have the happiness she'd found, to regain the passion that had been so fulfilling in high school. What did surprise Harlow was Wade's reaction to her answer. His gaze darted to her, and he seemed startled, as if learning this information for the first time.

Letting you go is the biggest regret of my life.

When she studied him closer, he quickly schooled his face …but not before Harlow saw a flicker of melancholy drift over his expression. He turned his back to her as he ended his call with Hannah saying, "Sure. Anytime. Kiss Lucy for me."

Sebastian gave Wade a few more last-minute directions, and they were soon on their way back to Wade's house.

Betty Jane crowded into the front seat with them, seemingly excited by the truck ride and the new adventure.

"Her heterochromia is kinda cool, don't you think?" Harlow asked.

"Her what?"

"Heterochromia. Her different-colored eyes."

Wade nodded. "Sebastian said it's not uncommon in huskies, especially since BJ is a mixed breed."

"Oh, so she's already BJ, huh?"

Wade shrugged. "Maybe."

When they pulled off the state highway and drove up the long driveway to Wade's house, an unfamiliar car was parked in front of his cabin.

Harlow stiffened, her senses going on full alert. As far as she knew, Wade wasn't expecting company. "You know this car?"

"Well, that didn't take long," Wade mumbled. He pointed out toward the shore of the lake just past his house to the two figures silhouetted against the afternoon sun. "Hannah and Lucy. Hannah said she might bring Lucy by to meet Betty Jane, but dang. She beat us here."

Hannah turned, obviously hearing Wade's truck, and as Harlow climbed out, holding Betty Jane's leash, she heard Hannah call to her daughter.

The small girl turned, spied Wade climbing down from the driver's side and squealed her delight. "Uncle Wade!" Lucy ran full speed, her pigtails flying, straight to her uncle.

Wade crouched so he could scoop the five-year-old into his arms, catching her against his chest with an exaggerated "oof!" when Lucy leaped into his embrace. The child's cheeks and nose were pink from the cold, and her eyes were bright with excitement.

"Hi there, Lucy Goose. I'm so glad you came to see me," Wade said, hugging her.

"Not you," Lucy said frankly, still balanced on his hip but casting her gaze about until she found Betty Jane. "I came to see your dog! Mommy said you got one of Uncle Sebastian's dogs."

Wade chuckled, then pretended to be crestfallen. "What? You didn't come to see your favorite uncle? I'm crushed!"

Leaning back in Wade's arms, Lucy framed Wade's scarred face between her mitten-encased hands and said with grown-up sincerity, "Don't worry. I still love you."

He tipped his head, a grin tugging his lips. "Do you? How much?"

Harlow acknowledged Hannah with a smile as she approached and bent to pat Betty Jane's head, but her focus was all on the interaction between Wade and his niece. The man and small girl entered a verbal contest over who loved who more that echoed books Harlow could remember from her childhood.

"Well, I love you to the sun and back," Lucy announced. "The sun is farther away than the moon."

"Hmm," Wade said, giving the child a thoughtful frown. "You're right. In that case, I love you to the end of the Milky Way!"

Lucy's eyes widened, apparently trying to decide what was bigger than Wade's offering. "Well, I love you this much..." Lucy proceeded to kiss Wade's scarred face, time and again in rapid fire, saying, "Mu-ah. Mu-ah. Mu-ah," with each smacking kiss to his cheeks and chin and forehead.

Beside her, Hannah tensed and called, "Be careful, Lucy."

But the man and child ignored Hannah. Instead, a chortle rumbled from Wade's chest and lit his face, and the joyful sound shook something loose deep in Harlow's core. She realized it was the first time she'd heard Wade really laugh, not just a wry snort, since she'd returned to Owl Creek.

Wade's laugh, his sense of humor and joyful disposition had been a large part of what had made her fall in love with him in high school. Hearing the laughter that had been missing in their earlier interactions only sharpened by contrast how much the interceding years had changed Wade. Or, perhaps more specifically, how the explosion had changed him, left him searching emotionally for a way forward.

Wade pulled Lucy close in a tight hug, saying, "And

I love you this much!" He made grunting sounds pretended to be squeezing her as hard as he could in the hug. The embrace was tight, but clearly not enough to hurt Lucy.

"Ack!" Lucy let her head loll and acted like she couldn't breathe, her tongue out as she panted. "Okay, okay, you win!" The girl wiggled. "Now put me down! I wanna pat your new dog."

Wade complied, his face still glowing with love and the reciprocated affection and teasing of his niece.

Because she doesn't judge me or treat me like I'm less of who I was before... Something deep in Harlow's core gave a painful throb.

When Lucy raced over to Betty Jane, who sat patiently on her leash, her nose up, sniffing the new smells of the lakeside terrain, Wade followed. "When you said you might bring Lucy by to meet the dog, I didn't expect you to beat me home."

Hannah shrugged. "What can I say? Lucy heard me say *Wade* and *dog*, and nothing would do but that we come immediately. She's been obsessed with dogs since her school friend got one."

"You must live close," Harlow commented. "We only had a ten-minute drive from Crosswinds."

Hannah chuckled. "You're in Owl Creek, Harlow, not Los Angeles, remember? Everything is close. But for reference, we just live that way along the shoreline about a half mile. You can see our storage hut from here, by the water's edge. If the ice were thicker, we could have walked across the inlet, as the bird flies, and it'd only be half that distance."

"But the ice isn't thick enough yet," Wade warned, "so don't try it."

Hannah gave Wade an I'm-not-stupid look. "Yes, big brother. I know."

Harlow moved closer to the lake and peered across the frozen water. "I see it. The gray building just there? Is that your storage building?"

"That's the one. It looks so innocent from here, but inside it's so...messy." Hannah sighed. "Well, that's a project for another day when I'm not so busy with single parenting."

"Oh, Uncle Wade, I love your dog! She's so soft!" Lucy hugged Betty Jane's neck, earning tail wags and a face lick in return. The girl laughed and stroked the husky's fur, beaming. "Mommy, look, she has one blue eye and one brown eye!"

"Sebastian said that's because she's a mixed breed. Her father might have been a malamute or German shepherd," Wade said, moving to the tailgate of his truck to unload the large bag of dog food, fleece-lined dog bed, and grocery sack with water bowls, brushes, and other accoutrements that went along with dog ownership, whether service animal or pet. He left the pile of supplies on the frozen ground while he fished in his pocket.

After pulling out his keys, he extended them to Harlow saying, "Here. You and Hannah can get out of the cold while Goose and I get this stuff inside and make sure BJ takes care of any business she needs to before we go in."

"Sure." Harlow offered the leash to Lucy, but the girl continued hugging and getting face licks from Betty Jane.

"Mommy, can we get a dog?"

Hannah bit her bottom lip, looking pained. "No, honey. That's not a good idea."

"I think it's a great idea. I love Betty Jane, and I'd love my dog, too. Pleeeease!"

Harlow could see refusing her daughter was difficult for Hannah, and she sensed there was more to Hannah's answer than simple logistics of dog ownership.

When Wade crouched to lift the large bag of dog food, Lucy flung herself on his back. "Can I have a piggyback ride? My daddy used to give me piggyback rides."

Now Hannah's face paled, and she fussed, "Lucy, no! Get off Wade's back. You'll hurt him!"

But before the little girl could wiggle off, Wade looped his arms under her legs and rose to his full height again, sending his sister a scolding glare. "Why don't you let me decide what I can and can't do." He shifted Lucy so that she bounced and giggled, and Wade cast a glance over his shoulder. "You holding on tight? This bronco's been known to buck!"

He jogged off with Lucy on his back and jostled and bounced his niece while Lucy squealed her delight. Betty Jane tugged on the leash and Harlow dropped it so the dog could scamper after them.

Harlow studied Hannah's frown as Wade trotted off with Lucy on his back. She debated whether she should say something to Hannah about how she and her siblings treated Wade with kid gloves. She didn't want to interfere, but the Coltons needed to understand that their coddling and overbearing caution with him were doing more harm than good.

Hannah sighed and shook her head. "I've told Lucy she has to be careful with Wade, that she can't rough-house with him the way she does with her other uncles. But she doesn't listen."

"Or maybe she's listening to Wade, where you and the rest of the family aren't?" she said, her tone gentle to offset the chiding.

Hannah refocused her frown on Harlow. "What do you mean?"

"He's chafing under all the overcautious treatment. He wouldn't have offered Lucy a piggyback ride if he didn't feel up to it. I've seen how you act toward him. All of you. I'm not singling you out. And I see how your walking on eggshells irritates him and makes him feel…belittled."

"But…" Hannah's face creased with pain. "Oh, Harlow, you didn't see him when he got home from the hospital. He was in such bad shape. We're only concerned that he not push too hard, that he heal properly."

"He's had a year and a half to heal since then, though. I know your caution comes from a place of love, but even love can be misused or become smothering."

Hannah seemed truly startled and chastened. "But we never wanted to— You think he resents us?"

"Well, I can hear the frustration in his voice when one of you tries to protect him or holds back somehow out of concern. Don't you think he's a better judge of what he can and can't do? What he needs most is your faith in him and encouragement."

Hannah looked back out on the yard where Wade and Lucy tossed a stick for Betty Jane, and he swung the little girl up over his head to peals of her giggles. "They are having fun. And he doesn't appear to be in pain."

"And he's laughing." A ripple of awareness and affection sluiced through Harlow seeing this hint of the old Wade. "How often does he truly laugh anymore, Hannah? I know he's been awfully somber around me. But with Lucy, he feels happy, safe, not judged or seen through the lens of his accident. He's more like his old self. She takes him at face value and treats him the same as she does her other family, like a whole person, like a beloved uncle."

Harlow shivered, not from the cold, but with a self-conviction. Had she treated him differently? Had she unconsciously measured Wade with a bias?

Hannah wrapped her arms around herself, her expression bereft. "The last thing I ever wanted was to cause Wade more grief. I just—"

Harlow sidestepped closer to her friend and draped an arm around her shoulders for a side hug. "I know that. And deep down, he knows that. But while he's making his own adjustments to a new normal, a new face in his mirror, new physical limitations from the loss of his eye, what he needs most from his family are support and faith."

Hannah exhaled heavily. "Of course. Absolutely. And I'll talk to everyone else. Mom has been especially worried, because—well, she's a mom. And mothers worry. But if she and I set the tone, I think everyone else will back off." Her friend chewed her bottom lip. "It's just with him keeping himself so isolated, it's hard to gauge where things stand with him."

"So ask him. Engage him like you would have before the accident. Tease him. Include him. Confide in him. Ask him for help fixing something at your house. He needs to feel needed, accepted, wanted...*normal*. Not damaged."

A male shout from near the lakeshore drew their attention back out to Wade and Lucy. Based on the way Wade was wiggling and tugging at his coat, Harlow surmised that Lucy had stuffed a handful of snow down the back of Wade's collar.

Betty Jane whined and poked her nose in the huddle of bodies, apparently agitated by the antics of Lucy and Wade. Did Betty Jane think Lucy was hurting Wade or vice versa?

A moment later, Lucy shifted her attention to Betty Jane, again enveloping the husky in an enthusiastic hug.

"So...that crew," Harlow nodded toward the man, child and dog, "may be a while. Why don't we each grab an armload from the truck and head inside? We can have hot chocolate waiting when they get in."

"Sounds like a good plan." Hannah put a hand on Harlow's arm as she moved away, stopping her. "And thank you for being frank with me. You're a good friend, and I've really missed having you to talk to."

Chapter 18

"So, what were the two of you gossiping about so seriously earlier?" Wade asked Harlow as he washed mud and dog hair from his hands while Harlow filled mugs with steaming cocoa from the stove.

"What makes you think it was gossip?" She gave him a side glance and a smirk.

"Because I remember all too well conversations I overheard between you and my sisters in the past. We grew up in a small town, remember? Gossip is kinda a hobby around here."

Harlow grunted. "I remember."

"Please, Mommy?" he heard Lucy say from the front room where Hannah was getting her daughter out of her wet coat and socks. "Bella's mom let her get a puppy!"

He carried a towel with him, drying his hands as he moved to the door of the kitchen to follow the exchange between his sister and niece. He curled his mouth to the side in a teasing grin, a quip on his tongue for his sister about fighting a losing battle, until he saw Hannah's expression.

"Baby, I'm sorry. We just can't. Not now. I've got too much on my plate these days to add a new dog to the mix."

Lucy scowled and stomped her foot churlishly, shouting, "I wish Daddy was here! Daddy would let me have a dog!" Whirling away from her mother, Lucy flounced off to throw herself down on the couch with a pout.

As bad as he felt for his niece, who clearly missed her absentee father, he felt worse for Hannah, who looked like she was fighting not to cry.

"Yeah," Hannah muttered under her breath, "A lot of things would be different if your daddy were here. But he's not, so…"

The pain lacing his sister's tone was so thick and heartbreaking, Wade's own chest ached as if slashed with sharp claws. He stepped over to Hannah and pulled her into a hug. "That bastard you married may have left you fending for yourself, but you are not alone. You have me. You have all of the Coltons. And we're a pretty formidable bunch when it comes to taking care of our own."

Hannah sniffled as she chuckled. "Formidable, huh? Yeah, I guess we are, huh?" She embraced him gingerly and then, as if thinking about it again, she squeezed him tightly, as tightly as Lucy giving one of her bear hugs. As tightly as his mother and sibling used to hug him before he'd come home with significant burns and scar tissue. And he reveled in the firm squeeze, the first peek at normalcy in his family interactions in too many months.

Over Hannah's shoulder, he spotted Harlow watching from the kitchen door, smiling. A niggle of intuition told him he owed this warm hug to the talk Harlow had had with his sister. *Thank you*, he mouthed to her.

She bobbed a nod with a satisfied grin.

Over the next few days, Wade divided his time among the ranch, Crosswinds and Harlow's house. Not wanting to leave his uncle in the lurch, he showed up at Colton Ranch early most mornings after dropping Betty Jane off for training with Sebastian and Della. He spent a few hours doing ranch chores, then returned to Crosswinds to get his own training, working with Betty Jane. In the afternoons, he and Betty Jane would arrive at the Joneses' house to wrap china or repaint bathrooms or bag clothes to be donated to charity.

During the hours he wasn't with Harlow, he encouraged Hannah or Vivian or one of his cousins to keep Harlow company and provide another level of security beyond the new cameras and alarm system.

On a Friday in mid-January, he arrived at Harlow's to find his mother and Lucy in the kitchen and the house smelling like fresh-baked gingerbread cookies. He gave his mother's cheek a kiss, then bent to unhook BJ's leash. "How exactly does baking cookies get the house ready to sell?"

"It doesn't," Jenny said, "but who can say no to warm cookies after a long day of work?" She offered a plate of the treats to him, and he helped himself to a few. "Besides," she said in quieter voice, "I'm babysitting for Hannah while she preps for a catering job, and baking cookies kept Lucy out of Harlow's way while she painted the trim in the guest bedroom."

"I see," he said as he shoved a whole cookie in his mouth at once. "Any problems here today?"

Jenny frowned. "Problems? Were you expecting there to be trouble?"

"Not expecting any so much as hoping to avoid it." When his mother gave him a look that demanded further explanation, he said, "Harlow's internet advice show,

Harlow Helps, has attracted negative attention from a listener."

"Oh, dear," Jenny said, lifting a hand to her throat. "Negative attention as in…?"

Wade glanced over at Lucy, who was draped over BJ, ruffling the dog's thick fur. "As in, that's why I've asked people to help with keeping Harlow company when I'm not here. I don't want her to be alone, just in case…"

"I knew it!" Harlow said from the kitchen door, her expression exasperated. "I was suspicious when I had a different visitor drop by randomly every day this week and stay for hours at a time." She wrinkled her nose, which had blue paint smudged on it.

"Which reminds me," he said, turning to his mother, "I don't have anyone scheduled for tomorrow. So can she come with me to the ranch?"

Jenny blinked and pulled an odd expression. "Well, why are you asking me?"

Wade placed a hand on his mother's shoulder and raised an eyebrow. "When are you going to give up the charade? I know you spend more time at Uncle Buck's than your own house. We're not blind to the looks you give each other."

"Looks?" Jenny's cheeks flushed.

Wade chuckled. "Just admit you have feelings for Buck and…well, make your relationship public. Date him without hiding it. You're not fooling anyone, and we're all happy for you both."

"You've talked about us to your siblings?" His mother looked startled.

"And the cousins." He popped another cookie in his mouth.

Jenny sat down hard in one of the kitchen chairs. "Oh.

Well, I..." She lifted her gaze then to Harlow, who stood at the sink, washing paint from her fingers. "Maybe I will, if you'll admit that the two of you still have feelings for each other."

Wade's cookie went down the wrong pipe. He coughed and met Harlow's wide-eyed look, before shaking his head and in a strangled voice saying, "What?"

"You two aren't fooling anyone either." Jenny stood and patted Wade's back gently as he continued coughing to clear the crumbs from his throat. "You're good for each other, and I haven't seen you this engaged and happy in months."

"Mrs. Colton," Harlow said, taking a towel from the counter to dry her hands, "we're not back together. I'm not staying in Owl Creek. In fact, I think the house will be ready late next week, and I'll officially put it on the market."

His mother's face fell, then lifting her chin and squaring her shoulders, she divided a look between Harlow and Wade. "Well, that's a shame. Anyone can see you two are perfect for each other." She glanced at her granddaughter, who was feeding dog treats to Betty Jane. "Lucy, dear, get your things together. It's time to go."

"Aw! I want to play with Betty Jane!" Lucy whined.

"Betty Jane is a working dog," Jenny said, putting a lid on a Tupperware box of cookies. "She not supposed to play with little girls."

"Even ones as cute as you," Wade added, ruffling Lucy's hair.

Shoulders sagging, Lucy got up from the floor and gave BJ a last pat.

"Now come get this box of cookies to take home. We'll

leave the rest for Wade and Harlow," his mother said. "We need to get on the road before the snow gets any worse. I hear we're supposed to get a foot of it by morning!"

Lucy's eyes brightened at the idea of a big snowfall. "Yea!"

"Speaking of tomorrow morning," his mother said, turning to Harlow, "why don't you take a break from the house and come visit with me at the ranch in the morning while Wade works? If what you're looking for is added security, where could you be safer than the ranch with all the extra men close by?"

Harlow shot him a look, then shrugged. "Why not? Sounds like a plan."

As promised, Harlow accompanied Wade to Colton Ranch first thing the next morning. While he prepared to help his uncle and the other hands deal with the snow and effects of the freezing temperatures on the livestock and equipment, Harlow headed toward the main house to visit with Jenny. This morning, his mother made no secret of the fact that she'd spent the night at Buck's, welcoming them warmly on the front porch, as if Buck's house were hers. Wade sent his mother a knowing look as the women headed to the kitchen for "hot coffee, fresh biscuits and juicy gossip," as his mother put it.

"I don't know what that look was for, Wade Colton," Jenny said, lifting her chin, "but I'll thank you not to track snow into the house." She made a shooing motion, adding, "Buck's waiting for you at the barn."

Wade left the truck keys with Harlow. "If you get tired of waiting for me, you can use the truck, but I'd rather you didn't go anywhere alone."

Jenny cocked her head and scoffed. "For Pete's sake, Wade. She's a grown woman. She's perfectly capable of going wherever she wants by herself." Turning to Harlow, she asked, "You remember how to drive in snow, don't you?"

"Well, it has been a while, but..." Harlow met Wade's gaze "I'll wait for you. I promise."

Ignoring the curious and hopeful look his mother shot him as he exited the house, Wade walked across the ranch yard, hiking up his coat collar against the frigid wind.

Buck greeted him with smile and an appraising look. "I hear Harlow's been staying with you. What's that about?"

"Long story, and not what you're thinking." Wade walked straight to the corral and got to work with the other hands.

Most of the heaters in the watering troughs had done their job, but Wade helped make checks to see that all the animals were fed extra forage. They also set up windbreaks, made with hay bales and tin sheeting, for the cattle to huddle behind. Next, he saddled Cactus Jack, preparing to ride out to check that the snow hadn't damaged any fences and to break the ice on the ponds where the cattle preferred to drink.

He was busy at one of the ponds late in the morning when he heard a shout from down pasture. He glanced up to see a lone rider headed toward him on Sunflower. He set aside the pickax he'd been chopping ice with and resettled his hat when the wind knocked it askew. When he recognized the coat and knit cap as Harlow's, pleasure spiraled through him, followed quickly by a prick of irritation. He strode toward the scrub tree where he'd tied

Cactus Jack and she was now dismounting Sunflower and squared his shoulders.

"Exactly what part of 'don't go anywhere alone' was unclear?" he groused.

She blinked at him, clearly startled by his salvo. "Whoa, cowboy." Narrowing a glare, she said, "And what part of 'you're not the boss of me' was unclear to you?"

He clenched his back teeth for a moment, then started again. "I'm just trying to keep you safe."

"I appreciate that, but we are out in the middle of nowhere after a snowstorm. There are hands back at the stable and scattered throughout the pastures, and Buck and Jenny are at the house. I'd think I was pretty safe."

He sighed. "You probably are, but…what are you doing out here? It's freezing!" He pulled her into his arms to buff warmth into her, but found she was the one warming him. His hands were stiff with the cold despite his gloves, and his face stung from the icy wind.

"Which is why Jenny sent you this." Harlow lifted the flap on a saddlebag and pulled out a large thermos. "Hot soup? You didn't come in for lunch, and we figured you had to be getting hungry."

Just the thought of some hot soup made his stomach growl. Loud enough for Harlow to hear.

She chuckled as she passed the canister to him. "I'll take that as a yes."

"That'd be a yes." He uncapped the thermos and tipped it up to drink, not even bothering with the small lid-slash-cup.

"So clearly your mom took your advice about your uncle Buck."

Wade coughed and had to wipe soup from his chin. "Why do you say that?"

Harlow grinned. "Because they're acting like lovesick teenagers back at the house."

Wade arched an eyebrow. "Really?"

"Yeah," Harlow sighed contentedly. "It's nice to see them so…happy."

When another strong gust of frigid wind buffeted them, Harlow shivered, and Wade put the lid back on the thermos of soup. "Listen, I'm done out here. Let's head in. We'll swing by to get BJ on the way back to your folks' house and get that last wall in the bedroom painted."

She tugged her knit hat lower on her ears. "Sounds good to me."

He gave her a boost up onto Sunflower, untied the reins for both horses and set out for the stable.

"I heard from Sloan this morning," Harlow said as they rode back. "She said her team has tracked the computer used to send the earliest threats from my stalker to the area around San Diego. They've been working with the LAPD, sharing the information SecuritKey tracked down to assist with the police's case."

"Good. Anything new on the cell phone numbers used to text you?"

She shook her head. "Just like I didn't want my traceable, apparently neither did my stalker. The numbers were burner phones apparently. They can track where they were used, where the number pinged on a cell tower, but nothing about who bought the phone."

He narrowed a worried look on her. "And where did the phone ping?"

She exhaled heavily, a large puff of vapor clouding around her. "Here. In Owl Creek. Just as we suspected."

His hand tightened on his reins. "That's it then. I'm not leaving your side until this guy is caught. And Fletcher needs to be updated. His officers need to be looking for strangers in town and checking hotels and rental houses and—"

"Wade, it's ski season. The hotels and rental houses are full of out-of-town travelers," she countered.

He firmed his mouth. "Maybe, but there's got to be something we can do to find him before he—" He couldn't bring himself to finish his sentence. The thought of harm coming to Harlow was too much for him to bear.

She was quiet for a moment, before she said, "Or I could leave. Move on to another town, another state, somewhere with no ties to my past or my friends."

Somewhere without me. His gut clenched. "Let's see what Fletcher says before you do that. I hate to think of you out there somewhere alone. Unprotected."

She cut a glance toward him, then gave a nod.

As they neared the stable, Cactus Jack and Sunflower picked up their pace, clearly ready to get out of the cold and get a snack. Wade turned to Harlow to say something about the eager horses, and he caught a movement, something dark and out of place at the edge of his vision. A prickle raced up his spine, a wariness he'd honed while in the Marines. Before the edginess could take form, before he could give voice to his concern, a loud crack of gunfire shattered the calm.

Chapter 19

A hot flash of adrenaline spun through Wade.

Sunflower reared, and Cactus Jack danced sideways in alarm.

Harlow gasped as her horse bucked, but she managed to stay seated. "What was—?"

Another crack echoed across the snowy landscape, and Wade reacted instinctively. Flinging himself off Cactus Jack's back, he shouted, "Get down!"

Harlow, who was struggling to bring Sunflower under control, shot him a startled look. "Wade?"

"Gunfire!" Reaching up, he grabbed a handful of her coat and yanked hard, dragging her out of the saddle. He caught her as she tumbled down. Cushioning her fall with his own body, he flopped into the snow and rolled with her out of the range of the horses' agitated hooves.

Free of her rider, Sunflower bolted toward the stable. Cactus Jack whinnied as he stamped his hooves.

Another shot rang out, then another. The bullets made dull thuds as they hit the ground around them.

Harlow jerked and gave a soft cry of alarm as each shot whizzed close to their heads.

Wade's heart slammed against his ribs. They had no

protection from the rain of bullets. He shifted, making sure Harlow was completely shielded. If he was hit, so be it. But he couldn't stand the idea of anything happening to Harlow. She was everything to him. She'd always been everything for him. Why hadn't he fought harder for her all those years ago? He'd been too proud, too stubborn, too hurt by her rejection of his career goals...

The sound of gunfire had alerted the ranch hands and family, and Wade could hear distant shouts coming closer. He raised his head, glancing toward the line of trees, the direction from which the shots had come. A figure clad in thick layers of dark outerwear and a ski mask stumbled deeper into the woods, out of sight.

"There!" he shouted to his cousin Greg and Uncle Buck as they arrived, bearing rifles. He pointed to where the intruder had been, and Greg and his uncle were gone in a heartbeat, pursuing the gunman.

"Call Fletcher!" he heard someone else shout.

Only as the reality that the danger had passed sank in did Wade allow himself to acknowledge the buzz of adrenaline in his ears, the tremor in his core and the black spots that danced at the edges of his vision. *No!*

He squeezed his eye shut and battled the rising panic. He gritted his teeth and struggled to draw deep, even breaths. Instead of the snow, he felt the scalding heat of flames and heard a deafening explosion reverberating in his head.

Beneath him, Harlow squirmed, and he used the distraction to jam down the roar of the fire and smoke in his brain. He drew a ragged breath and rolled to a seated position, letting Harlow up. Shaking himself out of his mental slide, he focused on Harlow's wide dark eyes. "Are you hurt?"

She took a few extra beats to answer, as if needing to gather herself before she could assess her physical condition. "I—I...think so." Her expression shifting from shock to concern, she reached for his cheek. "You're bleeding! Were you hit?"

Wade touched his face and found a spot with sticky warmth. "I don't think this is from the shooter. Cactus Jack may have cuffed me a little. Or a scrape from the ground." He motioned to the ice and rock uncovered as they'd rolled in the snow. He didn't tell her that his facial cut could have been a ricocheting bit of bullet, ice or rock thrown up when one of the sniper's shots hit near their heads.

She sent a lingering scrutiny up and down the length of him, clearly checking for other wounds. "Wade..."

He caught her hands between his. "I'm okay...as long as you are. Honest. My face is so numb with cold right now, I don't even feel the cut."

Slipping her hands from his grip, she threw her arms around his neck and hugged him. Tight. Like one of Lucy's bear hugs that nearly squeezed the breath from you. He squeezed back. The notion that he'd been so close to losing Harlow forever moments earlier terrified him. If the shooter had had better aim, if he hadn't gotten her off Sunflower and on the ground as quickly as he did, if he hadn't been with her...

"Hey, are you guys all right?" Greg called as he hurried up to them—or hurried as much as one could through the calf-deep snow.

"Thankfully, yes." Wade shoved to his feet and offered a hand to help Harlow rise. She dusted caked snow from her coat and jeans before turning her ministrations to the back of his jacket. He turned his gaze toward the woods where the dark-clad figure had disappeared. "What happened with the shooter? Did you catch him?"

Greg shrugged one shoulder. "Don't know yet. Dad, Malcolm and some of the guys went after him. Dad sent me back to check on you. Your mom's called 911. I've texted an SOS to Fletcher."

"A very efficient Colton crisis response," Harlow said with a strained smile. She was shivering. Probably post-adrenaline tremors as much as cold, Wade suspected, drawing her back into his arms.

"I'm afraid the Colton crisis machine has become well-oiled in recent months," Greg said, his tone dark. "Thanks to the bastards in Acker's cult—" Greg glanced at Harlow and twisted his mouth to the side "Pardon my French."

She waved off his apology. "Sometimes French is called for."

"I know Jessie threatened retaliation when you met with your lawyer about Uncle Robert's will, but sending a cult member to shoot up the ranch is just—" Greg clamped his lips in a tight scowl of disgust.

Harlow blinked, then divided a look between Wade and Greg. "So then…do you think that's who it was? Someone from that church Jessie is involved in?"

Wade could see something akin to hope in her expression. Knowing Harlow, knowing personal trauma, knowing his own jumbled feelings about who the shooter might have been, he could guess the source of that hope. If the shooter was from the Ever After "church," then it wasn't her stalker, wasn't personal, wasn't directed at her. And she could better distance herself from the frightening event, better shut it away, more easily move on.

Greg flipped up a gloved hand. "Who else would it be? Marcus Acker and his lackeys have been behind most of the sh—stuff that's happened to the family this year. We know he wants to take our land, push us out, steal the money from your father's estate."

"*Jessie* wants to steal Dad's money," Wade corrected.

"For Acker!" Greg said. "If she gets any of Robert's money, she'll give it to Acker and his minions in a hot minute. She's deep under his sway."

Wade nodded. His cousin had a point, but he still couldn't sell himself on the idea of the cult's culpability in this instance. He'd be remiss to dismiss the possibility the sniper was Harlow's stalker. They knew he was close by, if not currently in Owl Creek. The cell phone ping and the snake in the mailbox were evidence of that.

"The thing is," Harlow said, her voice shaking, as she backed out of his arms to face Greg, "the shooter may have been after me." She paused and cleared her throat before explaining her situation to Greg.

His cousin divided a concerned look between Wade and Harlow. "Does Fletcher know about this?"

Harlow nodded. "I asked him not to worry the family with it, knowing how much else was on your minds, what with the Acker church—"

"Cult," Greg interrupted. "Calling it a church is a disservice to churches everywhere."

Harlow nodded her agreement. "My point is, it's possible—likely even—that I was the target."

"I hate to hear that. I wish we'd known. When a member of this family is threatened, we rally. This year has taught me that for sure."

Harlow gave a weak half smile. "But I'm not a Colton."

Greg tipped his head, raising an eyebrow. "Aren't you, though? As good as?" He gave Wade a meaningful look before returning his gaze to Harlow. "Family can include people not related by blood. It's more about love."

The sound of voices and snowmobiles behind them hailed the return of the men who'd chased the shooter. Wade wanted to talk to them about what they'd seen, where the gunman had gone. He saw Fletcher pull up in his squad car, lights flashing, and Wade jerked his chin toward his brother. "Come on. We'll talk to Fletcher, then I'll take you home."

Harlow sat next to the roaring fire in Buck's living room but couldn't seem to chase the chill that had settled in her bones from moment the first shot cracked across the ranch yard. She listened with only half attention as Wade, Fletcher, Buck and his male cousins debated the next steps—for finding her stalker, for protecting the family, for resolving unfinished business with Marcus Acker. She'd brought danger to the Colton Ranch, to a family she cherished as much as her own. Why was she still in Owl Creek? As soon as she suspected the stalker had found her, the same day the snake showed up in her mailbox, she should have packed her bags and left town. So what had kept her here? Why had she risked exposing the Coltons, and especially Wade, to the danger her stalker presented?

Wade's mother sat beside her, a calming presence,

but the worry knitting her brow only made Harlow feel more guilty for the threat she'd brought to the Coltons.

She glanced across the room where Wade was engaged in deep, serious discussions with Fletcher and the others, and as if he felt her eyes on him, Wade turned his head and met her gaze.

His expression asked, *You okay?*

She flashed a weak smile and gave a nod, which seemed to mollify him for the moment.

"Other than tracks in the snow, we don't have a lot to go on," Buck said to Fletcher. "By the time we reached the road, the guy was gone."

"Can you do anything worthwhile with the boot tracks he left in the snow?" Wade asked.

Fletcher shrugged. "I've sent a guy out there now to see if any of them have a clear tread we can match. We can measure for boot size and stride length. Beyond that, we can get a ballistics report on the bullets, but without a weapon to match them to, ballistics won't go far until an arrest is made."

"I still say we shouldn't rule out a link to Acker," Greg said, his tone vehement. "Is it possible that Harlow's stalker is connected to the Ever After Church and Acker's minions?"

The men glanced to Harlow, and she perked up. "I can't imagine why he would be. This all started before I arrived in Owl Creek."

"But if the shooter knew you were once involved with Wade…" Jenny offered.

Fletcher shook his head. "That's rather a stretch, Mom. I mean, we'll keep all possibilities on the table, but there are more likely scenarios that bear more attention."

Buck folded his arms over his chest, scowling. "The hell of it is, the more things like this shooter crop up, the more your attention is diverted from finding proof that Acker killed Robert and is behind the other crap that has happened this year. We need Acker in custody!"

Greg and Malcolm both nodded their agreement.

"What else can be done to resolve the case against Acker? What can *we* do that we aren't already?" Malcolm asked.

"Be patient. Acker is smart, but he's not bulletproof," Fletcher said, then winced and cast Harlow an apologetic look as if realizing how harshly that phrase might resound for her. "In the meantime, if you want me to move you to a safe house outside town, I can do that."

Harlow swallowed hard, considering another relocation.

"Or you can stay here," Jenny offered, consulting Buck with a glance. "Surrounded by several Coltons and all of the ranch hands, you'd be plenty safe."

Harlow gripped Jenny's hand but shook her head. "Thank you for the offer but... I'm settled at Wade's now and..." She met his gaze again, and a thread of warmth flowed through her, remembering how he'd pulled her off Sunflower, covered her with his own body, held her in the aftermath of the chaos and numbing fear. "I feel safe with him."

Wade's head came up, and his startled look morphed into what she could only call resolve. Gratitude. Relief. Shoulders squared and jaw firmed, he nodded to her.

An hour later, they were back at his rental cabin with Betty Jane and a takeout order of burgers from Tap Out Brewery.

"Thank you for what you said today." Wade dragged a french fry through ketchup and popped it in his mouth. "About feeling safe with me."

Harlow took a small bite of pickle and ignored her burger. Unlike Wade, who'd only had a few sips of soup for lunch after a morning of manual labor, she had no appetite. Getting shot at had a way of doing that. "I do feel safe with you. Your quick response saved my life this afternoon."

He shrugged. "I mean I appreciate you telling my family. They were ready to take over and push me aside today when—"

"Wade." She tipped her head. "They were doing what any self-respecting, worried family would do. Offering help. And since I have no family of my own anymore, I was touched by their concern." She reached for his left hand as he ate another fry. "And I do feel safe with you— as safe as I can feel until Chris-whoever-he-is is caught."

She squeezed his fingers. Abandoning his meal, he turned to meet her gaze. "Nothing is more important to me than keeping you safe."

A smile pulled at the corner of her mouth. "Can I say that is a very sexy thing to hear without surrendering my independent woman card?"

"Oh yeah?" His eyebrow sketched up, and his expression brightened. "How sexy?"

Scooting closer to him, moving to the edge of her chair, she leaned forward. With her palm, she stroked the side of his face, then dragged her fingers over the day's growth of beard. "This sexy."

She touched her lips to his, barely brushing his mouth with hers, but it was if she'd struck a match and dropped it in gasoline. Heat rushed through her blood, and desire blazed at her core.

Wade canted toward her, capturing her lips again with a deeper kiss and cradling the base of her skull to hold her close. He drew on her lips hungrily, his kiss rousing all the feelings she'd worked these past weeks to deny. The yearning she'd shelved years ago in order to survive her life without Wade roared back from the shadows.

Maybe because she'd had a brush with death today, maybe because her life was still in danger from her stalker, but tonight she wanted to feel fully alive. She wanted to reclaim the earth-shaking experience of being one with this man, of having all of her senses awakened and sharing with Wade the life-confirming and joyful sensations that were as old as time. One look at the passion in his blue gaze told her he needed the same—that he needed to feel deeply human, entirely alive and intimately connected to her.

With her hands framing his face, she simply whispered, "Yes."

Beneath her palms, Harlow felt his tremor in response. He pushed to his feet and scooped her into his arms. With long strides, he carried her to his bedroom and followed her down as he set her on the bed. "There's been no one else for a very long time, Harlow. No one else ever meant what you did, and I quit looking for—"

She silenced him with her lips on his, her legs wrapping around him and her arms circling his neck. She broke the kiss only long enough to rasp, "Same here." And by silent agreement, they knew that was all that had to be said.

They took their time, slowly peeling away each other's

clothes, rediscovering each other's bodies, relearning each other's preferences. With her fingers, she traced the scars on his chest and face, then followed the path with her mouth, her tongue. Wade groaned his pleasure, and the rumble quivered in her belly and roused her all the more.

When he tugged her shirt over her head, exposing her midriff and bra, he dipped his head to rub his cheek on her skin. The scrape of his one-day beard sent tingles deep into her womb. "You're so warm, so soft, so precious to me," he murmured, trailing kisses up to her collarbone. He cupped a breast with his hand, and the stroke of his thumb shot such sweet torture through her that she writhed and gasped. "Please, Wade. Now…"

But he took his time, teasing her, working her to the edge of madness before he sheathed himself and made them one. Tears of happiness prickled in her eyes as she held him close, savoring the sensation of being near him, of moving with him in a rhythmic sway and undulation. And she cried his name when her world exploded in a thousand brilliant stars and a vortex of pure pleasure.

They made love several times before fatigue and the pull of slumber overtook them. She dozed briefly before Wade's snore woke her, and she snuggled close, smiling at the memory of their joining.

For the next couple of hours, Harlow lay awake, listening to Wade's heavy, steady breaths, staring into the darkness. After a while, the sweetness of their night together gave way to the bitter fear of the day. The terrifying moments as bullets had whizzed past her replayed in her mind's eye.

If she'd had any morsel of doubt that her stalker meant her harm, the hail of bullets this afternoon had erased all suspicion. The jerk with a violent vendetta against her meant business. Not only had he had managed to track her to Idaho, he'd made not just one but two attempts on her life—because the rattlesnake had clearly been the stalker's handiwork as well.

What frightened her even more was the fact that any of those shots aimed at her today could have wounded Wade...could have *killed* Wade. A muffled whimper escaped her throat before she pressed her lips tight and forcefully shoved gruesome imagined images from her mind.

Beside the bed, Betty Jane lifted her head, her dog tags jingling.

Harlow angled her head to peer over at the husky and whisper, "Good girl," before rolling to her side to try again to fall asleep.

The click of claws on the hardwood floor preceded the touch of a cold nose, the nudge of a warm muzzle. Harlow smiled as she rubbed Betty Jane's ears and neck. "I'm okay, sweet girl."

But Betty Jane hopped onto the bed and settled in the small space between Harlow and Wade, draping a paw on Harlow's leg.

"Really?" Harlow whispered to the dog. "Isn't three a bit crowded for this bed?"

Betty Jane chuffed and put her head down on her outstretched legs, her mismatched eyes watching Harlow. Sinking her fingers into the dog's warm fur, Harlow inched over to give Betty Jane more room, then, feeling more settled, tried again to find sleep.

She must have dozed eventually because some time later, a groan and the slap of a thrashing arm woke Harlow. She dragged herself awake as more moans and writhing alerted her to Wade's nightmare. Betty Jane shoved her way up from the foot of the bed to Wade's side and lay down across Wade.

Wade's brow was damp, his legs kicked and his face furrowed with anguish.

Harlow felt an answering twist of sympathy in her gut. "Wade, wake up!"

Betty Jane gave a soft bark, licked her owner's face and continued to nudge Wade's chin with her nose. Harlow held her breath, watching the companion dog work until Wade woke with a startled gasp. His gaze darted around the room, his confusion obvious even as Betty Jane gave another quiet chuff and wiggled higher on Wade's chest, pawing his cheek softly and bumping his hands and neck with her nose. Betty Jane's insistent but gentle nuzzling soon earned a pat from Wade. The ragged saw of air he gulped calmed to an even rhythm, and he dug fingers into Betty Jane's fur as if clinging to a life raft.

After a moment, Wade pushed Betty Jane aside, murmuring, "Good girl. I'm okay now."

He fumbled in the drawer of his bedside stand and found a baggie of dog treats. He gave BJ a couple treats, stroking her head and repeating, "Good girl."

"Are you really okay?" Harlow asked.

He swung his gaze toward her as if only then remembering she was there. He frowned as if embarrassed and glanced away. "I wish you hadn't seen that."

"Oh, Wade." She grasped his arm. "Do you really believe I'd think any less of you because you have nightmares? You went through something horrible that no one should ever have to experience. Nightmares are a normal response to a trauma."

"Maybe, but—" he exhaled a choppy breath "—that doesn't mean I want you to witness my struggle."

She looped her arm around his neck and snuggled closer. "If you can't share your struggle with me, then who can you share it with?"

He wrenched free of her embrace, growling, "No one! I can handle this by myself!"

Betty Jane, clearly sensing Wade's continued tension from his tone and body language, moved close to Wade again and pawed his leg until he stroked her head.

Harlow said nothing, giving Wade a moment to compose himself. But after a few deep breaths, he cut a side glance at her and said, "I'd like to be alone for a while. Would you…go back to the other room?"

Pain pierced her heart. Not only was Wade continuing to isolate himself, she'd thought when they'd made love that she'd finally reached him, made the connection she wanted that would warrant changing her life plans to give their relationship another shot.

But here he was holding her at arm's length again. Pushing her away. Closing himself off. That was no way to build a future together. If he couldn't trust her enough to share all of himself with her, how could she open herself to him again?

She gave Betty Jane's head a pat, picked Luna up from the chair where she slept and carried her cat back to the guest room to finish the night alone.

She was fooling herself thinking she had any reason to stay in Owl Creek. Her parents' house was ready to put on the market. Her stalker was clearly in town, lurking, waiting for another chance to hurt her or someone she cared about. And Wade was no closer to sharing his life with her in the open and honest way she needed than he had been eleven years ago.

In the morning, she would pack her things and move on. She would find a new city to take refuge in and put away the false hope of a life with Wade Colton.

Chapter 20

Wade spent the final hours of the night tossing and turning, trying to quiet the turmoil in his head and heart. After making love to Harlow, he'd thought they'd finally reconciled and found a way forward. But when Harlow had pressed him to talk about his nightmare, while the haunting shadows and screams were still so vivid in his brain, he snapped at her and pushed her away.

Why couldn't she just let him heal at his own pace? He was doing his best. He had already talked to her more openly about the day of the explosion than he had to anyone else. He'd gotten Betty Jane. He'd made progress with his family.

And it was still not enough for her.

Even as he tried to justify his actions, his conscience pricked him.

You were rude to her. Too harsh when she only wanted to help.

Wade groaned and threw an arm over his eyes. Betty Jane snuggled closer, pushing her nose into his hand. He stroked the husky's head idly and took a few calming breaths. When the first weak rays of sunlight seeped through his window and he felt more in control of himself, he finally got up and went looking for Harlow.

He found her in the guest room, tossing clothes into her suitcase. His heart squeezed. "What are you doing?"

She stilled for a moment before resuming her packing. "Leaving."

Wade's pulse spiked, and he blurted, "Hell no. Not with that lunatic still after you."

She scoffed and spared him a brief side glance full of irritation. "Maybe I'm going *because* of my stalker. If he's here, I should leave."

He shook his head, too gobsmacked by her decision to process it fully. "Wh—where will you go?"

"I haven't decided. Anywhere that is not Owl Creek."

He snorted and smacked the frame of the door with his open palm. "That's rich."

She paused again from her packing and faced him. "Pardon?"

"Eleven years ago, I asked you to marry me, to go with me when I left for the Marines, and you said you couldn't. You said Owl Creek was your home, and you would never live anywhere else." Frustration soured his gut. He moved closer, glaring down at her. "Of course we now know that was a lie, seeing as how you left for college in California and never moved back. That you avoided Owl Creek until a few weeks ago when you had to come to close out your parents' house."

She straightened her back, her face flushing as her mouth tightened. "That is not what happened."

"Really?" Wade folded his arms over his chest knowing his tone was bitter and wanting to reel it back, but somehow not able to stop the poison that spewed from him. "And just what did I get wrong?"

Harlow's shoulders sagged as if reluctant to dive into

this argument, but after taking a slow breath, she raised her chin. "First of all, what I said the night we broke up was that for the first time in my life I had a place in Owl Creek that felt like home. You knew I'd spent my childhood moving as an Army brat. I was trying to explain to you that I finally felt like I had some stability and consistency in my life in Owl Creek. I had friends I considered family. Your family! But you were asking me to give up that safety net, the sense of home I cherish for the same transient life I'd grown to hate."

"I was asking you to trust *me* to give you stability and safety. I wanted to be your home, to be your husband!" Hurt welled in him as it had that night long ago. "I wanted to matter enough to you, I wanted to *be* enough for you…but you rejected everything I was trying to offer you. My heart, my life, my future."

Her face fell, and she shook her head slowly. "And yet…that same night you told me you didn't really love me. You broke up with me and pushed me away saying horrible mean things."

Wade grunted and balled his fist. "I didn't mean those things! I was angry and hurt. In the moment, I thought it would make it easier for us both to move on if you hated me."

"I didn't want to move on!" she shouted, her voice thick with tears. "I wanted time for us to figure out a way to compromise, to salvage our relationship as we both worked toward our dreams."

"You never said that!"

"I tried to but—"

"You can't expect me to buy some revisionist version

of what happened and think it excuses everything that happened and that it erases the years of pain and regret."

"No. Nothing will change the past. But we can see the truth with more understanding and forgiveness...if you're willing." Harlow raked both hands through her hair. "God, Wade, we were still kids. Teenagers are notoriously self-involved. We were both selfish and unprepared for the realities of marriage. We both made plenty of mistakes. Obviously, we let our emotions and blind spots push us into defensive corners rather than listen to each other."

Wade gritted his teeth. "Seems as though we still are."

"Well—" she returned to her packing "—since I've been back in Owl Creek, I've tried to reach out to you and have the open and honest conversation we need to repair the past, to find common ground."

"So once again, it's my fault."

Harlow stilled for a moment, then threw the blouse in her hand onto the bed with a growl. "I didn't say that!" She stomped toward the door and pushed past him.

"Where are you going?" He dogged her steps, his insides a knot of pain and confusion and fear. Yet when he should have been showing her that he wanted to change, that he wanted to find a way back to her, his frustration boiled up instead. "Running away from this conversation like you're running away from me and Owl Creek?"

She only slowed down enough to snatch her coat and hat from the peg by the door. "We both need a minute to cool down. I don't want to leave town with angry words between us again."

"Harlow, don't—"

She strode briskly outside, and the door slammed shut behind her.

* * *

Harlow stomped through the snow, seething with hurt and frustration. She didn't stop until she reached the edge of Blackbird Lake, where she stared out over the flat expanse of ice. The empty, frozen lake reminded her a bit of her future. Nothing there. No one in sight. Sure, she still had her show, but a Facebook advice show didn't keep her company at night or share her dreams of children. She'd warned herself that letting Wade back into her heart was dangerous, but she'd been foolish enough to believe—

The crunch of footsteps in icy snow yanked her from her deliberations, and she spun around, half expecting Wade, half fearing her stalker.

Instead, she met the pale blue eyes of a late-middle-aged woman in a black coat and knit hat. She exhaled her relief—until she noticed the pistol in the woman's hand.

Confusion mixed with the shot of nervous energy that rushed through her blood. "What…who are you?"

"I'm your reckoning," the woman said hotly, her eyes narrowing. "Sharon's vengeance."

And it clicked. With a spurt of adrenaline that balled like ice in her gut, she knew. "You're Chris72583?"

"*72584!* Her birthday! July 25, 1984."

"And… Chris?"

"Short for Christina. It's what Sharon called me," the woman said, her voice breaking.

Even with the confirmation, Harlow goggled and fumbled to process—her stalker was a woman? Her mind whirled trying to reassess everything she'd assumed, everything that had happened—

The woman took a step closer, and Harlow shifted

all of her focus to the weapon aimed at her, the hatred blazing in the woman's expression. "Wh-what do you want? Why—"

"My baby sister is dead because of *you*, because of your terrible advice," Chris snarled.

Harlow raised a hand, palm out, hoping to signal a truce, a plea for calm. "I'm so sorry for your loss. Truly. Maybe if we talk about—"

"Ha!" Chris barked bitterly. "Your turn for talking is long over, *Harlow*." She gritted her teeth as she grated out Harlow's name like a curse word.

Swallowing hard, Harlow cast a quick glance toward Wade's cabin. From this angle, could he see her out his window? Probably not. And he'd closed the curtains overnight to help conserve heat and block drafts. Should she scream for help? Stay cool and try to talk Chris down? Panicking wouldn't help, but without signaling Wade in some way—

Chris surged forward, grabbing Harlow's arm and jabbing the gun under her chin. "If you make a sound, I'll kill your lover boy, too, just for sport."

Kill Wade, *too*? Harlow gulped. So murder was what Chris had in mind, just as the threats had promised. While her gut swooped with dread, her heart clenched at the notion of doing anything that would put Wade in danger. More danger than she'd already put him in...

"Got it?" Chris asked, shoving her nose close enough to Harlow's that she could smell a hint of coffee on the woman's breath.

Coffee. A flicker of recognition teased Harlow. "You were at the coffee shop... I mean, the bookstore the other afternoon."

"I was. Close enough to kill you, even then…if not for all the other people that would have hampered my get-away. But we're all alone now…aren't we?" Chris hissed, poking the underside of Harlow's chin harder with the muzzle.

Harlow nodded. She had to think of a way to reason with Chris, to find a solution that didn't involve blood-shed—hers or Chris's.

Chris took a moment to glance around, frowning. "I can't do it here in the open. Lover boy will hear and come running."

"You don't have to do it at all," Harlow said gently. "If I could do something to make amends for—"

"You can't! Not unless you can bring my baby sister back from the dead!" Chris choked out the words, then drew a deep breath, composing herself as her gaze landed on something in the distance. Something in the direction of Hannah's house. "Come with me."

"Where…?" As Chris dragged her by the arm, shifting the weapon to the base of Harlow's skull, Harlow angled her head and spotted their likely destination. Hannah's storage building at the end of her friend's short fishing pier.

A new location, hidden from Wade's view. Nothing about that was good. Harlow braced her legs, refusing to walk, but her feet slipped in the icy snow. She went down, dragging Chris off-balance as well. Her captor only stumbled and soon had righted herself, only to lash out at Harlow. She smacked Harlow across the cheek with the butt of the pistol.

Pain ricocheted though Harlow's jaw, and she tasted

blood. The cry of anguish slipped from her lips before she could catch it.

"Shut up!" Chris said through clenched teeth, then smacked her again, hitting Harlow in the temple this time.

Harlow's howl this time was as much rage and frustration as pain. "Stop it! Just…stop! I'm sorry your sister died, but blaming me, killing me solves nothing." She took a trembling breath as Chris hauled her to her feet again.

Mustering her courage and her wits, Harlow turned, facing the woman squarely. If she kept her talking, had more information, maybe she could find a way to negotiate with her. "Tell me what happened. How did your sister die? Why do you think I'm to blame?"

"Because she called in to your show." Chris seized her arm again and dragged her forward. "She *told you* how dangerous her husband was, and you told her to leave him. She *told you* how mad he'd be, how he'd come after her and kill her, and you didn't listen!"

Harlow tried to sift through her memories of the calls she and Wade had been replaying, analyzing. Had there been an abused woman named Sharon? She recalled counseling several people, men and women, concerning domestic violence, always counseling safety for the party involved above all else.

Harlow stumbled along with Chris, moving farther away from Wade's cabin and the hope that he'd see her, see Chris and the gun. Her mouth was sore from the woman's blow, dry with fear, numb from cold. She licked her chapped lips and said in the calmest voice she could muster, "If she called about a violent partner, I would have wanted her to remove herself from the situation for her protection. If I told her to leave her husband, it was because I believed she'd be better off—"

"Dead? Better off dead? She *told you* he'd kill her, and you told her to leave anyway." Chris stopped suddenly and whirled to face her, growling, "I raised Sharon after our mother died. She was like a daughter to me! I loved her more than anyone on earth." Fury darkened Chris's face. "My Sharon's blood is on your hands!"

A pang of grief and guilt spun through Harlow. The absolute worst-case scenario for her was always that her counseling failed and a client was injured or killed. Even if the loss of life came because the client ignored her advice, Harlow felt a sense of failure. While her training taught that she couldn't be blamed for other people's actions, that ultimately every individual must be accountable for themselves, the losses hurt. She wouldn't be in this business if she didn't truly and deeply care about her clients. She couldn't bring Sharon back for Chris, but could she do something, say something to ease the sting of the woman's grief?

"Chris, I understand that you are hurting. Losing a loved one is difficult. Especially—"

"Shut up!" Her captor jerked hard on her arm and shot her a poisonous glare. "You had your chance to—" Chris's step faltered, and an oddly smug look crossed her face. "Fine. You want to talk? Then you will." Planting a hand in Harlow's back, she shoved her forward.

With her arm free of Chris's grip, Harlow recognized her chance to attempt an escape. She *almost* ran. A tingle of energy shot down her legs to her feet that she reined in at the last second. She couldn't outrun a bullet in her back.

Instead, she plodded on through the wooded property between Wade's cabin and Hannah's house. And what about her responsibility to this grieving woman? If she spent a little time with her, could she help Chris find a path through her suffering? Sure, the woman had committed several crimes—not the least of which was threatening her life and Wade's when she shot at them. Chris would have to answer to the justice system for her wrongdoing, but she didn't have to add murder to her rap sheet—not if Harlow could talk her down.

Chris grabbed Harlow's coat at the nape and, shoving her to a faster pace, guided her to the door of the storage house. The latch wasn't locked, and Chris was able to open the door. With a jerk of her head, Chris said, "Inside, Harlow. We have business to take care of."

Wade paced the living room floor, debating whether to follow Harlow or give her time to calm down before he tried again to explain himself. As he stalked restlessly back and forth, Betty Jane treaded along by his side. She tried to block his path, tried to get his attention with soft whines and hand nuzzles. He acknowledged Betty Jane, giving her a treat, but walked around her to continue his pacing. He replayed Harlow's parting words and wrestled with his accusation that she was running away. But was he the one who was running away? Not literally, perhaps, but by avoiding hard topics, ignoring difficult truths?

He'd always believed his choices, the way he'd handled everything in their relationship had been about protecting Harlow and giving her the best chance for the kind of life she wanted, even when those decisions and actions cut him to the bone. How could she call that selfish? How could his willingness to sacrifice for her and let her go be rooted in fear?

He shoved the suggestion aside. It was preposterous!

And yet...a strange nagging sensation chewed at his belly. He had been dealing with a lot of unsettled feelings, anxiety and self-imposed isolation since coming back from the Marines. He had to admit he had been more anxious in recent days because of the rising stakes with her stalker, because of the reminders of the relationship they'd lost, because of the incidents that had stirred up his PTSD nightmares and flashbacks.

God, could she be right? The last thing he wanted, as a Marine—because though he'd left the service, he was still always a Marine in his head and heart—was to be labeled frightened. Marines didn't do scared. Marines faced intimidation with their teeth bared and a growl in their throat. *Oorah!*

Huffing out a breath of frustration, Wade dropped onto his recliner and rubbed the heel of a hand into his good eye. His shoulders drooped as he took a hard look at his life, at the changes that the past years had wrought and the way he'd dealt with his injuries and guilt.

Betty Jane propped her chin on his lap and bumped his elbow with her nose until he patted her head. "Good girl," he said, retrieving another dog treat from the drawer of the lamp table beside him. With a soft chuff, he acknowledged that stroking Betty Jane's head and having her warm body snuggled sympathetically close *did* ease the tension wound through his chest.

Sebastian and Harlow had been right about the service dog helping him. On the heels of that admission, he allowed himself to consider what else Harlow had been right about. He leaned his head back on the chair and closed his eye. He sat like that for several moments, taking slow breaths and trying to refocus his thoughts, trying to search his heart and word an apology to Harlow. But then Betty Jane's head jerked up, her tags jangling. She glanced toward the back window and whined.

Wade studied his dog's behavior. "Betty Jane?"

The husky licked his hand but continued to send agitated glances toward the back window. What could have bothered her? A squirrel? Harlow walking the yard as she fumed?

Sebastian had said the dog's training included teaching Betty Jane not to let other animals, people or noises distract her from her job of guarding and aiding Wade. Wade was about to correct the dog, run through the steps that Sebastian had given him for refocusing the young service dog.

Then he heard it, too. A cry. A panicked shout. Harlow.

He bolted from his seat, nearly tripping over Betty Jane in his haste to get to the door. As he snatched his coat from the wall hook, he shoved BJ away from the door. "Stay!" he told the dog and raced outside.

He visually followed the path of Harlow's footprints, which wound around the side of the house, before he set out, but the next noise he heard, a distant, angry voice, came from the opposite direction. Wade needed no further information. He hurried through the snow and ice, crunching across his yard, tracking the voices, scanning the surroundings as he trotted.

When he found footprints coming from the woods close to the road, he rushed over to them for a closer look. Again, he visually tracked the path of the depressions in the snow toward the edge of Blackbird Lake until he spotted a second trail of footprints joining the first set.

Cold dread settled in Wade's chest. Harlow's stalker? He struggled to keep his panic at bay. Harlow needed him to focus, to think, to act.

At the edge of the lake, the prints became messy, snow scattered as if there'd been a tussle, and his gut roiled with dread. Moving quickly, he tracked the footprints in the direction of his sister's house. Could the second set of prints be Hannah's? Had Hannah recruited help from Harlow because something happened to Lucy?

A fresh wave of concern flowed through him at that notion. But...if Hannah or Lucy were in trouble, they'd have called 911, not come for Harlow. And the second set of prints came from the road, like the shooter had yesterday at the ranch. Hell! He trotted faster, the possibility of slipping and falling on the slick ice his only concession to speed.

Wade skirted the edge of Blackbird Lake as he rushed toward his sister's property. He'd traveled about half the distance when a sobering thought pierced his panic, and he hesitated to take a mental inventory. He was unarmed. He had no backup. He was blind in one eye and headed toward an unknown, likely dangerous situation.

Did he go back to the cabin for his service weapon? He'd run out the door without his phone, too. Damn it!

Going back would eat valuable time, and Harlow needed help *now*.

Another loud, distressed cry settled the matter. He didn't have time to equivocate. Picking up his pace, Wade continued following the footprints.

Harlow hesitated on the threshold of the dim building, dreading what would happen, shut away from view. At least outside, there was a chance Hannah would look out her window and call 911. Or Wade would realize how long she'd been gone, step out in his yard and see her with her abductor.

"Go on! Get in there. Hurry!" the woman said, jabbing Harlow's nape with the cold muzzle of her gun.

The inside of Hannah's storage building was dark and musty-smelling. The walls were lined with shelves, loaded with plastic storage bins and dishes, and the center of the floor had four sawhorses supporting two canoes. Harlow shuffled in, dread coiling in her gut.

Behind her, Chris found the light switch and a fluorescent glow blinked on, illuminating the dank space. Harlow faced the woman, trying not to stare at the gun aimed at her. She needed all her confidence and composure to address her volatile captor. "Chris, I know you are hurting. Grief is difficult, and everyone has to grieve in their own way."

Chris's face darkened. "You don't know squat about what I'm feeling! And I didn't ask your opinion." While holding the gun leveled at Harlow with her right hand, she fished a cell phone from her pocket with her left. "You like preaching to people on the internet? Well, we're going to make a little video, right now, that I'm going to blast all over the web."

Harlow stilled, her mind racing. If she complied, could she buy time for Wade to realize she was missing? She thought about the angry words she'd thrown at Wade before she stomped out. Why had she let her temper, her pain, her frustration get the better of her? The wedge that had divided her and Wade for all these years couldn't be wiped away by snapping her fingers. Reconciliation would take commitment, understanding and effort from both of them.

"You're going to tell the world how you were responsible for Sharon's death," Chris said, bringing Harlow's focus back to the problem at hand.

Before she could resolve things with Wade, she had to survive this confrontation with her stalker.

"You're going to tell the world how your horrid advice got my sister killed. How Sharon's death deserves to be punished," Chris said, "And that you're taking your own life because of your guilt."

Alarm streaked through Harlow. "What? No!"

Chris took a long step closer, jamming the gun in her face. "You will! Your screwup cost me everything I love, and you're going to tell the world you were to blame!"

Harlow raised a shaky hand, signaling for calm, for patience. "Chris, please, put the weapon down. Shooting me will not serve any purpose. It's not too late to rethink this situation."

"I've done all the thinking I need to. You got Sharon killed, and for that you deserve to die!"

"I'm sorry Sharon was killed. So deeply sorry. I never wanted that to happen. I only ever want to help my callers and ensure their safety."

"Fat lot of good your sorry is worth now! She's *gone*!" Tears pooled in Chris's eyes. "I have to make you pay for what you did! I have to give my Sharon justice!"

"Chris," Harlow said, infusing her tone with warmth and compassion. "You're not a killer. You don't want to go to prison. Sharon wouldn't want that for you, would she?"

"Shut up! You're not worthy to speak her name!" With the back of her left hand, Chris swiped the tears from her cheeks.

"Chris, Sharon wouldn't—"

"Shut up!" Chris shouted—and fired the pistol.

Chapter 21

Wade studied the tracks in the snow as he moved stealthily along the frozen shoreline. The two sets of footprints were practically on top of each other rather than side by side now. Whoever was with Harlow was walking behind or in front of her, not beside her. Why—

The sound of a gun firing echoed across the water and ricocheted from the line of trees. Wade skidded to a stop, his heart rising to his throat. Horror choked him. He couldn't be too late. Couldn't! *Please, God, let Harlow be okay!* He set off again at a run, his feet sliding on the icy snow.

As he neared Hannah's property, the storage building at the end of her pier, he heard voices again. Women's voices. He frowned. He'd thought the person with Harlow was her stalker, but—

He grimaced and whispered a curse under his breath. He'd assumed her stalker was a man. Statistically speaking, it wasn't a bad assumption. Except making assumptions was usually a mistake. And his mistake could now cost Harlow her life.

Pressing his back to the outside wall of the storage building, he eased to the corner where he could peer around the edge. The door stood ajar, and he saw shadows shifting inside. Straining to listen, he followed the conversation to get a read on where things stood inside, what he was walking into, who was standing where relative to the door.

"Next time it will be in your brain," the unfamiliar voice said, her tone dripping menace. "Now the only talking you're going to do is for your confession. You'll say exactly what I tell you and nothing else. Understood?"

Confession? Wade frowned. *What the...?*

As he crouched at the corner of the storage building, he heard a noise to his left and glanced to Hannah's back door. His sister had stepped out, clearly concerned by the gunshot, and called to him. Rising to his feet, he signaled her urgently with his hands to stay back and be silent. Then he made a gesture like using a phone and held up his fingers signaling 9-1-1.

Pressing a hand to her mouth, Hannah nodded and disappeared inside. He hoped that Hannah would call Fletcher first, knowing their brother and his men could get here faster with a direct call rather than waiting on 911 to collect information and reroute the call.

Taking a breath, he refocused on the sounds coming from the storage building. He needed to get in there, unseen. If he could move in from behind and take the stalker down, even if he got hurt in the process, it would be worth it to save Harlow. Harlow was what mattered.

And in that instant, he knew that his life, his future happiness depended on having Harlow beside him. Whatever it took, whatever words she needed, whatever changes to his life he had to make, he would do it to keep

Harlow close. He'd give anything to have the woman he loved safe, fulfilled and at his side.

From inside the storage building, he heard the other woman say tightly, "I am responsible for the murder of Sharon Wilson. Because of my reckless and unprofessional advice that she leave the marriage, her husband killed her. I am to blame for—"

"No. Chris, Sharon's ex is the only person to blame. I did what I was trained to—"

"Say it, or I swear I will kill you!"

A chill slithered down Wade's spine. He needed to get in there and stop this standoff before the unstable woman did something rash, something deadly.

"Don't you plan to kill me after I make your video? Why would I give you a false confession if you're going to shoot me anyway?"

He heard the woman growl her frustration. "I want to hear you say it! Tell the world what you did to my sister or…or…" There was a pause, and in the silence, Wade could hear his own heartbeat pound in his ears as he eased along the side of the storage hut.

"Say it, or I'll hike back over to that little cabin and kill your boyfriend," the woman said, her tone gloating.

Wade pulled up, startled by…what? Being called her boyfriend, or by having his own life used to bait and influence Harlow?

"I don't have a boyfriend." Harlow's voice trembled, and the fear he heard stabbed Wade's gut. She was trying to protect him, deflect the threat even at the cost of her own safety. He was filled with an odd cocktail of loathing for the woman who'd put Harlow in this position, who even now was threatening her, and a pang of despondency over Harlow's denial of their relationship.

Wade gritted his back teeth and shoved the swirl of emotions aside. He couldn't let his feelings distract him. His distraction eighteen months ago had gotten a soldier in his charge killed. He had to do a better job now. Harlow's life depended on him getting it right. *Stay focused.*

"Mr. Eye Patch?" the woman with Harlow squawked. A chuff of dismissal. "Maybe he's not your boyfriend, but I'm not blind. I've been watching the two of you together."

This bit of news rankled. They'd been *spied on*, and he'd missed it. He'd failed Harlow, damn it.

"You love him," the woman taunted. "And why should you have someone you love when you cost me the person I loved most?"

Wade rounded the corner of the building, stepping slowly to minimize the crunching of the snow under his feet.

"Why do you get to be happy when I've been left in misery because of *you*?"

"Killing me, killing…anyone…is not the answer, Chris."

Back pressed to the front wall, Wade peeked inside the storage room.

Harlow held both hands in front of her, palms out in a *stop* gesture. "If you put the gun down and walk away, I promise not to press charges. I can get you help for your—"

Harlow stopped abruptly as her gaze flickered to him in the door. Wade gave a quick shake of his head and touched a finger to his lips.

"Help? Like you gave Sharon?" The woman cackled derisively. "No, thank you!"

The subtle shift in her expression told him Harlow was making mental calculations in light of his arrival. She was still at the business end of a pistol. She was still negotiating with an irrational and dangerous woman.

"The only thing I want from you is retribution. And a public admission of fault. I don't want anyone else's baby sister following your horrid advice and dying."

"I don't want anyone to die either, *Chris.*"

Wade picked up on the subtle emphasis Harlow put on the name, understanding the message she was sending him. *This is the stalker.* He gave a small nod, then pulled back from the door as he weighed his options. He felt sure that with the element of surprise, his Special Ops training and his size and strength advantage over Chris, that he could overtake and disarm Harlow's stalker. But...

Chris was a panicked finger squeeze away from shooting Harlow. He needed to signal Harlow, warn her of his intentions, instruct her to get down, to ball up and protect her vital organs.

Waving the cell phone in her left hand, Chris grated again. "Say the words! Say you are responsible for my sister dying!"

Wade edged from the outside wall to fill the doorway, praying the stalker didn't notice the shifting shadow as he blocked the outside light. He lifted a hand, waiting for Harlow to glance over again. She was obviously trying not to give him away, trying to ignore his presence. But damn it, he had to get her attention! He gave her a stilted wave, and as soon as her eyes flickered toward him, he pointed at the ground, then clenched his fist.

Please understand what I'm telling you.

He repeated the signal.

Harlow gave the merest of nods as she said, "All right. I'll make the video. I'll apologize."

"Any time," Chris said, "I'm already recording."

With a long stride up behind the woman, Wade swept his arm from high to low, knocking Chris's gun arm down. As expected, Chris yelped her surprise and fired the gun, even as Wade completed the downward arc of his arm with a hooking twist. The motion brought Chris's arm behind her back, the gun within range of Wade's grasp. He reached for the weapon, but possession of the gun was not so easily won. Chris spun around, following the tug on her arm until she faced Wade. Her alarmed expression quickly morphed to rage, and a battle for possession of the pistol began.

As soon as Wade made his move, Harlow dropped to the floor and curled in a ball, covering her head. She gasped as the gun fired again. Something stung her as it grazed her cheek. She heard the scuffle of feet and angled her head to find Wade and Chris grappling for the pistol.

"Wade!" she cried as she pushed to her knees.

"Stay down!" He backed Chris against the shelving that lined the walls, and dishes rattled as they jostled and jockeyed.

Despite his directive, Harlow hated the idea of staying on the floor, cowering and unhelpful. She moved to a crouch, ready to spring up or drop again as the situation merited. She cast her gaze about for a tool, a makeshift weapon, *something* she could use to defend Wade and swing the momentum in their favor. Spying a kayak paddle propped in the back corner, she rose to her feet but only made it one step before Wade's voice echoed through the small room. "Freeze! Get on the ground!"

And Harlow pivoted toward him, her breath stuck in her lungs.

Wade didn't want to hurt the woman, but if he had to, he would incapacitate her, injure her in a way that would bring the situation under control. The woman's stubborn refusal to release the pistol made the necessity of stronger force more and more likely. Chris grunted and growled her outrage as he pinned her against the shelving unit and forcefully peeled her fingers away from the weapon. If he had to break a finger, so be it. He had to neutralize the threat of the gun. One on one against him, Chris was outsized, out-skilled, outmaneuvered. Once unarmed, Harlow's stalker could be taken into custody easily.

But she wasn't going quietly. Chris screamed and bit and thrashed and slapped as he fought to wrench the gun from her. Finally, he managed to pin her scrabbling limbs enough to twist the pistol out of her grip. Howling her frustration, Chris clawed at him and fought to regain possession of the pistol. He held it above his head, out of her reach, until he could break loose of her battling hand and take a determined step back.

She lunged toward him, and in order to stop her—and *only* to keep her in line and exert his control over the situation—he aimed the pistol at Chris and shouted, "Freeze! Get on the ground!"

For a moment, Chris stilled. But in an instant that

caught Wade off guard, she reached for a tray on the shelving unit, snatched up a large butcher knife and held it up in front of her.

A curse word flittered through Wade's brain. Why did she have to make this difficult? He could shoot her, end this standoff now, but that wasn't how he wanted things to go. He wanted no part of ending another life. He already had to grapple with his part in Sanders's death. Through clenched teeth he snarled, "Drop the knife, or I *will* drop *you*."

He saw the flicker of fear in the woman's eyes. Recognized the moment her resolve hardened stubbornly. Her mouth firmed. Her eyes blazed.

And with a couple quick, backpedaling steps, she seized Harlow, shoved her in front of her as a human shield, and pressed the knife to Harlow's throat so hard she drew a thin trickle of blood.

Ice shot to Wade's marrow, and adrenaline kicked his pulse into overdrive.

Focus, he reminded himself, even as a roar like fire exploded in his mind. *Don't get distracted.*

"Drop the knife," he repeated, his tone commanding, despite the frantic pulse in his veins.

"Give me back my gun," Chris countered. When he didn't flinch, the stalker added, "I will cut her throat! I swear I will!" Chris's volume was rising even as her patience was clearly eroding.

"Chris," Harlow said, her voice somewhat strangled by the pressure against her windpipe. "Please. This doesn't have to end badly. You can still do the right thing. Sharon wouldn't have wanted this for you."

"Put the gun on the floor and kick it to me." Chris

shoved Harlow forward, closing the gap between the women and Wade. "Now!"

Wade stood his ground until it occurred to him that outside, Chris wouldn't have the variety of further make-shift weapons. If, between him and Harlow, they could disarm the irate woman...

Harlow must have been on the same wavelength, because at that moment she threw her head back, hard, smashing the back of her skull into the other woman's nose. The move gave Harlow just enough advantage to wrench her hands up around the knife handle and push the blade away from her throat. Once free of the blade's threat, Harlow stomped on the other woman's instep.

Wade goggled, admiring Harlow's grit as he watched her twist and jab her elbow, employing classic self-defense moves.

Enraged, Chris fought back, and Wade decided his best move with the least bodily harm was disarming the stalker. But first...

"Chris! You want your gun?" he shouted as he walked backward out of the storage building.

Chris paused, lifting her head toward him. Harlow seized the chance to dig her fingernails into her opponent's wrist and pry the knife from Chris's hand. Standing between Harlow, wielding the butcher knife, and Wade, holding the pistol, Chris panted for a breath and glared.

Before she could rearm herself with another knife, Wade knew he had to draw the woman away from Harlow. He set the gun on the ground, just beyond the threshold, and stepped back, his hands up and empty. "Here it is. Come get it."

Chris scowled, staring at him as if trying to work out the trick. Then, giving herself away with a glance toward the pistol, she lunged for the gun. Wade was faster. He stepped forward and kicked the gun from her reach. In the same forward motion, he knocked Chris to the ground. While Chris scrambled to stand on the slick icy snow, he snatched up the pistol again. With a windup and pitch that would have made his Little League coach proud, Wade threw the pistol far out onto the ice-covered lake.

From the frozen ground where she'd landed, Chris's eyes widened and fury pinched her face. "Nooo! You son of a bitch!"

Harlow emerged from the storage shed, her fingers wiping blood from the small cut on her neck, and handed Wade the knife. "You can get rid of this, too. But maybe don't throw it on the lake and lose it permanently. I'm guessing Hannah still wants it."

He bobbed a nod of agreement and turned to fling the large knife toward Hannah's house to be retrieved later.

He'd only just released the knife, watching it hurtle through the air, when snow crunched behind him.

Harlow gasped. "Wade!"

Before he could turn, he was struck, low and hard, as Chris plowed into him, her shoulder lowered. He stumbled forward, his feet slipping on the packed snow, and went down. His breath whooshed from his lungs, and a searing pain shot through his shoulder. He gasped like a fish out of water, unable to move his arm. Before he could regain his breath and warn her away, Harlow rushed forward to assist him, attempting to grab her rage-fueled and vicious stalker.

* * *

Harlow grabbed the sleeve of Chris's coat, shouting, "No! Chris, stop this! Now! It's over."

But instead, her stalker spun toward her and grabbed a fist full of Harlow's long hair, winding the tresses tightly around her hand. A thousand pin pricks stung her scalp, and Harlow cried out in pain.

"Nothing is over!" Chris jerked hard on Harlow's hair, towing her toward the edge of the frozen lake.

Tears filled her eyes as Chris tugged brutally, grabbing more and more of Harlow's hair into her fist as she marched briskly across the snow.

"Stop! Ow! What are you doing?" Harlow panted as she stumbled, bent over at the waist, while Chris dragged her to the lake's edge. Harlow battled Chris's hands, but her opponent had wrapped the strands tightly, tangled her fingers in Harlow's hair. "Please stop!"

"I'm getting my gun," Chris said, "and then both you and the pirate are going to die."

When Chris took her first few steps onto the ice at the edge of the lake, a fresh terror swamped Harlow. It hadn't been cold enough, long enough for the lake ice to support the weight of an adult...much less two adults.

"Stop! The ice is too thin!" Despite the pain of her hair pulling, ripping out at the roots, Harlow struggled against Chris's grip. "We can't go out there. The ice will break!"

"Shut up!" Chris growled, yanking harder on Harlow's hair, plodding faster across the ice.

Bent over at the awkward position she was in, Harlow couldn't tell how far out they'd come, but she knew with every step the danger to them grew—the ice would be thinner, the shore would be farther, the water would be deeper.

"Please," she begged, tears of pain and fear filling her eyes, "Please go back! It's too dangerous to be out here!"

"I'm getting my gun!" Chris grated.

And Harlow heard the first pop, the cracking sound that shot cold terror to her bones.

Chapter 22

Both winded and with his arm dislocated, Wade was slow getting to his feet. Too slow. By the time he'd struggled to his knees, using only one arm for balance as he rose, Chris had dragged Harlow to the shore of Blackbird Lake. He realized the stalker's intent immediately but couldn't get the air in his lungs to shout a warning.

How far out were Fletcher and his men? An ambulance? Had Hannah reached them and requested backup?

If they weren't here now, they were still too far away.

"Wade!"

He angled his head toward Hannah's house as his sister burst through the back door and ran across her lawn to him. "Are you all right? Who is that woman? I called 911, but—"

"No!" he gasped thinly, waving her off. "Go...inside."

"You're hurt!" Hannah shoved her phone in her pocket and used both hands to help him gain his feet and traction. "Oh my God! Your arm!"

"Get...inside!" He sucked in a thin breath as his lungs finally loosened. "Call... Fletcher and...keep Lucy out of harm's way!" He shoved his sister back toward the house, but she twisted free of his grasp.

"Fletcher is coming." She pulled the phone out of her

pocket and told the person on the line, "My brother's injured. I think his arm is dislocated!"

He pushed Hannah toward the house again. "Get inside, damn it!"

Hannah's gaze flickered to the lake, and she gasped. "Harlow! Oh no, no, no! The ice—"

"I know." He staggered toward the lake, cradling his injured arm, and he called over his shoulder to Hannah. "Tell them we'll need an ambulance!"

He'd only made it a few loping steps, each one jarring his throbbing shoulder, when he heard the loud crack that echoed from the trees across the lake. His heart stilled, and his gaze darted to the two figures on the ice. In the next moment, the ice beneath them shattered, and the freezing water swallowed Harlow and her scream.

The icy blackness closed over Harlow's head. She could feel the thrashing of Chris's limbs as her captor fought to free her hand—now needed to save her own life—from Harlow's hair. The sting of ripping hair paled in comparison to the suffocating bite of the icy water. The lake was so cold it hurt. Instantly and deeply. She could feel the numbing, paralyzing ache of cold sinking quickly to her core.

Air. She needed air.

As much as the freezing water hurt, the ache in her lungs for oxygen seared as harshly. Worse.

She finally broke the surface and gasped in air. Once. Twice. She was hyperventilating, panting from fear and shocking cold. She tried to tread water, but her arms and legs were stiff, slow to move or obey the command of her brain. She managed to use her feet to push off her snow boots, lightening the weight that dragged at her. When with a final rip of hair, Chris pulled free of her, Harlow flailed her arms, groping blindly for the edge of the ice. Chris's weight pulled her down. Her captor's thrashing was breaking more and more of the ice ledge.

No! her brain screamed. She couldn't die like this, not when her last words to Wade had been so cruel. So untrue. Of course she loved him! Of course she wanted a life with him! She had to get out of this water, had to tell him that. If she died today because of her stalker, because of this frozen lake, so be it. But Wade had to know the truth.

The instant Harlow disappeared under the ice, Wade sprinted for the lake, his dislocated shoulder all but forgotten. All that mattered was Harlow. He had to get her out of the icy lake before hypothermia took her from him.

"Wade, stop!" Hannah shouted. She was on his heels, grabbing at his jacket. "You can't go out there! You'll fall in, too!"

He stopped at the edge of the ice, pulling off his heavy boots. "I need a rope. A long, strong one." He turned to his terrified sister. Hannah was shaking her head, clearly worried for him. Gritting his teeth, he growled, "I will not let the woman I love die! I have to try!"

Hannah's mouth opened, as if to argue, tears filling her eyes, then she sighed and said, "Rope. What else?"

Wade sorted through his tumbling thoughts, forcibly quashing the panic that would steal his ability to reason and act judiciously. "One of the kayak paddles. A carabiner or two. And blankets and heat packs. Lots of them. Hurry!"

She ran for the storage building, and Wade took a few tentative steps out on the ice. After a few feet, where the ice was thickest, he lay down his stomach, which distributed his weight over a larger area of the ice. His body prostrate, he pulled with his good arm and pushed with his feet, scooting across the frozen surface. He was approximately halfway to the hole where the women splashed and struggled when Hannah shouted from shore. "Wade!"

He twisted enough to look back just as she half threw, half slid the paddle to him with remarkable aim. Hannah had known to tie one end of the sturdy rope to the paddle, and Wade sent up silent gratitude for his sister's instincts and quick response. Scooting the paddle in front of him as he inched across the ice, he shouted, "Harlow!"

Drawing nearer to the hole, he saw a floundering hand, a flash of her dark hair as her head bobbed up then sank again. Hypothermia happened so fast. He couldn't remember the statistic in the moment, but he knew he had a frighteningly small window to get her out of the icy water before her body shut down.

When he'd moved as far out on the ice as he dared, he paused to tie a lasso at the end of the rope and shove the loop to the end of the paddle. Extending it toward the hole, he shouted again, "Harlow, grab the rope! Put the loop around you, an arm through it."

When her head rose at the edge of the hole and she dragged her arms to the top of the ice, a small frisson of relief and hope spun through him. Quick as it came, the relief died. Harlow was far from safe yet, and her clock was ticking.

* * *

An odd calm settled over Harlow after a couple of minutes. The icy water was still horrifying, still dragging at her, but the initial gasping panic had passed. The freezing lake had numbed her skin. Chris, too, had stopped flailing, and with a side glance Harlow saw the other woman groping methodically for purchase across the growing hole in the ice. Chris hoisted her body halfway out of the water, only to have the ice break and send the woman back into the slushy lake.

"Harlow!"

She lifted her gaze to find Wade, his body low to the ice as he belly-crawled toward her. A poignant cocktail of gratitude and dread spun through her mind, her brain too cold and slow to sort out any reasoning behind her feelings. "W-Wade," she rasped, her voice thready as the cold stole her breath.

He shouted something to her, and she tried to focus, to stay conscious as the paralyzing cold made it harder and harder to concentrate. A kayak paddle poked her hands, and she saw the rope draped on it.

Grab it! a voice in her head said. Or maybe it was Wade's voice.

She reached for the rope with trembling hands, her arm heavy and weak. When she couldn't close her hand around the rope, she struggled to pull off her sodden and refreezing mitten. With her fingers freed from the mitten, she curled her fingers enough to hook around the rope, drag it closer. She had to rest. She paused and closed her eyes.

So cold...

So stiff...

So tiring to move...

"Harlow!" Wade's voice cut through her drowsy lethargy. "Don't you dare leave me, damn it! I need you! I love you!"

Love...you...too. The words were there. On her tongue. But stuck. Frozen.

Something deep within her rallied. She had to stay alive...had to tell Wade...had to apologize. She seized the flash of determination and pulled the rope closer. Tried to move it over her head. Couldn't. Put an arm through it. Then the paddle lifted from the ice and bonked her head as it wavered and dropped the rope over her head. With small choppy movements, she wiggled the rope down, under her armpit.

"Kick your legs!" Wade shouted. "Get as flat as you can and hold on!"

Kick? She wasn't even sure she could move her legs.

Wade pulled on the rope, and it tightened around her, pulled her higher out of the water. When she tried to push, to lift herself out on the edge of the ice, the shelf crumbled. Frustration flared in her gut, and she tried again. Again, the ice chipped and collapsed under her.

"Kick your legs! Get flat!" Wade repeated.

And somehow through the fog in her brain, she recalled the technique they'd learned in high school that called for distributing one's weight as much as possible over the weak ice. She needed to leave the water as horizontally as possible, not with a vertical push.

Kick your legs...

She focused all her energy, all her concentration on moving her numb legs. Her limbs were heavy. Ached.

But with effort, she managed a weak scissor kick. Then another.

Wade tugged harder on the rope and shouted, "Come on, Harlow, kick! Harder. You can do it, love."

Love? The term of endearment pierced the muzziness that swamped her. Her eyes prickled, and his plea prodded her to give more effort.

Kick. Kick. She heard the splash that said her efforts had brought her legs to the surface.

"That's it. Keep kicking!"

She groped with her arms as she slid higher, then slowly across the ice.

"Can you roll, Harlow? Roll to me!" Wade called.

She tried. Got about halfway over. The tug of the rope helped pull her over. Between Wade's pulling her and her sluggish assistance, he slowly dragged her to the edge of the lake. By then her entire body was shivering violently.

"Thank God!" Wade said, his voice choked with emotion as he gave her an awkward embrace. "Harlow, stay with me."

Then Hannah was there, helping him peel off her wet coat and clothes.

Her teeth chattered so hard she thought she might bite her tongue, but she tried to speak. "H-h-h—" Her throat wouldn't let her form the harder consonant she wanted, and she whimpered in pain and cold.

"I'm here, love." Wade bent and kissed her forehead.

She tried again, struggling to get any sound from her throat. "Ch-Chris."

Wade met her eyes, and she knew he understood. "Promise not to leave me?"

She managed a small nod, and after placing another kiss on her lips, Wade headed back out onto the ice.

Chapter 23

Wade belly-crawled back out to the hole in the ice, picturing Private Sanders in his mind's eye. No way in hell would he let anyone die on his watch again, not even someone who'd tried to kill Harlow. Let the stalker pay for her crimes in prison, not with her life. Not while he still had a chance to save her.

He looped the rope on the paddle again and shouted toward the hole. "Chris! Can you hear me? Lift a hand or shout if you can."

He got no response. He inched closer, his progress impeded by his throbbing shoulder. No time to dwell on his own injury. He drew on his Special Forces training and used his mental reserves to help him ignore his pain and solve the problem he faced. One step at a time.

"Chris!" he called again as he reached the edge of the hole. He tossed the lasso, and the rope landed, circling her shoulders. "Chris, hook your arm through the rope!"

But the woman was unresponsive, and Wade watched in horror as she slid deeper into the icy water. He shifted, trying to catch her arm, a handful of her coat…something.

Crack!

The heat of adrenaline shot through Wade as he recognized the sound of the ice breaking. Before he could wiggle backward, he plunged into the icy lake. He shuddered with the shock of the freezing lake but kicked hard to get his head above water.

He grabbed the edge of the ice and gathered his wits, even as the cold tried to steal his breath. He panted a few times, sucking in shallow gulps of air, then forced his brain to focus. He turned to find Chris sinking even farther into the lake. Damn it!

"Wade!"

He blinked hard as he moved his gaze to the lakeshore where several figures now stood. Fletcher, Malcolm and Sebastian were among the men helping Hannah with Harlow and making their way, well spaced out, across the ice to him.

Moving hand over hand to pull himself to Chris, he hauled the woman up and fumbled the rope under her arm. Chris was shaking hard now, still unresponsive. But the tremors said she was still alive.

Malcolm, on his belly, reached the frozen rope and paddle first. "Are you tied on?"

Through chattering teeth, he replied, "Th-the woman f-first."

Fletcher, also flat on the ice, positioned himself a few feet down the rope and added his strength to the pulling. Sebastian was on shore with his feet braced as he tugged.

Wade's hold slipped, and he went under briefly, but as he kicked to the surface, he grabbed Chris's leg and shoved it upward. The added horizontal angling of the woman's body allowed their rescuers to haul her out of the lake.

Malcolm removed the rope and tossed it back to Wade. "Your turn, hero."

Wade growled in frustration as he worked the rope over his head and under his dislocated arm. At least the icy water had numbed the shoulder pain. Small favor. Exhaustion dragged at him when he tried to kick again, his legs finally rising to ease his exit as his family pulled him from the lake and across the ice. When he reached thicker ice, Fletcher hooked an arm under Wade's bad shoulder help him sit up. Wade gritted his teeth and growled his pain.

"I know, man. But you're safe now." Fletcher was unzipping Wade's coat and getting him out of his wet clothes.

"H-Harlow—"

"Awake and waiting for you in the back of the ambulance. You've done well, brother. Really well. Now let's get you warmed up."

Chapter 24

"And how are my favorite human Popsicles doing?" Fletcher asked as he poked his head around the door of Harlow's hospital room.

Wade, whose shoulder had been reset and was feeling much better, squeezed Harlow's hand. "Thawing."

"And no one will lose any fingers or toes to frostbite. That's a blessing," Harlow added, then her expression sobered. "What about Chris? Did she live?"

Fletcher hesitated, then shook his head. "No. She, of course, stayed in the lake longer than either of you and apparently had a preexisting cardiac condition, which made her heart more susceptible to failure."

Harlow sighed. "While I'm glad that she can't terrorize or threaten me anymore, I'm sad that it ended so tragically. She was hurting and lost after the death of her sister. I know that doesn't excuse her actions, but with help, with proper counseling or medical intervention—"

"You're awfully forgiving, considering all the trouble she caused you." Wade creased his brow as he studied Harlow, marveling at her kind soul.

"Well." Harlow dropped her gaze to her covers and plucked at a loose thread on the blanket. "Forgiveness is the healthier option. Harboring a grudge just means holding on to stress and anger and pain." She lifted her eyes to him. "Forgiveness doesn't excuse wrongdoing, but it frees you to move past the offense, not let the person *continue* hurting you. I mean, look what vengeance and anger did to Chris."

Wade considered her point, and with an exhale, nodded. "You're a wise woman, Harlow Jones." After a beat, he continued, "Any chance you could forgive me while you're in this merciful mood?"

She tipped her head. "Forgive you for what? Wade, you saved my life. You got Chris out of the lake despite the risk to your own life and your injured shoulder. You did everything right."

"Agreed, brother," Fletcher said, folding his arms over his chest as he leaned back against the wall. "I couldn't have done better myself." Then with a lopsided smile, he added, "Oorah!"

Fletcher's approval and nod to Wade's career with the Marines warmed Wade better than any blanket or heated IV drip. With a lopsided grin, he chuckled and teased, "Thanks, but...that was the weakest *oorah* I ever heard."

Turning to Harlow, Wade brushed back a lock of her chestnut hair that had curled around her cheek as it dried. "I meant I want you to forgive me for breaking your heart after high school. I should never have broken up with you. Never hurt you. Never said the terrible things—"

"Wade..." Harlow's eyes filled with tears.

"Um." Fletcher pushed away from the wall and moved toward the door. "This sounds private. So... I'll go now. I only wanted to make sure you were both on the mend.

The waiting room is full of worried Coltons needing a report."

Harlow gave a small wave. "Thank you, Fletcher."

The brothers exchanged a nod and smile, and when Fletcher reached the door, he paused and looked back over his shoulder at Wade. "I know this isn't the time for a full conversation about it, but...the Owl Creek PD could always use good officers...if you'd be interested."

Something akin to an electric shock zipped through Wade, and he sat taller as he stared at his brother. Join the OCPD? He'd never considered law enforcement as a career, but...the idea had merit. The suggestion...felt right. "I...maybe. Yeah."

Fletcher's face brightened. "We'll talk."

When he faced Harlow again, her eyes were bright with tears, and a smile tugged her lips. "You'd make a great policeman, Wade. And don't miss what Fletcher was really saying just then. He believes in you and your abilities."

Wade's chest tightened with emotion, and he had to clear his throat before he could speak. "I know. And that means...a lot." He exhaled and took both her hands in his, careful not to squeeze the IV needle in the back of her hand. "But more important, this morning has made something else starkly clear. The idea of living without you for even another day scares me more than any nightmare, or stalker, or explosion ever could. I never stopped loving you, Harlow, despite what I said as a confused and hurting teenager."

Fresh tears bloomed in her eyes. "Oh, Wade, I love you, too. And I'm sorry for pushing you away instead of embracing your dreams of the Marines."

"You're forgiven. And I should have seen how important having a place to call home was for you. I should have listened better, been more understanding."

Harlow wiped a tear from her cheek. "You're forgiven." She touched his cheek, adding, "I thought I needed a town to call my home, but the truth was *you* were my home. You were what I needed to feel rooted and secure. And you still are."

Wade's heart stilled, and he sat taller, his gaze narrowing on Harlow's dark eyes. "What exactly are you saying? Because... I don't want a misunderstanding or selfish argument to ever come between us again."

She gripped his hand tighter, a clear sign her strength was returning, and she smiled. "I'm saying I've decided not to sell my parents' house. I want to live in Owl Creek and do *Harlow Helps* from here. I want to wake up every morning next to you and never let you out of my life again."

A grin bloomed on his lips, and he chuckled his joy. "Same here. You are everything to me, Harlow Jones, and I made a vow this morning that I intend to keep," Wade said, and a shudder rolled through him as he remembered the terror he'd felt earlier when Harlow was in the frozen lake.

"A vow?"

He nodded. "To do whatever it takes to be with you. I'll move to LA. I'll get PTSD counseling. I'll share my deepest secrets with you, so you'll know I trust you completely. I'll—"

She touched a finger to his mouth to silence him. "No to LA. Our family is in Owl Creek. Yes to the counseling and honesty between us. But—" she leaned in for a quick kiss "—there's one more thing I want you to do."

"Name it," he said eagerly.

"Marry me."

Shock waves more powerful than a blast of dynamite shook Wade to his core, and he took a moment to catch his breath. In a flash, he could see his future clearly— growing old with Harlow, raising a family, exploring a new career and making Owl Creek his home for years to come. Happiness coursed through him, and he threw his head back to laugh. "You have a deal, my love. It's you and me forever."

* * * * *

Don't miss the stories in this mini series!

THE COLTONS OF OWL CREEK

MILLS & BOON

A Spy's Secret

Rachel Astor

MILLS & BOON

Rachel Astor is equal parts country girl and city dweller who spends an alarming amount of time correcting the word *the*. Rachel has had a lot of jobs (bookseller, real estate agent, 834 assorted admin roles), but none as, *ahem*, interesting as when she waitressed at a bar named after a dog. She is now a *USA TODAY* bestselling author who splits her time between the city, the lake and as many made-up worlds as possible.

Visit the Author Profile page
at millsandboon.com.au.

Dear Reader,

I can't wait for you to meet Ava and Zach, a sunshine/grumpy pairing if there ever was one. But truth be told, Ava's sunny nature and her appreciation for life is new, born out of dark secrets in a past she was lucky to escape. And even though Zach has little patience for the tourists who flood to town during the annual Apple Cider Festival, he will always be one of those guys who will do anything for anyone, even if he throws out a few complaints while he's at it.

When Ava's past comes back to haunt her, everyone in town is put in danger, and Ava and Zach have to work together to set everything right again...all while navigating new layers of a relationship that has always been firmly planted in the friend zone.

Fun fact: *A Spy's Secret* is my first story set in the quaint fictional town of Ambrosia Falls. I have so many ideas for this little town (and even a couple outlines already written) and hope someday I'll get to tell all the stories from this charming place filled with lovable and quirky characters.

Thank you so much for reading!

Rachel

Prologue

Something had been off with Justin for weeks.

The change was subtle—most people would never notice—but the Sparrow's training taught her to spot inconsistencies. She couldn't pinpoint what it was, exactly, but he was acting strange. And when he kissed her goodbye that fateful Tuesday morning, a thought hit her like a truck, filled to the brim with trepidation.

Oh God, he's going to ask me to marry him.

Was that even something she wanted?

Judging from the way her stomach flopped when the thought crashed through her brain, it wasn't. Except, Justin was the best guy she knew. She only trusted two people in the world, and he was one of them.

In their business—a business literally built on lies— trust was in short supply, only coming after years of earning it. And Justin had earned it. He'd been her partner for four years before they ever got romantically involved. It was inevitable the relationship would eventually turn into something more.

But they'd only been a couple for eight months.

Of course, time acted differently when you were in the spy business. Forced to depend on someone to keep you safe when they held your life in their hands made everything more intense, heightened. And as her communications tech for years, he'd kept her safe through inconceivable danger.

Lately though, things were less…exciting. Which of course had been inevitable too.

Maybe she was reading too much into things. They'd only been living together a few months, after all. And even that had been more out of convenience when the lease came up on his apartment. She owned this huge, beautiful place with plenty of space, and it seemed like the logical thing to do. But now that the thought had entered her brain, she needed to know.

Justin wouldn't be back for hours.

So she began to search.

Thoughts jolted through her. Thoughts like *too soon, bad timing* and…*I have to get out.*

Sparrow's training taught her how to conduct a thorough search while making sure to keep everything intact. Neat. No suspicion aroused.

She came up empty in the house. Deep down she suspected she would. If a ring existed, she knew where it would be.

The shed.

Justin had the small building delivered when he moved in.

"I could never do this stuff in my old apartment, but I've wanted this for years," he'd said.

And it didn't matter to Sparrow. Her property had plenty of space, tucked out of the way from prying eyes, far away from the city. She loved being lost in the desert. And so, the shed was installed. A dark room for his photography. No matter how advanced technology got, Justin swore something about film was truer, more real. There was an art to it.

Sparrow thought his passion was endearing.

What would she do if she found a ring? Make hints that it was too soon? But how could she possibly do that without rousing his suspicions that she'd discovered it? Justin was trained to spot lies too.

Sparrow flung the shed door open and flicked on the light. Everything appeared in order. *Exacting* order. One more thing that differed between the two of them. Sparrow wasn't messy, but she wasn't anal either. Working undercover meant blending in, and she always thought Justin's obsessive neatness was too over-the-top to blend. But no one would ever discover his perfectionism way out here, so she let it go. Although, when she routinely found her toiletry bottles lined up with the labels all facing front and in order from shortest to tallest, she always wanted to mix them all up into a disorganized group. One time, she did exactly that. He'd come up behind her, grasping her in a tight hug, as if he was physically trying to stop her. "I love that you love a little chaos," he'd said.

"It's hardly chaos," Sparrow replied, pulling gently out of his grasp.

The bottles were once again lined in military precision the next time she came into the room.

The urge now to mix up the shelves of chemicals, film and tools was immense, but she was far too professional. Start at one end and be methodical. Leave no stone—or bottle—unturned.

I have to get out.

Stop, she told herself. *Things are fine. Why do you always search for trouble whenever things are going well?*

Unfortunately, she knew the answer. Because she always found trouble. And when she tipped over a black plastic chemical jug in the middle of ten other black plastic chemical jugs, hearing a telltale click of a door unlatching, she realized she'd found it once again.

For a second, she actually wished she'd discovered what she'd gone looking for. She'd realized in the past few minutes, with absolute clarity, she did not want to marry this man, but still, a ring would have been so much better than this.

Sparrow shot off a quick text before she pulled the trapdoor, which had unlatched from the floor when she tilted the bottle. Annoyance rolled through her. The bastard did this on her own property right under her nose, probably during the Marseille job when he claimed he was sick. She should have caught it. She'd been trained to catch things like this. Trained not to trust anyone. But she did. She trusted Justin. Sure, he had his idiosyncrasies, but this was Justin.

I have to get out.

Sparrow grabbed for her gun, but it wasn't there. Of course it wasn't. All her weapons were in the house. But she couldn't turn back. Irritation and curiosity fueled her forward.

Until a moment ago she believed she had control. Of her life, her career, of everything. But suddenly nothing was true anymore. And with the passion of a thousand sports fans whose team had just lost, she hated that she'd been played.

The bunker was pitch-black. She lit the screen on her

phone to search for a switch, but there was only a simple light bulb with a string. She pulled it, sucking in a breath, bracing herself for anything.

Still, she was not prepared for what she saw.

Surveillance.

A typical spread. Photos of the target. Maps of where they'd been. Movements tracked down to the minute. Schedules.

But it was the face of the target, staring back from all those photos, that almost broke her.

Her face.

Some of the pictures were from before she'd even met Justin. Years before. Of her shopping, eating…sleeping. Newspaper articles from when her parents were killed ten years ago. Family history. Not that there was anyone left anymore.

The pictures and articles grew older as she moved down the wall.

She reached up to pull the string on the second light above her.

Click.

No light came on. In an instant she understood her fatal mistake. A barely audible squeal pierced her ears. And then the blast.

Blinding, deafening, jolting her forward. Backward? She didn't know.

Pain.

And as the world began to go black, Sparrow had only one thought left.

I have to get out.

Chapter 1

Five years later...

Zach was annoyed. This time of year was always so... much. Everyone in town seemed to think the annual Apple Cider Festival was the best thing ever, and sure, most of the people in town made half their year's salary during the week as several thousand people from all over the state and beyond flocked to town, so he could kind of understand, but man, all these tourists were just so...touristy.

The bell above the coffee shop door chimed, his shoulders rising further toward his ears. It was the third time in the last five minutes he'd heard its tinkling ring, messing with his focus.

"Oh my gawd, this place is so stinking cuuuuute," the woman who'd entered said.

Zach closed his eyes and pulled a long breath in through his nose. *Breathe*, he tried to encourage himself, *just breathe*.

"Welcome to The Other Apple Store," Ava said from behind the counter.

Somehow, she actually seemed to enjoy when these people barged into her life and her store. Of course she did—that was Ava Katz. Good with everybody. Always kind. Always patient. Although she'd only been in town for five years, and he'd been here his whole life, so maybe the novelty hadn't worn off for her yet.

The woman whose jangle interrupted Zach turned to her friend, gasping with excitement fit for a teen pop concert. "Did you hear that? The Other Apple Store! Like the computer one except, like, this one actually sells real apple stuff."

"I know!" her counterpart squealed.

They erupted into a shriek slash giggle slash "oh my gawd" fest. And Zach just knew they'd gone shopping for their Apple Cider Festival uniforms of cable knit sweaters, boots with wool socks peeking out and winter hats with giant pom-poms at some overpriced hipster store too. A small growling groan escaped him before he could catch it.

Ava beamed while Zach tried not to say anything more under his breath. She caught his eye and pumped her eyebrows at him like she was having the time of her life.

Which, knowing Ava, she probably was.

It was one of the things he loved most about her—she seemed to find genuine enjoyment in almost anything.

He shook the thought from his head, reminding himself he wasn't supposed to love anything about Ava. She was off limits—too important a friend—a friendship he couldn't risk with silly, romantic notions.

Maybe if he'd made a move in those first months after she'd arrived in town…but that time was long gone. He remembered the first time he saw Ava, laughing and joking with the movers like she'd known them all her life.

She'd stopped him in his tracks.

She was beautiful, but it wasn't just the way she looked. There was something about the way she treated the movers. Like kindness was her religion.

But Chloe had been his focus, only five back then, and time for romance didn't exist. Now, all these years later, Ava and Zach had both put each other so wholly in the friend zone it was far too late for anything else. Besides, he'd learned that lesson with Kimberly. Never date a friend. There was too much to lose.

And he honestly didn't know who he'd be anymore without Ava's friendship.

It was too important.

She was too important.

Another flurry of giggles shocked him out of his thoughts, the ladies trying—and failing—to pick something out at the bakery counter.

"Everything looks so goooooood," one of them said.

Zach couldn't stop his eyes from rolling. They weren't wrong, but why did they have to be so loud and all "Look at me! Look at me!" about everything? But Ava never lost her hundred-watt smile, her patience rivaling that of a saint. She shot him a quick wink, which reminded him he didn't have to be such an old curmudgeon about the festival, but honestly, these people were a nightmare to deal with. He thanked his lucky stars he didn't have to work part-time in the gift shop anymore like he did in high school. Talk about a horror show.

"Apple Fritter, Caramel Apple Cake, Apple Spiced Cookies. You sure do have a lot of apple stuff," the second tourist said.

"Well," Ava replied, still genuinely charmed by the

women, "it is the Apple Cider Festival after all." Her smile grew even wider, and her eyes sparkled.

"Oh my gawd, you're right!" the first woman squealed. She jump-turned toward her friend and gasped. "I just had the *best* idea. We should buy one of everything!"

Her friend's eyes went wide as if the woman had discovered gold or cured cancer or something. She began to nod vigorously. "We totally should! We are here all weekend, after all!"

Ava packed up their enormous order and sent them on their way with complimentary cups of apple cider you would have thought were filled with diamonds the way they'd reacted.

"This town is so friendly! No wonder Trixie and Alistair recommended this place so highly."

Zach had never been so happy to hear the little bell over the door as he watched them walk out. The sigh he let out might have been a bit more audible than he'd intended.

"You okay there, Zach?" Ava called from behind the counter.

He looked at her, more serious than he'd ever been. "I honestly don't know how you do it."

She shrugged. "I'll never get sick of this. All the people, the energy, the excitement…the apples," she said. He didn't know how she could routinely make her eyes twinkle the way they did, like a kid on Christmas morning. "And speaking of apples," she continued, sneaking into the kitchen and returning with a plate covered in a napkin. "I present to you—" she paused both for effect and to fling off the napkin with a flourish "—the Apple Butter Glazed Spiced Pecan Blondie!"

He stared at her, expressionless. "The name's a bit of a mouthful, isn't it?"

But Ava simply grinned. "Not as much of a mouthful as you're about to have," she said, grabbing the fork off his plate and shoving a bite into his mouth before he could say another word.

And of course, the dessert was perfection. Like everything she baked. As he chewed the buttery, sweet goodness, he couldn't help but wonder how he'd gotten so lucky as to be her resident taste-tester.

"That is good," he said, "really good. But how come you're always trying your new stuff out on me?"

"Ah, there are two reasons," Ava said. "First, you're always here."

He tilted his head in agreement. He basically considered The Other Apple Store his unofficial coworking space.

"And second," she continued, her smile widening, "if even you, Old Mr. Grumpy Pants, like something, I know I've got a winner."

And as Zach's eyes rolled so hard he nearly saw his brain, hers sparkled brighter than ever.

Honestly, Ava loved how grumpy Zach was. Like her very own little Grumpy Cat in human form. He came off unbearably gruff to new people, but once you got to know him, everybody loved him—even his grumpy ways. Especially his grumpy ways. Because he was the most generous, empathetic, helpful old grump anyone could be lucky enough to know.

"Besides, you were the first person to welcome me

to Ambrosia Falls, so I guess I have a soft spot for ya," she said, shoving his shoulder a little.

He smiled.

She remembered the first time she'd seen that smile. Her first day in town had been a long one…after an even longer month. She'd been holed up in the safe house all alone—not supposed to even glance outside, though she obviously took a peek once in a while. A person isn't meant to not see the outdoors, to not get a glimpse of sunshine.

She didn't get much of a say in what her house would be like—she couldn't exactly leave protection to go house shopping, but she did get to pick out her furniture—thank you online shopping! She could only hope everything would go with whatever house she landed in. Ava purposely picked things different from her old place, which had been minimalist, stark and modern, and thank goodness she did. The giant old Eaton farmhouse would have looked ridiculous decked out like that. But she'd chosen comfortable and cozy things, and after a bustling day of movers and unpacking, things felt more settled.

But it had been so…quiet.

Alone again, Ava thought. Hadn't she always known she was destined to live like this? To always be on the outside looking in? Why would a new town be any different? Except she was out now. She wasn't a spy anymore. She wasn't Sparrow. Relief and a little sadness washed over her. For a while she had loved that life. The excitement, the danger…but it got old faster than she had thought.

In theory Ava didn't have to worry about letting people get close anymore. That version of her disappeared off the face of the earth, replaced by this new "normal" person.

But what did that even mean?

And then Zach showed up at her door with a welcome to the neighborhood gift, a six-pack of beer. The night had been so hot the flyaway tendrils that had escaped Ava's ponytail stuck to the back of her neck as she opened the door and got her first glimpse of the man who would become so important to her.

"Hey," he'd said and introduced himself. "This, uh… this was all I had." He lifted the six-pack, looking a little sheepish. "I wanted to bring a bottle of wine or something, but the store was closed and I figured it was better than nothing…"

"It's perfect," Ava said, charmed by the way his words trailed off and he rubbed the back of his neck, clearly uncomfortable. But with the impeccable manners of someone raised in a small town where community meant everything, he couldn't leave a new neighbor waiting without something to welcome them home.

Little did he know how perfect the gift really was, at the perfect time in the perfect little town.

They didn't chat much that night, but his smile, along with the beer, did make her feel welcome. She'd been so terrified normal wasn't possible, yet here she was, normal flourishing all around her.

The bells chimed above the door again, and Zach's face grimaced automatically, but when he saw who entered, his expression quickly changed.

Only one person could put a smile on his face like that. Sadly, it wasn't her, Ava thought.

"Hey, Chloe," she said, not having to turn to know who'd come in.

"Hey, Ava," came the adorable chirp of a voice. "How is your day going?"

Ava turned and smiled. Chloe had to be the most adorable kid ever. Ten going on thirty, she loved to spend time at the coffee shop, preferring grown-up conversations to the ones with her friends. What kind of kid asks the adults in their life how their day is going before the adults get the chance to ask first?

"Even better now that you're here, kid," Ava said, then gave Chloe a sideways, mischievous look. "Got a new one for ya." She held the blondie plate out and grabbed a clean fork off the counter.

Chloe's eyes got wide as she slipped into the booth opposite her dad. "A new one?"

Ava nodded, opening her mouth to speak, but Zach interrupted her.

"Don't ask her what it's called unless you have until next Monday for her to tell you. Just eat it, trust me."

Chloe laughed and nodded, knowing full well how Ava liked to name her recipes after the long list of ingredients. "Don't worry, we'll come up with something amazing."

"I'm counting on it, kid," Ava said, glancing up out the window.

She loved this time of year. The festival helped stoke a tiny longing for something else in her life—something a bit more exciting. She loved this new life, but it was so very opposite of how her world used to be. And sure, a small-town fruit festival wasn't exactly the epitome of intrigue, but the whole town came to life with activity, and that was good enough to quell the yearning.

But as she took in the view of Ambrosia Falls—the glorious colors on the autumn trees, the ever-growing groups of tourists, everybody working hard to erect temporary tents and booths—something seemed...off.

She crossed her arms and tilted her head, trying to figure out what bothered her.

She moved slowly away from Zach and Chloe, toward the door, opening it slowly, the gears of her mind cranking.

The seasonal water tower. Was it...swaying?

Ava glanced at the trees surrounding the town and while a few leaves fluttered gently in the light breeze, it certainly wasn't enough to make the enormous makeshift water tower—filled only once a year to cover the needs of the town as the population quadrupled in size—sway.

And then she heard the groan.

Ava's eyes darted to the tents and cloth-roofed booths near the bottom of the tower.

"Move!" she yelled at the top of her lungs, her feet already in motion.

People turned to see what the commotion was about, but not a single soul appeared the least bit alarmed. "Move!" she screamed again, realizing Annie's booth—the one filled with a year's worth of crocheted sweaters, both for people and pets, as well as hats and baby booties—stood directly under the tower.

The tower began to tilt.

Ava kept screaming, "Move! The tower! Move!" as a few people started to figure out what was going on, their eyes nearly popping out of their heads before they turned to flee.

Annie would never be able to get out of harm's way

in time. She didn't have the best hearing, and the fact she needed a walker definitely wouldn't help.

The sound of wood splintering must have finally reached Annie. She began to turn, trying to see what was going on behind her, but there was no time.

Ava dove at her, circling her arm under Annie's the way one might saving a drowning victim and pulling her as far away from the inevitable disaster as she could, hoping she wouldn't do any physical damage to the poor woman.

The sound of the crash brought with it a flashback of the fateful night back at the desert bunker when Ava's whole world imploded, both literally and figuratively. Screams erupted as water exploded from the enormous plastic tank, drowning the street, the booths, and soaking all of the people standing nearby.

An explosive squawking came from Miss Clara's booth as her prize rooster, Captain Applebottom—the fair's unofficial mascot for the past three years running—was hit with the surge. Feathers and water flung from the cage violently before Miss Clara rushed to soothe the poor creature who was somehow, miraculously, still clucking.

When the water finally settled, flowing rapidly over Ava's feet and into the sewer grates on the edges of Main Street, Annie turned to Ava, blinking. "Are you alright, dear?" she asked, calm as could be.

Ava nodded, although she felt more than a little bit away from alright. "Yeah," she said, still panting. "Yeah, I'm alright. Are you?"

Annie looked down at herself as if checking to make sure. "Yes, yes, I think so, dear. Thank you for saving me."

Ava gave the woman a hug—more for her own benefit than Annie's—and said, "Yeah, of course. Anytime."

"Ava!" Zach's terrified scream rose above the rest.

She turned as Zach rushed up to her, putting his hands on her shoulders and surveying her head to toe. "What the hell were you thinking, running in like that?"

"Well." Annie's reply came quicker than Ava could form words. She always had that trouble whenever Zach touched her, no matter how innocent it was. "She was saving my life, of course," Annie said, as if delivering any old sentence.

Ava supposed poor Annie was a bit in shock, looking at her booth. The creations she'd taken all year to make with love and craftsmanship had become flattened mats of soggy yarn, floating pitifully in the muddy water.

"I wonder how on earth something like this could have happened," Annie said, expressing the words everyone was thinking.

Chapter 2

Zach was more than a little relieved everyone appeared okay as he tried to process the situation. Ava had just... taken off. Dove headfirst into danger. He thought he knew her pretty well, had spent nearly every day of the past five years with her, but he honestly would have pegged her as a flight-er, not a fighter.

He was also embarrassed to admit he was more than a little turned on by her bravery and, holy mother-of-pearl, the way she looked with her clothes soaked and clinging to every inch of her. He shoved those thoughts as deep and as far into the corner of his mind as possible.

He still held Ava's shoulders, double- and triple-checking that she was all in one piece. One nonsmashed piece. The water tower had come so close. From his angle he swore it came straight down on them. Right on top of poor Annie and... Ava.

What if something had happened to her? The thought made him instantly sick, and that realization made him even sicker. He'd been working so hard to keep her at arm's length, to center himself solidly in the friend zone.

He lowered his arms and took a sheepish step back, clearing his throat.

"We need to figure out what happened here," Barney from the candle stand said. "Do you think this was an accident?"

For the first time, Zach considered the possibility it might not be.

"Of course it was an accident, you fool," said Miss Clara, the one person in town you could count on to always give Barney a hard time.

"You know, Clara, contrary to your belief, there are things in this world even you don't know every answer to," Barney said. Unfortunately, you could always count on Barney to volley that hard time right back.

The two started bickering like they were in grade school, the volume rising quickly. Others tried to jump in and calm them down, but Zach had watched the scene play out a hundred times before, and it would never work. He raised his hands to his mouth and let out a deafening whistle, quickly regretting it when every eye in town turned toward him.

"Look, none of us knows what happened here. Maybe instead of arguing all day, we could, I don't know, examine the tower and see if we can figure it out?" He glanced from one person to the next to the next, but not a single one backed him up.

Until he locked eyes with Ava. "Sounds reasonable," she said, her breath surprisingly back to normal already, not at all like she'd recently dead-sprinted to save a friend. Suddenly, everyone standing on the street agreed. Zach tried not to take it personally that he'd lived in Ambrosia Falls his entire life, was related to some of these people, yet the moment Ava opened her mouth, they hung on her every word.

Not that he could blame them.

"Well, you guys take care of it then," Barney said, apparently all too happy to spout on about needing to figure everything out, but not too keen on actually doing it.

"Um, who's taking care of it?" Ava asked.

"You two," he said, vaguely waving toward Zach and Ava.

"Makes sense to me," Miss Clara said. "You're the mystery expert, after all."

Zach closed his eyes. "Seriously? The first time in the history of the world you two agree on something, and that something is to send a mystery writer off to solve a real mystery?"

"Sure," Barney said, without a hint of irony.

Zach opened his mouth to argue, but the crowd had already started dispersing, beginning the cleanup before more tourists could arrive.

Ava put her hand on his shoulder. Her touch sent an all-too-familiar jolt through him. "It's fine," she said. "Maybe the whole thing was engineered poorly or something. I mean, a giant tub of water on those spindly wooden legs. This was bound to happen at some point."

"Shouldn't we call the authorities or something?"

Ava shrugged. "I guess if we find something suspicious, but you know as well as I do that unless something catastrophic happens, we're so far out in the middle of nowhere we don't hit anyone's radar."

He let out a long, slow breath. "Yeah," he said, remembering the time Hanson's horse got stolen. The law took six days to come out to investigate, and even then, it was a reserve officer who'd come…one Hanson suspected was sent due to some kind of a hazing situation.

"Honestly, I think we're about as good a choice as any," Ava said. "At least we'll keep it together. Imagine some of the conspiracy theories Jackson or Mae might come up with?" she asked, the spark back in her eyes.

Zach sighed. "Fine, let's get this over with."

They made their way through the rubble, mud and flurry of townsfolk cleaning up with no regard for the fact they might be ruining evidence. They eventually got to the area where the wooden stumps of the base were still sticking out of the ground, the wood splintered and shattered.

"Doesn't look like the legs were cut or anything," Zach said, easily pulling a sharp piece of wood from the jagged stump.

"Termites?" Ava asked.

"I don't know. Might be rot, but either way this doesn't look like anything too nefarious, other than an incredible lack of safety inspection."

Ava nodded. "Well, case closed, I guess. Come on, I'll buy you a beer for the good work. I feel like we both deserve one."

"Yeah." Zach watched as Ava moved back toward the coffee shop, tucking a piece of wet hair behind her ear as she carefully picked her way through the wreckage.

But something still felt off about the whole thing. The water tower was quite literally on its last legs, but still. Why today? The wind wasn't blowing that hard. And what were the chances the tower would fall in the exact direction to put people in harm's way?

He shook his head and threw the splinter to the ground.

Perhaps he wasn't the best person to do any investigating. His writer's imagination definitely got the best of him sometimes.

* * *

Ava watched as the last of the vendors closed up their booths for the night. The rest of the afternoon had gone by in a blur of mud and tourists and baked goods. Zach had been surprisingly focused after the incident, incredibly productive over in his corner frantically typing the afternoon away.

She flipped the sign on the door to Closed, then finally cracked the beer she had promised Zach and set it on his table. She cracked another for herself and slipped into the booth opposite him.

"Well, that was a day," she said.

He slid his laptop aside and pulled the beer toward him. "Definitely something."

Ava took a swig. "Looks like the excitement gave you a shot of inspiration though," she said, motioning to his laptop.

"Yeah, I guess so. Powered through a chapter and a half."

Ava raised her eyebrows. "Nice."

They talked about what happened, then a bit about the festival, and went on to everything else under the sun. Chloe's grandma was with her for the evening, so Zach was in no hurry.

Funny, no matter how much time they spent together, they never ran out of things to say.

But Ava always wondered about one thing, and with three beers behind her, she found the courage to bring up the subject that had been on her mind for years.

"You've never told me what happened with Chloe's mom." She held her breath.

For as long as she'd known Zach, he had been single, and she was more than a little curious why. Then again, she supposed she hadn't been involved with anyone either.

She expected him to wave her off, but to her surprise, he let out a breath and began to speak.

"I thought we wanted the same things. Kimberly was a little hard to please, but I felt like I pulled it off, at least at first. My debut book had been moderately successful, and some real money started to come in, so we were living the dream, I guess," he said, shrugging.

Ava nodded, not wanting to say anything, scared to break the spell.

"We'd been best friends ever since we were kids. She lived down the street, and we'd known each other since before we started grade school. Then when we did go to school, we kept being best friends. We depended on each other for everything."

"Sounds perfect," Ava said, nodding for him to continue.

"It was…mostly. She was adventurous, you know? And I was too for a while. After graduation we went on all these trips…white-water rafting, mountain excursions, zip lining, that sort of stuff. Life was fun, don't get me wrong, but I always felt like I was playing a part. Like it wasn't really *my* life."

Ava could relate so much more than he would ever know.

"She liked the lifestyle more than I did, but we were best friends, and making her happy made me happy." Zach squirmed in his seat a little.

"You know, for someone who makes their living as

a storyteller, you don't seem to be all that comfortable when you're telling one out loud."

He grinned. "That's the beauty of the computer. No one to judge until you know you've got it right. I can make as many changes as I want until I'm satisfied."

Ava's neck went hot, trying not to think about what Zach would look like satisfied. She cleared her throat. "I'm not judging you, Zach."

He nodded. "Yeah, I know." He took a long swig of his beer.

"So you were living the dream. What happened?"

Zach tilted his head. "I don't know exactly. I mean, we never discussed having kids, but I assumed, like a fool, I guess, that we both wanted the same things. She got pregnant and, well, it spooked her. She wasn't sure if she wanted a baby, but me," he said, staring off, a grin—elated, but somehow with a sadness to it too—spread across his face, "after knowing a part of me was growing into a tiny human, I couldn't think about anything else. I thought I wanted this life of adventure and travel and freedom, but the second even the *idea* of a kid entered the picture, I became obsessed."

Ava smiled. "Sounds about right."

He nodded. "It's who I am now, but I was a different person back then. I was scared too, but I convinced her to have the baby. And Chloe came along, and we tried for a while, Kimberly tried for a while, but motherhood didn't come naturally. She said she was never meant to be a mom and she left."

"I can't imagine how someone could leave their child."

Zach shrugged. "She was never cut out for it. I suppose I shouldn't have pushed, but I wanted to be a parent so badly. And Kim tries. I mean, she's a parental disaster, but she sends Chloe letters and presents and tries to stop in once in a while, but for the most part, Chloe and I are on our own."

Ava felt a squeeze in her heart. This man she admired so much—tried so hard *not* to admire as much as she did—had done such an amazing job raising a great kid all by himself. "Must have been hard on you all these years."

"The dad part hasn't been hard at all. I feel like you just love your kid and try to make good choices and do your best. The hardest part was losing my best friend, you know?"

Ava didn't know. She couldn't remember ever having a best friend, but she nodded anyway. "I'm sorry. It's hard to lose people." That she did know.

Zach nodded, drifting in his own thoughts. "Maybe Kimberly and I were never meant to be romantically involved. We probably should have stuck with being friends. Everything got screwed up once we became a couple."

Ava nodded. "There's always the chance you're going to lose the friendship if things don't work out."

"Exactly," Zach said. "But I did get the most important thing in my life out of the deal, so I suppose it was meant to be."

Ava smiled. Nodded. *Meant to be.* How nice to live a life where you could believe in "meant to be" and "happily-ever-after" and all those fairy-tale notions.

"Well, I guess I better leave you to it," Zach said, probably realizing she still had a lot of cleaning up to do before returning at dawn to start tomorrow's baking.

And the day's baking would be intense. Two assistants were coming in at 5:00 a.m. in order to keep up with the demand.

"Thanks for the beer," he said, packing up his computer.

"And thanks for the story," she said. "I thought I knew almost everything about you, but I guess there's always more to learn."

She hated all the secrets she would never be able to tell him.

As Zach stood to leave, a frantic knock sounded at the door.

Zach sighed. "What now?"

Ava shot him a twinkling smile and went to unlock the door. Miss Clara burst through, nearly knocking her over.

"Miss Clara, what is it? Are you okay?" Zach asked.

"No! No, I'm not okay. You guys…" she said, trying to catch her breath, clearly beside herself. "Captain Applebottom is missing!"

Chapter 3

"This can't be a coincidence," Miss Clara said, looking around as if she might find Captain Applebottom right there in the room.

"A coincidence with what?" Zach asked.

"The water tower, of course," Miss Clara said, though Zach couldn't, for the life of him, figure out what one could possibly have to do with the other. "This has to be the work of those Pieville hooligans."

Zach nearly spit out a laugh trying to imagine the charming older ladies of Pieville creeping around town all dressed up in "hooligan" outfits, which, in his mind, consisted of head-to-toe black, perhaps with those eye masks that tied in the back of their various gray/purple/blue and heavily permed hairstyles. But he couldn't even get a snort out before Miss Clara went on.

"Everybody knows they've been trying for years to take over the festival scene around these parts—I mean, they changed the name of their entire town just to wrangle a few tourists—but if they think they can beat our cozy charm and friendly atmosphere, they have another thing coming."

"Friendly atmosphere. Right," Zach said, risking a

glance at Ava, who looked like she was enjoying every second of Miss Clara's rant.

He couldn't understand how Ava never seemed to tire of the ridiculous, and endless, "emergencies" the people of this town overreacted to on the daily. Or how she seemed to be enchanted by it instead of the correct reaction, which was, of course, exasperation.

"I'm sure Captain Applebottom is fine," he said in his most soothing voice.

Ugh, he hated saying the name of that damned chicken. The bird itself was okay, and he got that it was an homage to the Apple Cider Festival, but why did Miss Clara have to go and name him something so embarrassing to say out loud?

"Fine?" Miss Clara said, her voice screeching a bit. "Fine? That poor creature experienced the shock of his lifetime when the water tower came down this morning, and on top of that, now he's been abducted! How could you possibly say you're sure he's fine?" She broke off, pacing and muttering something under her breath that sounded a bit like, "Don't these people have any idea how important my sweet boy is to this town?"

"But we checked the tower, Miss Clara. You know we didn't find any signs of foul play," Zach said.

Miss Clara stopped her pacing to squint at Zach in a way that revealed how little she thought of his detective skills. "Yes, maybe the wood was rotting a little on the tower, but that does not mean there was no foul play! Anyone could have pushed it over."

Zach tried to picture what that would entail, but came up a bit short. To even think of standing under something, with all that weight teetering above—knowing the structure was so rickety it could simply be pushed over—a person would have to be about as smart as a Popsicle stick…or have gargantuan balls of steel. Or a death wish, he supposed.

"I bet it was that dastardly Mayor Harlinger," Miss Clara continued. "She's been after this town for years."

Dastardly?

Pieville's Mayor Harlinger was a kindhearted seventysomething woman who originally hailed from the Deep South, which she loved to tell everyone about as often as possible.

"Miss Clara," Ava said, grabbing the woman's hands to get her to focus.

And thank goodness for that, Zach thought, since he had no idea what he was supposed to say after the "dastardly" comment.

"I know this is incredibly upsetting," Ava continued. "I'm upset too—and I can't imagine what Captain Applebottom is going through, but if we just think for a moment, we'll all realize that if someone has actually taken him, it's probably because they love him so much and just want a little quality time with him."

Miss Clara blinked at Ava a few times. "You might be right," she said. "Captain Applebottom is a good, good boy, and he loves everyone. But—" tears starting to glint in her eyes "—but what if I never see him again? He's everything I've got in this world."

If asked, Zach would never have admitted it, but he had to swallow a bit of a lump forming in his throat.

Over a chicken.

But damn it, he was a pretty cool chicken. And Zach had no idea how he would ever tell Chloe if something bad happened to Captain Applebottom. The girl had a soft spot for every animal she'd ever met.

"And you're sure the cage wasn't accidentally left open?" he asked, bracing for the full impact of Miss Clara, who let out a tired sigh.

"Of course I'm sure the cage wasn't accidentally left open."

"And there was no ransom note or any other clue?" Zach continued, quite bravely, if he did say so himself.

"I'm pretty sure I would have noticed something like that," Miss Clara answered, and to her credit, she barely even rolled her eyes.

Zach figured he'd better not press his luck by mentioning the unhelpful thought about vagrant coyotes that happened to be flitting around in his mind.

"Come on," he said, holding his elbow out to Miss Clara. "Why don't I walk you home? It's going to be a long day for everyone tomorrow, especially Ava here, and we should all get some sleep. None of us will be any good for—" he cleared his throat "—Captain Applebottom if we don't get some rest."

Miss Clara nodded absently. "Yes, I need to be at my best for the captain," she said. "He's going to need me more than ever tomorrow."

Zach turned back to give Ava a wave good-night, trying his best not to wish it was a very different woman walking out on his arm.

Ava waved and mouthed a quick *thank you* as Zach escorted Miss Clara out of the store. She had a few things left on her list of things to do before she crashed for the night, but if she hurried, she figured she could still get in six solid hours before the alarm went off again. In about equal measure, she was both thankful and bummed that the Apple Cider Festival only came around once a year.

And even with the drama of the day, she still had the baking contest to think about. Sure, the Apple Butter Glazed Spiced Pecan Blondie could be a contender, but she didn't think it had quite the wow factor to win. And being the owner of the town's bakery/coffee shop, she had to make a good showing, or she'd never live it down. And frankly, it wouldn't be great for business, either. Not that it would stop people from coming—she was the only bakery in town, after all—but it would be a year of listening to people be all like, "This is okaaaay, but it's not like she won the contest or anything," and trying to get Ava to lower the prices on her "subpar" baked goods. On top of that, depending on who did win the contest, there could be an entire year of razzing to put up with, and Ava had to admit there were people in Ambrosia Falls she'd gladly take a razzing from, and people she would prefer...um, not to.

But she was way too tired to think up any more apple-liciousness tonight, even if she only had a few more days to figure it out. Maybe her subconscious could work on it while she slept.

Ava lowered the blinds, locked the front door and turned off the lights as she made her way through the kitchen to the back door, where her car was parked. She grabbed her purse off the coatrack and came to an abrupt halt.

The back door wasn't locked. Which was completely weird, since the back door was always locked. The kitchen was often empty since she spent so much time out front with customers, so she never risked having it unlocked. And as far as she knew, no one she ever had as extra help on busy days had ever forgotten to lock it either. In fact, none of her fill-in staff even used that door. Unless someone had propped the door open to get some air flow or something, but it kind of seemed strange they wouldn't ask first.

Still, nothing else seemed out of the ordinary and nothing seemed to be missing, so Ava made a mental note to talk with the girls about it, then headed home to catch some much-deserved and much-needed z's.

The large floor-to-ceiling windows in the coffee shop made it easy for the Crow to execute his surveillance. These past five years of searching had been the longest of his life, but as he watched from his nesting spot in the bushes across the street, he was finally getting a good look at the Sparrow's every movement.

Sloppy.

Someone like her should know better than to be in the open like that. Of course, it had taken him five years to track her down, so maybe hiding in plain sight wasn't as terrible a strategy as he always assumed.

But none of those thoughts were taking up the most real estate in his mind.

That honor went to the man.

The lackluster nobody of a small-town guy nowhere near exciting enough for the Sparrow. The man who was clearly putting on airs when he made a big show of escorting the old lady home.

Pathetic.

The Crow didn't want him to be of even the slightest consequence—he certainly didn't seem worth it—but after seeing the way the Sparrow interacted with him, the Crow knew something was up. He'd been watching the Sparrow for so long, far before she even knew who he was, far before he'd made her fall in love with him. And if there was anyone on this earth who could read her body language and those sparkling expressions on her face, it was him. He liked to think he knew her better than she knew herself.

Which was how he knew precisely what was going through her mind at that exact moment. She'd be wondering how the darn back door had gotten unlocked. She'd try to explain it away, of course—maybe she'd simply forgotten to lock it herself—but it would niggle at her.

Exactly the way he planned.

He was fine playing the long game. It had been a hell of a long game so far. A few extra hours or days certainly weren't going to bother the Crow. He was a professional who never missed his mark.

Especially now that he'd finally found the only mark that mattered. The mark that had gotten away.

Chapter 4

A couple days later Zach stared out the window, wishing he had a cup of coffee in his hand. It was the same thought he had every morning. He knew he could easily just make it and put himself out of his daily misery, but the payoff when he finally did get that first morning sip was too good to change his routine. Because if he was being honest with himself—something he tried very hard not to do most of the time—he couldn't live without the other payoff of waiting.

Seeing Ava.

Without the excuse of the coffee, he'd have no reason to go to The Other Apple Store until at least lunchtime, and then what would he do with his mornings? Sit at home and try to write? It was plausible, certainly. There was a whole room on the second floor of the house that he'd made into an office. It had an incredible view of the forest behind the backyard, and he'd spent months picking out the right chair that was both comfortable and something he deemed worthy of an author—a high-backed leather number with carved wooden armrests. Any old office chair would not be fit for writing the Great American Novel, after all.

He almost laughed at the thought. He'd never get a word down in that room upstairs. No, he was one of those writers who apparently needed a muse. A damned muse. The notion of it made him feel ridiculous, like a kid who was way too old believing in the tooth fairy, but he didn't know what else to call it. All he knew was after Kimberly left all those years ago, he thought he might never be able to write another word. And he didn't...for a long time. Not until a certain someone moved in next door and all of a sudden Zach felt an itch in his fingertips to write again.

On the days he was being *very* honest with himself— an extremely rare occurrence if he could help it—somewhere deep down he understood it was really that he'd finally found another person who was not so much a muse, but more of a "reason" to do what he did. An inspiration to do something productive with his life. Someone to impress, he supposed. And whenever Zach was around Ava, he simply wanted her to see how hard he was working, which, in turn, made him actually work hard. A convoluted way of getting things done, but effective nonetheless.

Of course, these were all fleeting thoughts Zach routinely pushed way the hell back to the far reaches of his mind, preferring silly notions like muses to explain the phenomenon of his productivity around certain...important people. Not that he'd ever tell another soul about the muse theory either, but it helped him reason away all the time he spent close to Ava.

All those unwelcome thoughts moseyed through his mind as he stared out his front window looking over at Ava's place. Another thought about the fog tried to weasel its way into his brain—something about it being out of place on the warm morning—but it didn't have a chance to settle in before his thoughts turned back to their previous subject. She wouldn't even be there at this hour, but still, he couldn't help but wonder what she was doing at that exact moment.

She'd have gone into the shop to start the day's baking a couple of hours ago already—he always heard her car door slam in the mornings. He knew she tried to be as quiet as possible, and he'd told her the thousand times she'd asked that he never heard a thing, but the truth was, over the years his sleeping pattern had adjusted itself so he would be awake to hear it. Not that it would ever happen in a million years, but it wouldn't hurt to be on similar schedules with Ava for…whatever reason might present itself down the road. Plus, you know, early bird, and worms and everything.

He allowed his mind to wander, an indulgence he only allowed himself once a day during his morning stare out the window, always wishing that bloody cup of coffee he wanted so badly was in his hand.

"Why is it smoky?" Chloe's voice jolted him out of his thoughts…and almost jolted him right out of his skin.

"Jeez, kid, you can't sneak up on an old guy like that."

Chloe rolled her eyes. "Well, if you'd stop daydreaming at the window every morning, maybe you wouldn't be so jumpy. And you're not that old, Dad."

For his own self-preservation, Zach tried to ignore the "that" in her sentence. "I am not daydreaming," he said.

"You were totally daydreaming," she said, and actually patted him on the shoulder. "But it's okay. I get it's part of a writer's job to be all up in your head half the time. Part of the job."

The job. Right. That's definitely what he'd been day-dreaming about.

"So what's with the smoke?" she asked again.

"Smoke?" Zach asked, turning back toward the window.

He supposed the fog did look a bit like smoke.

"Yeah. Since you were staring at it so hard, I thought you would have figured out where it was coming from."

It was a bit strange the way it was hovering there, floating ever so slowly like it was just out for a stroll.

He leaned in closer to the window. "I think that actually is smoke," he said.

"Uh, yeah," Chloe said—for a ten-year-old, she really did have the sarcasm of a teenager already. "That's why I was asking."

Worry started to fill Zach's mind. Where the heck *was* it coming from? Suddenly he realized there were few explanations for the smoke that could end well.

"Come on," he said, handing Chloe her lunch as she was grabbing one of Ava's famous apple cinnamon bagels off the counter for breakfast. "We can check it out on the way to school."

Chloe let out a groan. "I don't see why we have to go to school when the only interesting thing that ever happens in this town is happening."

It was the biggest point of contention between the adults of the town and their kids. All the kids figured the Apple Cider Festival should be held before school started up again, not two weeks afterward. Of course, the real point of contention was really that most of the kids simply wanted an extra couple weeks of summer vacation, but that was never going to happen.

"It's not my fault the apples aren't ready in time," Zach said, using the same old line his parents used to give him when he complained.

They hurried out the door, the smell making it even more obvious the haze was definitely smoke and not fog. In fact, Zach couldn't believe he'd thought it was fog at first, or that it took him until Chloe said something to figure it out, but that was kind of what his brain was like when he was letting it run wild. Far too focused on one thing, the rest of the world falling away. It was why he only let his mind go there once a day, then pushed those thoughts aside for the rest of the time. Mostly.

Zach took the long route toward Main Street since much of the direct route was blocked off for the festival. All of Main Street was blocked off as well, but he wanted to get close enough to see what might have been on fire.

"At least it's not getting worse," Chloe said, saying the exact thing Zach was thinking.

"Yeah, couldn't have been too bad," he said, hoping it was true.

Still, it was a fair amount of smoke—it had to be something more than a barbecue or something.

The smoke began to dissipate a bit as they neared the center of town. The fire had clearly been put out, and there seemed to be just a bit of smoldering going on. Still, Zach couldn't help the knot balling up in his stomach the closer they got. There were too many buildings in the way to see for sure where it was coming from, but the smoke seemed to be located somewhere near The Other Apple Store.

Almost immediately his brain started to go off on a tangent about Ava and what would happen if she were in some kind of danger, which of course sent him spiraling to the moment when the water tower had fallen all over again. He swallowed hard, hyperaware Chloe would be able to pick up on any fear, and she'd already seen enough of his panic over the past couple days.

He cleared his throat, hoping to dislodge the lump sneaking up out of nowhere, and pulled his truck over to the curb as close as he could get to Main Street. Which wasn't all that close since he and Chloe were definitely not the only people who wanted to see what the heck was going on.

"Stay put," he said to Chloe, whipping his door open.

"But I want to see!" she said, putting on the "I can't believe you're doing this to me" voice that usually made Zach want to give her everything she'd ever asked for and then some, which was also the surest indication he absolutely should not do anything of the sort.

But he somehow stuffed his panic down long enough to turn back to Chloe. "I'm sorry, sweetheart, but I need to make sure everything is safe before I let you get near where the fire was, okay?"

Chloe did not look at all pleased, but she knew there was no convincing him otherwise when there was even a sliver of a question over her safety at stake. She sighed heavily. "Fine."

"Thank you. Please lock the doors behind me."

The moment Chloe started to nod, Zach took off down the street, headed toward the lingering bits of smoke, desperate thoughts running through his mind.

What seemed like minutes later, though must have been only a few seconds, Zach rounded the last building blocking his view of the coffee shop. Once he hit the sidewalk of Main Street, he skidded to a halt. The Other Apple Store looked...fine. Exactly as he'd left it last night. But there was something else that was definitely not the same as it had been the night before.

The temporary staging area for the annual baking contest had disappeared. Or rather, burned to the ground. The local volunteer firefighters were on scene and had done a good job of containing the blaze to the staging area, which was no small feat considering it was sandwiched into a small lot between the hardware store and the local insurance place.

Several people were milling around the smoldering area, and it only took a moment for Zach to spot the person who mattered the most.

She would have been just as home in jeans and a tank top, and hell if she didn't look damn good in those, but today she was wearing a sundress, white, with a few lacy bits here and there, and cowboy boots making her look every bit the small-town girl she'd become. Her hair was partially tied back, but it was the pieces that escaped, the ones she was always trying to smooth back, that he liked the most. They always blew in the slightest breeze and he wondered if they tickled her sometimes. Of course, even with those stubborn tendrils, Ava was put together as always, and doing what she did best—helping people. Which that day meant handing out coffees while everyone else stood around in shock.

Zach took a furtive look around to make sure no one

had witnessed his panic, then turned and walked calmly back to his truck.

He had a worried kid to reassure and get to school on time.

Handing out a bit of coffee was the least Ava could do under the circumstances. She was the one who'd had to wake up half the town since she'd been the first on the scene that morning. The timing was strange, although she supposed she didn't know exactly when the fire started, but she luckily noticed it long before it hit its most violent moments. When she'd dialed the emergency line, there had only been a small flicker in the darkness. In fact, it was only because it had still been so dark out that she saw it so quickly.

It almost seemed like the electrical issues were waiting for someone to be there before they made themselves known. Because it had to be something like electrical issues, right? The problem was, no matter how hard she tried to convince herself it was innocent, just an accident, a heavy sense of unease wouldn't let her go.

She'd run out with her kitchen fire extinguisher, but by the time she hung up and gotten the bloody thing off the wall, the fire was in full swing, and she looked ridiculous holding the small canister.

And now she and the team were way behind on the day's baking, not to mention coffee sales were going to be a bit slower considering she was handing it out for free, but it was the least she could do for the town that had saved her life.

Miss Clara stood alone, staring at the charred remains of the temporary staging area.

"Hey, Miss Clara," Ava said, coming up behind her. "Would you like some coffee?"

But Miss Clara looked like coffee was the last thing on her mind. When she turned, Ava could see her eyes were glistening. "This can't be a coincidence," Miss Clara said.

"I'm sure there's an explanation," Ava replied. "It was a temporary stage. The electrical is older and maybe not exactly up to code."

"Maybe," Miss Clara said, "but when you put it together with the water tower and Captain Applebottom…" Her words fell away as she choked up.

Ava had never had a pet, but she could imagine what it must be like to not know where the creature that mattered the most in the world to you was. A pang of guilt shot through her for not taking Miss Clara's loss more seriously last night. Even if the chicken was safe, the poor woman was still going through a terrible time. "I'll help you find him, Miss Clara. Maybe he just needed a break from all the commotion going on."

Miss Clara sighed. "It's alright dear. You've got a business to run. I've got Carol and Eunice coming to help me search down by the river later this morning. If we need more help, I'll be sure to let you know."

"Okay, Miss Clara. But please let me know if I can do anything. Anything at all, okay?" She practically forced a coffee into Miss Clara's hands, feeling like she had to do something, anything, to help pull her out of her misery. Not that the coffee would do much, but it was all Ava had at the ready to give.

Miss Clara wandered off, hunched over a little more than usual and another pang shot though Ava. She made a mental note to have some baked goods delivered to her house later. If anything, maybe Miss Clara could drown her sorrows in a little home-baked comfort.

."We should see what we can do about getting this cleaned up ASAP," Donna Mae from the antique store said, easing up and gratefully taking a cup of coffee. "Or at least covered up somehow."

Ava nodded. "I suppose it won't look good for the tourists if we have a piece of the festival all charred up at the end of Main Street."

"Exactly," Donna Mae agreed.

Just then, something caught Ava's eye.

It was the same damn thing that caught her eye every day. The same damn thing she tried to make sure did *not* catch her eye every day.

Zach.

He was in her favorite pair of jeans, the ones that were just a little snugger than the rest he usually wore. He didn't wear them often—she suspected they were his laundry day jeans—but when he did, Ava made a point of silently appreciating them.

She sighed.

"Mmm-hmm," Donna Mae said, holding her coffee cup close to her lips but not quite taking a sip. A quick glance confirmed her eye had also caught the man in question, still halfway up the street. "I wholeheartedly agree."

"Sorry?" Ava asked.

Donna Mae gave a knowing smirk. "If I were fifteen years younger, I'd be sighing like a schoolgirl when Zach came around too."

Yikes, apparently the sigh had been a lot more audible than Ava thought. She was going to have to work on her reactions when it came to Zach, or she'd have the whole town talking. Although considering they were two of the very few eligible singles in their age demographic in all of Ambrosia Falls, the whole town had probably been talking nonstop about them for years already.

"Donna Mae," Ava said, rolling her eyes." You know Zach and I are just friends."

"Oh, I am aware, but I can't for the life of me figure out why." Her eyes sparkled at Ava as she finally took her first sip of her coffee.

"Hey," Zach said, finally reaching them. "You guys seem deep in conversation."

"Yup, very deep," Donna Mae said helpfully.

Ava cleared her throat and handed Zach the last coffee from her tray. "We were talking about how we should try to mask this whole scene so the tourists don't get antsy."

"Good idea," Zach said. "I don't think we should disturb anything yet, but we could build some kind of temporary fence across the front of the lot to hide it as best as we can."

"You are brilliant," Donna Mae said, eyes still sparkling as she gave him a playful swat on the forearm. "I'll leave it up to you all to figure it out." With that she was off like a rocket. A very satisfied rocket whose job there was done.

People in town were always doing that. As soon as Zach joined a conversation, they would make some weird excuse and hightail it out of there. Of course, it happened just as often when Ava joined some conversation Zach was having. If Ava didn't know any better, she'd think the whole town was trying to get the two of them alone as much as possible. Which was absurd considering all the time the two of them spent in the coffee shop when Zach was there working and Ava was holding down the fort.

"Why, whenever there's something to do in this town, does everyone else disappear and we're left in charge?" Zach asked.

Ava made a murmuring sound. "I'm going to take it as a compliment. We're the ones everyone thinks are the most capable."

Zach's retort was less of a murmur and more of a grumpy growl. "I think everyone around here might be a little too lazy for their own good."

"Well, the vast majority of them are retirement age so I suppose they've earned it."

Zach tilted his head in agreement. "At least the hardware store is right there. I'll run in and see if Jackson has any scrap lumber he's willing to donate to the cause. If you can get a couple guys on board to help, we could have it up in less than an hour, I bet."

"See, that's why people leave it up to us. We *are* the capable ones around here," Ava said, shooting him a wink before she headed back to the coffee shop to refill her tray. Maybe she'd be able to bribe a guy or two with some morning caffeine.

She couldn't help but smile as Zach let out another grumpy groan before he headed off to see Jackson, wondering if it was weird that the sound soothed her.

Twenty minutes later Ava was back in the kitchen making a batch of her famous Choco-Jumble cookies, which were pretty much basic chocolate chip cookies except they were her way of using up all the extra bits and chunks of leftover chocolate at the end of a baking day.

There was nothing apple about them, so she wouldn't be putting them out in the display case for this week, but they were Zach's favorite, and she decided they could be a special treat to reward the guys building the fence.

Once they were in the oven, she headed to the front of the shop to check the progress of the fence. Amazingly, they were almost done with it. Perfect. The cookies would be ready just in time, and they could have them while they were still warm out of the oven.

Her eyes gravitated, as they so often did, over to where Zach was working. Some of the other guys had shed their shirts as the morning sun's rays got stronger, but sadly, Zach was still fully dressed. She'd only seen him with his shirt off once in all the years she'd known him—the time she happened to be at the pool when Chloe had Lil' Duckies swimming lessons and the parents had to be in the pool with the kids. She didn't know Zach well back then, but that didn't stop the moment from leaving a mark on Ava's memory.

She'd been waiting for an encore presentation ever since.

Stop. Just stop, she scolded herself. She could not go there.

Yes, of all the people in the world who could be trusted with someone's heart, Zach was at the top of the list. But she'd thought that about someone else once before, and look where that got her. Though from her view out her window, the way Zach had bent down to hold a board in place while someone else wielded the drill, the place it had gotten her wasn't so bad.

She tilted her head a little. Not so bad, indeed.

Not sure how long she'd been staring, she blinked

when Zach stood up and looked straight at her, giving her a little wave. Caught staring, she had no choice but to sheepishly wave back, dying a little inside, then force herself to get back to work.

Chapter 5

Once the temporary fence was done, Zach eased into his regular booth, laptop in hand. No one else in town even bothered trying to sit there anymore, which made it feel like the spot sort of belonged to him. He liked the thought of a little piece of Ava's place belonging to him.

Ava set down a plate of four cookies.

"Holy mother of all things majestic. Choco-Jumble. You are a goddess," he said.

And even though it was only a silly little remark, Ava gifted him with a smile that could flash-melt the heart of a snowman.

It seemed like everything had been weird lately—the tourists, the town, the strange occurrences, but one bite of a Choco-Jumble and the world was made right again. He tried not to let out a moan of ecstasy, but it didn't work out.

Ava shot him a little smirk, but then her face morphed into something else. Intrigue? Nah, maybe she just had gas or something.

Once all the other cookie bandits/fence builders had left and her helpers in the kitchen were gone for the day, Ava came to sit with Zach.

"Give me a sec," he said, typing in a sudden flurry

until he finished the section he was working on—things never did turn out the same if you didn't finish the thought in the moment—then flipped his laptop closed. "What's up?" he asked.

"Nothing really," she said. "I just…" She trailed off.

"You just what?" he asked, after her pause became less of a pause and more of a longish silence.

"I don't know. It's just—" She sighed. "Is all of this starting to feel a little fishy to you?"

"Fishy?"

"Yeah. Like with the water tower. And Captain Applebottom. And now the contest staging area. All of it put together, it's…starting to feel a little less like a coincidence than I would like."

Zach worked his jaw, staring at her for a minute. He'd been trying all day to push the same thought from his mind, but his brain wasn't having any of it. "The same thought crossed my mind," he said. "I guess I was hoping I was the only one who thought so."

Ava let out a long sigh. "Same here. But at least I feel like I'm not overreacting if someone else thinks so too."

"So what should we do?"

"I don't know. I mean, if anything else happens, I'll feel bad if we don't do anything."

Zach nodded. "You ever get the feeling we hold the fate of this whole damn town in our hands?"

Ava laughed a little, and the sound was like magic being injected straight into his veins. He hadn't meant to use the word "we," like they were in this thing—this moment? this situation? this life?—together, but truthfully, he quite liked the idea of it.

"It is starting to feel like a 'what would they do without us?' scenario," Ava said, still smiling.

"Well, as much as I love this town, how about we do something about that?" he said.

"What are you thinking?"

"I think it might be time to get the authorities involved," Zach said.

After another pause, and some weird expressions weaving their way across Ava's face—he knew every one of those expressions, but he was pathetic at trying to decipher them, even after all these years—she finally conceded. "Yeah, I guess it's time."

Zach pulled out his phone and searched for the authorities in the nearest city. The place was only two hours away, but he suspected a few small incidents in Ambrosia Falls would barely register a blip on their radar. They might even garner a chuckle or two. He'd bet his life what they considered a serious incident was a whole lot different from what the people of his town did.

Still, like Ava said, if something even worse happened and they hadn't at least tried, they'd never be able to forgive themselves.

"Sheriff's Office," came a gruff voice from the other end of the line. The kind of voice that made a person want to immediately hang up for fear they've done something wrong.

But Zach steeled himself and cleared his throat. "Uh, this is Zach Harrison out at Ambrosia Falls."

"Ambrosia what?" the guy on the other end said more impatiently, if that was even possible.

"Ambrosia Falls. Small town about ninety miles north of you. You're our closest law enforcement office."

"Okay?" the man said, making it sound like a question.

"So yeah, anyway, we were hoping you could send someone out to investigate a few incidents that have happened out here over the past couple of days."

There was a hearty sigh on the other end of the line. "And you're sure you're in our jurisdiction?"

"Yes, sir, I'm sure," Zach said, shooting an eye roll Ava's way.

By the look on her face, she was having a grand old time. Honestly, he should have made her call. He'd bet anything that she'd be more successful at convincing these guys to show up. Unfortunately, it was a bit late to decide that now.

"Fine. Let me get something to write on."

He covered the phone with his hand. "He's getting something to write on," he whispered to Ava, whose eyes widened in what seemed to be a surprise/confused combo.

"How could they not have something to write on by the phone at a sheriff's office?" she whisper-yelled with over-the-top drama thick in her voice and a laugh behind those gorgeous deep brown eyes.

"Alright, what is it?" the guy asked.

The guy's voice was something to marvel at, and Zach wondered if he should put the call on speakerphone so Ava could get the full experience of it too, but he decided against it, doubtful whether they'd both be able to keep a straight face.

"Okay, well," Zach began, the guy had a knack for making a person feel nervous, "we have the annual Apple Cider Festival in Ambrosia Falls every year and due to the increase in population, we always have a temporary water tower installed and filled, and the other day the water tower toppled over, nearly taking out a few of our citizens with it."

"How many were injured?" the man asked.

"Well, we got lucky, and no one was injured," Zach said.

"No one was injured," the man said, his waning patience becoming a substantial component to his voice.

"That's correct," Zach said, forging on. "But that isn't the only thing. We also have this makeshift stage where we host our annual Apple Cider Festival baking contest, and this morning it burned to the ground."

"A makeshift stage," the man said.

Zach couldn't help but be annoyed with the way the man kept repeating his words back to him, only in a way that seemed to imply Zach was the biggest chump in the world for bothering him with such petty matters.

"That's right."

The sigh on the other end was even heavier this time. "And did anyone in your—" he cleared his throat "— little town there, bother to take a look at what you think the cause of these…incidents might be?"

"Um, yes."

"And what did y'all come up with?" he asked.

"Well, the water tower seemed to be in a bit of disrepair and so at first we didn't think much of it, but now with the fire, it seems a bit suspicious."

"Uh-huh," the guy said. "So…just so we're all on the same page here, you've had a decrepit water tower, which you only fill once a year, fall down, and then you've had a fire that originated on…what did you call it, oh yes, a makeshift stage. Is that correct?"

Zach was starting to get annoyed with the way this guy was treating the situation. "Right. And there was a third incident as well."

"A third incident, you say. Well, I am utterly on the edge of my seat."

Zach sighed. "Our festival mascot was stolen."

"Your mascot."

"Correct."

"Like, some stuffed apple or something?" the guy said, clearly amusing himself.

"No, our mascot is a live chicken. Um, his name is Captain Applebottom."

This was the point when the laughter started, followed soon after by an alarming amount of wheezing. When it all finally subsided and the guy caught his breath again, he came back on the line.

"Okay, sir, uh," he said as the sound of a page being flipped came over the line, "Zach. I have your number here on the call display. I can't say when we might be able to send someone out to investigate your water tower situation, or your little fire, or," he said, clearing his throat again, "the disappearance of Captain Applebottom—"

Another pause ensued for a bit more laughing, and Zach tried to keep his cool. By the heat in his neck, he had the distinct feeling his annoyance might have been close to reaching the surface.

The man took a few deep breaths to compose himself before continuing. "But I'll be sure to send someone out to your neck of the woods as soon as we can spare the resources."

"Yeah. Thanks," Zach said with little feeling and hung

up with even less hope that anyone would ever actually arrive.

"That did not sound promising," Ava said.

Zach shook his head in both frustration and disbelief. "Sounds like it could be days before anyone even thinks about coming…if they decide to come at all."

"Incredible," Ava said. "What if something actually urgent ever happened?"

Zach shrugged. "I guess we're on our own."

She shook her head a little. "Well, I guess I should get back to it. The display case is looking a bit sparse after the lunch rush. Better go see how much stock is left back there and get a start on some fresh batches for the late afternoon crew."

"Sounds good. I'll just be here," he said, motioning to the general area of his booth. "If that's alright with you."

"Wouldn't have it any other way," Ava said, making something swirl a little in Zach's stomach.

And that was when—right after Ava disappeared behind the kitchen door and Zach had barely opened his laptop again—the worst sound he had ever heard reached his ears.

The sound of Ava's blood-curdling scream.

Flashbacks of the night five years ago flooded Ava's brain. Pain. So much pain. She'd forgotten what that kind of burn felt like. She hoped she'd never feel it again.

Zach burst through the kitchen door, his eyes frantic, searching.

"I'm okay," Ava said, "I'm okay."

But with the amount of pain she was in, she honestly

wasn't sure she was okay. The last time she'd felt this kind of pain, she'd been pretty far from okay.

"Show me," Zach said, his voice gruff and demanding.

But there was only fear in his eyes. A fear that hit somewhere deep inside Ava, making her angry that she was the person who caused fear in this man she cared for so much, but also elation that she had the power to make him feel so deeply.

She held her arm out to Zach, who took it gently, peering closely.

"What happened?" he asked.

"I went to check my phone and leaned on the counter with my arm. Except it wasn't the counter, it was the stove I guess, and the burner was on."

"How was the burner on when no one was even in here?" Zach asked, though he was only half listening, clearly far more concerned with inspecting her arm.

"I don't know," Ava said. "It's never been left on before. And I can't even think what the girls might have been using the stovetop for this morning."

In her mind, Ava began to go through the list of baked goods on the menu that day.

"Here, sit," Zach said, pulling up a stool, then turning to the cupboard where he already knew the first-aid kit was kept, having had to grab a bandage every now again, usually for Chloe.

Ava did as she was told, her mind still taking stock of the morning's menu items. "No, there was nothing that needed the stove. The filling for the Candy Apple Glazed Donut Supreme was made ahead of time. I can't figure out why anyone would have turned it on."

"Could someone have bumped it?" Zach asked, coming back to face her, taking her hand gently again.

Ava shook her head. "I don't think so. You have to sort of push in the knob before you turn it. It's a safety feature meant to stop accidents from happening."

"You're lucky there wasn't another fire," Zach said, checking through the contents of the first-aid kit.

"Yeah, I guess so," Ava said, though something about Zach's words sent a sliver of dread down her spine.

"We should clean this," Zach said, gently guiding her off her stool and over to the sink as Ava's mind kept whirling.

The cool water sent a new wave of pain through Ava, shocking her back to the present. He was so close, using his hands to lather the soap before gently rubbing them on the burn. The gentle pressure momentarily hurt, then subsided as she closed her eyes, concentrating on how his hands felt on her skin. How gentle he was.

This close, she could smell him, a woodsy clean scent she'd come to associate with comfort, though she didn't often get to be so close to it, and she couldn't help but lean in a little more.

"Come," Zach said, and there was so much feeling in the single word as he pulled her gently back toward the stool.

She opened her eyes as they moved, and suddenly the room felt thick with emotion, so thick she could barely breathe.

And so of course she went and ruined it by speaking. "Well, with this and the stage burning down, I guess I won't have to worry about the baking competition." She let out a slight chuckle.

Zach drew his attention away from her hand to her eyes. "Were you seriously worried about it?"

She shrugged. "I always want to make a good showing since I'm the one charging for my baked goods in this town."

Zach grabbed a roll of gauze from the kit and looked directly into her eyes. "Ava, it wouldn't matter what you came up with for the competition. You would have won."

"That's not true," she said, but he cut her off quickly.

"You've won the past five years in a row," he said.

"Only because I stress over it for months in advance," she said. "Except this year, all the stressing didn't even do me any good."

His brow furrowed. "I never knew that about you," he said. "You always seem so carefree. I didn't think you stressed over anything at all."

If only he knew.

"Sorry to burst your bubble," she said, then put her best carefree face back on.

Well, as carefree as someone who'd just burned the hell out of her arm could be, anyway.

But Zach just made a murmuring sound and got back to work, carefully spreading a thin layer of antibacterial ointment across her forearm. His hands were soft and gentle and felt like they always belonged there…touching her skin. She had a brief thought, wondering how she could have survived this long without that touch to soothe her, and she realized then she never wanted to let the feeling go.

He laid a nonstick sterile pad over the worst of the burn and began to wrap it with gauze, careful not to hurt her. The concentration on his face, so careful, the way he bit his lower lip drawing her attention there, his bottom lip full and looking so soft.

She wondered what his lips might taste like.

Heat began to build deep in her center and she closed her eyes again, inhaling deeply, wanting to savor the moment, knowing she'd want to look back on it for a long time to come.

"Does it hurt?" he asked, and Ava realized he was finished with the bandage.

She blinked her eyes open, and he was there, right in front of her, still holding her arm, taking care of her.

"Hey," he said, his voice so soft. He tilted his head slightly, with a little smile, like he was wondering what was going on in her head.

"Hi," she said, giving him a tiny smile back.

They stayed like that for a moment, volleying silent questions back and forth with their eyes until one of them—Ava didn't know if it was her or Zach, maybe it was both—closed the small gap between them, their lips finally, blessedly meeting.

Ava's mind filled with thoughts. Was this really happening? After all the time spent wondering, resisting, pushing him out of her mind, he was finally here, right in front of her. The moment was surreal and unbelievable, and felt like she had finally found a home in this world.

Zach wrapped his arms around her, deepening the kiss as Ava leaned into him. She let go and fell into the abyss of nothingness that could only be found in the safety of someone who was trusted so deeply the rest of the world suddenly didn't matter at all.

He pulled her closer, onto the very edge of the stool, though it felt like she'd never been so stable in her life.

Her arms wrapped around the sturdiness of him, one hand moving down the taut muscles of his back while the other was desperate to find his head, to pull him closer.

And that was the moment the cruel world came crashing back down on her, the pain searing through her arm, shocking her back to reality. A small, gasping wince escaped her lips before she could stop it.

Zach stiffened and pulled back, though he kept his arms around her. Still protecting. Always protecting. "Are you okay?" he asked, the concern heavy in his expression.

"Yeah, sorry. Just forgot about the arm."

And she wanted to keep kissing, to fall back into the oblivion of a first kiss that makes you feel drunk, but the moment was broken. Zach smoothly propped her back onto the stool and pulled away from her.

The moment his touch was gone Ava missed it, and was only slightly consoled when he took her bandaged arm, inspecting it once more.

"It looks okay," he said, finally meeting her eyes again.

"Okay," she said, unsure where everything was supposed to go from there.

Holy shit. She had just kissed Zach. Like really kissed him, and now everything was going to change. And it felt so right, like the change was going to be an incredible thing. But she was scared too. What if he had gotten caught up in the moment and didn't feel the same way about her? What if he regretted it already?

But the thing was, he didn't look like he regretted anything. He looked…happy. Or maybe her happiness was oozing out all over the room and coating him too. Maybe his wasn't even real at all.

Except there had always been…something between them. The kind of thing you knew you couldn't act on until you were ready. Until the time was right. Until all the stars aligned.

And damn if it didn't feel like every star in the universe had lined right up especially for them.

Hadn't she always known they were putting off whatever was going to be between them because they knew as soon as that "whatever" started, it was going to be forever?

She looked down at her arm, which Zach had been holding, then looked at him. He looked like he might have been having the same sort of thoughts running through his mind, but didn't quite know what to do with them either.

What he did do was take a step back, then put his hands into the back pockets of those fantastic jeans and sort of lean back on his heels. "Um, so…" he said, trailing off and looking toward the door to the front of the shop.

Ava tried to smile, but it ended up a little sheepish. "So," she said back, shifting slightly on the stool.

The moment stretched into oblivion.

She opened her mouth to say something, though she had absolutely no idea what that something might be— she just felt like she needed to fill the silence. But Zach apparently had the same thought at the same time, and they both spouted some incomprehensible jumble before each stopped short.

"Sorry, you go," Ava said.

"No, you go," Zach said.

"Um, okay, except I have no idea what I was even going to say." She smiled.

And then he smiled back. "Me neither."

Her shoulders relaxed. He was still Zach. Her best friend.

"So... I guess that happened," she finally said.

He let out a chuckle and pulled his hands from his pockets, taking a tentative step toward her. "Um, yeah. It really did," he said.

Ava thought he was going to come back to her, to give her the one thing in the world she wanted most, which was obviously another long, and hopefully even more passionate kiss—if that was even possible—when his eyes suddenly went wide.

"Is that the right time?" he asked.

Ava's eyes followed his to the clock on the wall. "Shit, Chloe."

"I gotta go," he said, and turned to dash out the door, but just before he reached it, he turned and ran back to her, grabbing her face in both hands and kissing her hard. It was a kiss that said everything Ava needed to know. Because it felt more like a promise than simply a kiss.

She smiled as he dashed through the door.

And smiled as he yelled, "I'll see you later!"

She was still smiling as she heard the tinkle of the bells above the shop door letting her know he had gone.

But then the smile faded as she spotted something on the floor near the other door. The back door. Something had been slipped underneath. But that couldn't be right. It was an outer door, sealed off. And she was sure it hadn't been there when she'd come into the kitchen and burned herself, which meant someone had opened the door while she and Zach had been right there.

Dread oozed up and filled every corner of the room

as Ava moved carefully toward the envelope, picking it up from the floor before she could give herself time to talk herself out of it. A quick glance told her the door was sealed tight and locked.

The dread grew thicker as she slipped her finger under the sealed end of the envelope and ripped, pulling the contents out.

And in that moment, she knew, without a shadow of a doubt, she would never kiss Zach again.

Chapter 6

Zach wasn't sure if it had been the best thing that could have ever happened to him, or the worst. Thoughts about how everything started to go south with Kimberly the moment they started being more than friends filled his mind with every doubt imaginable.

But Ava was not Kimberly.

Maybe this time could be different.

And he had to admit. This time felt different. He was feeling things he'd never felt with Kimberly. Maybe it was because he'd known Kimberly his whole life that the relationship didn't carry the same kind of...spark. That was the only word he could think of to describe it. And my God, did the kiss have some spark in it, although it would be better described as lightning, if he was trying to be as accurate as possible.

He'd thought of a kiss like it so many times, pushed away those fantasies just as often and then the moment—the real moment—had completely snuck up on him. Maybe it was the emotional roller coaster he'd been going through when it came to Ava these past few days—the water tower, and then this morning before he knew she was safe from the fire. The last incident with the burn must have been more than his poor heart could take.

Although he wasn't entirely sure if he'd been the one to initiate the kiss or if she had. He was damned sure thinking about it, that was for certain, but he didn't know who'd actually closed that last, tiny, excruciating gap.

But it wasn't just the kiss that felt different. It was the way he felt inside too. Like the world had a glimmer to it…a lightness. Like he was invincible. No, like he and Ava together were invincible.

Apart, he was just him. But around her, he became someone he liked a whole lot more.

"What's up with you?" Chloe asked, climbing into the truck. "You're never late. I was starting to get worried, you know."

She wasn't necessarily scolding him, but she wasn't *not* scolding him either. Zach decidedly did not like this new side of her. But he *had* been late and couldn't really give her a good excuse.

"I'm sorry, I lost track of time."

Chloe narrowed her eyes. "You never lose track of time."

"I know. I was helping Ava with something, and I forgot to watch the clock."

"So you forgot about me," she said, and Zach couldn't tell if she was legitimately annoyed or if she was just giving him a hard time.

The kid was way too smart, and way too wise for her age.

"I did not forget about you," he said.

Finally, mercifully, she cracked a grin his way. "So…

you were hanging out with Ava, hey?" she said, a tone of amused curiosity in her voice.

Zach couldn't help but feel like he was right back in grade school alongside his daughter. "Chloe," he said, rolling his eyes.

"And you lost track of time," she said, implying something was definitely up.

Zach sighed. "She hurt her arm, and I was helping her."

Chloe's eyes grew wide. "Is she okay?" she asked, a note of concern in her voice now.

"She's going to be fine, don't worry. Has anyone ever mentioned you worry too much for a ten-year-old?"

"Yes. You, pretty much every day," she answered, shooting him a side-eye. "And like you're one to talk," she said.

"But I'm a creaky old adult. It's my job to worry. For the both of us."

Chloe rolled her eyes. "How about we agree it's nobody's job and both stop worrying? Besides, you're only just starting to get a little creaky around the edges."

Zach chuckled a little, amazed, as he so often was, at this kid of his. "Yeah, okay. Deal."

They drove in silence for a couple blocks, then Chloe spoke, spotting the coffee shop up the road. "Can we go get something from Ava's?"

"Not today kid," he said. "I've got stuff to do at home."

He did not, in fact, have stuff to do at home. But he was worried about what seeing Ava again so soon would do to him. That kiss pretty much wrecked him, and he was worried he might lunge for her again the moment he saw her. Which would not be a good look in front of his kid.

And he definitely wasn't going to stare at The Other Apple Store as they passed. Except he found he couldn't stop himself, feeling like a damn teenager desperately hoping to catch a glimpse of his secret crush.

I am in so much trouble, he realized as he craned his neck even further to watch the store for one more second.

It's over, Ava thought. *It's all over. He's found me and I have to go on the run again.*

She shuffled through the pictures one more time. The first, a shot of her hugging Annie moments after the water tower had fallen. Then one of Ava—before the firefighters had even arrived on scene at the contest stage—holding her pathetic little fire extinguisher, knowing it was pointless. Next came shots of the back door of The Other Apple Store, as well as her stove, which Ava took to mean that whoever left these photos was taking credit for the strange, seemingly unexplainable incidents in her own place of business.

And then the final shot, which must have been taken with an instant camera, of her and Zach, locked in the kiss they had shared just moments ago.

The bastard had been right there.

It had to be Justin, and he seemed to be having a grand ole time toying with her. Just like he always used to do. It was the one thing about him that bothered her back then—the way he seemed to get pleasure out of making his targets uneasy.

She wondered how long he'd known where she was. Had he been lying in wait all this time? Waiting for proof she'd moved on with her life? That she actually had a life—one she wouldn't want to leave.

She supposed the kiss with Zach would have proved to Justin that she wouldn't be willing to go easily. He wanted her to be comfortable and let her guard down before he made his move.

He wanted her to suffer.

Tears came to her eyes. She should have known better. She came into this town vowing never to get attached. Sure, she could have friends, ones she would always hold a bit at arm's length, but she would never really let them into her soul. But so much time had passed. Ava didn't know when Zach had wriggled his way straight into the middle of that soul, but she couldn't deny that's exactly where he lived. And somehow, after one person had gotten in, the floodgates opened and now she was pretty much in love with the whole damn town.

She blinked the tears away. This was not the time.

She had work to do.

First things first. Protection.

She went out front to lock the door, putting out a Back in 15 Minutes sign. It wouldn't keep Justin out if he wanted in badly enough, but she couldn't have people wandering in off the street while she did what she had to do. She moved to the closet where they kept the cleaning supplies, conveniently out of sight from any of the front windows, and pulled up a few of the carpet squares she'd laid down to disguise the hatch, quickly pulling it open.

The space wasn't really a basement—more like a glorified crawl space, but it was good enough for what she'd needed it for.

Things she couldn't let others know about.

Ava collected the items she needed, both for protection and for what she knew she'd have to do that evening, then headed back upstairs and took the sign off the door, hoping it would seem to the town that nothing was out of the ordinary.

She had one last important task. A message to send to one of the most important people in her life. The only person who'd remained from her life from before. The one contact in her old life even Justin hadn't known about.

George.

Ava still didn't know how George had managed it. Pulled her from the flaming bunker all those years ago and gotten her to safety and to medical help. She couldn't imagine the strength it must have taken to go down into a smoke-filled hole in the ground to see if there were any signs of life. Then find the will to pull her unconscious body up the steep stairs and back out to the world again. At the age of seventy-five.

He must have been running on pure adrenaline.

Ava opened the browser on her phone, loading up the Buy & Sell page for an obscure medium-sized town somewhere in the heart of Oklahoma. She'd never been to the town, and neither had George as far as she knew, but the online space was where the two of them had communicated for the past five years. They couldn't risk direct contact, of course—George was aging and sometimes needed medical care, so being invisible was no longer an option for him. Thankfully, Justin still didn't know of George's existence, probably still wondered how the hell Ava ever got out of the bunker alive, and so he was relatively safe. Still, Ava couldn't risk Justin even suspecting she'd had help that awful, fiery night, so they kept their communication on the down low.

Ava quickly went into her routine of computer precautions she always took—masking her IP through a VPN and creating a brand-new, encrypted burner email address that would delete itself the moment she hit Send. It wasn't foolproof, but without the tech experts she used to have at her fingertips, it was the best she could do.

She used the email to set up a new account with the site and logged into the Buy & Sell. George knew what to look for. Avocado pits for sale. Ava had noticed a strange trend of people giving away their discarded avocado pits so others could use them to start an avocado plant. Which struck Ava as incredibly strange considering anyone who liked avocados enough to want to grow them would likely have avocado pits of their own to start their plants, but it was, apparently, a thing. Most importantly, a thing easily skimmed past. And in order to make sure she didn't actually get any inquiries about the avocado pits, she put a price tag on them. A small one, about the cost of an actual avocado, which would deter anyone in their right mind from actually being interested in the ad.

But it was what George knew to look for. If Ava ever needed him, she would post about the avocado pits, and vice versa, which would open up a line of communication difficult to trace. Ava spent countless hours skimming that silly Buy & Sell with only the occasional check-in from George. But it was the way it had to be. Anything more direct would be too risky.

She quickly typed up her ad:

Avocado pits, cleaned and dried, healthy? And ready for planting. UnCompromised pits, disease free. Perfect for all you avocado lovers. Call to arrange pickup.

Ava normally wouldn't be so bold as to add the question mark and capitalize the *c* in *uncompromised*, but it was the only way she could figure out how to get her message across to George. If she had a bit more time, she could think of something better, but of all the considerations in a situation like the one she found herself in, time was the most critical. She needed to know if her friend was healthy, and he needed to know she was compromised.

In truth, George had always been much more than a friend to Ava. He was more like a father figure. He'd been her first handler when she'd become an operative and helped her through those first difficult years. And the years had certainly been difficult. Yes, she'd lost her parents years before and had been a ward of the state for a long time, which meant she didn't have a whole lot in the way of family connections, but still. She had a few friends, and when a person agreed to do the kind of work required—lots of unexplainable travel, frequent changes of appearance, and a sudden influx of money— a person had to let things like friendship go.

Thankfully, George had a huge heart and a soft spot for Ava, and Ava knew no matter what went down in her world, there was a single person she could always count on.

George.

And if anything had happened to him, she wasn't sure she could live with it.

For the next few hours until closing time, Ava waited. The more time passed—each minute seeming like an hour—the more worried she became. The only thing keeping her going was the steady stream of customers thanks to the Apple Cider Festival, a welcome distraction.

She must have checked the Buy & Sell page over a hundred times before she finally got a reply.

All good here, do you need me to come?

Ava felt like she could breathe again, and the weight of about three tons of avocados was lifted from her shoulders. She quickly typed into the Buy & Sell instant messaging window.

Hold tight. I'll keep you posted.

Because before she called in one of the most precious people in the world—especially one who wasn't in the best health—she needed to know exactly what she was up against.

Her first thought was to run. Pack a small bag and get the hell out of Ambrosia Falls as fast as she could. It was exactly what she would have done if she was confident Justin had nothing in the town to hold against her, but Ava realized, with a sick feeling swirling in her guts, there was so much in the town he could hold against her. So many people who mattered.

She shouldn't have let it happen. It was Spy 101—never get attached. Never give your enemy something they can manipulate to get to you.

She'd been sure after being shuffled from house to house as a teenager, and then working diligently not to make personal connections all the years she'd been active, she supposed she didn't think she was capable of those feelings anymore, so they kind of snuck up on her.

It was a monumental mistake, and one she'd regret

for the rest of her life if she didn't make this right. And making it right meant one thing…going back to a life she never thought she'd be a part of again.

She needed to bring Sparrow back from the dead.

Chapter 7

Zach felt like a total creeper staring out the front window. He tried to convince himself it wasn't because he was waiting for Ava to pull up to her house—*just checking to see what the weather's up to!*—but even he wasn't buying it. Thank goodness Chloe was busy doing homework in her room or she'd 100 percent start asking him all kinds of questions.

By now, he knew her schedule almost better than she did, not that he was keeping tabs, or anything, and the strange thing was, she was never this late getting home. He wondered if he should start to worry.

He sighed. Ava was a grown-ass adult, and she didn't need some snooping neighbor wondering what she was up to every waking moment. Even one she'd shared an incredibly passionate kiss with earlier in the day. Heat rose up his torso thinking about the kiss, and he tried to tamp it down by gulping a huge glass of ice water. As fast as he could. Unfortunately, a massive case of brain freeze was all he got for the trouble. Those damn swirly emotions were still lurking in his guts.

But honestly, where could Ava be? Sure, it was possible she had plans with someone else in town, but since

Zach was always at the coffee shop, he usually knew about changes in her schedule. He wondered then, if the amount of time he spent around the poor woman might be considered stalking in some circles. And then he wondered if it was a bad thing this was only the first time he'd even thought to consider the notion. Was he being a total pain in Ava's butt all the time? A flurry of panic whirred through his chest until he remembered the kiss. And the way she was completely comfortable around him. And the way she used him as a guinea pig for her recipes.

No, he realized, if she thought he was a big pain in the butt, none of the above would be happening. Still, as if he were back in grade school, he couldn't help but feel like he was doing things all wrong. That's where his mind went when he was all alone and spending way too much time with his thoughts.

When he was around Ava, he felt different. He wasn't nervous. He wasn't worried. He was just him. She had a way of putting him at ease. Maybe that was why he craved being around her so much.

Well, that and the fact he could spend an eternity staring at her and never get tired of the view.

Another hour passed and Zach began to pace. Normally, he would try to pry Chloe away from her phone and get her to do something with him. But he could barely focus long enough to force himself to walk to the back of his house, before rushing back to the front to check the window yet again.

Finally, well after dark, Ava's car pulled into her driveway next door. He breathed out the longest sigh of relief he'd ever expelled in his whole life, then suddenly wondered if he'd left his wallet in the car and headed out to check, careful not to glance her way. The last thing he needed was for Ava to think he'd been waiting for her to come home.

Only after Ava pulled into her garage and her car door slammed, did he allow himself to look up. God, he was being ridiculous, crushing like a thirteen-year-old, desperately wanting to find out if she liked him. He supposed it had been so long since he allowed himself to go there it was expected, but it didn't stop him from feeling incredibly silly and lame as hell.

"Oh hey," he said, as she came out of the overhead garage door, as if he'd only just noticed she was there.

Yup, absolute loser.

Ava looked tired, but eventually gifted him with one of those smiles that reignited the annoying swirly action in his guts, as she hit the button to close the garage. "Hey," she said back.

For the past several hours, Zach had been playing this exact scenario over in his mind, with slight alterations each time it played. Sometimes Ava would come rushing up and fling her arms around him—those were the best ones—and sometimes she would saunter up, all cool-like, with a look in her eye that reminded him they had an exciting little secret. But in none of those fantasy scenarios did she look like she wanted to flee.

Which was exactly how she was looking now. Eyes darting, shifting from foot to foot, and generally seeming as though she was stuck in the most uncomfortable situation she'd ever experienced. It made Zach feel completely awkward and uncomfortable too.

He rubbed the back of his neck. "So, uh, long day, hey?"

"Yeah," she said, nodding a little too vigorously. "Really long day."

Zach had been hoping she'd expand on where she'd been half the damn night, and reminded himself one more time it wasn't any of his business. A concept he hated with the fiery passion of a thousand Red Hot candies and a chaser of Fireball. Should he bring up the kiss? He wanted to bring up the kiss. Except…she wasn't bringing up the kiss, so he probably shouldn't bring up the kiss. If she wanted to talk about the kiss, she would say so.

She shifted her weight one more time.

And then, right after he decided not to say anything, his damned mouth opened itself and started spewing anyway. "So, uh, this afternoon…" he said.

It was barely noticeable, but Zach swore Ava jolted ever so slightly.

She cleared her throat. "Um, yeah…"

"That was, um——"

"Probably a mistake, right?" Ava jumped in, cutting him off and quite soundly crushing his soul into oblivion.

"Right," he said, with an awkward little chuckle. "A mistake…"

"I mean, because we're such good friends and everything," Ava said, her words picking up speed.

Zach nodded in kind of a full-body way, rocking back on his heels. "Yeah, we, uh, wouldn't want to mess anything up."

"Right! Exactly!" Ava agreed, her words full of over-the-top enthusiasm.

And then there was nothing else to say. Just the two of them standing there, staring at nothing, and definitely not looking at each other.

"Um, so... I should be getting in. Kinda tired...you know how it is," she said, along with another weird nodding routine.

"Right, yeah." Zach shook his head a little. "Sorry to keep you," he said, backing away a step and giving her this strange little wave the likes of which he'd never done in his life.

Zach watched as Ava went up her front steps and into her house. She turned back once, giving him a look filled with regret, making him wonder if she regretted this moment, or the one between them that afternoon.

He went back inside, thoughts racing faster than a bird trapped in a house with the homeowner chasing after him.

"Whatcha doin' outside?" his daughter asked in a small voice, startling him out of the mental hamster wheel.

"Oh..." He looked around.

Why had he gone outside?

"Right, I was looking for my wallet."

Chloe glanced over to the console table by the front door. "That wallet?"

Zach followed her gaze, seeing that his wallet was right in the center of it beside his keys...the keys he was currently holding in his hand and must have picked up from *right* beside the stinking wallet before he'd gone out.

Chloe giggled a little. "A bit absent-minded today?"

Zach forced out a small chuckle. "Yeah, I guess so," he said.

He felt like a damn fool.

But unfortunately, it wasn't because of any wallet.

Ava couldn't bring herself to think about Zach. Walking away from him, telling him the kiss was a mistake... it was, inconceivable. Cruel. Both to her and to Zach.

So she just wasn't going to think about it.

How could she? There was something bigger at stake than his heart.

His life.

The fact that the Apple Cider Festival was going on was in Ava's favor. Every Airbnb and rental property in town had been booked up for Apple Cider months in advance, so Justin would never have found a place like that to stay at. And he would have never held out this long before confronting her if he'd known her whereabouts months ago. Of course, Ava wasn't sure he would have even tried any of the legitimate places to stay anyway. It wasn't his MO.

As the Crow, Justin always thought it was much more badass to hole up in abandoned or unused buildings. Ava had always disagreed with him on the matter, thinking it too risky—it was much easier to spot suspicious activity at a place everyone knew was supposed to be empty, and it had once been a huge point of contention between them. And that day, she decided, it was going to be his downfall, like she always suspected it would be. Especially considering she knew Justin was a bit posh, not likely to use some run-down building as the place he went if there were any other options. And Ambrosia Falls definitely had other options. She could think of at least three gorgeous vacation homes that sat empty this time of year—families who didn't love the crowd of the Apple Cider Festival, but also didn't rent their houses out to tourists.

She had a good idea which houses were empty—she was still the Sparrow after all, trained to remember details—but all evening she'd been confirming with some of the locals. Just "making conversation" in order to substantiate what she already knew.

The rest of the daylight was used to prep for the next day's customers. She knew she'd be out late and would never make it back to the shop early for the morning's baking. So with one last pit stop to give Maureen—her main baking assistant—a key and the code to the alarm system, she headed home to prepare for what was to come.

She'd considered Maureen's safety, of course, wondering if she should be worried about her opening by herself in the morning, but she decided if her evening was successful, there wouldn't be anything to worry about anymore.

Her plan had been coming together for hours. Desperate to find some way—any way—to stay in Ambrosia Falls, she had landed on an idea. One chance she might not have to run. If she were to simply take Justin out, make it so he couldn't hurt anyone she loved, she could go on with her life as it was. She could stay in town, keep everyone safe, and most importantly, figure out what everything meant with Zach.

She didn't take the job lightly. She was a different person than she'd been five years ago, but she still had the training. Still had the ability to do what she needed to do for the greater good. It was just that this time, the greater good was keeping herself and all the people she'd grown to love safe instead of someone else.

Running into Zach outside her house had thrown her off though. Seeing the look on his face when he noticed her there—excited, loving, hopeful...all at the same time—she'd panicked. If her plan for Justin didn't work, she needed to keep her distance from everyone in town. Especially the ones who mattered as much as Zach. Plus there was the little matter of making sure Zach didn't catch a glimpse of the weapons she had concealed around her body. Most people would never notice, but if Zach got close enough to touch her, she'd have a whole lot of explaining to do.

So many feelings had flooded her when she saw Zach—fear something might happen to him, a fierce sense of having to protect him and a heavy dose of straight up lust, something she hadn't allowed herself to wholly feel about him before. But that flipping spectacular kiss had awakened something in her. Something that had been dormant for a very long time.

Had it really been five years since she'd had sex? Good Lord, no wonder her nether regions were churning up a storm of hormones, the likes of which she didn't even remember having as a teenager.

But she had to leave all those feelings behind her.

There was a job to do, and she would only be able to allow those feelings back in if she was successful. It was something she was good at—pushing her own emotions away to do what had to be done.

Ava piled supplies into a large duffel bag. The sooner she could get this over with and didn't have anything to worry about anymore, the better. But her burned arm was not making things any easier. It was amazing how a person could take for granted something as simple as packing without thinking. But with her arm in so much pain, it was no simple feat at all, not to mention the bandage around her arm getting caught in her bag. She thanked her lucky stars that at least it hadn't been her shooting hand.

Once she finally got the damn bag shut, she turned out all the lights in her house, including the outside light. She hoped if Zach or Chloe were watching, they'd assume she'd gone to bed. Not that she thought they'd be paying any attention, but she had to admit, if she didn't have so many other things on her mind, she'd probably be staring out the window toward a certain house, wondering what a certain person inside said house was thinking right at that moment.

Giving it a few more minutes to be sure, she finally slipped out the back door of her house and through the main door to her garage, thinking the whole routine would have been a hell of a lot easier if she'd had an attached garage. After collecting a few more things and stowing them in her trunk, she hit the button for the overhead door, cringing at the loudness. But the noise couldn't be helped.

If she got through this, she thought, she'd get something quieter. Then she realized, if she got through the rest of the night, she would no longer have to worry about it.

As she backed down her drive and out onto the street, Ava let out a long, slow breath, trying to calm her vitals, knowing she would need a steady hand—and a steady mind—for what came next.

She would stake out each of the three properties one by one, starting with the biggest. If Justin was still using the same tactics, chances were he'd pick the fanciest place he could get away with.

She headed to the Williams residence first. It belonged to a kindly older doctor and his wife, who loved to have the place on the river to go boating with their grand-kids. There was a cluster of trees on the edge of the large semirural property. That was where Ava headed, park-ing a half mile down the road where her car would blend in with the others on the street, then made it the rest of the way on foot. Not an easy feat considering the heavy duffle she carried. But the one thing it seemed she had done right was stay in decent shape—not prime form, but decent—which made the trek manageable.

Inside the trees, she set up her surveillance, starting with recording equipment she would leave in case Jus-tin was staying there but not present at that moment, then placing her infrared camera to pick up any heat signatures.

She left her sniper rifle in the bag for now, wanting to get a read on the area and the situation. She sat for twenty minutes, barely moving a muscle. Justin was not there.

She left the recording equipment and made the trek back to her car, scanning the area the whole way. She re-alized, for all the hunting she'd done before, she'd never known she was the one being hunted. She'd been sur-veilled back when Justin had been watching her all those years, but she'd been oblivious. It was a very different situation when you knew you were being watched. Every sound, every movement in the shadows had her on edge, and it was starting to play with her mind.

Ava moved to the next house on her list, the Batras place on the other side of Main Street. She didn't know much about the Batras family, only that they came to town about three times a year for a week. She knew them to see them although she hadn't had much chance to chat with the family. But she knew where they stayed. Ambrosia Falls was small enough that most anybody knew where most everybody lived, and she made her way close within a few minutes and surveyed the scene.

There wasn't as obvious a hiding place on this property, since the immediate area was more populated than the Williams place. The park across the street would be risky, but it would have to do.

She made her way to the top fort-like area of the slide, somewhat hidden by the heavy boards all the way around. She'd seen many a kid peeking through the boards, only their curious eyes in view, and now she was about to do the same thing. It was just unfortunate she wouldn't be able to place recording equipment here, since kids would no doubt be back as soon as the sun came up. As it was, she was lucky there were no teenagers hanging in the park that night.

After twenty minutes she was certain Justin was not there. She began to wonder if she had it wrong. Maybe he'd changed his ways, after all, or changed them up since he was dealing with someone who'd once known his routine—but she still had one more place to check.

Lawson's.

This property was the most rural of all, but Ava hadn't gone there first because it had been vacated for the least amount of time. The couple lived in town year-round and loved Ambrosia Falls, but they disliked when the tourists "took over the place." Honestly, they could give old Mr. Grumpy Pants Zach a run for his money when it came to complaining about tourists. They "got the hell outta Dodge," as they liked to say—as often as anyone would listen—the day before the tourists started arriving and were back the day after the festival ended.

Ava assumed Justin had been in town planning and scheming long before the first "strange" occurrence, which didn't seem so strange anymore. But maybe he'd been chomping at the bit and was doing things quickly as ideas presented themselves. It would be the best possible situation really, since it would mean he'd be sloppy, and sloppy was almost always what got a bad guy in trouble.

On foot again, Ava moved in closer to the Lawson residence, her hopes falling the closer she got. Justin would have to be reckless to use this place as his center of operations. It was too secluded, too surrounded by trees—he'd be far too exposed. There were a hundred places Ava could hide and he'd never have a clue she'd been there.

Still, she had to check.

Not worrying too much about where in the trees she settled, she quickly pulled out another set of recording devices and placed them on a tree branch where they wouldn't easily be seen by anyone who happened to be hiking, even though she assumed that didn't happen a whole lot, especially with the Lawsons away. She climbed a separate tree and got her infrared out, her stomach jolting when a very bright, and apparently very warm, figure flashed up on the digital screen.

Someone was most definitely home.

There was always a chance the Lawsons had come home early, but there was only one heat signature—exactly what Ava had been trying to find.

Still, she had to be sure. She was always thorough and didn't make many mistakes. This was not going to be the day that changed.

Her next plan was born when she saw the large rock about ten yards away. The moonlight was strong enough to discern the outline of the large boulder. When she was a kid, she would have loved it. There was something about giant rocks that made her feel like they needed to be climbed and sat on. Being seated on a piece of history, something that had been there for thousands of years felt powerful somehow, especially if it was just high enough not everyone would be able to climb it.

Since she wasn't a kid anymore, Ava didn't have as strong an urge to climb it, but she did wish it was a foot shorter so she could comfortably rest her sniper rifle on it for a stable shot. Then again, nature sometimes had a way of solving problems, and a few minutes later her rifle was planted on that rock, her feet balancing on a large fallen tree. It had taken most of her strength to shimmy over to the rock, but the result was worth it.

She'd have a clear line of sight, and if she could see without a doubt that it was Justin inside those walls, she'd have a clear shot too.

Then, as she gazed through the scope, her heart clenched.

The profile she hadn't seen in years, back to haunt her, as if in a waking dream. And then he turned, facing her fully. She was shocked at how brazen he was, how

open and careless he was being. He had essentially announced he was in town. It wasn't like him. Even if he
had never been as careful as she was, he'd never been
this easy to get to.

Something wasn't right.

But she would never get another chance like this. She
couldn't walk away without taking it.

Ava gave herself a few minutes to work through it
in her mind, coming at it from every angle, but could
not think of a single reason he would purposely be so
careless. Maybe he was losing his touch. Sometimes
she wondered if he ever had the operative's touch, often
wondering if he'd been paired with her back in the day
because she would ensure he'd be careful. He was always the brazen one, the one who wanted to charge in
without thinking everything through. She'd thought he'd
learned a thing or two from her, but maybe he'd gone
back to his old ways. His sloppy ways.

Whatever the case, the situation was as it presented
itself, and she would not waste this chance at saving the
life she'd created these past five years.

She rechecked the wind and stilled her body using
the breathing techniques she'd once used on the regular,
slowing her heart rate. Justin moved around the kitchen,
going from the stove to the fridge to the counter, clearly
making a late-night snack.

Still hardly able to believe he was exposing himself
the way he was, Ava went into Sparrow mode, clearing
her mind of all thoughts, her only focus on the chest
of the man inside the house. And then in her mind, the
man wasn't a man anymore. And he certainly wasn't

the man she'd once shared her life with. Shared every secret with. Almost.

He was only a target. It was the way she was able to get on with what she had to do. Depersonalize the situation. Make it a job. Compartmentalize.

One more slow breath in, and then out through her mouth so slowly, so still...only her finger moving ever so slightly.

The shot was quiet—the silencer doing its job. The only sound was glass shattering as the bullet hit the window and in the same moment, the target went down.

She got him straight to the chest, exactly as she'd intended.

Ava didn't smile. Tried not to think.

It was always that way after a hit. Emotions were tricky things in the moment, and she used all her energy to keep them pushed as far away as possible, focusing on the rest of the job. Putting away her equipment, making any sign of her having been there disappear.

Thankfully, the emotional distress only lasted a short while. Some kind of primal reaction that faded quickly if she didn't let it take hold. By the time she made it into the Lawson house, any residual pangs had wafted away. It was one of the reasons she was good at what she did. Had stayed human enough to stay on the right side— some operatives were apt to switch sides on a whim...or financial incentive—but detached enough to be able to sleep at night. She understood what needed to be done, and not everyone had the capabilities to do it.

Truthfully, she hadn't been sure she was still capable after living in the world she'd been living in the past five years, allowing herself to get close to people again, to let real emotions in again. But it was the same as it had ever been.

She eased into the Lawson house, quickly and quietly. In theory, there should be no one to be quiet for, but it had always been her way. Soft and quiet as a tiny bird, disturbing as little as possible.

She wouldn't be able to clean up completely—the broken glass of the window would stay, but she couldn't leave a body for the poor Lawsons to find. Though as she crept though the house, something felt wrong. She knew it immediately.

And as she moved into the kitchen where all she found was a disturbing lack of a dead body, her heart sunk. She grabbed for the firearm at her side, even as she knew there was no point.

She could feel it as surely as she felt her heart speed in her chest.

The Crow was long gone.

Chapter 8

Zach was at a loss.

He'd practically worn the finish off the patch of floor he'd been pacing for the past two hours, not knowing what to do, trying to convince himself there had to be a reasonable explanation for what he had seen.

Ava sneaking from her house—just an hour or so after she'd told him to his face that she was tired, implying she was headed to bed. And she should have been headed to bed considering she'd have to rise again at the crack of dawn, if not sooner, in order to start her baking for the festival guests.

But that was very much not what she had done.

Zach hadn't meant to be watching, but something in him was drawn to his windows that night, even after he'd turned his lights off and "gone to bed" too. He hadn't really gone to bed. All he'd done was tuck Chloe in, and then head to his room. Yes, he'd had intentions of turning in, but with all that had happened, there was no way in hell he was going to fall asleep anytime soon.

Still, he didn't want Chloe to worry, so he turned off his light and lay on his bed hoping by some miracle he'd actually drift off. But after lying there for a good fifteen minutes with thoughts rolling through his head, picking up speed as if they were on a runaway, downhill trajectory, he was even further from sleep than he had been when he lay down.

And then he heard the noise.

It wasn't a particularly loud noise, but it was very familiar.

For a moment he wondered if he was losing it. Had he fallen asleep and not realized it? Because what he heard was a sound he heard almost every day…but never until morning. Ava's garage door.

He checked the time on his phone.

Not quite midnight. Okay, so he wasn't losing it.

He got out of bed and moved the curtain a hair, just in time to see Ava's car backing out of her garage, down the driveway and out onto the street…all without turning on the headlights of the car.

Which was incredibly weird.

Because she wouldn't have anything to hide, right? And then, in a moment of extreme clarity, Zach realized she did have something to hide. She'd been acting weird ever since the kiss. And yeah, that kiss had changed everything, and maybe Ava was scared of what it meant—God, knew Zach was scared too—but Ava had never been one to hide from what worried her. She was more of a "get it all out in the open" kind of person—something that had given Zach more than his fair share of uncomfortable conversations.

Like the one he'd had the other night with her about Kimberly. The conversation he'd avoided like the plague for years. The one he knew would make him and Ava grow even closer because it was one of those "vulnerability moments," which he hated with the absolute breadth of his being, but apparently one that his subconscious was willing to have because maybe, just maybe, he was ready to move on. And damn it, if he was going to move on, he wanted to move on with Ava.

After Zach paced in his room for twenty minutes, a thousand scenarios running through his head with possible explanations for Ava sneaking out of her house in the middle of the night, he moved downstairs. Much more room to pace there.

But after another hour with no sign of Ava returning, he still hadn't come any closer to an explanation that made any sense.

Why would she feel like she had to sneak out? It wasn't like she answered to anyone, let alone Zach, who was likely the only person who might even notice her leave. He'd never ask that of her. But what was with the timing? All these years, he hadn't let himself go there, then lately, things had started to feel different. Like maybe he didn't have to be alone for the rest of his life. Like maybe, if he gave love another shot, it wouldn't have to end badly.

And then the kiss happened, and everything changed. Like the universe was confirming yes, finally, he could have something good without worrying it was all going to leave him. The kiss felt like a forever. Like everything in the world was clicking into place. Like he'd finally found a way to feel "right" when he'd always felt a little bit wrong somehow.

Zach could feel himself starting to spiral. The thoughts entering his mind barely even made sense anymore, but he was having about as much luck stopping them as he would stopping an avalanche with his bare hands.

He was also starting to feel a sense of panic, an urge to get out into the open air. The house was closing in on him. But there was Chloe to consider. She was usually a heavy sleeper and rarely woke up during the night, but if she did, he couldn't let her find the house empty.

He had an old baby monitor in her room, which he'd been meaning to get rid of for years, but just for one night, he could sneak in and turn it on. But then he'd risk waking her.

He could leave a note, he supposed. He paced some more, trying to think of what might happen if Chloe woke up. She'd probably be headed for the bathroom and then straight back to bed, which wouldn't be an issue. But if she woke up and came looking for him, he'd feel like the world's worst dad if she couldn't find him and thought she'd been left alone. If that was the case, she'd go straight to his room, so he quickly wrote a note saying he'd be out in the front yard.

At least out there, he'd have room to pace. Room for his thoughts to—well, to what, he wasn't sure, but he supposed he hoped they'd leave or work themselves out or something.

He wrote two more quick notes—one for the kitchen in case Chloe went for water, and one he taped to the inside of the front door, in case she somehow missed the other two notes and made it all the way to the point she would head out the door. It was definitely overkill, but he wasn't going to take any chances stressing his kid out.

Outside, the air was cool, and it suddenly felt like he could breathe again.

But the thoughts still swirled, spreading like wildfire, becoming increasingly more intense by the second.

One minute he was almost convinced Ava had just left to check on the stove or something at the coffee shop. The next he was in a full-blown panic imagining Ava being so disgusted by his kiss that she packed up and fled in the night, never to be seen again.

Unfortunately, he couldn't make any of the believable—or even a single one of the truly ridiculous—scenarios add up. It didn't make sense that she snuck out with no headlights if it was something innocuous, like checking the coffee shop, and, well, the wild scenarios didn't fit Ava. She wasn't a runner.

A brief thought flitted through his head. The way she arrived in town had been sudden and unexpected, and for the first time he wondered what the circumstances had been. It hadn't been so out of the ordinary that he thought anything of it at the time, but…could there have been something off about her late in the day arrival? Or the fact he never saw anyone take a look at the house next door before the moment she moved in. Was that a thing? Did people buy houses off the internet without going to see them in person? Seemed like a rash, irresponsible thing to do—and Ava certainly wasn't that. But still, he supposed it was possible.

He rolled a dozen more scenarios over in his head. Reasons someone might buy a house sight unseen. Running from a domestic situation, financial instability—but then, how would one afford a house?—evading the police…

They were all terrible. Unless there had been some sort of bidding war over the house. But he was sure he would have heard about it if there had been. Not to mention the local Realtor, Sandy St. James, was not particularly known for keeping secrets under wraps. Half the town would have kept him in the loop on that one. Hell, probably 99.8 percent of the town, considering it affected him directly, being next door and everything.

He was so lost in his thoughts, still pacing between his house and hers that it took him much longer than it should have to hear the crunch of the gravel on the street, nearing Ava's driveway. There was no way to run back across to his place without being seen, but he didn't particularly love the idea of being caught out there pacing in the middle of the night either.

Ava had made it clear she wasn't interested in being anything more than friends, and pacing in front of her house was a look that was a hell of a lot more stalkerish than Zach preferred.

In a panic, he strode up the steps of Ava's front porch, clinging to the shadows.

And the moment he got up there, he realized he was trapped.

She was still driving with no headlights, and worse, she was already out of the car to lift her garage door manually, he assumed, so it would make less noise.

There was no question. She was absolutely hiding something. Most likely from him.

And, even though his curiosity had never been so piqued, he wished, more than anything, he could disappear into thin air, just for a couple of minutes.

Ava drove into her garage, and Zach wondered if he should make a break for it. Unfortunately, by the time the thought could fully form, she was already coming back out of her garage to close the door again.

He skulked farther into the shadows, wishing he was

back to feeling as creepy as he had staring out the window earlier. Because his "I am such a creeper" factor had gone way up since then. It was shocking how easily he'd turned into an irrational being when all his life he'd been rational as hell.

Ava made her way across the short expanse of grass, then up the stairs, headed for her front door. Zach began to believe maybe, just maybe she would simply go inside and never know he'd been there at all, pleading to the heavens that if he were to escape this humiliation, he would never, ever do anything so stupid again in his life.

Her keys jingled as she reached toward the door, and Zach's heart began to soar. It was happening! He was going to make it out of there unscathed!

And then, in a final second of absolute horror, mixed with a hearty dose of confusion, a light burst on out of nowhere, throwing them both into a dizzying flash of movement and terror. Zach terrified of getting caught, but realizing poor Ava was probably in fear of her life.

Although, as he stared down the barrel of the gun she'd pulled out from somewhere in her jeans' waistband, so fast he'd barely even seen her move, perhaps she hadn't been quite as caught off guard as he thought.

In the split second that passed, Ava fully expected to see Justin's steely blue eyes staring back at her, but those eyes were not the frigid blue she anticipated at all. They were warm and kind and…well, truth be told, looking fairly terrified.

"Jesus, Zach!" Ava yelled, quickly lowering the gun and shaking it a bit, like it was hot and she could only touch it gingerly. "What the hell are you doing? I could have killed you!"

She was out of breath, her heart beating fast after being jolted into action. It was only thanks to her training that she'd taken the nanosecond before she blindly reacted and pulled the trigger.

So close. Way too close.

The thought of losing Zach was too much, but imagining it could have been her own fault made her instantly sick. She moved closer to the porch railing to lean on it, feeling rather unsteady on her feet.

Zach stood speechless for a bit, hands in the air like someone in a damn movie "stickup" scene or something. Slowly, he lowered his hands.

"Um, sorry." He cleared his throat. "Didn't mean to startle you," he said weakly, lowering himself into a nearby chair, looking a little shaky and a little green around the edges.

Ava leaned hard into the railing she'd been clutching, her adrenaline waning fast, suddenly feeling exhausted and wondering what time it was. It had to be at least two in the morning if not later.

"Zach, what are you doing on my porch in the middle of the night? In the dark," she added, to make sure she pointed out how weird it really was. Maybe to make herself feel better for pulling a gun on her best friend.

Who, she realized, after what had gone on earlier, and then over the past couple of minutes, was maybe not actually her best friend anymore.

Zach had been staring at his quaking hands and finally looked up, a little dazed. "Um… I," he said, and looked around like he was trying to come up with some kind of plausible explanation, but then his shoulders dropped, and he let out a long sigh. "This is going to sound dumb, but I was out here getting some fresh air."

"Some fresh air," Ava said, the doubt heavy in her voice. "On my porch."

"No. Well yeah, but…" Zach trailed off again.

"Zach," Ava said, moving to sit across from him. She needed to be at eye level. "Talk to me. What's going on?"

He looked into her eyes then, and Ava wanted nothing more than to close the two-foot gap and latch on to those soft lips again, but there was no way they could go there. Not ever again.

"I just—" he let out another short breath, like he was giving up on trying to make it look like anything other than it was "—I was out here pacing, okay?" he said. "I saw you."

Ava's brows furrowed together, her brain scrambling to figure out what, exactly, he had seen. Her stomach instantly seized, thinking the worst. What if he had seen her shoot at the Lawson house?

"I saw you leave. In the dark. With no headlights on."

Oh.

To his credit, the words weren't accusing, just had a sense of…hurt or something behind them.

"Zach, I—"

He held up a hand. "It's none of my business. And I have no business being here right now either. I don't know what I was thinking." He moved to stand.

"Zach," Ava said, her heart hurting, stretching as if it were trying to reach for him. She should let him walk away—it would be better…safer for everyone—but she couldn't do it. Couldn't leave him like that. Couldn't let him think whatever the hell he might be thinking about her. And the kicker was, it shouldn't matter what he thought. But right then, it was the only thing that *did* matter. "Can you please sit? I… I don't know if we can figure all this out, but can we at least try?"

Zach settled back into the seat and nodded.

Ava looked around, suddenly realizing they were exposed out there. "Where's Chloe?" she asked, trying to keep her voice steady.

"Sleeping," Zach said.

"Let's go over to your place and talk," Ava suggested. "I wouldn't want her to wake up not knowing where you are."

"Yeah, okay," Zach said, and there was still something unsure in his voice, almost zoned out.

Ava let Zach lead the way down the porch steps as she took a long look around, searching for any sign of movement—a flash of metal or glass in the moonlight, an out of place rustling of bushes—but she didn't sense anything.

She probably wouldn't even if there was danger. Justin was usually too good for that.

Which only sent her thoughts whirring again. Had he meant for her to see him back at the Lawson house? He had to have been wearing a vest to have gotten away. There hadn't even been any blood at the scene. Which meant what? Had he planned the whole thing and she'd completely fallen for it?

She felt like a damn fool. And the two of them absolutely, 100 percent, needed to get inside the house immediately and get the curtains shut.

Once inside, Zach seemed to get a little clearer, pulling some whisky out of the cupboard and pouring it into two small glasses while Ava shut the curtains.

"We should move to the living room," she said.

They'd be farther away from windows than at the kitchen table.

Zach didn't argue, just set the glasses down on the coffee table and put his head in his hands, pulling his fingers through his hair slowly before taking a sip from his glass and leaning back heavily into the couch.

After checking each window in the room, making sure everything was shut, locked and covered, Ava finally came to sit across from him.

"Ava, what's going on?" Zach asked. "Why do you have a gun?"

She knew it would be the question on his mind since the moment it had been pointed in his direction, and she couldn't blame him. Guns weren't especially common in the town of Ambrosia Falls, unless someone was using a toy one for a target practice game at the fair.

There was no way out of it, she decided. She was going to have to come clean.

Mostly.

She took a slow sip of the whisky, feeling every inch of the burn from her lips to her stomach, letting it take over and fill her with something, anything other than the dread of what she was about to say.

"When I came to Ambrosia Falls," she said, "it was because I was running from something. Well, someone, I guess."

Zach nodded, like he'd suspected her to say exactly that. He also looked like he was itching to jump in and ask a million questions, but he stayed quiet. Still.

So still it made Ava nervous, and she marveled at how often this man made her nervous. No one had ever done that to her before. No one had ever been so important.

"I was involved with a man," she began, hating how the damn story was already making her sound like a victim. She had never allowed that term to be something used to define her. But she sure as hell couldn't tell him the whole truth. She couldn't bear what he might think of her then. "He was great at first…you know how the story goes. And then he tried to hurt me, and he had powerful allies and so I was put into witness protection."

Zach's mouth opened slightly in surprise, but he remained quiet.

"And, as I'm sure you've guessed, after all these years, he's found me."

Finally, Zach spoke. "So, the fire. And the water tower? That was all…this guy?"

Ava nodded.

"Shit," he said. "He broke into your place."

Ava nodded. "Looks like it."

"And the police are on their way," he said. "Maybe."

"I wish we had never called them now," Ava said. "Knowing what we're up against, the police might be more in the way than they are of help. They'll think this is just some regular guy, not someone trained."

"Trained?"

Ava nodded. "Justin's…well, he's sort of an operative."

There was a pause that went on long enough to make Ava a touch queasy.

"Like CIA or something?"

"Kind of. He's more of an off-the-books kind of operative."

Zach let out a slow breath. "The kind that does the work the sanctioned operatives can't really get away with without certain people and agencies asking too many questions?"

"Exactly."

"So we have one of the world's most dangerous men after us? Here, in Ambrosia Falls?" His voice rose a bit at the end, and as much as Ava hated that she was freaking Zach out, it had to be one of the most adorable things she'd heard in a long time.

"He's not after us," Ava corrected. "He's after me. And I plan to fix that as soon as the sun comes up."

Zach looked a little panicked. "What does that mean?"

"Zach," she said, "I have to leave. It's the only way."

He shook his head, the panic morphing into a resolve that had Ava's heart melting faster than butter on a cooktop.

"No. You are not leaving. We've finally, I don't know, started to figure out what this is," he said, gesturing between the two of them, "and I'm not about to let that go."

A sting formed behind Ava's eyes. The last thing she wanted was to never be able to see it through with Zach, but there was no other way."

"I've already tried to fix it, Zach."

"What do you mean you've already tried?"

"I tried to find him. To take him out." She hated that the way he thought of her was probably changing by the second.

"Like kill him?" he asked, saying the last words in a whisper.

She sighed. "Yeah."

He ran his fingers through his hair. "Why the hell

would you do something so dangerous by yourself?" he asked, his eyes wild.

Ava contemplated coming clean. All the way clean. Contemplated filling him in on the fact that she was more lethal than Justin. That she'd had so many more years' experience behind her. Though that might not be true anymore, considering her experience had come to a standstill once she moved to Ambrosia Falls. She wondered what Justin had been up to since that fateful day five years ago.

"It's fine," she said. "I've learned to take care of myself."

"Well, you don't have to anymore."

"Of course I do, Zach. This is ridiculous. I'll go and everyone here will be safe. I wouldn't be able to live with myself if anything bad happened to the people here. Knowing it was my fault and I could have stopped it by leaving."

"You can't start over all over again," Zach said.

"I can," Ava replied. "I've done it before, and I can do it again."

"Well," he said, breathing hard. "Then I don't think I can start over all over again."

"Zach," Ava said, moving to turn away. She couldn't take the look in his eye. The one saying she meant everything to him. Of course, she only knew the look so well because the feeling was disastrously mutual.

Zach grabbed her arm and turned her gently to face him.

"Like it or not, it's not just you that you have to think about anymore. This town, all of us…we're your family now. And even if nothing more ever comes out of you and me, I'm your family now. You're my best friend, Ava. We're going to figure this out together."

Chapter 9

Strangely, Zach was relieved. He'd obviously known something was up, and the fact it had nothing to do with the kiss made everything okay again.

Well, maybe not everything, considering Ava's life was being threatened by a professional damn spy or whatever, but he'd be lying if he said he wasn't relieved all of it meant that he and Ava might still have a chance to be together.

"Maybe he's already on the run," Zach said. "If you tried to take him out."

Ava shook her head. "I think he knew I was coming. He must have had it all planned out. He's messing with me."

"Jesus," Zach said. "This guy is sick."

"And," she said, "he's not playing by his usual playbook."

"So, what now?" Zach asked.

"The smartest thing is for me to get out of here—"

"Stop," Zach said. "You aren't going anywhere. We just need to find a way to get the cops out here faster."

Ava shook her head. "That will put them in danger too. They won't understand how Justin is. He's smart. He's more dangerous than anyone they've come across before."

She gave him a serious look, like they should give up too, but Zach hadn't waited five years with a massive crush to let it go the exact day he finally decided to do something about it.

"Okay, so where would Justin go?"

Zach hated the way this guy's name sounded in his mouth—he'd honestly love to get his hands on this guy who'd hurt the most important person in his world—but he pushed the feeling aside. For now.

Ava sighed. "In the old days, he would find someplace nice. Someplace that wouldn't be roughing it too much. Let's just say Justin likes his amenities. I found him in the Lawson house."

Zach raised his eyebrows. "He was in Gus and Millie's place?"

Ava nodded.

"So are we looking for another place like that?"

"I doubt it. He knew I was coming. Had taken precautions."

"So he knew you'd know his regular routine and was counting on you coming after him."

"I guess so," Ava said. "I thought he'd be just cocky enough to stick with his routine."

"I'm surprised he'd even think you'd come after him like that."

"Um, yeah," Ava said, shifting a little, like she was uncomfortable.

Zach figured he'd be a little uncomfortable too if something like this suddenly sprung up from his past. And even though Ava was a victim, she thought she was safe and had finally let people back into her circle again. Had finally begun to trust again, and now her whole world was imploding.

And if he knew Ava at all—which he liked to think he did—she would even be a little embarrassed she hadn't been able to take care of it on her own. The woman was nothing if not fiercely independent. It was a quality he admired about her, a quality that, frankly, made him even more attracted to her, but at some point, she had to realize she didn't have to do everything on her own.

At least he hoped she would, since there was nothing he wanted more in the world than to take care of her in every way she'd let him.

He wasn't sure what the hell he was going to do once they found this guy, but he was anxious to make a plan and get it over with. More importantly, he was anxious to get on with his life with Ava. Assuming this whole thing with Justin was the reason she'd blown him off earlier.

Except…what if it wasn't?

Shit.

"Um, can we pause for a second and get something straight?" Zach asked.

"Um, sure?" Ava said, phrasing it like a question.

Zach stood and started to pace. Lord knew he'd done enough pacing for one night, but there was no way he could sit still and say what he was about to say. "Okay. So, the, um…" He cleared his throat and stopped pacing, turning to Ava. "The kiss."

Ava nodded once. "The kiss."

Zach's pacing resumed. "Yeah, so I'm just going to lay it all out there and say I don't actually think it was a mistake. And maybe you still do or whatever, or maybe you said it because of this Justin thing, but I thought we should, like, get on the same page about it."

He stilled. Turned. Looked at her, his heart filled with equal parts dread and hope.

Ava stared back. For what seemed like an impossible amount of time, though it might have only been a heartbeat. And then she smiled. A shy smile Zach had never seen on her—she was always the least shy person in the room—but somehow it made her look more like...herself.

Zach held his breath.

"I don't think it was a mistake either," she said.

Zach felt every speck of stress release from his body in a giant wave of relief, and for a moment, everything was right with the world. And then, knowing the seriousness of the situation they were in—a place where she could be taken from him at any moment—every muscle tightened up again almost as quickly as they had relaxed.

"Okay, good," he said, his voice serious. "Then we have to concentrate on getting this guy so we can, you know, do that some more."

Ava looked like she was working hard to hide a smile, and somehow almost even managed it. "Okay," she said. "Sounds reasonable."

"As reasonable as talking about taking out a guy can sound, I suppose," Zach said.

"Indeed," Ava agreed.

"Okay, so now that we have that out of the way," Zach continued, "I'm guessing this Justin asshole needs another place to hide out then."

"Probably," Ava said, deep in thought.

"Probably?" Zach asked.

"Yeah, but it doesn't matter where he is," Ava said, as she noticed the first traces of the rising sun break past the edges of the curtains in Zach's living room. "Because we're going to make him come to us."

Ava needed sleep badly, but a quick glance at her watch told her it was time to get up. Except she hadn't actually gone to bed. It was a damn good thing she worked in a coffee shop, because she was going to have to be mainlining the stuff for the rest of the day.

"What do you mean, he's going to come to us?" Zach asked.

"It's the one thing he won't expect," Ava said. "He's going to assume I'm either going to run or try to go after him again. And since he's been a step ahead of me this whole time, he'll probably continue being a step ahead of me. So we have to do the one thing he doesn't think we'll do."

"Which is…nothing?"

"Exactly. At least for now until I can work out a real plan. If there's anything I know, it's that plans made under duress or exhaustion are never as good as plans that have had plenty of time to be thought through."

"So, what…we just go about our day as usual?" Zach asked, looking slightly horrified.

"It's me he wants, and I know how to be careful," Ava said.

"There is no way I'm going to let you out of my sight for a second," Zach countered.

Ava only rolled her eyes a little. "You're going to have to let me out of your sight for at least a second. Like, for example, when I go home in a few minutes to shower and change."

His lips twitched up into a half grin. "I mean, are you sure you don't need any supervision for those, um, difficult tasks?"

The thought of Zach watching her shower sent a thrill through Ava's body, but she managed to keep the crimson of her face tempered. "I'm pretty sure I can manage," she said, though she gave him a little smirk back that hopefully said once all this was over, she might be game for some sudsy supervision.

"Okay, I'll let you go get ready for the day, and I'll do the same over here, but you have to stay on the phone with me the entire time."

"Don't you think that's a little overkill?" Ava asked.

"Do I think it's overkill to take the absolute minimum amount of precaution when we know there is a trained killer after you? One which you've recently poked like a damn bear, except instead of just poking him you actually shot him?" He raised his eyebrows as if waiting in great anticipation for her answer.

"Um, okay. You have a point," she reluctantly agreed. "Even though I still don't think he'll do anything."

"But that's what I don't get. Why don't you think he won't do anything?"

Ava shifted. "Because he's toying with me. The water tower, the fire, the pictures he left on my doorstep…" She decided not to let Zach in on the fact that the pictures had actually been left right there in the room while they were busy making out. "I'd bet my life he's not done yet. He has a plan, and if there's one thing I know about Justin, it's that he will not be satisfied unless his plan is acted out to perfection. It's why we're taking today to regroup and do nothing. It's going to drive him to a tizzy wondering what the hell we're up to."

"I gotta say, it's probably not going to be a tizzy-free kind of day for me either," Zach admitted.

"I know. It's going to be tense. But we'll be on alert and make the best of it for now. If we get any time to ourselves at the coffee shop, we'll think about what our next steps will be—maybe even get a chance to talk them through."

Zach nodded. "I don't like it, but I'll agree to your plan."

"Good," Ava said, turning to head to the door.

"I just have one more question."

She turned back and he grinned.

"Would it be okay if I kiss you?"

Ava couldn't stop the smile from creeping across her face. "Um, sure," she said, cool as ever even though her mind was screaming *yes, yes, yes!*

He stepped toward her, then slowed, grabbing hold of her arms lightly, his hands shaking a little.

"I'm so nervous," he said, then let out a little chuckle.

She laughed a little too, her insides vibrating—the excited feeling that made a person shiver as if they're cold. "I'm still me," she said, though the idea made her feel guilty. She was still hiding so much from him.

"I know, that's why I'm so nervous," he said, his face inching closer until finally his lips met hers and she let out a tiny sighing moan, relief flooding over her.

Strange that relief was the sensation she felt, though she supposed she'd been building the moment up for so many years, and then there was the whole roller coaster of the day—yesterday now, she supposed—making every emotion hover so close to the surface that none of them would really be a surprise. Grieving the idea of losing Zach only moments after it felt like she really found him, and then the hope blooming again...it was all so much. And she knew she couldn't quite trust any of it.

Justin had to be dealt with first.

But Ava was determined to savor the kiss, trying like hell to burn it into her mind and make it last forever. But it's funny what the brain did when those moments were happening though. Almost the precise second a person decided they wanted to really remember something because it's so damn good, or delicious, or perfect, that betraying brain tended to check out like a traitor, making the moment fog up and become hazy, leaving only a vague whispery essence of the real thing. It was why Ava knew she would crave that kiss forever.

The kiss was soft, not as urgent as the one in the coffee shop, but still, it felt familiar. Not because it was their second kiss, but because it felt like Zach. This had been exactly the way she'd imagined being with him would be. Sure. Steady. Gentle, but strong at the same time. Where the first kiss had been a whirlwind, a frenzy, this one felt a whole lot like being safe.

Of course, brains didn't only betray with memory, but with recollection too. And again, with its precise timing, the moment even the idea of safe popped into her mind, she immediately remembered how very unsafe things were right then.

She pulled gently out of the kiss, reluctantly blinking back into the room.

"Well, that's a good start to the day," Zach said with a grin, his arms still around her.

She smiled and nodded. "It definitely is."

"Okay," Zach said, taking a step back, which only made Ava want to take a step forward to close the gap again. He pulled out his phone and started typing, and while Ava was still trying to figure out what he was doing, her own phone started vibrating.

She hit the button to answer. "Am I supposed to say hello?" she asked, smirking.

"No, you don't have to talk. Go get ready like you normally would. Just don't go out of reach of the phone."

"Got it," Ava said, nodding, then headed to the door and straight out, turning only to wave her phone in Zach's direction, letting him know she would keep it by her side.

Outside, Ava scanned the area for threats. If Justin was out there and had a scope on her, there was little she could do. But not seeing anything obvious, she made her way back to her place, thinking about what she'd said to Zach.

She didn't know if what she said was true—about how Justin wouldn't do anything rash because he was still toying with her. Hell, she'd shot him, riled the bear, and frankly had no idea what he'd do now—Justin had never been known for being the calmest agent out there, but she didn't have a plan and needed time.

And in the meantime, she would keep a closer watch on this town than anyone ever had before.

Chapter 10

If Zach thought the bell over the door at The Other Apple Store had been bad before, it was absolutely driving him up the wall now. Never in his life had his senses been on such high alert, and he was suddenly suspicious of everyone, even people he'd known all his life. Which was ridiculous, but it wasn't like he could make the feelings go away.

And since it was the Apple Cider Festival, that damned bell kept chiming almost nonstop. A group of women would come in, and Zach would be suspicious of them, even though he knew Justin was a guy. A senior couple strolled in, and he'd be suspicious of them too. What if Justin had coconspirators of the geriatric variety? A family of four strolled in and Zach was especially suspicious...like seriously, why weren't those kids in school? Did we all just take our kids to random towns in the middle of the school year now? *Come on, people!*

The worst part was, he knew he was being ridiculous, but he couldn't help it. This thing with Ava was too important. He couldn't risk anything happening to it before it even got started. If they didn't see it through, he'd always wonder. And then his thoughts turned to the kiss that morning. It had been so different from the one yesterday. Maybe there hadn't been as many sparks flying as with the first one, but Zach kinda loved that. Because he knew sometimes their life could be full of passion, sometimes full of friendship, and sometimes simple appreciation and love. It was the perfect blend...much like the perfect cup of coffee, he thought, as Ava walked up and jolted him out of his daydream.

"Whatcha thinking about?" she asked.

"Um, nothing," Zach said, bringing the cup to his lips a little too quickly and sloshing coffee over the edge of the cup, thankfully missing his clothes by about a millimeter.

"Yeah." Ava nodded. "I've been thinking a lot about, um, nothing too," she said, and even shot him a wink before she moved on to the next table.

Cripes, Zach thought. Here he was daydreaming when he was supposed to be figuring out a plan to save the love of his life.

Wait. Love of his life? Was that what Ava was? No, it was way too early to know for sure. Of course, when does anyone ever know for sure, really?

Damn it! He was doing it again.

He shook all thoughts out of his head and concentrated only on finding a plan. A way to find this guy. A guy he didn't have even the slightest clue what he looked like, what he sounded like...nothing. Zach's shoulders slumped.

He'd never felt so helpless in his whole life.

The jingle of the bells above the door interrupted his thoughts for the thirty-eight millionth time. A man, all alone, which was suspicious for the festival. Most people came with their family, or a group of friends, usually the ladies, or with someone who had newly become special to them. The Apple Cider Festival was nothing if not "the perfect weekend date destination," as the regional papers loved to tout.

Zach watched him closely. The man could have ducked into the coffee shop while his wife and kids were off bobbing for apple-themed prizes or perusing the local apple butters and honeys. Lord knew it was exactly what Zach would be doing if he was forced to attend some weird town's festival against his will.

But the man wasn't looking like he was having a crappy time. In fact, he looked downright cheerful, which Zach would have loved to say was strange, but in this town, cheer was basically the religion. The damn guy looked like he fit in perfectly, which was just so annoying. But Zach was used to pushing little annoyances out of the way, so he decided to give the guy the benefit of the doubt. Who knew, maybe the poor guy was just happy not to be stuck in some work cubicle for the day.

The man gave his order of coffee and an apple fritter—a little basic, but a solid order nonetheless—to Maureen, who was manning the counter while Ava no doubt created some delectable concoction in the back.

Zach pretended to be engrossed in his computer screen as the man sat, choosing the table directly across from him so they were facing each other.

Zach could never understand this move. Why, of all the places in a restaurant or café, would someone choose to sit staring straight at another human? Talk about awkward. He supposed some people did it on purpose, since they loved to chat with strangers…another thing he couldn't figure out. Ava would love it, Zach thought, then suddenly realized that could be a real benefit to him once they were officially together, since she could be the one to field all the awkward "people encounters."

Zach pretended to work for a while, keeping a keen eye on the stranger across from him, even though he'd pretty much decided the guy was harmless. Of course, it wouldn't hurt to know for sure, so he decided to take a sip of coffee, which he'd been avoiding since it would mean taking his eyes off his screen and potentially engaging with those around him, including the man in question. Which, if he was trying to glean any kind of information—like whether he was a cold-blooded, murderous spy—it would probably be the quickest and easiest way. Well, quickest, anyway. There was nothing easy about talking to strangers in Zach's book. He moved his cup to his lips and took a long sip, gazing all around until finally his eyes landed on the man.

"You look pretty deep in thought there," the man said the literal second Zach acknowledged his presence.

Zach had known it. The man had been waiting all along to talk to someone. Which Zach always thought of as kind of insulting, since it wasn't Zach this person was particularly interested in talking to—he could have been absolutely anyone in the world and this man would have been perfectly happy. Like, if you're perfectly fine talking with just anyone, it had to mean you really only wanted to hear yourself talk, right?

"Um, yeah, I guess so," Zach answered.

"Got a deadline?" the man continued. "I assume you must be a writer by trade if you're working that hard in the middle of a Wednesday," he said, grinning.

At least, Zach thought, it wasn't a goofy grin. The guy seemed like a normal guy.

"Uh, no deadline. Well, at least not yet," Zach answered. "Just kicking around a few ideas, seeing what they might turn into."

"Nice," the man said. "I used to write. Wasn't as good at it as I wanted to be, unfortunately."

Zach knew the feeling well. He was pretty sure every writer knew the feeling, really, and after the little nugget of common ground, he found he was the one who was suddenly asking questions. "What did you write?"

The man shrugged. "Nonfiction stuff mostly." He grinned. "The problem was the research. I hated the research. So much time spent feeling like you're not actually accomplishing anything even though you're laying the groundwork, or whatever."

Zach tilted his head back and forth in agreement. "Yeah, not my favorite either. Although there's still some research involved in fiction."

"Ah, fiction. Yes, that's true I suppose," the man said. "But it's not all research, all the time."

"So, were you a journalist then?" Zach asked, finding he was actually enjoying chatting with the guy.

"Educational books," he said. "And then creating online courses for schools after that."

"Interesting," Zach said. "Sounds like it would require a lot of—"

"Research," they both said at the same time, then shared a small chuckle.

"Nothing against the educational sector," the guy said, "but lately I've been craving something a bit more creative."

Zach nodded. "So what's next then?"

"Well, I don't know, to be honest. I've been toying with the idea of a novel."

"Also not easy work," Zach said, "but it is rewarding...mostly."

"I bet," the guy said, a bit of a gleam in his eye now.

"Tell you what," Zach said. "Why don't you we exchange numbers, and if you do decide to take that route, let me know. I'm happy to lend a hand where I can." Writing was such a solitary practice, and could be discouraging, especially when starting out. If he hadn't had the help of a few key people early on in his career, he never would have gotten to where he was. He liked to pay it forward whenever he got the chance...as long as it wasn't someone who seemed like they were going to take advantage. Which, by now, he could usually spot a mile away. But this guy seemed genuine enough.

"That's very generous of you," the man said, pulling out his phone.

Zach did the same and they exchanged electronic business cards. "'Glen Abrams,'" Zach said, reading the info aloud.

Glen nodded. "The listing has my previous educational work info attached, but the number's still the same. This way, you'll have a better chance at remembering who I am down the road." He stood and moved closer to Zach's table, holding out his hand.

Zach stood and took it. "Perfect," he said.

"Well, I better get going," Glen said. "The wife's probably out there figuring a way to convince me we need to move out to the country," he said. "Not that I don't love the country, but I think I'm more of a city guy."

"Fair enough," Zach said, thinking he wished there were a few more guys as down to earth as he was in this world.

Ava's stomach seized, her lunch threatening to make an encore appearance as she stood in the shadows watching Zach shake hands with the man who wanted to kill her.

Had tried to kill her and was back to finish the job.

The moment their hands touched, a lightning bolt of clarity shot through her.

What the hell was she doing?

Every moment…every second she stayed in town was another moment she was putting the people she cared about at risk.

How could she have been so careless? She should have been packing the moment she discovered she hadn't taken Justin out back at the Lawson house.

She knew Justin would try something else to mess with her—that he wanted nothing more than to make her suffer the way he must believe he'd been suffering for the past five years—but she didn't think he'd go after the people around her. Not the ones closest to her. Sure, he put people in danger with the water tower and the fire, but those were simply potential innocent casualties—something Justin never cared enough about.

But she was the Sparrow, trained not to get close to people. Trained to easily walk away the moment it was time. Trained to never let her feelings get in the way.

Of course, if Justin had been watching her for any length of time, a thought making her intensely queasy all over again, he would know she'd dropped that notion a long time ago. Longer than she was even willing to admit to herself.

Worse, it was the reason she was still in town when she should have been long gone.

And she'd bet her life Justin had known exactly what he was doing. He knew the moment the people who were really in her life were threatened—something that happened simply by being in the same room with Justin—she would have no choice but to leave.

He was smoking her right out of her town. Right out of her new life.

She wanted to drop everything and go, just turn around, walk right out the door of that kitchen and never look back. But that wasn't how the town of Ambrosia Falls worked. In about two minutes flat, someone would wonder where she'd gone. And about one minute later, someone would ask Zach if he'd seen her. And then he would come after her. She wouldn't even have a chance to pack the essentials—namely the supplies and weapons she had stashed in various corners of her house—before he'd be on her. Telling her she couldn't go. Telling her they were in this together. Telling her all the things that terrified her to her core.

Because they could not be in this together. Not really. Zach was a capable guy, but he wasn't trained like she was...or like Justin was. He wouldn't stand a chance out there. And she couldn't deal with him out there either. She'd be far more worried about protecting Zach than she'd ever be for herself. She didn't know what she'd do if something ever happened to Zach.

She could never live with herself.

A plan quickly formed in her head. She hated when

plans came so easily. The easy plans were usually only easy because there was a lack of options. And this time, she only had one option—run—and Justin knew it as well as she did.

The afternoon went by quickly. Too quickly.

Ava was going back and forth in her mind about how to say goodbye to Zach. Imagining not saying goodbye to him was inconceivable but telling him she was leaving was not a choice either. He'd try to talk her out of it, or worse, try to follow her.

The only thing she could do was sneak away in the night, being far more careful this time to make sure he wouldn't see her leave. When she'd first arrived in town all those years ago, she'd made several contingency plans, and she still had a beat-up old Chevy truck in storage across town. She'd have to pack up the things she needed and make her way there on foot. It wouldn't be easy, since she wanted at least a few days' worth of supplies, but she'd been in worse situations.

If luck were on her side, maybe Justin wouldn't catch on about her other mode of transport right away. He'd know she was gone in the morning—right along with everyone else in town and probably within a twenty-five-mile radius too—but half a day's head start might be the best she could do. Especially if Justin didn't know what she was driving or which direction she'd gone.

Still, she couldn't leave without saying something to Zach. She couldn't be that cruel.

Around the time Zach packed up his stuff and was heading out to get Chloe from school, the idea of a letter came to her. And if she left it in his mailbox, he wouldn't see it until he checked for the mail in the morning, or hopefully longer. It would be perfect. She'd be long gone, and he wouldn't have too much of a chance to worry.

Then, of course, her thoughts started churning over what to write. It wasn't like she could just be all like, thanks for everything, byeee! Ugh.

But how could you tell someone how much they meant to you in one little letter? She hoped he already knew—at least somewhat—how large a role in her life he'd come to play, but she was sure he didn't fully understand how much he meant to her. He couldn't understand that he was everything, and everything was something she'd never even come close to before.

She had closed herself off her entire life, even with Justin, she realized. Coming to Ambrosia Falls she'd seen how the real world could be—simple, even if it wasn't easy, and filled with a comfort she had never known before.

It was like the town—and Zach—had woken her from a hazy dream world and, for the first time in her life, filled everything with color.

After the rush of folks buying their breads and desserts to take home for dinner, Ava locked up the store the same way she did every evening. She didn't take anything extra with her—everything she would need was back at her place. Her supplies were mostly ready to go. She just needed to gather them all from their hiding places around her house, then slip out into the night. Fingers crossed she'd be unseen, by Justin and, most especially, by Zach.

She drove home and parked her car in the garage like she always did, then went into the house and texted Zach first thing.

Hey, I'm home, but I'm beat. It was an easy excuse, considering neither of them had gotten any sleep the night before. I've double-checked all the doors and windows and have the security system on. Gotta get some sleep. Have a good night.

Short, sweet, and just familiar enough he wouldn't get suspicious. Even though everything had changed between them in the past couple days, they'd never texted each other anything more intimate than the sort of message she'd just written, so she hoped it would work.

A minute later, her phone dinged with a text.

Me too. Please be careful. See you in the morning.

You be careful too, she typed, feeling a twinge of guilt at the see you in the morning part.

She avoided the letter writing as long as she could, going around the house and collecting only the essentials—small weapons she could easily carry, food supplies meant for backwoods camping, a couple changes of clothes and a second pair of sturdy shoes in case the whole thing went south, and she had to make her way on foot. The final things she packed were various forms of ID—with several different aliases—and some thick rolls of cash she'd been slowly adding to each week over the years.

And then it was time. She set her bag by the back door and sat down at her kitchen table with a pen and paper. She'd gone back and forth all day about what to write, finally deciding she owed it to Zach to lay it all out there. Not the stuff about her history or why Justin was so focused on her, but about the way she felt.

Dear Zach,

By the time you see this letter, I'll be gone. Long gone, I hope. But I couldn't leave without saying goodbye. I know I'm robbing you of your chance to say it back, and I'll forever be sorry for that, but I couldn't figure out any other way.

I had to go. I love you and Chloe too much to keep putting you in danger.

You might notice I used the word *love*. And I want you to know I don't mean it in the way you love your parents or your friends. Yes, you are my best friend, but I also want you to know I've been madly, head over heels in love with you for years. Maybe since the moment I laid eyes on you. The problem was, I didn't really know what love was. I'd never let myself have that before, and I guess I kind of thought I'd go the rest of my life without it.

I haven't told you everything about my past, but what you need to know is this: you were the reason I kept going. This interesting guy next door. The one who was so good with his kid, the one the whole town loved despite his efforts to push them all away, the one everyone knew they could count on. The one who made the days go by effortlessly, the one who gave me the inspiration for my recipes, the one who, without my even realizing it, was the reason I did everything I did.

Because that's who you are, Zach.

The one.

I thought love was something you *let* happen to you. I didn't know it could come along and hit you over the head, forever changing you whether you liked it or not. I was arrogant. I didn't think I could ever be touched by the big L word. But I was 100 percent wrong, and it's fine if you don't feel the same way back—in fact, I *hope* you don't, because leaving is going to be the hardest thing I've ever done and I do not want that for you.

I never want you to hurt. I never want Chloe to hurt.

Which is, of course, the very reason I have to go.

This whole town has stolen my heart, but the biggest chunk of it will always be set aside for you. Never change, Zach. Knowing your kind, incredible, grumpy self is still out there living, breathing, thriving, will be the only thing that continues to keep me going.

Kiss Chloe for me and please, do everything you can to live your best life.

With my love forever,

Ava

Ava didn't realize she was crying. She had to move. She had to keep the important people safe.

She decided to leave the letter in Zach's mailbox. With any luck he wouldn't think to check the box for a few days. The only tricky part would be getting it there without him noticing. Unfortunately, Zach liked to watch out his kitchen window. She knew this because she was also a watcher, and now that she thought about it, her watching was aimed way too often at Zach's house. She would sit several feet back from the window, so anyone glancing over wouldn't immediately see her, and watch him standing at that kitchen sink lost in thought.

But he wasn't there now.

It might be her only chance. Every part of her screamed to put it off, but she might not get another shot. She had to go now, before she lost her nerve.

She stuffed the letter in an envelope, scribbled his name on it, checked the window facing Zach's one more time and snuck quietly out her front door, stepping carefully to make as little noise on the gravel as possible. It had never bothered her that the mailboxes were all the way at the street before. It wasn't much of an inconvenience to walk the thirty or so steps to retrieve the mail, but in that moment, the distance seemed like miles.

She reminded herself to breathe as she moved. That was the thing about sneaking...your instinct was to hold your breath, which was, of course, the worse thing a person could do when trying to be quiet. Finally, she made it, pulling the mailbox open slowly. It squeaked a little, but she slipped the metal flap shut and turned back toward her house.

A few more steps and she'd be home free.

Which was precisely when the door to Zach's house burst open and he came flying down the stairs, a look of pure panic on his face.

"Zach?" she said, and as he ran toward her, the terrible empty feeling of having to leave morphed into something else. Something along the lines of nauseated terror. "What's wrong?"

"She's gone," he said, out of breath, jumpy and looking like he was on the verge of tears. "Chloe is gone."

Chapter 11

"Okay, let's not panic," Ava said, though it made it a hell of a lot harder for Zach not to panic when Ava looked like she was about to panic too.

His mind swirled. How could he have let this happen? He knew there was a dangerous person in town, and he hadn't even thought to make sure his daughter was by his side at all times? What was wrong with him? Sure, he'd grown up in this lazy small town his whole life and had literally never seen anything dangerous happen. There'd been some tragedies, of course. Accidents and weather-related catastrophes no one had seen coming. But the thought someone could do something to hurt the people of Ambrosia Falls on purpose…it didn't seem real.

Except he had known there was a threat. He should have been more vigilant.

Thought he had been, to be honest, though he supposed he didn't have it in him to think like a bad dude and had been so focused on keeping Ava safe he would never, in a million years, have thought Chloe was in danger.

"Let's get inside," Ava said, glancing around in a way Zach did not like.

He couldn't give two shits about his own well-being, but at least had the presence of mind to know he couldn't help Chloe if he became incapacitated somehow, so he let Ava lead him up his front steps and into the house.

"Are you certain she's gone?" Ava asked, guiding Zach to a kitchen chair. "Like, does she have any hiding places or anything?"

Zach shook his head. "She's never really been a hiding kind of kid."

Ava started to pace. "What about friends? Would she sneak out to go see anyone, do you think? Was she mad about anything?"

"Mad?" Zach asked, putting his elbows on the table and leaning his head in his hands. He was having trouble catching any of the thoughts pummeling through his head.

"Like, did you guys get in a fight or anything?"

He looked up from his hands. "What? No. We weren't fighting. We had a normal dinner, the same as we do every day, and then she went upstairs to finish some homework. She was working on some big project for science class or something."

"So, she was up there for a while," Ava said.

Zach nodded. "At least I thought she was." He put his head back in his hands. "Oh God," he said, his voice strangled.

"Did you hear anything during the time she was up there?"

Zach shook his head. "Nothing. Which maybe should have clued me in? But I thought she was sitting at the desk in her room working. It's not like she would normally be roaming around or anything. And then I went to check on her and she was just…gone…" he said, his voice trailing off.

"Okay, so is it possible she could have simply come downstairs and headed out without you knowing?"

"She's never done anything like that before," Zach said. "I mean, she walks to her friends' houses all the time, and to Mom's, but she's always told me where she was going."

"Maybe she forgot this time," Ava said, and Zach could tell the hope in her voice was false, even if it did inject a tiny spurt of it into him too.

"I guess. I mean, it would be the world's worst timed coincidence, considering all the other stuff going on around town and what's going on with…you," he said, not sure how else to say what he was thinking.

That this was no coincidence at all.

"I agree," Ava said, "but we have to cover all our bases, right? It's the smart thing to do."

"I have to get out there. Start searching," Zach said, getting up from the table and starting to pace along with Ava.

"But," Ava said quietly, "search where?"

Zach stopped midstep. It hadn't occurred to him it might be pointless to rush out of the house and start randomly driving around. Where would he go? What would he do? And now that it was dark out, how would that even work? "Well, I have to do something," he said, trying to keep the anger out of his voice, though it wasn't working.

"I think we should at least call around to make sure she hasn't gone to a friend's house or your mom's or something before we jump to conclusions. I agree the

timing is terrible, and we have to consider all the possibilities, but this is at least a place to start."

Zach swallowed hard, not liking any of it one bit.
But he didn't have any other ideas. At least not any rational ones.

"So let's call around and see if anyone knows where
she is. Just casually, you know, so more people don't get
freaked out," Ava said. "Because if this is who we think
it might be, we're going to want to keep this as simple as
possible. We can't have all the people in town freaking out
and getting in the way if we need to move to a plan B."

"Yeah, okay," Zach said.

At least it was something to do. There was absolutely
no way he could do nothing. He just wasn't sure how
he was supposed to keep the fear out of his voice as he
called around.

An hour later Zach's panic was going into full-blown
freak-out mode. No one had seen Chloe. Deep down,
he'd known all along they wouldn't get anywhere with
the calls, but they had to try.

"At least we managed not to freak anyone out, I guess,"
he said.

"I'm so sorry, Zach," Ava said, her eyes red as much
from emotion as from exhaustion.

"It's not your fault," Zach said.

He wanted to be angry at Ava. To be mad she ever
came to this town and put all of them in this position,
though of course he couldn't be. She had been a victim
in all this as much as anyone. More than anyone. She
was the innocent bystander who did nothing besides
being in the wrong place at the wrong time and getting
involved with the wrong dude. And Zach knew a little

something about getting involved with the wrong person. A person who turned out not to be who he thought they were at all, so he could hardly get mad at Ava for doing the same thing.

"This is definitely my fault," Ava said, a tear falling.

She looked like she was about to crumple, but Zach couldn't let that happen. He needed her to keep it together. Because if Ava fell apart, there was no way he wasn't going to follow.

"Nope," he said, putting his arms around her and pulling her close. "First of all, this isn't your fault. This is all shit you had no control over. You are not putting all this on yourself. And second, you simply can't go down that rabbit hole because I need you to keep me calm. If we both lose it, we have no chance. We have to keep it together for Chloe."

Ava pulled in a deep breath and nodded. "You're right. I'm just going to put all these feelings aside and deal with them later."

"Yup, we will deal with them later," he said. "Okay, so what's next?" he asked, as they broke apart from the hug.

"I'm not sure what we can do before the sun comes up," Ava said, making panic flash though Zach's eyes again. She put her hands up. "I'm not saying we're going to do nothing—I'm just saying things are going to be limited."

"I'm not going to sit here all night," Zach said.

"I know. I'm going to go upstairs and check Chloe's room, see if there are any clues there."

"Right, okay. I'll go check outside, under the window of her room—see if there's anything there," he said, heading for the door.

But before he got two steps out of the house, something stopped him cold.

An envelope—bright white contrasting against the dark porch floor.

"Ava," he called before she got too far away. "I think I found something."

This was 100 percent her fault. It killed her to keep the real her a secret from Zach, especially with everything going on, but she couldn't come clean now. If she did, Zach would hate her, which she could live with, but she couldn't live with anything happening to Chloe. She needed Zach to trust her, to work with her, for their best chance at getting Chloe back.

She was halfway up the stairs when he called to her, his hands shaking as he turned toward her with an envelope in his hands.

Ava's stomach seized.

Zach came back into the house in a daze, shutting the door absently.

"Do you want me to open it?" Ava asked.

She wanted to be the one to handle whatever was going to be inside that envelope. She was trained to preserve evidence, to keep her cool no matter what the contents might be. But Chloe was Zach's daughter, and she had no right to be the first to see, even if this was about her in the end. Right now, all that mattered was Chloe. And Zach.

Ava cringed as Zach ripped into the envelope, thinking about all the things that could happen. There could be a dangerous substance, or worse, some kind of explosive even though the envelope appeared to be flat from where she stood.

Zach pulled a photo from the envelope, and Ava rushed over, praying it would be proof of life and not something much, much worse.

She let out a breath when Chloe's scared, but very much alive face looked back from yet another instant camera print.

"It's proof of life," Ava said quickly. "It means she's okay."

"Okay?" Zach said, his voice hitching. "She's tied up. There's a gag in her mouth."

"I know. And that's obviously bad, but it's not Chloe he wants."

"She looks so scared," Zach said, running his finger along Chloe's face in the picture.

"We're going to get to her," Ava said. "We just need to find out where he's keeping her, and I'll surrender. He'll hand Chloe to you and this will all be over. Easy peasy," Ava said.

"That is not easy peasy," Zach said, an angry edge to his voice. "I'm not going to hand you over to this guy."

"It's the best option, Zach," Ava said, and she meant it.

She would do anything to save Chloe, and if that meant the end of herself, so be it.

"I don't care about easy," Zach said. "I care about getting Chloe back *and* keeping you safe."

Ava waved away his comment. "Whatever, either way we need to figure out where this is," she said, poking at the photo, "and get to her."

Zach flipped the picture over. *Don't even think about the cops, Sparrow.*

"Sparrow?"

"It's, uh, what he used to call me," she said, hoping he wouldn't ask too many questions.

"This guy is getting weirder and weirder," Zach said. "Although he clearly didn't do his research if he thinks cops are going to be a problem around here."

Ava took the picture from Zach to study it closer, starting to pace, hoping it would help her think.

"If he wants you to come and find her," he asked, "why doesn't he just tell us where she is? You'd think he'd have had plenty of time to set up traps for us or whatever."

Ava shrugged one shoulder. "That's not how Justin works. He only feels powerful when he's playing people. When he's messing with their minds."

"Is that what he's doing to Chloe?" Zach asked, with something wild behind his eyes.

Ava shook her head quickly. "I don't think he'll hurt her. Not if we do what he says. I mean, I don't think it's impossible, but Chloe isn't who he's after. He's doing this to hurt me."

"Okay, I get that, but how in the hell are we supposed to find her from this?" Zach asked, pulling the photo right out of Ava's hand, which, given the circumstances, Ava wasn't going to fight him on, no matter how much she needed to study it and hope for a clue.

"He must think we'll be able to figure it out somehow," she said.

Suddenly Zach stopped. "This was taken in the daylight."

Ava moved beside him, close enough so they could both see. "Right, I didn't even think of that. So if she was still here for dinner, that doesn't leave much of a time frame for it to still be light out. What time did you eat?"

"It was late. I cooked a roast, which always takes a while, but it's Chloe's favorite."

"So we're looking at a window of like, two hours, tops."

"Which means she can't be far, right?" Zach said, a tiny sliver of hope trickling into his voice.

"Yeah, if he got her to this...whatever this is," Ava said, motioning to the photo, "and then came back here again so quickly, it was only about an hour that we were making calls before we found the envelope."

"Jesus," Zach said, running his fingers hard through his hair. "I just realized this asshole was right here. We could have had him." Zach raced back to the front door and whipped it open.

Ava wasn't sure if he was expecting to find Justin right there on his doorstep, or what, but she knew he was long gone. Justin didn't take chances. He likely would have waited until he had a full view of the two of them to risk creeping up to the door. He was good at what he did. Damn good.

Ava just hoped she was still better.

Zach shut the door again and threw out a string of curses that would make a sailor blush.

"We should try to get some sleep," Ava said.

At a time like this, it was unlikely to happen, but she knew from experience sleep would make everything so much easier and the likelihood of success much greater.

"We can head out as soon as the sun starts coming up."

Zach flopped onto the couch and let out a half-hearted chuckle. "I can't see how there's any way I could sleep knowing Chloe is out there, scared and alone."

"I know," Ava said, "but we should try anyway. We'll be better for helping Chloe that way."

"We don't even know where we're going," Zach said.

"We'll figure it out."

"How though? We have no idea where to start." He held up the photo of Chloe. "This could be pretty much anywhere."

"We'll find her," Ava said, with as much confidence as she could muster.

"You don't know that. You can't know that," Zach said, a hint of anger breaking through the fear in his voice.

"I do know it," Ava said. "Because I know you, and I know me. And we aren't going to stop until we do."

Zach slumped his shoulders and nodded. Ava knew his mind would be reeling all night. She glanced at her watch. It was about five hours until the sun came up again.

And it would be the longest five hours of their lives.

Chapter 12

Zach knew he needed sleep but knowing that didn't get him any closer to actually getting any. Still, he tried to rest as much as possible as he studied the photo of Chloe. He could hardly stand to look at it, almost relieved she was gazing slightly away from the camera—he wasn't sure he'd be able to take seeing her fear head-on. Which made him feel like a coward, but his heart was already ripping in two catching even a glimpse of her.

He hoped Chloe would be able to sleep...at least she'd get a bit of a break if she did. She had to know he was coming for her, right? He hoped it would be enough to keep her spirits up, to stay strong and positive. A tiny smile played at the edge of his lips. He would bet his life Chloe was giving this Justin jackass a piece of her mind. Maybe that's why she had the cloth around her mouth. Chloe was a fierce, determined kid and would likely not be making it easy on the guy.

Of course, that realization terrified Zach, and he sent a silent plea out to the universe to keep her safe. He couldn't lose her.

He just couldn't.

Zach leaned his head back and closed his eyes, picturing Chloe's sweet face laughing at the dinner table. She'd been humoring him after he'd told a particularly bad joke about a snowman and "the Winternet," and she'd played right along even though she was way too old for the joke. She was so good at that. The bad dad jokes were kind of their thing. Sure, she—rightly—made fun of him over it, but she never told him to stop, even when her friends were around. And yeah, she might roll her eyes every now and then, but that was part of her charm. And part of what made it so fun to tell the stinkin' jokes in the first place.

He let out a heavy sigh as a tear escaped his eye, rolling down his cheek and toward his ear, but he couldn't be bothered to wipe it away. It didn't matter. Nothing mattered except finding Chloe.

Chloe, Chloe, Chloe. He had to find her…

Should they start with places close to town? She couldn't be more than two hours away, given the time frame they'd worked out earlier. Maybe they should start at the far end of that window—drive an hour out of town and work their way in? But which direction? And more importantly, how much ground could they cover before the sun went down again?

Zach's eyes snapped open.

"Hey," Ava said. Somehow, she was sitting in the chair across from him even though he hadn't heard her sit down. "You've been out for a few hours."

"I have?" Zach asked, then wiped a bit of drool from the corner of his mouth. "It didn't feel like I slept. The last thing I was thinking about was how much ground we can cover before sunset and then…"

A jolt went through Zach. "Where's the picture of Chloe?" he asked, a note of desperation in his voice.

Ava leaned over and grabbed it off the coffee table, holding it out to him.

He plucked it out of her hand and studied it. But this time he didn't look directly at Chloe. He looked past her, above her head to the window. It was how they'd known it was still daylight when the picture was taken. There it was.

"Look at this," Zach said, pointing to the direction the light shone in through the window. "The sun's coming in from this direction," he said, motioning to the area out past the left perimeter of the photo.

Ava let out a little gasp. "And we know the sun had to be close to setting when he took the picture."

"And the sun sets in the west...so this has to be west." He made the motioning gesture again.

"Which means this is north, east and south," Ava said, pointing to each edge of the photo as she said the directions.

"Which means this picture was taken somewhere south of town."

"Holy shit," Ava said.

Suddenly they were getting somewhere, Zach thought. "It's mostly woods out that way, which would make sense. I haven't gone hunting in years," he said. "Never liked the idea of shooting living things, you know? But I used to go with my dad when I was a kid. I think there are still a few hunting shacks out there."

"That's exactly what this looks like," Ava said, pointing at Chloe again. "It's small, likely one room, but has an area for a cot here and I'm assuming a bit of living quarters behind the photographer."

Zach knew Ava was avoiding saying kidnapper so he wouldn't get all worked up again, but avoiding it only served to bring it straight back to the forefront of his mind. "We need to get out there," he said, getting up.

"The sun will start coming up in about an hour. We can gather supplies, and by the time we're ready to leave, it will be close to rising."

"Sounds good," Zach said, heading upstairs to get changed. Ava headed toward the front door. "Wait, where are you going?"

"Home. To change and get ready," she said, pointing toward the door.

"I don't think we should split up. I can change quickly, then we can head to your place where I can stand watch while you get ready."

Ava raised her eyebrows and opened her mouth as if she were about to argue but must have thought better of it. "Sure, sounds good," she said. "I'll go see what you have for food and water."

Zach nodded and continued up the stairs to put on a few layers. In his experience, the woods could be either way too hot or way too chilly depending on the time of day and the direction of the sun. He tried to think of every possible scenario and couldn't help but feel underprepared for all of them.

He headed back downstairs and fished in the closet for his hiking boots he used occasionally when he and Chloe decided it was time to get outside and see some nature.

Ava handed him a couple bottles of water and kept

two for herself. "I'm pretty sure I don't have any of these at my place," she said, heading for the door.

Zach grabbed his keys and followed, letting her lead the way over to her place.

As they walked, Zach was on high alert. With the lights from their houses, they'd be sitting ducks if someone decided to shoot from out of the darkness. He strained to hear any noise that might be out of place but could barely think over the sound of the crickets. Had they always been that loud? A friggin' elephant could charge past and barely be heard over the damn things.

But in a few steps, they'd made it to Ava's and Zach was safely closing the door behind them.

Ava went toward the back door to her house and re-trieved a large backpack.

"Were you planning on going somewhere?" Zach asked.

Ava looked momentarily surprised, then gave him a little smile. "I learned a long time ago it's good to be prepared, that's all," she said with a shrug.

But Zach had been in her house dozens of times, and there had definitely not been an already packed bag lean-ing up against the back door. "Jesus," he said, rubbing his face. "You were going to leave."

Ava pulled in a long breath. "It's the only way, Zach. And this…what happened to Chloe only proves it. As soon as we find her, I'm either going to have to go with Justin, or if we get very lucky, I'll make it out too and can get a head start on him."

"You can't leave," Zach said.

Ava stood in front of him and looked him straight in the eye. "Except I have to."

Zach shook his head.

"We can't waste time arguing about it," Ava told him. "I have a second gun at the store. We should stop by and grab it before we head out."

"Why do you have even one gun?" Zach asked, but Ava just gave him a look.

Of course, he knew the answer. The guy who now had his daughter. It was going to take a while to rearrange the ideas he'd had of Ava's life before Ambrosia Falls into the truth he now knew. Trying to picture her under the influence of this guy, helpless and desperate, didn't compute with anything he knew about her. She'd always been so confident, so strong. He couldn't reconcile any other thoughts of her, no matter how hard he tried. And the way she was checking and double-checking her gear, which included doing a safety and ammo check on her handgun, did not make the visual of a helpless Ava any easier to grasp onto.

"How much gas do you have? Your truck will do better out on the rougher roads," Ava said, zipping her backpack with finality.

"Yeah, we should be good. Filled up a couple days ago."

"Great, let's go," Ava said, and Zach marveled at her businesslike tone.

Like she was a completely different person. Except, she wasn't a completely different person. This was just another side of her. A side that, even though it was jarring, made a hell of a lot more sense than some damsel in distress scenario.

A few minutes later they pulled up to the coffee shop, both jumping out of the vehicle. Zach was not about to leave Ava by herself for even a second. He didn't know what this Justin guy was capable of, but he was not going to make the mistake of underestimating him.

Zach thought he had been prepared for anything, but as he went to close the truck door, the silence-shattering siren and the red and blue lights bursting out of nowhere definitely caught him a teensy bit off guard.

And like a damn fool, he promptly stuck up his hands.

Zach was not good at attempting to look innocent.

It was a good thing the guy was a writer, because he would certainly not make it as an actor, or you know, any profession requiring even the slightest hint of faking anything, anywhere, at any time.

"You okay there, man?" the officer said as he stepped out of his vehicle.

Ava shot Zach a look that she hoped conveyed he needed to lower his arms, and she hoped the officer wouldn't pick up on it in the early morning light.

"Oh, uh, yeah, sorry," Zach said sheepishly, lowering his arms. "You, uh, startled me a bit."

The officer nodded. "Yeah, sorry about that. I like to see how people react. Tells me a lot."

"Does it?" Zach asked politely, not doing a very good job at hiding the panic on his face.

"Is there anything we can do to help you out, Officer?" Ava quickly interjected, desperate to take the focus off Zach so he could hopefully regain some semblance of composure.

"Y'all are up a little early, aren't you?" the man asked.

Ava shrugged one shoulder. "I'm always up this early," she said. "Bakery owner." She motioned to the store.

"Ah," the officer said, raising an eyebrow. "Looks like a nice store. Was thinking I might have to come in for a coffee when you open."

"We'd love to have you," Ava said, turning on her small-town charm.

Which was strange. She'd settled into the small-town charm persona so fully over the last couple years it became who she was, except…she realized now she'd been in a different mode ever since she learned about Justin's reappearance.

Sparrow mode.

"And you?" the officer said, turning back to Zach.

"Oh, uh, just helping out a bit," he said. "You know, the Apple Cider Festival and all."

"You help with the baking," the officer said, a sarcastic lilt to his voice.

Zach's brows furrowed together, and Ava held her breath, terrified he was going to say something even more suspicious, but he simply said, "Of course," effectively conveying he couldn't understand why that would be strange at all and putting the sexism right back in its place.

"Got a lot of gear in there for a coffee shop," the officer said, flicking on a light and shining it into the second-row seat of the truck.

"Yeah," Zach said, "we were out hiking yesterday. I was a little tired afterward, and I guess I got lazy about putting our stuff away."

The guy nodded and took a step back. Ava got the feeling he decided they were harmless. "I hear there's been some trouble up this way," the officer said. "You guys know anything about that?"

"Sure," Ava said, jumping in. "Who doesn't? The water tower. The fire at the baking competition stage. Gotta say, I'm pretty bummed about that one." She leaned in close to the man. "I usually make a pretty good showing."

"I bet you do, what with being the town baker and all," the officer said, giving her a courtesy smile. "But you don't have any insight beyond the basics? No ideas as to how any of it happened?"

"Oh," Ava said, doing her best to look surprised, "unfortunately no. It's all just so…strange."

"And you?" he said, turning to Zach.

Zach shrugged, and it only looked a little forced. "No idea. Nothing like it has ever happened around here before."

"You lived here long?"

"All my life," Zach said.

The officer nodded, looking Zach up and down, making him squirm all over again.

"I'm sorry," Ava said. "I wish we could help, but if there's nothing else, I really do need to get started on my day."

"Right, no problem," the officer said, pulling a card out. "I'll be nosing around town a bit today, so if anything else out of the ordinary happens, I'd appreciate it if y'all could let me know."

"Sure thing—" Ava took the card and peered at the name "—Officer Banyan," she said, shooting him her best "no need to worry about me, I'm just an innocent baker" smile.

He tipped his hat and got in his car, backing away as Ava and Zach went into The Other Apple Store.

"Holy shit," Zach said, the moment they were safely inside. "What the hell do we do now?"

"We're going to have to make it look like we're doing exactly what we said we'd be doing. I figure there's another hour before the town starts coming to life and he'll have other things to be focused on. We can't risk moving your truck right away. I say we wait it out for a bit, then you calmly head out by yourself—it'll look like I'm staying here—make sure the coast is clear, then come around back and pick me up."

"I don't know if I can wait an hour," Zach said, starting to pace.

"If you're going to look all nervous and guilty, can you at least come back to the kitchen and do it?" Ava asked, pulling him toward the kitchen doors. "Officer Banyan is probably looking at us right now."

Zach let out a groan. "I am so bad at this," he said as they moved to the back.

"Not that bad," Ava said. "There were moments out there I almost believed you."

Zach rolled his eyes. "Almost? Great. I wonder what I looked like to a trained professional."

As a trained professional, Ava thought he'd done okay. Unfortunately, she couldn't exactly explain that to him.

"Jesus. Of all the times for the cops to show up," Zach said, able to pace freely now that they were out of view.

"I know, but I think we're fine. This might be better, anyway. Maureen will be here right around the time it should be safe for us to go. I'll tell her I have a migraine or something and ask if she can run the store for the day. I was planning on closing, but this will be better. It'll keep the town gossip down a bit."

Zach nodded. "Okay, yeah, you're probably right. But how in the hell are we going to kill this hour? I'm dying here. I have to do something."

"Easy," Ava said. "If the store is opening today, we have to get some baking done."

Zach looked as terrified as she'd ever seen him. Which, given the past several hours, was saying something.

"It's fine," she said. "I'll find you some easy stuff to do."

An hour later the place was full of baking smells and Zach still looked just as nervous. Ava couldn't fault the guy—he was hardly in an ideal mindset to be learning the ropes of a bakery, especially given that it had been a while since he'd had a proper sleep.

While he was watching over the mixer, adding dry ingredients a small amount at a time, Ava took a moment to retrieve the gun she had hidden in the back closet on the top shelf behind a box of old marketing materials. She wished she could go down into the crawlspace and really arm up, but that might be a little hard to explain to Zach.

When she got back to the kitchen, Maureen had arrived and was grilling Zach about why he was there.

He seemed to be doing about as good a job at improv with Maureen as he had with good ole Officer Banyan.

"I'm helping a bit. Ava's, um, not feeling well," he said, swallowing guiltily.

"Hey, Maureen, I'm so glad you're here," Ava said, trying to look exhausted.

Which, she had to admit, wasn't much of a stretch.

"I woke up with a migraine this morning," she continued. "As you can see, I roped Zach into helping. Is there any way you can run the store today?"

Maureen looked from Ava to Zach, then back to Ava again. "So you called Zach? That seems a little weird. Unless you already knew he was up or—" Her eyes grew wide.

At first Ava wasn't sure what Maureen had figured out, panicking that somehow she knew about Chloe. About Justin. About all of it.

And then Maureen smirked. One of those knowing smirks that said loud and clear she knew you were up to something, and she knew exactly what that something was, wink, wink. And then her expression changed to something akin to pure glee. "Sure. Yeah definitely. I can run the store today," she said, then added a quick, "It's about time," with a happy sigh.

Oh, jeez, Ava thought. *This'll be flying through town faster than wildfire once the store opens.*

It was taking a little longer for Zach to catch on to what was going on. "What's about time?" he asked.

"Nothing," Ava said, grabbing his arm and leading him toward the door. "Would you mind giving me a ride home? Maybe grab your truck and come around back to pick me up?" Ava said, lifting her eyebrows with a look that said, *Just go, I'll deal with this.*

"Yeah, sure," Zach said, still a little dazed as she pushed him out of the kitchen.

"Omigod, spill!" Maureen said the second Zach was out of earshot.

Ava groaned. "Maureen, it's nothing. It's not what you think."

"Mmm-hmm," she said, not believing it for a second.

Ava wished a secret affair was the only thing she'd be dealing with over the next few hours, but she supposed a little rumor was the least of her worries, even though it was…embarrassing somehow. Not that Zach would be embarrassing to be with—definitely not—but the fact the whole town was going to go nuts over the whole thing, all thinking like they knew better way before either of them did. And yeah, that might actually be true, but they didn't know the half of what had been holding them back from exploring the possibilities.

She sighed as she stepped out the back door of her shop. Zach was already waiting, looking tired, worried and so heartbreakingly handsome behind the wheel of his truck. If only there was a chance to properly explore those possibilities someday.

"She thinks there's something going on between us, doesn't she," Zach said, looking like he both wanted to kick himself for not figuring it out sooner, and like he wanted to crawl under the nearest rock and hide for a very long time.

"She does," Ava said, staring straight ahead.

"This is not good," Zach said. "The whole town is going to be talking."

Ava waved the comment away. "It'll be okay. In fact, it might be good. It will keep everybody distracted, at least for today. We'll have time to get to Chloe, I can get out of town, Justin will follow and forget Ambrosia Falls even exists and everything will be fine."

"How would any of that be fine?" he asked, his eyes wild.

"I'm sorry you'll have to deal with the fallout of all

the gossip, but after I'm gone for a few days, everyone will forget all about it."

"That is not happening," Zach said.

"Zach, it's the only way. You know it's the only way."

"I absolutely do *not* know that it's the only way. And yeah, I'm good with focusing on Chloe for step one, but I'm not okay with you being bait for this guy to hurt yet another person I care about."

"You need to stop," Ava said.

"Stop what?"

"Caring about me. It's just not going to work."

"You and me won't work?" Zach said.

"Exactly."

He let out a hard breath. "Fine," he said, though he looked hurt. "That's not even what I'm worried about. And I'm not worried about any ridiculous gossip fallout either. This is about you being safe. Whether our friendship could ever become something else doesn't matter right now. What matters is the friendship itself, and frankly I'm pissed you're treating it like it's nothing."

"I know it's not nothing, Zach," Ava said, turning away, focusing on the passing landscape. "It's everything," she whispered.

Silence fell in the truck for the next several minutes.

Finally, Ava spoke. "Let's focus on Chloe. Nothing else matters if we don't get this next step right, okay?"

"I know, but...we're going to try to get this guy, right?"

Ava nodded. "In an ideal world, yes. But we can't assume we'll get close enough. And you said yourself you don't like the idea of hurting things. You won't even hunt, Zach."

"Innocent animals hunted for sport are very different from someone who is trying to kill the people I love."

Love.

Ava let that sit there, not knowing what to say in return. Especially since she wanted to scream at the top of her lungs that she loved him too.

"Just focus on Chloe," she eventually said instead.

Zach nodded. "Focus on Chloe."

And then I'm gone.

Chapter 13

"I think we're a few miles out from the first shack," Zach said after they'd driven for more than an hour.

"We shouldn't get too close," Ava said. "He'll hear us coming from miles away if we pull up in a one-ton truck."

Zach pulled to the side of the road. "Do we try to hide the truck?"

Ava looked around. "If you can find a place, it might help."

"There was a trail about a half mile back," he said. "We could go a little way down there."

"Yeah, that would be better," Ava said, her eyes scanning as much of the terrain as she could see, which wasn't much considering they'd been on a forest road for the past fifteen minutes. "Will we be coming back to the truck after we check out the first shack? Or going on foot?"

"If I remember correctly, this road ends not too much farther from here. I think we're on foot from here on out."

Ava nodded. "Carrying packs is going to make it harder, but we'll have to suck it up. How many shacks are there?"

"Only three I know of, but that doesn't mean there aren't more. Like I said, this isn't really my world."

"Fair enough. With any luck, there will be trails lead-ing to any shacks you don't know about."

They heaved their packs over their shoulders and headed out. Ava followed Zach since he knew the ter-rain better than she did.

After hiking in silence for about twenty minutes, Zach held up his fist military-style to alert Ava to stop. They moved much slower then, and as silently as pos-sible, though Ava couldn't help but feel like Zach could use a little more training in being stealthy. Or you know, any at all.

Zach ducked behind a tree, and Ava followed his lead, easing behind another where she had a good view of both Zach and the tiny cabin in the distance.

"Okay, so how are we going to play this?" Zach asked.

He had imagined a scenario where he'd quietly charge forward, gun in hand and eyes darting, scanning for po-tential targets. And he had to admit, that's pretty much the way the whole thing went down, except he was still back behind the tree thinking it all through while Ava whisper-yelled, "Follow me," and then moved out exactly the way he'd envisioned himself doing it.

He had no choice but to follow, watching Ava aim her handgun steadily in one direction and then the other, stepping lightly but quickly, nearly silent on her feet, moving closer and closer to the shack.

One thought kept repeating in his mind. *How is she so good at this?*

She paused at one last tree, pointed in the direction she was about to go. She motioned for him to move in the opposite direction, which he did, the adrenaline pumping.

Even though Ava had the longer route, she somehow made her way around the shack first, seamlessly ducking under the single window in the back, then moving around to the front. While all this was going on, Zach felt like a lumbering bear as he made his way much more loudly around the closer side of the shack, thankfully not having any windows to avoid, and got around to the front in time to watch Ava take her last couple steps toward the door, lunge back, then kick her leg near the handle of the door. With wood splinters raining, the door burst open, and Ava stepped inside, pointing her gun first to the right, and then immediately to the left as Zach finally bumbled in after her like some kind of clueless old-timey deputy.

"Clear!" Ava yelled, as if she'd done it a hundred times before.

Jesus.

"Um, okay," Zach said, standing there blinking, his mind moving in all kinds of directions.

He was upset and pissed that Chloe wasn't there. He wanted all this to be over. He wanted to know the people he loved were safe.

And he also wondered how in the fiery depths of hell Ava was so calm under pressure, seemed to know how to expertly handle a weapon, not to mention maneuver like some kind of tactical genius.

"Um, what was that?"

Ava turned to him. "What do you mean?"

"That," he said, waving his arm in a circular gesture. "Like the whole…rushing in like you're some kind of navy SEAL or something."

It was Ava's turn to stare and blink for a moment. "Um, I guess I was copying people on the TV," she said, shrugging. "Did it look ridiculous? It probably looked ridiculous. I'm sorry, that's so embarrassing. I guess I...kind of got caught up in the moment or something."

Zach squinted at her. "No. No, it looked very believable," he said. "Like, weirdly believable."

"Huh," Ava said, nodding slowly. "Okay then, um, that's good I guess."

They stood for a moment, then Ava spoke again. "Well, this clearly isn't the shack in the picture—the view out the window isn't the same at all so, we should get going."

"Right," Zach said, hiking his pack a little higher on his shoulders. "There's one a little farther toward Aspen Hill."

"Great," Ava said, "lead the way."

Thirty minutes or so later they slowed again, hiding in the trees several dozen yards from the shack Zach led them to.

"I have a feeling this could be the one," he said.

Ava nodded, working her jaw. "Okay, let's take it slow...be extra cautious."

Zach was still nodding when Ava was on the move again. *Shit.* He hurried after her, trying to be as quiet as possible, but it seemed to be one of those situations where the harder you tried at something, the worse you were at it.

He pulled in a deep breath, letting it out slowly through his mouth, trying to calm his racing heart, but by the time they neared the shack, he was breathing like he'd just run up ten flights of stairs.

Like the last time, they paused to get their bearings.

And that's when Zach saw it. A small, red shoe. Exactly like a pair of Chloe's.

Saliva filled his mouth as his stomach performed an impressive reenactment of one of those spinning teacup rides.

Strange that the man would have the presence of mind to grab shoes for her as he somehow stole Chloe out of her second-story bedroom window. The planning and precision it would have taken was enormous. Sure, Chloe's bedroom window looked out onto the forested edge of town, so it wasn't likely he'd be seen, but he had to be quiet enough that Zach wasn't alerted, and with a kid like Chloe, that couldn't have been easy. To think of him gathering up shoes on top of it all was wild. Like the man had thought of everything, including precisely how to execute his plan.

It was not a thought that comforted Zach.

Ava was signaling to get his attention. She'd seen the shoe too. This was definitely the place. She put her finger over her lips to signal silence, then began to move. They followed the same procedure as at the last shack, though now that Zach knew what to expect, he was able to round the front of the building at the same time as Ava.

Still, she was the one who got to the door first and gave it a kick that might have been even more intense than the one at the last shack. She whipped her gun right, then left, then once again…and to Zach's horror, yelled "Clear!"

"What do you mean, clear?" Zach asked, rushing inside, his eyes frantically covering every inch of the room. "She was here. This has to be the place. Look at the window, it's the same as in the photo." He dug into the side pocket of his cargo pants to retrieve the photo even though he already knew he was right. "Her shoe is outside. She has to be here."

* * *

Ava's heart sank, though she knew what she was feeling was nothing compared to what Zach must be feeling. Justin was an absolute bastard for putting them through all this. Not to mention what Chloe must be dealing with. She must be so scared. All alone with that jackass of a human who probably didn't know the first thing about kids. Ava could only hope he was feeding her decently and keeping her warm.

The silver lining was, she didn't think Justin would actually hurt Chloe…not yet, anyway. None of this was even about Chloe. It was about Ava, and Ava alone. Chloe was just another ploy. Another way to toy with her, to make her pay for finding him out and escaping all those years ago.

Zach started rummaging through some of the stuff in the cabin, lifting relatively recent food containers from the small counter, then throwing them back down again in disgust. He moved over to the bed and lifted the pillow, which was when Ava heard it.

A quiet, almost imperceptible high-pitched squeal. A squeal Ava had heard only once before…five years ago.

"Get out!" she yelled, yanking the back of Zach's shirt with more might than she knew she was capable of, and dove for the doorway, dragging Zach behind her.

He didn't question—didn't have time to question—following her lead as she turned and dove through the doorway as the first boom sounded, then a second… pieces of the shack exploding in every direction. Wood splinters shot through the air, then rained on them as Ava covered her head with her arms, hoping nothing more substantial was on its way down.

Since the shack didn't have much to it, the raining debris didn't take long to clear. Ava rolled onto her back to survey the damage. Her first thought was that the thing had been obliterated so fully that, if there hadn't been a black mark of ash where the shack once stood, no one would have known anything ever stood there at all. Her second thought was to wonder where the hell all the blood was coming from.

"Shit, Zach," she said, scrambling over to him.

He was breathing and conscious, but clearly in a lot of pain. The blood was pouring from his thigh at the base of a five-inch shard of metal still lodged in his leg.

"Don't move," Ava said, scrambling into her pack.

But Zach, of course, moved. And in the worst possible way too, realizing what was causing the blood... the pain. His hand flew to the shard and yanked, tearing the metal free from his leg.

The blood gushed faster.

Ava had never been one to get queasy at the sight of blood, but apparently when it's the man you've recently come to realize you loved, it wasn't so easy to keep your wits about you. Ava wanted to panic...had started to panic, but quickly realized she was all Zach had.

Come on, Ava, she said to herself. *Do not lose it. Keep your shit together and save the love of your life.*

An unexpected knock came at the front door.

The little girl's eyes grew wide...hopeful. Silly little bird, the Crow thought.

He picked the girl up off the sofa and carried her to a closet, tucking her gently inside.

He spoke quickly and quietly. "If you make a sound,

it will be very bad for both you and your daddy." He looked straight into her eyes as he finished speaking. "And believe me, you do not want that."

Needless to say, the hope vanished from the girl's eyes, replaced by a fear that sent a satisfied calm through him. He was in control of the situation. All was going as planned.

He just needed to take care of whatever this little problem was knocking on his door.

He wasn't worried. He was trained for this and would handle whatever stood in his way. He would not fail this time.

"Hello there," he said, a pleasant smile pasted on his face. The Crow was surprised, but not rattled, to see a uniformed officer standing at the door. "How can I help you?"

"Officer Banyan," the uniform said. "I'm checking on some leads in the area." He peered over the Crow's shoulder, looking for clues, perhaps anything suspicious. Looking for mistakes.

But the Crow did not make mistakes. "Oh?" he said. "What do you mean by leads?"

"Well, there have been a few odd occurrences back in Ambrosia Falls, and I ran into a fellow from—" he flipped back a few pages in his notebook "—Pieville, down there at the apple festival thing, and he remembered something strange. He said the property in the woods should be empty right now. Said the owners headed down to Florida for a couple of weeks. But then he saw smoke from an outdoor fire the other day, and thought it was strange. And since I was asking him about anything strange he might have noticed, he filled me in," the officer said. "Thought I ought to come out here and take a look."

Damn snoopy small towns, the Crow thought, but he pulled out his best acting chops and feigned relief to the point of almost chuckling. "Well, I suppose that makes sense. I'm Jonathan, the Millers' son. And you're right, my parents did head down to Orlando for a bit. They asked me to come house-sit, though I didn't think I could until the last minute. I suppose that's why no one in town knew about me coming to stay." He finished off with a shrug he hoped said the whole thing was no big deal.

The officer nodded, buying his story hook, line, and sinker. *Sucker.* The Crow found people were quite trusting if you were nice to them. Even trained professionals.

Of course, no one ever expected anything bad to happen in a place like Ambrosia Falls, which made the whole thing about ten times easier. If it hadn't been for the real prize—the Sparrow—he wouldn't even consider a job like this that was, frankly, a waste of his talents.

But this was the job he'd been thinking about for five years. On top of the years he'd put into the target before that. So much time invested. So much at stake.

The only one that really mattered.

"The Millners' son, you say?" the officer asked.

Typical. The man was testing him.

"Miller," the Crow replied, trying not to take offence at the juvenile treatment. Reminding himself the man was simply doing his job.

"Miller, right, right," Banyan said. "And you're the son?"

"Right. Jonathan, sir."

"And you're out here all by yourself?"

"Just me and my typewriter," he said. "Taking the opportunity to do a little work on the old memoirs."

The officer raised his eyebrows, then wrote the information in his notepad. It was unlikely he'd call around to check on the story of Jonathan Miller, but the Crow had done his research anyway. Art and Eliza Miller did indeed have a son named Jonathan, and the Millers only bought the place in Ambrosia Falls a few years ago. The folks in town likely wouldn't know what Jonathan looked like. Even if word got around the son was staying at the property, the Crow had no doubt he could deal with a few nosy neighbors. Maybe he'd tell them he was there for some peace and quiet and wasn't interested in getting to know the locals. The people in town wouldn't understand. Small-town people tended to live in small towns because they liked the socialization of knowing everyone around them, but they would let it go. They certainly wouldn't want to be accused of being something so heinous as "rude." They'd chalk it up to him being a "big city person," accompanying the phrase with knowing looks to their fellow gossips.

Even if a neighbor did show up, word would get around fast and that would be the end of it.

"So, uh, what did you mean about odd occurrences?" the Crow asked.

It was always better to keep a person talking, and not give them too much time to think. All the better for making people believe you're friendly and concerned, and if you were friendly and concerned, you were no longer a person worthy of suspicion.

Banyan waved a hand as if it were no big deal. "Some small petty crime stuff. Nothing major. Kids, I suspect."

The Crow made an agreeing, musing sound. "Probably bored in a place like this," he said, smiling at Banyan like he knew what he was talking about.

Banyan played right along as if the Crow had scripted the whole thing. "You got that right," he said with a chuckle. "Sorry to have bothered you. You have a good night now."

"Will do. Thanks, Officer," the Crow said, giving the man a wave as he turned to leave.

What a doofus, was all the Crow could think as the officer stepped off the porch and headed to his car.

Chapter 14

Officer Banyan got into his car, careful not to look back at the house too much.

He had good instincts, and those instincts were telling him the man in that house was not telling the whole truth. In fact, he'd be surprised if he'd been told even a sliver of truth.

It wasn't so much that the guy was suspicious, it was that he was too smooth about the whole interaction. People tended to be nervous around the law, like that guy back at the bakery, but this guy was a little too sure of himself.

Banyan turned around in the wide yard and made his way back down the drive. He was out of sight of the house in a few seconds, the forest swallowing his car. He drove another minute before he got to the side road he'd seen earlier, and turned onto it, pulling his car to the edge to make a call.

"Hey, Vince," Jennifer, the dispatcher, said from the other end of the line. "How's it up there in Appleville, or whatever it's called?"

"Hey, Jen. It's…interesting."

"I bet," she said. "What can I do for you?"

"I need a lead checked out if you have a minute. There's a couple out here—Art and Eliza Miller. I've got a guy here who says he's their son staying on the property. Can you find out if there's anything I need to know about this Jonathan Miller? Something's got my spidey senses twigging about him."

"Well, you do have the best spidey senses around," she said. "I'll see what I can find out."

"Thanks, Jen," Banyan said, and hung up.

Research always took its sweet time, and Banyan had never been very good at waiting. Besides, with all the convenient forest surrounding the house, it would be a real shame to let it go to waste. There weren't many surveillance opportunities better than the one presenting itself to him on a silver platter.

He quickly collected his supplies and headed into the trees.

The pain in Zach's leg made every minute feel more like an hour, and every step he took—leaning much more heavily on Ava than he would have liked—was like a fire poker being slowly inserted into his muscle, then down into the bone.

Ava had been incredible under pressure. The picture of calm in a world suddenly filled with pain and chaos and confusion and hurt. His thoughts circled around Chloe and what she must be going through, then to the pain in his leg that would not be ignored for more than a moment at a time, and then back to Chloe again.

The first-aid kit in his pack was almost used up, and they had to get to better supplies sooner rather than later.

"You're doing great," Ava said as she helped him hobble along through the rugged terrain.

She had to be as exhausted as he was, but she was much better at hiding it.

The trip back to the truck took far longer than the trip into the woods, and it was afternoon by the time they finally made it back.

"What are we going to do now?" Zach said, his voice choking.

Ava was helping him into the passenger side. "We're going to get you patched up, regroup, and decide what our next move is."

"We don't have time. We have to get to Chloe," he said, wincing as Ava started backing the truck out of the rugged terrain.

"I know," Ava said, "but we also have to stop the bleeding or you're going to pass out. And you're obviously no good to Chloe if you're unconscious."

No matter how much he wanted to argue, Zach knew she was right. He was weak and tired and needed to regain his strength.

It took several minutes to move through the not-quite-trail in reverse, but soon they were back on the road and rolling toward town. Somehow through the pain, Zach was able to find a few short bursts of something close to sleep—an intense sort of focused rest where he thought only of Chloe...of how they were going to get her back.

The trip felt long, but the clock confirmed they'd made good time. Ava must have driven way past the speed limit, and Zach was grateful for it.

Thankfully, their houses were at the end of their lane and backing the forest, so no one was around when they got back. Ava helped Zach out of the truck, his leg feeling like it had been lit on fire all over again.

"I have a good supply of first-aid stuff," Ava said, as she pointed him toward her house.

Zach didn't argue. Couldn't argue, really. Maybe it was the pain or maybe it was the stress, but he could hardly focus, let alone come up with a plan.

The bandage around his leg was soaked through as Ava helped lift him up each step, and slowly, painfully, they made their way into her house. Ava sat Zach down at the kitchen table.

"I'll be right back. Don't move," she said, as she went in search of supplies.

Moving was both the last thing Zach wanted to do, and the only thing he wanted to do. He had to get to Chloe. He leaned his head back, resting it against the wall behind him, no longer able to stop the tears from flowing. He wasn't sobbing, just a stream coming from the corners of his eyes as if he'd turned on a faucet.

"I'm so sorry, Zach," Ava whispered as she knelt beside him to deal with his leg. "I'm so sorry I've done this to you and Chloe."

Zach raised his head, about to speak, and realized Ava had her own tears teetering on the edge of her lower lids. But she was keeping herself busy, cutting off his pant leg and pulling the used bandage away from his wound, which was enough to shock him straight out of the conversation. He tensed and ground his jaws together, trying not to scream out with the pain.

But oddly, it seemed to shock his brain back into working again. "What about a drone?" he said, gritting his teeth.

"For?" Ava asked, unscrewing the cap from a bottle of something Zach was pretty sure was not going to feel all that wonderful.

"It can cover a hell of a lot more ground than we can," Zach said, just before he shouted a curse as the antiseptic hit his leg.

"That could work," Ava said, moving quickly to dry the gash as best as she could.

She grabbed a large wound closure bandage, adhering it to one side of the gash and then the other, then pulling the wound closed, the whole thing holding it shut like a series of connected butterfly bandages.

"This should hold for a while," Ava said, as she covered everything with a large gauze pad, then neatly wrapped it.

His leg still hurt like hell—was going to hurt like hell for a while, Zach knew—but it was clean and closed and, with any luck, would hold until he could get proper stitches. At least the damn air was off it anyway, and he could maybe have a chance at saving his daughter.

"Okay," Ava said, putting her hands up as if to surrender. "So, drone, then. You have one, right? You any good at flying it?"

Zach gave her a side-glance. "I'm okay," he said. "And I'm all we've got, so I'll have to make damned sure I'm at my best."

Ava nodded once. "Great, let's do it before we lose the light. Can you walk?"

Zach leaned heavily on the table as he made his way to his feet. He was going to walk one way or the other. "Yup, I'm good," he said, only wobbling a little when the head rush hit him.

He paused for a second, steadying himself, then headed toward the door. "I'm going to need help with the drone."

Ava followed, and ten minutes later they were loading the drone case into the truck. It was about the size of a carry-on suitcase but was reinforced with metal and was heavier than it looked.

"Let's go," Zach said, heading toward the driver's side.

"Not so fast," Ava said. "First off, you are not driving with that leg, and second, we need to gear up."

Gear up? Zach thought. Wondering if maybe she wanted to gather more food, some more water, which would probably be smart.

The pain in his leg had morphed into something more like a heavy, pulsing ache that was much better than the gaping wound had been. He limped up the porch stairs and stopped in the doorway as Ava pulled a large painting—apparently on hinges—from the wall and began punching numbers into a large safe behind it.

"Okay," he said, looking behind him, then quickly closing the door.

"There are some duffel bags in the chest behind you," she said, opening the door to the safe.

But Zach was too stunned, watching Ava pull weapons out of the safe, a handgun and several knives. She followed up with a magazine of ammo and what looked like a...grenade?

"What the hell?" Zach asked.

"I'll explain in the car," Ava said. "But we need those bags."

Zach nodded, then turned to the chest, lifting the lid to see four large duffels.

"We'll need them all," Ava said, heading to the kitchen table with her haul.

Zach looked at the duffels, then at the items Ava was carrying, then back at the duffels. There was no way what she was carrying would come close to filling one of the bags, let alone four, but he grabbed them anyway, his mind spinning.

Ava set everything on the table and moved to the stove, bending to open the warming drawer on the bottom. It didn't look like there was anything inside, but she reached under the lip of the drawer, struggling a bit with her burned arm, and released something with a soft click. The floor of the drawer lifted to reveal a false bottom from which Ava proceeded to pull four shotguns.

"Um, okay then," was about all Zach could say.

She didn't stop there. Moving to the living room, Ava lifted the seat of an easy chair to reveal yet another secret compartment, this one filled with what looked like high-tech equipment.

"Night vision with heat signature capabilities," she said, as casually as if she were reading the day's specials at Margie's Diner downtown.

Zach added the goggle-like contraptions to one of the bags.

Next, she moved the coffee table and pulled up the area rug, revealing a cutout in the floor. She pulled the switch completely off a nearby lamp and inserted it into a hole that looked like a knot in the wood. The switch became a handle, which Ava quickly pulled, revealing two more guns and some body armor.

Of course.

"Put this on," Ava instructed, tossing what Zach could only assume was a Kevlar vest his way.

Around the house they went, Ava revealing compartment after compartment filled with rations, weapons and ammo until each of the duffels was full and Zach was feeling a bit like he'd been launched off the planet and had landed in a different world.

Zach and Ava stood staring at the bags, so full it was a miracle the damn table was even holding.

He glanced at Ava, then looked at the bags, then looked at Ava again. "Who are you, and what have you done with my happy-go-lucky, always positive, charming and harmless best friend?"

Officer Banyan was perched in a prime spot inside the tree line overlooking the Miller property, which consisted of a few small outbuildings and a large barn, but he kept his eyes trained on the house. There hadn't been much movement, though he supposed there wouldn't be if the guy inside had been telling the truth and he was in there working on his memoirs.

He settled in to wait, binoculars in hand.

But it didn't take long to spot movement in the house.

The man, Jonathan, moved to one of the front windows and looked out. Then strangely, he moved on to another window on the side of the house that didn't even face the driveway and looked out that one too. He moved to the next window, went out of Banyan's sight for a few minutes—about the length of time he might need to look out a few more windows—then came back to the front of the house, looking in that direction one more time.

The man could have been admiring the scenery, Banyan supposed, but the way he was so methodical about it, almost tactical, something had to be up.

He lifted the binoculars and peered in, studying every detail in every corner of the house that was visible through the windows. He was about to pull back the binoculars and sit back for a bit when he spotted something rather disturbing.

A foot. And it most definitely did not belong to the man who answered the door. It was far too small, not to mention clad in a rainbow-striped sock. Banyan was the first to admit he didn't always catch every single detail, but he was sure he would have noticed bright, rainbow-striped socks if Jonathan—though he was beginning to doubt that was his real name—had been wearing them.

Unfortunately, the rest of the body the foot belonged to was out of sight.

He must have stared at the foot for ten minutes straight, until finally it twitched ever so slightly. Banyan let out a long breath, relieved the worst-case scenario, which had been strolling through his mind, was not reality.

Still, the man told him straight to his face he was there alone, and no matter which way you cracked that particular egg, the man had lied.

A few minutes later Banyan's phone vibrated.

"Hey, Vince," Jen said from the other end of the line.

"Hey, Jen," Banyan replied.

It was stunning how silent it was this far from civilization, and even though he was barely talking over a whisper, his voice cut through the quiet like a gunshot.

"I have your confirmation about that guy Jonathan,"

Jen said. "The Millers do, in fact, have a son by that name."

"So, he was telling the truth?" Banyan asked.

"Well, he didn't seem like a liar when I was talking to him."

"Wait, you talked directly to Jonathan Miller?"

"Just got off the phone with him," Jen confirmed.

Banyan's eyes shot back toward the forest house. "And did you happen to catch where he was at?"

"Sure did. Says he's packing for a trip to see his folks down in Florida. Leaves tomorrow," Jen said. "And Vince?"

"Yeah?"

"He says he's never been to his parents' place up in Ambrosia Falls. Been meaning to get there, but he usually just meets up with them in Florida once a year."

"I'll get back to you," Banyan said.

"Be careful out there, Vince," Jen said, hanging up.

Banyan's mind was whirling a mile a minute when he spotted movement in the house again. He quickly lifted his binoculars. The man—not Jonathan Miller, apparently—was bringing a plate of food over to the person who was just out of sight. The person did not reach for it, so the man eventually set the plate on the floor. Banyan peered through those binoculars so hard he forgot to blink, but the peering paid off. A few minutes later the person with the rainbow sock finally leaned forward to check out the plate of food.

Banyan wasn't sure what he'd expected, but an adorable preteen with an incredibly defiant look on her face had not been it.

Sure, a preteen could aim a defiant look at a parent,

but there was something in the way they interacted. This girl was not that man's kid.

It took Banyan about zero point five seconds to decide he had to get to her.

The correct thing to do would be to call for backup, but he decided he couldn't wait. He shot off a quick text, hoping it would reach its destination—cell service was spotty—then began the descent toward the house.

Still inside the protection of the trees, Banyan double-checked his equipment—handcuffs, gun loaded, holster unsnapped. He didn't like the feel of any of it. The remote location, the eerie silence, the child in harm's way. It was a cop's nightmare scenario, the kind that tested the mettle and let you know if you had what it took. And Banyan knew there was no way in hell he was turning around and leaving that little girl behind.

He considered how to approach the situation. He could simply walk up and knock on the door...a better option if he had his squad car with him. But out here on foot, he still had the element of surprise working for him.

Best case scenario would be if he could get the girl and haul ass out of there before the man even knew she was gone. But hiking a scared kid through dense forest after she'd been abducted and through who knew what was probably not the best situation either.

Banyan took a deep breath. There was a very good chance he was going to have to take a shot at the guy. With any luck, he wouldn't have to take a fatal shot, but he needed to prepare himself in case it came to that.

Banyan pulled the gun from his holster and stepped out into the clearing. He moved quickly and quietly toward the structure, flattening himself against the house near one of the side windows, hoping he'd catch a glimpse of the girl. He needed to know exactly where she was before anything happened. He couldn't risk hurting her and didn't want to traumatize her more by witnessing a shooting if it could be helped.

He tried to figure how an abduction of a girl could relate to the other incidents in town but couldn't understand what the connection might be. What he did know was, it was too small a town and too small a time frame for all of it to be coincidence. Something worse than anything the residents of a town like Ambrosia Falls had likely seen was happening, and the man inside was the key to unlocking it all. If Banyan could, he'd like to take the man alive, but the girl was the priority...if she was in danger, he would do what he had to do to ensure her safety.

There was no movement visible inside. Banyan made his way toward the front door, ducking under windows, then climbed the steps silently. He reached for the knob, which turned easily in his hand. He supposed the man inside wasn't too worried about security way out there in the middle of nowhere.

Banyan eased himself inside, gun at the ready, heart beating a million miles a minute. It took a few moments for his eyes to adjust to the dim entrance, but soon he was moving into the living room where he'd first seen the girl.

She was no longer there.

He moved stealthily across one wall of the living room, making his way toward the kitchen area, gun leading as he rounded the corner. Quickly and methodically, he cleared the room, moving deeper into the house, entering a hallway.

He was about to pass the first bedroom on the right, peeking in and seeing it was empty, when something caught his eye. Something flickering inside a smaller space—a closet—on the other side of the room. He moved toward the lights, realizing the flickering was a security setup. He moved closer, entering the walk-in closet. If he could get a good look at the monitors, maybe he could find the girl.

Three screens sat on a small desk. The first showed four views of the inside of the house—the living room, the kitchen and a couple bedrooms. The second monitor showed various sections of land surrounding the property. This was when Banyan's tap-dancing nerves began to whirl their way into a frenzy. The third screen showed flashing words. *Perimeter Breach, Northeast Quadrant.*

That was the moment he knew. The moment he realized he had lost the very second he stepped out of the trees.

He turned to leave the closet. To give himself a chance to get out of there alive, but the small space was already going dark. The door was shut, then bolted behind him even though closet doors didn't typically have bolts on them.

The man had prepared the closet for this exact purpose. To lure anyone wanting to help straight there. And as a fog-like substance began filling the small space, the feeds on the first monitor changed, the girl popping up clearly on the screen. She was in a dark space, alone and looking pissed off...and scared. Banyan called out to her, yelled that he was there to help.

But he couldn't help. And the girl showed no signs of having heard him before his head became heavy and he slid down the wall.

His last thought before everything went black was, *I failed her.*

Chapter 15

Ava and Zach were heading back to the forest. Unfortunately, they didn't have a specific target this time.

What they did have was about half an hour before they reached the last clear area appropriate for launching a drone before the forest got heavier.

Zach finally broke the silence. "So, I'm guessing there's a little more to your past than you've led me to believe."

Ava let out a long, slow sigh. This was the moment she'd been dreading for five years. The moment the people important to her found out she wasn't exactly who she said she was. She wasn't anything even close to the person she appeared to be.

"I'm so sorry, Zach. It was all part of the conditions of being in witness protection. Though it's not strictly witness protection in my case, more like asset protection."

"So you're an asset of the government."

"I used to be," Ava said. "But I haven't been active since I came to Ambrosia Falls. Everything about my life here has been legit since the day I arrived."

She hoped he understood that meant her feelings for him too—especially her feelings for him.

"So...judging from the arsenal you've got back there, were you some kind of assassin or something?"

Now that she had come this far, she couldn't lie to him anymore. Found she didn't want to keep anything from him anymore.

"Sometimes," Ava said, watching him out of the corner of her eye, but his face remained neutral. "And sometimes I was recon, and sometimes I was asked to be security, or backup, or sometimes I was needed for my expertise."

"Expertise in what? Were there a lot of national baking emergencies?" Zach asked, though his voice sounded more baffled than angry. More stunned than sarcastic.

"Baking has always just been a hobby," Ava said.

"Could've fooled me," Zach replied, and Ava smiled.

"I have an advanced degree in geology. I specialize in forensic geology, using trace evidence to track down suspects or persons of interest. I often got asked to assist in time-sensitive searches for victims or sometimes perpetrators. I have some sharpshooting too, so that was a big part of my job."

Zach swallowed hard.

"I'm still me though," she said.

"Still you. Right. You just have a little forensic geologist slash sharpshooter experience to pad your résumé with. No big deal, right?"

"I'm serious, Zach. This doesn't change who I've always been to you."

Zach shook his head, still clearly trying to wrap it around everything.

"And now that you know," Ava continued. "it means I don't have to hide any of this—" she waved her hand toward the bags in the back seat "—and we can go in there and get Chloe back using everything we've got available to us."

"That's the other thing I've been wondering about," Zach said. "Why the hell didn't you tell me all this when Chloe got taken? Why did we go up to that shack and make damn fools of ourselves falling right into his trap?"

"That's on me," Ava said. "I didn't think Justin would be so organized, so prepared. None of that was ever his strong suit. It's why he and I worked so many jobs together. I was the one who checked and rechecked each tiny detail of every job. He was the one who was good at storming in and causing chaos, which is a surprisingly rare quality to have, and if there was ever a master at it, it was Justin. This whole…careful, methodical, calculated side is something I've never seen from him before."

"So you underestimated him," Zach said, his voice accusatory.

"I'm not so sure it was underestimation so much as it was familiarity and knowledge of past behavior and skills. You want to know a target inside and out, which is why I thought I had an advantage here, but clearly Justin has changed as much as I have. Maybe more."

"Well, you did get one thing right, at least," Zach said. "This is all on you. And I may never see my daughter again. Sometimes, I wish I'd never met you."

The words stung. More than stung, they obliterated. And the worst part was, he was absolutely right.

Zach hated himself the moment the words left his mouth. He was hurt and angry and maybe a little embarrassed it had taken so long to catch on to the truth of who Ava really was. And worse, he was running on fear, terrified something unthinkable could have already happened to Chloe.

They drove in silence for a while, but when they neared their destination, Zach couldn't take it anymore. "I'm sorry," was all he said.

Ava shrugged one shoulder. "You're not wrong. I did do this. I came into this town and into your lives out of nowhere. You didn't ask for any of it. I knew the risks, and I decided to get close to you and Chloe anyway. And as long as I live, it will be the biggest regret of my life."

Oof. Zach knew Ava was talking about putting them in harm's way, but it still stung to hear the woman he loved say she regretted ever knowing him. Of course, he had just told her the same thing only more harshly, so yeah. He could only hope she meant the words about as much as he did, which was not at all.

"And don't worry," she continued. "As soon as we get Chloe back, you'll never have to see me again—but I am trained for this sort of thing and probably your best chance at getting her back."

"Ava, that's not what—"

Ava put up a hand. "It's fine. It's…whatever. Right now, we need to focus on Chloe. She's all that matters."

Zach certainly couldn't argue with that, and they were nearing the edge of the trees anyway, so he let it drop. Ava pulled the truck into an approach off the road, stopping before they went too far down the rugged trail leading into a wheat field.

Ava opened the tailgate and pulled the drone case to the edge. Zach took over from there, opening the case and pulling the drone from the protective foam padding. He was about to walk it a few paces away, but Ava took it gently from his hands. Walking was not his strong suit at the moment.

Zach powered everything up, and within a few minutes, the drone was airborne, hovering high over the trees.

"This could take a while," Zach said. "There's a lot of area to cover in these trees."

Ava nodded. "It's what makes it perfect for hiding." She shook her head. "I should have anticipated this. The people who put me here should have anticipated this."

"I'm not sure there's a place in the world that doesn't have trees close by."

"Not this kind of dense forest though. A person could get lost in this indefinitely."

Zach focused on flying the drone and trying not to get discouraged. Not yet.

Ava shook out her body. "Okay, this isn't helping. I need to think. Think like Justin, only not exactly like Justin since he's been ahead of us this whole time."

"Okay, so what's his usual MO?"

"He's never been good at being uncomfortable," Ava said. "Or at being wrong. Which is probably why he's still after me after all these years."

"Why was he after you in the first place?" Zach asked.

It was the question he'd been wondering since he found out someone had been after her. He'd assumed she'd gotten swept up in the wrong crowd and witnessed something she shouldn't have, but that theory didn't really fly anymore.

"I can only assume he was an enemy operative. A sort of double agent, I guess, although we don't use that term in the real world. It's more of a TV thing."

Zach nodded, thinking over all the things that meant. "And you were with him for a while?"

"Years," Ava said, rubbing the bridge of her nose, like she was trying to stop a tingle. "I found his stash of surveillance on me. All the years we'd been together, and for a while before that even. He'd been gathering data, intel for who knows what purpose. He had a thousand opportunities to kill me... I don't know why he never did. I almost wish he would have," she said, trailing off.

There was a pause as Zach looked at her—beautiful, vulnerable, still the Ava he knew, just...with a few additional skills.

"I'm glad he didn't," Zach said.

Maybe it was the hope talking, but he couldn't bring himself to believe he would never see Chloe again. And knowing what he knew about Ava now actually made him feel better about the situation. Yes, he was still terrified beyond belief, but in a way, none of it seemed real. He still felt Chloe's presence, and he was going to cling to that feeling as hard as he damn well could.

Ava began to pace, thinking, mumbling a bit to herself, though Zach couldn't catch any of the words. He was busy trying not to let his drone crash. It had been a while since he'd been out flying, and the machine took more concentration than one might think.

"You wanna talk it out?" he asked.

Ava stopped and turned to him. "Maybe."

"Okay, so it was a surprise to you that he headed for the shack, I'm guessing."

"Very much so," Ava said, "but I figured he was trying to throw me off his trail. And I hate that it worked."

"It's smart, but we can be smarter. So, he had it pretty cushy at the first place he was at...the Lawson place."

Ava nodded. "It made sense because it was close. It

was cushy enough for him…barely," she said, rolling her eyes, "and the family was going to be away for a while."

"But he likely guessed you'd know all that about him, so he set it up so you would think you were getting the jump on him, when really, he was ten steps ahead."

"I hope not ten," Ava said, "but yeah, sounds about right."

"And then the shack."

"Which we can assume he only went to long enough to plant the explosives and take the photo of Chloe," Ava said.

"Right. And had we been thinking in terms of Justin, we might have realized it was a trap, but we were so focused on Chloe. I'd bet my last dollar he purposely got the window in the picture so he could throw us off the scent of where he was really staying."

"So where would he really be staying then?" Ava asked, more to herself than to Zach.

She started pacing again.

"Well, we know he likes a luxurious place if he can get it," Zach said, the wheels starting to turn a little faster up in the old hamster wheel of his.

"But we thought he'd stay close to town, which is why I headed to the subdivision on the lake first," Ava continued.

"But then he headed for the woods, which was smart. Easy to get lost. But if this was the place he'd planned on staying for the major part of his, what would you call it?" Zach asked.

"Operation," Ava said.

"Right. For the major part of this operation, I'd bet he'd still be looking for a nice, cushy place."

"If that even existed," Ava said, still pacing.

"Ah, but it does," Zach said, his heart rate climbing with a little zip of excitement. "The Miller place," he said, with a big smile.

"Who are the Millers?" Ava asked. "I thought I knew everyone in Ambrosia Falls."

"You do, but the Millers get their mail in Pieville."

Ava's eyes grew wide. "Can you find their place with the drone?"

"I think so," Zach said, quickly changing course.

Several minutes later Zach was maneuvering the drone over a patch of forest about twelve miles away. "I don't know exactly where it is, I've never been out there, but Arnie Jackson was out helping build it about ten years ago. Said the place was huge. They built it on an old ranch site, apparently."

"Sounds like it would be the perfect place for Justin," Ava said, looking like she didn't particularly like the taste of his name on her tongue.

"But wouldn't he realize we'd figure it out eventually?" Zach asked, his eyes glued to the monitor, praying for a break in the trees.

"That's exactly what he's counting on," Ava said. "He wants me to come to him."

Zach swallowed. He very much did not like the sound of that.

Just then, off to the far side of the monitor, Zach spotted something. The edge of a clearing. He quickly maneuvered the drone toward the clearing, hoping the machine was too high for the whir to be heard from the ground.

"I've got something," Zach said.

Ava came to stand beside him, leaning toward the small screen.

"That's got to be it," she said.

"Has to be. There's a vehicle in the drive."

"Could be the Millers'," Ava said.

"Could be," Zach agreed. "I wish I knew more about them."

"Wait, what's that?" Ava asked, pointing to something shiny in the trees.

Zach changed the path of the drone again, centering over the object in question. "Is that a car?"

"I think so," Ava said. "Weird place for a car. And what's that dark strip on the top?"

"Holy shit. I think it's a police vehicle," Zach said, panic sneaking into his voice. "The asshole said no cops. Why the hell are there cops?" He turned to Ava, his eyes wide. "Maybe they have Chloe already. We have to get out there."

Ava remained silent.

Chapter 16

At least we have a new target, Ava thought as she steered the truck toward their destination. But she was worried. The police car presented a whole host of new problems, and she did not like adding variables to the mix. And a cop was a huge variable.

Sure, there was a chance the officer had somehow caught on to Justin, taken him down and rescued Chloe, but that was very unlikely. Still, the police vehicle was well hidden from both the road and the place where Justin was squatting, so maybe he or she was just watching. Waiting for backup. Of course, that meant another set of eyes on their rescue, which could go either way. A cop could think they were the bad guys and keep them from doing what they needed to do. Or they could decide to help.

The fact that Justin specifically said no cops did not put her at ease. He would have to know she had nothing to do with this officer showing up—they'd been trained to work outside the confines of organized law enforcement, at least the kind the public knew about, anyway. The "no cops" thing had been for Zach's sake. People who'd lived their whole lives following the law would automatically think to phone the police, but Ava was far beyond any of that. If there was anything she couldn't take care of herself, she had resources beyond typical law enforcement.

Maybe the whole police vehicle thing was another ploy by Justin to throw her off her game. She just couldn't figure out what the reasoning behind it might be.

It took time to get out to the remote location. More time than it did getting to the place they could park before they went on foot to the shacks, but this time they wouldn't have to trek so far through the forest.

"I think we should stay away from the police car," Ava said. "On the off chance it's a plant by Justin to mess with us, we won't want to get too close."

"A plant?"

Ava shrugged. "I can't figure out any good reason to do something like that, but if there's one thing I've learned over the past few days, it's that I do not have as much insight into Justin's thinking as I thought I did. It could simply be something he's using to distract us, so we'll miss something else. We need to stay alert…be ready for anything."

"I don't know how to be ready for anything," Zach said.

"Just try not to be too surprised, no matter what happens."

Zach raised an eyebrow. "Considering our current situation, and the things I've discovered about the person I'm closest to, I'd say you could pretty much send a steamroller right over me and I'd say it was par for the course."

"Good," Ava said, trying to ignore the sarcasm laced in his words.

It would be good if he was angry. Even better that he

was angry with her. It would mean Chloe was his only priority. Maybe, with any luck, he wouldn't worry too much about what she was doing.

Because she was going after Justin. And she wouldn't let a little thing like her personal safety get in the way. She would end this one way or the other. If Justin was gone, there'd be no more threat to Chloe and Zach. And the same applied if she was the one who was gone instead. Either way, she was going to make sure Chloe and Zach were safe.

"We're getting close," Zach said, watching the pin he'd dropped on his phone map based on the drone footage. He hoped he wouldn't lose the signal, since cell service was pretty spotty in the area.

"The police car is in there, I think," Ava said, pointing to the recently car-trampled grass leading into the ditch.

A short distance later they approached the gravel drive leading into the acreage and up to the farmyard. From the drone, it had looked like the house was about a half mile in. The place must be a nightmare in the winter. A person could be stranded there for days if they didn't have a snowplow of some sort.

"I'm going to go past. See if there's somewhere we can ease into the trees like the police car did."

Zach nodded, his neck craning to see as far as he could up the drive, which, given the sharp curve near the entrance, was not far at all.

About a quarter mile past the turnoff, Ava eased the truck off the road and into the ditch, continuing through a small break in the trees. She weaved a little way farther until she was sure the vehicle couldn't be seen from the road. The grass would be trampled, just like with the police car, but there wasn't much she could do about that.

"We need to go up the hill and try to get a read on the place," Ava said. "Figure out what our next move is going to be."

"I don't like this," Zach said. "Chloe is in there all alone. He's one guy. With all this firepower, we should be charging in there and taking him down."

Ava shook her head. "That's way too risky for Chloe. What if she got caught in the line of fire? Justin may know he needs Chloe for leverage to get me out here, but once I'm in his line of sight, he won't think twice about using her for a shield."

Zach cursed under his breath. "I hate this."

"I hate it too," Ava said. "We can't carry all this up the hill. Take what you're comfortable with and follow me," she told him, tucking a handgun into the back of her pants and a knife at her ankle. She hung the infra-red goggles around her neck.

"We'll come back for what we need once we know what we're up against."

Zach rummaged through the bags while Ava double-checked her ammo. "Do you need help with any of that?"

"I think I'm okay. I haven't used one of these in years," he said, checking a gun of his own, "but I do know a bit. Like I said, I used to hunt."

Ava nodded once. "Sounds good," she said, hoping Zach would not have to use his weapon. If the guy was against hunting animals, who knew what it might do to him to aim at a person.

They moved up the hill quickly, slowing as they neared the top. Staying low, Zach followed Ava as she crept to the point where she could see the farmyard. All was still and quiet.

Ava put the goggles on, then began to whisper as Zach crept up beside her. She lowered to her stomach and Zach followed suit.

"So, these don't work like they do in the movies," Ava said. "We're not going to be able to see the outline of a person unless they're outside. Through walls we have to use our best guesses. Walls are insulated and aren't the best way to get a good read, but we might get lucky and catch someone walking past a window or something."

Zach was disappointed, but realized there wasn't much he could do about it. He nodded and put his goggles on anyway.

"I can't stand sitting here waiting for something to happen," Zach said. "I need to get to Chloe. She must be so scared."

"I know," Ava whispered, "but this is the way it has to be. If we go in there unprepared, the person we're putting most at risk is Chloe, and that is the last thing we want to do."

"I get that in my head, but this is killing me. I need to know if she's down there."

"Give it a few minutes," Ava said, studying every inch of the yard, searching for anything out of the ordinary. "Looks like there's a heat spot inside the barn."

"Just one?" Zach asked, turning his attention to the barn.

"I think so. Like I said, it's hard to tell through walls."

"So, let's go in there and get him," Zach said.

"Except we don't know it's him. It could be Chloe, or even an animal."

"If it's Chloe, that's even better, we can grab her and get the hell out of here."

"Assuming it's not a trap," Ava said.

Zach let out a long sigh. He just wanted to know his kid was okay and get her to safety.

"Look, I know this is hard. It's killing me too," Ava said. "But we have to play this smart. If it's Chloe, great, but there's no telling what kind of trap he may have set. And if it's Justin in there, things could get ugly fast, and if he goes down—" she let out a long sigh "—we need to know where she is before anything can happen to Justin."

Zach understood what Ava was getting at then. "In case he has her stashed somewhere it'll be hard to find her."

Ava nodded, not looking at all happy he'd arrived on the same page.

They lay in silence for a few minutes, watching… waiting. Zach's thoughts jumped from being certain something catastrophic could have happened to being so sure Chloe was alright. Because she had to be. Any other outcome was unthinkable. Any future without her was impossible. And then his thoughts moved to scolding. Cursing himself for even thinking about any of that when all his attention should be 100 percent on getting to her. Rescuing her. Making sure she was okay and spoiling her for the rest of her life. And yeah, in his head he knew spoiling her wasn't good for her in the long run, but that didn't stop him from making pleas with the universe that if she ended up okay, he would do anything and everything in his power to make this up to her.

But being stuck inside his own head was not helping anyone, least of all Chloe.

"What are you thinking?" Zach asked.

"It's so quiet. Too quiet," Ava said. "Too still."

"Do you think he's not even here?" Zach asked, his disappointment already rising.

"No, I think he's here somewhere," Ava said. "It's like I can feel him, but something isn't right. If he had a plan, there would be something obvious, or at least a hint at something. I can't figure out what his strategy is."

"I bet that's exactly what he's hoping for," he said. "Get you off your game. Get you lost inside your head, guessing what his next move is going to be."

Ava nodded. "Yeah, and I've been thinking about that. Trying to decide whether he'd do something exactly opposite of what I would expect, or if that's too predictable now too."

"If it were me, I'd do both," Zach said.

"Me too," Ava agreed. "Which means we have nothing. No strategy."

"We have instinct," Zach said, "and mine is telling me to get back to the vehicle, load up with as much shit as we can possibly carry, get Chloe out of there and end this bastard."

Ava nodded. "I guess waiting isn't getting us anywhere at this point. You sure you're up for this? Going up against Justin is no joke."

"I couldn't give a flying rat's butt who we're going up against. It's not about him."

"I'm not sure there are flying rats—at least I hope to hell there aren't—but I get what you're saying," Ava said, easing her way down the low hill a bit, then slowly standing.

Zach followed, but he had only taken a few steps before the ground beneath them shook. The world in front of them lit up in a series of flashes, one after the other. The noise was booming, shattering the serenity of the forest.

"Holy shit," Zach said.

Ava stood motionless, mouth hanging open.

"Ava?" Zach asked. He'd never seen her in shock like this, and if she—the trained spy-type professional person, or whatever, exactly, she was—was in shock, things must be very bad indeed.

"I think we can assume Justin knows we're here," Ava said, her eyes still wide with a sort of faraway look in them. "I'm pretty sure that was your truck."

"Along with all of our ammo and guns?" Zach asked, his voice squeaking a little.

Ava nodded.

"We have to get to Chloe now!" Zach said. "Please tell me we can go find her now. We have to get her away from this guy."

Ava looked from Zach to the area where the truck had exploded, then back to Zach again, her face finally morphing from shock to something closer to determination. "Yeah, we gotta go now," she said, turning toward the house.

Zach was on her heels. "What's the plan?"

"I have absolutely no idea."

Chapter 17

Since Justin clearly had the advantage of location and planning, Ava had hoped to even the playing field with the element of surprise and sheer firepower, both of which had just blown up right in front of her face.

He'd known exactly what her plan had been. It was a thought that sent stone-cold fear through every inch of her body. She always thought she'd be able to outsmart Justin when the time came, but she realized he'd had five years to plan what to do when he found her. Five years she'd spent rebuilding her life instead of thinking about Justin.

They'd been the best five years of her life, and she wanted to end this asshole for making her go back to her old life. How could she have fallen for his BS in the first place? She'd always been the better operative—more careful, more intuitive, more prepared. But now she wondered if all that had been true, or if he'd played it that way all along and she was simply the world's biggest sucker.

The worst part was that now—when her skills and confidence mattered the most—was not the time to start doubting her abilities, to start feeling inadequate.

She had to save a beautiful, smart, hilarious little girl,

and save her dad while she was at it. If she could just do that, she'd gladly lay down her life and give Justin what he wanted. What happened to her after Zach and Chloe were safe mattered exactly zero percent.

"Are we going for the barn?" Zach asked.

"Probably," Ava said, slowing down as they neared the edge of the trees.

She motioned for Zach to stop, as she eased behind a large tree. Zach did the same a few feet away.

"I want to check the heat signature one more time," she said. "Might look different now that we're closer."

She pulled the googles up from around her neck. Zach did the same with his.

"Shit," Ava said, closing her eyes to the blinding light.

Zach made a surprised sound as the same glare burned into his eyes. "Jesus, what the hell is that?"

"He must have lit a bunch of fires in there," Ava said, trying to blink the bright spots from her vision.

"How is it not burning down then?"

"Not sure," Ava said. "They must be contained somehow. Maybe in metal containers or something."

"I am really starting to hate this guy," Zach said, throwing out the greatest understatement Ava had ever heard.

"Yeah, welcome to the club," she said, with a half-hearted smirk.

"He clearly wants us to go into that barn," Zach said. "Which means I am highly disinclined to do so."

Ava thought for a moment. Zach was right. Justin obviously wanted them in the barn…using the fires as a sort of calling card slash bait situation. So that was exactly where Ava was going to go. But she sure as hell wasn't letting Zach get anywhere near it.

"Let's go for the house," Ava said. "Stay low. You go around the front, and I'll take the back. With any luck we can catch him by surprise from one angle or the other."

She pulled the gun from her waistband and nodded for Zach to do the same.

"Promise me one thing," she said. "If you find Chloe first, get her out. Don't worry about where I am. Your only job is to get her out—I'll be right behind you."

The moment Zach gave his nod, Ava sprinted from the trees and headed toward the back of the house, clearing the corner of it in seconds. A quick glance back assured her Zach was headed toward the front of the house. She waited a few more beats, hoping to hell it would either take Zach a bit to get inside, or there wouldn't be a good view toward the barn from in there. She didn't need a lot of time, but if he spotted her, everything would be lost. There was a still a chance she could handle Justin if left to her own devices, but she definitely wouldn't be able to handle him if she had to make sure Zach was safe too.

If she knew Justin at all—though after the past couple of hours, she wasn't sure she ever did—he would be focused on one thing and one thing only.

Her.

And maybe it was instinct, or maybe it was the fact that she felt like she did still know the Crow, at least in the most fundamental sense, but Ava somehow knew Chloe was not in that barn. He would be keeping her somewhere that wouldn't be easy to find. He wanted to keep Zach busy…keep him away.

And to have her, his Sparrow, all to himself for one last fight.

* * *

Zach tried like hell to get his hands to stop shaking but was having no luck. It had to be the nerves or adrenaline or something, but either way, he took a moment—just a second—to breathe and try to center himself. The life of his daughter depended on what he did in the next few minutes.

Thank the Lord Ava was right there with him. He wasn't alone. Chloe wasn't alone.

Two breaths in, two breaths out, then he tried the door.

Locked.

He wondered if the real owners of the house ever locked their doors. They were so deep into the middle of nowhere it seemed impossible some random criminal would stumble upon the place, but he supposed no one was ever completely immune to the outside world encroaching into their existence. The current situation was proof enough of that.

There was little reason to worry about noise—Justin clearly knew they were there—but Zach's instincts told him to be as quiet as possible. Still, the only way in seemed to be to break one of the small windowpanes on the door and reach in to unlock the door like they always did on TV. He was about to do it too, when he noticed an open window halfway down the side of the house. He figured it would be a whole lot quieter to cut through a window screen than it would be to smash a damn pane of glass.

He just needed to find something to step onto to get up to the window. Anything would do, like…one of the chairs sitting around the firepit a few yards away. He rushed over and grabbed one, hoping Ava wasn't already inside and wondering where in the hell he was.

He made quick work of the screen with his pocketknife and eased one leg over the windowsill, pushing off with his other leg to sort of jump up there. And damn if it didn't hurt quite a bit more than he expected with the gaping wound that had only been closed a short while earlier.

He bit his lip through the pain as he struggled through the window.

It was not a graceful endeavor.

He glanced around, taking in the room, half expecting Ava to already be far enough into the house to catch a glimpse of her, but she was nowhere to be found. Maybe she was halfway to clearing the whole place by now, Zach thought, and figured he'd better get a move on if he was to be of any use at all.

He began on the main floor, moving through the living room, eyes darting, ears perked, skin prickling with adrenaline and anticipation. Easing his way toward what he thought might be the kitchen, he peeked around the corner. It was, in fact, a kitchen, and it was very empty and very quiet.

Zach let out a long, slow breath, trying to find his composure, his bravery, his wits. And while he was pretty sure he didn't actually find any of those things, desperation and fear propelled him forward anyway.

Where the hell was Ava? He did not think he would be doing this alone.

But he was so close to Chloe now. He could feel it.

Moving back through the living room, he started down a short hallway. Peeking into the first room on the right, he found a bedroom. Nothing seemed out of the ordinary. Without going in, he moved on to the next bedroom down the hall. Same thing. The third bedroom was as empty as the others. His frustration grew as he moved to the bathroom at the end of the hall, even flinging the shower curtain open and half-expecting someone to jump out at him.

He had "cleared" all the rooms and come up with nothing. But of course, he hadn't really cleared them completely, had he? He'd determined there was no one obvious lurking in any of them, but he had to look closer. Closest to the third bedroom, he moved into that room first, gun at the ready. He whipped the door back and pointed his gun in that direction, heart beating hard and feeling like an absolute imposter. Who was he trying to kid? He had no idea what he was doing. Still, what other choice did he have?

Zach ducked and lifted the bedspread, readying for the jump scare of his life, but again, nothing happened. He moved on to the closet, taking a deep breath before thrusting the door open then aiming the gun into every corner.

Empty.

He really hoped no one was watching him, because this whole daring rescue thing was making him feel like the biggest amateur on the planet.

He moved into the next bedroom across the hall, going through all the same motions with the same result.

Zach headed down the hall, backtracking his way to the first bedroom. He did the behind the door thing, the under the bed thing, then moved on to the closet. But this time, when he moved to the closet, he wasn't met with nothing.

There was a latch on the door.

On the outside. His heart began to race. There would never be a latch on the outside of a closet door unless someone on the outside was keeping someone on the inside against their will.

Zach slowly opened the latch, visions of Chloe jumping into his arms already rolling through his mind as he whipped the door open.

The first thing he registered was that Chloe was not there. His heart fell straight to his feet and through the floor.

The second thing he registered was even though Chloe wasn't there, the closet was not empty. A man lay on the floor, and Zach couldn't tell whether he was dead or passed out. A strange shot of excitement moved through him…if this was Justin, then maybe everything was already okay. Maybe Ava had somehow gotten in there and secured him in the small space, perhaps already on her way to Chloe. Unfortunately, the third thing he registered was that the man was wearing a police uniform, and also, that he looked familiar.

Shit.

The cop from that morning in town. Banyan?

He had no idea how the officer had gotten to Justin ahead of them, but it actually made Zach feel more secure, his shoulders easing a bit. The police knew what they were doing. Except, he realized in the next heartbeat, even if Banyan had found Justin, he hadn't fared too well going up against him, and the low vibration of dread in his stomach started all over again.

Guess they knew the origin of the police cruiser in the woods now.

And then, as these things rushed through his mind, Zach registered a fourth thing. There was a strange smell in the room…a little bit earthy, and a lot chemical. He looked at the officer on the floor. Had the man been gassed?

Without thinking, Zach just moved. And yeah, probably not the best idea to go rushing into a small space that might still be filled with gas, but that apparently didn't matter to his brain. He shoved the gun into the back of his pants, then grabbed the man under the armpits, gathering all his strength to pull him out of there.

The thought had occurred to him that maybe it was already too late, and perhaps he shouldn't be moving a body—especially if this place was about to become a crime scene—but even as he was thinking those things, Zach knew he couldn't leave a defenseless man in a situation like that, even if it might already be too late.

After a few strong heaves, Zach maneuvered the officer out of the closet and into the bedroom. He thought about putting him on the bed, but all of a sudden, he was feeling a little…dizzy?

His breathing was heavy from the excursion. Which meant he'd taken in some of the gas. He hoped to hell it wasn't lethal, and hoped to even deeper depths of hell this asshole hadn't done anything like this to Chloe.

Zach had never been so scared, so full of adrenaline, so motivated to…he wasn't sure what. Find Chloe, for sure, but then he wanted to do something else. To find this man who had his daughter and make sure he never did anything like this to anyone ever again.

He did not like the feeling. It wasn't him.

The air in the bedroom was probably already compromised, but in Zach's mind, it only made sense to shut the closet door and keep as much of it contained to that small space as possible. But when he moved toward the closet, he saw the screens. Four of them, clearly receiving pictures from surveillance cameras around the property.

He was torn. This could be the answer to exactly where Chloe was, not to mention where Ava had gotten to, but getting close enough to see, and maybe even figure out the basics of the system, would mean going all the way inside the closet and risking getting caught in there himself…maybe permanently.

The room seemed to tilt around him.

But the other choice was to continue wandering around the house aimlessly, and then move on to the grounds if he had no luck. But all of this was already taking too long. Every second Chloe was out there, scared and alone, was one second too many.

He almost decided it wasn't worth the risk. He was of no use to Chloe or anyone else if he was unconscious… or worse, and he moved to close the door, ready to seal it shut and latch it back up, but then a flash. Movement across one of the screens and he was pulled in, as if he had no control over his feet. He yanked his shirt up over his nose, realizing it wasn't going to help much, but it was all the protection he had and peered into the screen.

But the screen was so dark, like maybe he hadn't actually seen anything at all.

He blinked, then blinked again, convincing himself it had been a trick of the eye. He'd wanted so badly to see something that he dreamed it all up.

He started backing out of the closet when the flash came again. Someone running across the top left screen. The feed was dim, but the place looked like...the barn. And someone had just moved from behind one large beam to the next.

Ava.

What the shit was Ava doing in the barn?

But Zach knew the answer with a certainty that sent a chill straight to his bones. She was going after Justin, and she was doing it alone. Except screw that, Zach thought, already halfway there in his mind. He didn't think about what he would do when he got there; he only knew he had to help.

And then the screens all flashed, changing to new feeds, and he saw the one thing he'd been hoping to see, so scared he might never see again.

The face of his beautiful daughter.

Chapter 18

The barn door slid open with a wail. So much for taking the sneaky route, Ava thought as she eased inside. Even though the sun was just beginning to set, the inside of the barn was incredibly dim, and her eyes needed time to adjust. Time she didn't have.

Ava's first instinct was to slide the door shut again, though it did cross her mind she might need a quick escape. But the thought of Justin being able to get out without her realizing it and going after Zach or Chloe won out, and she squeak-slid the door shut again.

Her eyes still a bit compromised, Ava felt like a fish in a fishbowl—vulnerable…exposed. She needed to find cover.

She began to make out shapes in the shadows. The place was a veritable smorgasbord of farm implements ranging from large tractors and machinery all the way down to pitchforks and rakes, and a million other potentially deadly instruments in between.

The infrared goggles were useless. Justin had set at least a dozen fires in the main open space of the barn, contained in old wheel wells on top of concrete blocks. It was a maze in there, with stalls running in one direction, then turning and continuing in another. Which would have been fine if Justin hadn't already had time to memorize the place.

First rule of operatives—know the territory. Which went hand in hand with the second rule—confuse your opponent whenever possible.

It was a built-in element of surprise situation on repeat.

"Hello, Sparrow," a creepily disembodied voice echoed through the barn.

What the hell had he done? Install a damned speaker system?

"I've been waiting for this moment for a long time."

It's funny the things a person forgot when given ample amounts of time. Ava was surprised to learn she'd forgotten his voice. Or not forgotten it, really, but it had been such a long time since she'd thought about his voice, the sound of it took her by surprise. Made so many memories come rushing back.

Funny thing was, very few of them were happy. Though she supposed that had a lot to do with the fact she rarely allowed herself to be happy back then. Given how she'd been living the past five years and how different her life was, the thought broke her heart a little. She'd never noticed it back then, but after experiencing a joyful life, she wasn't sure she could go back to a life like her old one.

"I haven't," she said under her breath, glancing around for any hint as to where he might be.

Her eyes landed on a speaker built into the wall. So, the intercom system was in place before Justin got there. Maybe it was a way to communicate between the house and the barn, or maybe they'd had ranch hands at one point and this was the easier way to get messages to their staff. With any luck, it would be an older system, which would mean there was likely a dedicated room where a person would have to make the announcements from. New technology was definitely handy sometimes but could be a real pain in the ass to trace with all the Bluetooth and wireless and everything.

She eased down the wall, glad she had dark clothes on.

Her eyes were finally starting to adjust, and she spotted a wire running up a post in front of her. Tracing the wire with her eyes, she moved farther down the length of the barn, following it to a small room built into the back of the structure.

Silently she moved into position outside the door of the room, kicking it open, so ready to shoot. So ready for all this to be done.

But the room was empty.

"Aw, Sparrow, you didn't think it would be that easy, did you?" came the disembodied voice.

No, Ava thought, but she'd be lying that she hadn't hoped he'd be that careless and underestimating of her.

And now she knew he was watching her too. Hard to track someone when they had eyes on you, but you had absolutely no idea where they were. But it was dim inside the barn, the windows shuttered, the only light coming from the fires.

Ava moved quickly, ducking behind the nearest fire. If he was using infrared to track her, she would use his own fire trick against him. She moved again to the next nearest fire, then the next. It wouldn't be impossible to track her, but she was damn well going to make it as hard as she could.

The real problem was, she had no idea where the hell Justin even was. And he probably had her exact location pinpointed.

She closed her eyes...had to think. If she were Justin, where would she go?

And then, with the intuitive clarity that used to fuel her every move, honed over years in her former life, she knew.

Up.

Justin would be somewhere above, in the loft. Advantage was at the high ground where you can see your enemy coming. Usually. She had to figure a way to go up without waltzing right into some trap he'd no doubt set for her. She desperately needed an advantage of her own. *She* needed the higher ground.

A quick glance around told her there were several ladders leading to the hayloft, and she'd bet her life each one of them was booby-trapped somehow. And if she knew Justin, those traps would do harm, yes, but it would not be enough to kill her—only to weaken her so he could toy with her some more.

Coward.

But Ava didn't need to get to the loft. She needed to get higher. She needed to get to the roof.

Of course, getting onto the roof of a barn was not an easy task considering a two-story barn was usually thirty feet up, and this one was no exception. She also needed to get there without Justin knowing what she was up to.

She needed a distraction.

And as the final rays of sun shone through the edges of the shuttered windows, the dust dancing around as it passed through the sun streaks, an idea started to form. Dust. So much dust. Highly flammable dust if given the proper variables.

And she'd passed a bunch of yard and lawn tools on her way into the barn that would come in very handy, indeed. Bags of grain lay stacked against the nearest stall. The feed looked like it had been there for a long time, as if the animals the grain had been intended for had been gone awhile and no one ever got around to getting rid of it. If Ava were very lucky, maybe the grain had even begun to form the dusty black mold that was very bad for a person to breathe in, but that would be perfect for her plan.

Ava crept back to the pile of yard tools and pulled out what she needed. The gas-powered leaf blower wasn't going to be quiet, but if her plan worked it wouldn't matter if Justin knew where she was.

Because she would not be there for long.

Making her way back to the sacks of grain, Ava pulled out the small knife from its sheath near her boot and made a long, quick slice down the front of each stack. Grain began to leak out. She put her knife away and pushed the primer button a few times before yanking the cord. It made a hideous sound, no doubt instantly alerting Justin to her location.

She pulled the cord again, and again—hideous sound, no start.

Scrambling came from above, and she knew she'd only get one more chance.

She yanked that damn cord with every ounce of

strength she had and the thing finally, blessedly, roared to life.

In one swift move, Ava kicked over the stacks of grain, causing a huge plume of dust to billow into the air as she pointed the leaf blower toward its destination—the nearest fire, and on the other side of it, a nice, convenient stack of hay, dry and brittle, and best of all, gloriously flammable.

It hadn't been Justin's best move to light those fires, Ava thought as she ran in the opposite direction toward one of the shuttered windows.

Even though they were behind her, Ava knew the flames were huge. The heat was heavy at her back, and as she scrambled the few feet to the window and pushed the shutter open, she risked a glance back and smiled as the flames licked their way around the edges of the haystack.

It wouldn't keep Justin busy forever, but if he had some master plan to deal with her in the loft, he'd have to put out the fire first. Footsteps pounded on wood somewhere deep inside the barn and Ava knew she was right.

She flung one leg over the windowsill, then eased to the ground on the other side, gently closing the shutter behind her.

Problem one down. Now there was just the little matter of how to get onto the roof of the exceedingly tall, and extremely daunting—now that she was getting a good look at it—building. She ran a full circle around the barn, pleased to see a bit of smoke billowing from the east side—Justin was no doubt losing his shit, which made her extremely happy—but there was no obvious way up the structure.

Scratch that.

There was one very obvious way, but Ava really did not want to take it. Unfortunately, there were no trees, or any structures around that might be hiding a handy-dandy ladder that might happen to reach all the way to the roof either, so it made her decision easy.

The decision was easy, but the execution definitely wouldn't be. Back when she was in the field, she might not give too much thought to it, but now that she'd let herself…soften for five years, she was not sure how this was going to go.

Off the front of the barn, there was a pulley system that must have once been used to transport feed, or hay, or who knew what up to the second floor of the barn. The heavy metal contraption was bolted above the second-floor door, close to the roof.

Ava took a deep breath and let it out in a big, determined whoosh. It was now or never, she knew, and jumped up onto the long rope dangling near the ground. Inch by inch she eased up the rope, moving hands above her head, then pushing with her legs, trying her damnedest not to look down. But the moment she had that pesky thought that she should not look down, the task, of course, became impossible.

Halfway up, Ava began to think the whole thing had been a very bad idea. Her arms, not used to the kind of stress, began to shake, but she tried to kind of zone out, to keep moving and not think too much. Eventually she made it to the heavy metal wheel part of the pulley and above it, the strong wooden post, about six inches square. She hadn't thought this next part all the way through. She was only taking it one step at a time, and with her arms as weak and spent as they were, she wasn't sure she could hoist herself up to the post. Although, given the situation she was in, so high from the ground, she wasn't entirely sure she could make it back down either, so again, easy decision…and a difficult execution.

She tried to visualize her plan. Maybe she could kick her feet up and go legs first, but the thought of dangling upside down made her shove that idea away pretty quickly. She honestly still didn't know if it was going to work when she decided to simply go for it, moving her legs up close under her, gripping the rope with her feet and pushing herself partway above the post, steadying herself by grasping the post and heaving her way the final few inches.

As she straddled the post, her heart raced, and everything else shook, and then, even worse, she accidentally looked down. A little zip of wooziness forced her to scramble up over the edge of the roof to its relative safety faster than she could say giddyap.

Which was definitely also faster than she could process that she just climbed to the roof of a barn that was, you know, on fire.

But a girl couldn't have everything. One step at a time was about all a person could handle in a situation where their ex-boyfriend slash stalker slash attempted murderer is after them and everyone they love.

Legs still shaking, Ava made her way to the first of two little vent stacks with the cute tiny roofs on the top of the barn. She supposed they had a name but had absolutely no idea what it might be. And absolutely no desire to care, what with the whole burning building beneath her and everything. Which was when she decided to risk a peek, leaning a bit toward the east side of the barn. There was smoke, but it didn't seem any worse than before, and since it wasn't streaming out of the vent she was currently leaning on, she figured Justin must have it under control. It would have been pretty careless to light a bunch of fires inside an old dusty barn filled with hay and not have a few extinguishers lying around.

The slats in the vent stack allowed Ava a bit of a view back into the barn. It was almost as dark in there as it was becoming outside, the last whispers of light melting into darkness as she rested, knowing that what had gotten her this far had been the easy part.

And then a shadow crossed as she watched, a darkness breaking the muted orange of the glowing fires. The path of the shadow was determined, confident, not evading or using maneuvers to try to stay hidden. Either Justin was very sure of his plan, or he had no idea about her perch above.

He moved fast, and almost instantly past where she could see, heading for the back of the barn. Ava got up and hung on to the vent stack as she eased around it. The roof was steeply pitched, but she was surprised at how steady she felt up there. Though she supposed anything would feel steady after the monstrous climb of doom she'd just performed.

Careful of making noise, Ava made her way down the roof, stepping carefully in the dark, testing each step before putting her full weight on it. It was an old barn, but it was sturdy, and she made it to the second vent stack in a minute or so.

Jackpot.

Justin wasn't directly below the vent, but he was in

her line of vision. Surrounded by monitors and electronic equipment, the guy had a whole intelligence center going on right inside that rustic old barn. She should have known. Justin wasn't one to trust his instincts, always preferring the backup of technology to show him the easiest way.

And then on one of the screens, she saw something. A man, wandering through the house, and she couldn't help herself—her body moving of its own accord—when she leaned in a bit further to get a better look.

And that's when she heard the big crack.

But she didn't have time to figure out where it was coming from before the world in front of her gave way, the vent falling in on itself.

Which was precisely when she began to plummet.

Zach knew only two things. He had to get to Chloe, then he had to get to Ava. He had absolutely no idea how he was going to do either of those things, but he was going to damn well do them anyway.

The screens flashed again, and Chloe's face appeared. She was somewhere dark. The grainy gray feed of Chloe's face looked like night vision, but the sun was still peeking out over the horizon, the setting sun coating everything in a sickly pink glow.

Which meant there weren't any windows wherever she was.

His guts started to churn. What if she wasn't in the house at all? Or anywhere on the property? The bastard had moved her at least once, even if it was stopping only long enough to take a picture at the old hunting shack.

But Zach knew he had no choice. He had to search

every inch of the property because, well, frankly he had no other option. So he began to search, knowing full well it was an exercise in frustration and he was going to descend further and further into panic the entire time.

The screens flashed once more and Zach trained his eyes on Chloe, studying every inch of the screen for some kind of clue to let him know where she might be. And then he saw it. A small circle a bit brighter than the rest of the feed, as if a tiny bit of sun was trying to break through. A knot in a piece of wood, maybe? Or even a crack? But before the screen switched again, Zach knew one small thing more than he did before. He'd had frenzied visions of underground spaces, bunkers, panic rooms impossible to get into, but now he knew she was in a space where there must be at least one window—a covered window, but a window nonetheless.

Zach took a big breath and screamed, "Chloe!"

He'd forgotten where he was and a wave of dizziness washed over him, making him thrust an arm out to grab the wall, nearly falling. He moved back out of the closet, stepping over the police officer and wondering how deadly the gas was. But the thought pushed to the back of his mind as he stumbled toward the door of the bedroom.

"Chloe!" he yelled again, the effort forcing him to pause and lean on the doorframe.

His vision swirled for a moment, then righted itself, like the worst head rush of his life. As long as the effects weren't permanently affecting him, he was damn well going to use every moment he had to get to his daughter.

He moved back toward the living room. There was a chance Chloe could be in the basement, and he wasn't about to leave the place without exhausting every possible chance he had at finding her.

As another wave of dizziness rolled through, his head feeling heavier, his body moving slower, his thoughts getting thicker, he made his way to the large windows. If the gas was this potent, and if there was any chance Chloe was anywhere nearby, he needed to air the place out. He thought about going back and closing the bedroom door the gas was coming from, but if there was any chance Banyan was still alive, he couldn't do that. The officer had clearly already been through a hell of a lot. Judging from the headache already threatening to strangle Zach's efforts at finding Chloe and Ava, if the officer did wake up, he was going to be suffering, and Zach couldn't bear to make that even worse.

He struggled with the old windows that clearly hadn't been opened for a while, but finally got the crank to move the tiniest bit. After another lurch or two, the window gave way, a whoosh of fresh air pouring in, aided by the window he'd climbed through on the other side of the room. He repeated the effort with one more window, then moved toward the basement stairs, which he'd seen near the entrance.

The stairwell was dim, but even as he was descending, Zach could already sense this wasn't going to be where he found Chloe. The light from the stairway would have illuminated the feed from the camera more, he was sure of it, but he supposed, in his hazy stupor, it was possible there could be a room built down there that was darker.

The sensation as he made his way down the stairs was similar to being drunk, with brief moments of clarity alternating with bouts of fogginess through which he concentrated hard, trying to find lucidity again. And then, without fully knowing how he'd gotten there, he was standing in the middle of an empty room, light streaming in through windows on all sides.

Chloe was nowhere to be found.

Still, Zach fumbled to open every door in that basement. He wasn't sure in the end how many there were, it felt like a hundred, but even he knew that didn't make sense.

He blinked a few times and shook his head, which seemed to help a little, then made his way back up the stairs to the main floor. The task took far more exertion than it should have, but he got the sense the toxin was already weaker than before, and maybe he was on the other side of it. His head still felt like it was in a vise and his eyelids were heavier than ever, but the fresh air as he crested the top of the stairs helped even more.

"Chloe!" he yelled one more time before reaching for the doorknob to leave.

He had no idea what his plan was, but he'd exhausted every possible hiding place in the house.

But as he turned the knob, a clunk sounded. A clunk from somewhere inside the house.

"Chloe?" he yelled again, this time more questioning, his heart starting to beat a little faster.

The clunk sounded again, and this time Zach was ready for it, listening intently for where it was coming from.

The ceiling?

It took Zach far longer than it should have to figure it out. How could he have been so dense?

The attic.

Zach figured it must be the gas, or at least that was the story he was going with as he stumble-ran through the house searching for an access panel. Living room, nothing. Kitchen nothing…he went through the bedrooms, even stepping over the police officer to peek into the closet of horrors, but still nothing until he reached the back bedroom on the left, tucked away inside the closet, where he finally found what he was looking for.

"Chloe, I'm coming!" he yelled, then ran back to the kitchen for a chair, positioning it under the panel and sliding it open.

But even with the chair he was still too far below the opening to see inside. With the still-foggy brain, Zach didn't know where he summoned the strength—it must have been pure adrenaline—but somehow, he jumped and pulled himself partway through the small hole, and still half hanging out, he scanned the dark space.

A scurrying noise came from somewhere in the shadows, and Zach braced himself once more.

But it wasn't an enemy to fight that he saw. It was his amazing Chloe—hands tied and a cloth around her mouth—but otherwise looking healthy and uninjured.

Relief flooded him, and he didn't even care how much he shook with the effort of hanging there as his daughter looped her arms around his neck and began to cry.

Chapter 19

Everything hurt.

Ava started to move slowly, trying—unsuccessfully—not to groan, unsure as to what might be injured or broken…or what might be coming at her next. Eventually she rolled onto her back, and nothing seemed to be broken, but her muscles screamed. This was going to hurt tomorrow.

If she made it to tomorrow.

A slow clap started from somewhere in the rafters. "You always did know how to make an entrance," Justin said.

Ava couldn't see where he was, exactly, but from the direction of his voice, she got the general idea of his whereabouts being ahead of her and to her right. She had seen him just before her fall though, so he couldn't have gotten far.

"Asshole," she said under her breath, realizing—as she picked a few splinters of wood from her shirt—that he had to have doctored the vent stack, set it to crumble.

The first one she leaned against had been as strong as the day it was built, but the second folded in on itself like the origami game she used to play as a kid to determine her future. She was still waiting on her "large fortune" and "many cats."

"I have to say, you've played into my plan exactly as you were supposed to," his voice said, faraway and tinny.

A speaker.

He'd known exactly what she was going to do before she did it. Of course, he'd had the advantage of time—scoping out the property and putting measures in place to ensure she did what he expected. She wondered if he'd even bothered to booby-trap the ladders or if he knew she'd assume they'd been tampered with.

Ava began to realize one thing. In the time she'd been slowly getting to her feet, Justin could have taken her out six times. But that wasn't what he wanted. He wanted to toy with her. To make her suffer—both physically and mentally. He wanted to control her.

And she hated that she'd played right into his game. Her face burned...with rage, embarrassment, she wasn't sure. Probably a combination of both. She used to be better than this.

She needed to be better than this.

"Where's Chloe?" she spat, wiping at the bit of blood on her lip.

"She's safe," Justin said. "Might take a while for that...gentleman of yours to find her though."

Of course. Justin would do everything in his power to keep Zach busy. To keep him away while he played out his sick game. To have Ava all to himself. To do what he failed at the first time.

But Ava wasn't going to make it easy. If it was a choice between saving herself or saving Zach and Chloe, it wasn't a choice. She'd gladly sacrifice for them, and she was prepared. But if there was a chance, a way to keep the life she'd built...well, she was going to bloody well try for it. And lucky for her, she didn't care about teaching anyone any lessons, or whatever the hell it was Justin was trying to do or prove. The first chance she got she would take him out. No questioning, no overthinking, no excuses. She reached behind her back for her gun.

Shit.

It must have dislodged in the fall. Ava glanced back to the pile of rubble wondering if it was worth trying to find, when a shadow jumped out at her. Except, of course, it wasn't just a shadow. It was the man she hoped she'd never see again. She was caught off guard, knocked to the floor, tumbling, tangling with him. She never wanted to be this close to him again. Had fiery, burning nightmares about it after the bunker explosion.

But as they rolled once more, Ava realized something. All those years spent worrying about Justin finding her, terrified about what might happen, were for nothing. In fact, now that he'd found her, she realized it was the best thing that could ever happen.

Because truly, this was the only way to end it.

She wrapped one leg around Justin's waist and used the momentum of the roll to heave herself to the top position. Justin anticipated the move and countered, but it was enough to untangle them and send her scrambling a few feet away.

Justin got to his feet quickly, but so did Ava, finally coming face-to-face with the man who'd very nearly killed her five years ago.

"Good to see you, Sparrow," he said, the words not so much being spoken as they were oozing out of him.

"Afraid I can't say the same," Ava said, "though it is a little alarming to see you this way."

"Scared?" he asked.

Ava scoffed. "I meant your appearance is alarming, not the situation," she said.

Justin had always been vain, and Ava knew how to hit him where it hurt. He was an attractive person, most spies were—it helped their marks trust them—and he would still be considered handsome. But he had definitely aged, and Ava wasn't above using any tactic she could to get inside his head.

His eye twitched and she knew she was on the right track, but then he smiled.

They were giving each other a wide berth, circling the loft of the barn. Ava's hands were out at the ready, as were Justin's, though he clearly had the advantage, considering the knife in his hand.

"It has been a long five years," he said, as if shrugging the comment off, but Ava knew better.

"Really?" she said, as if she didn't have a care in the world. "Because they've been the absolute best five years of my life."

She wasn't lying either…she'd give anything to go back to her warm little Ambrosia Falls house and be quite content for the rest of time. She'd kind of fallen into being an operative in the first place. It was cliché, a recruiter singling her out in college, citing her advanced marks and athletic abilities, but even then, Ava knew her desirability as an agent had more to do with the fact that she didn't have any close family left, or many other connections for that matter.

Ugh, and she hated to admit it, but all that was probably how Justin had been able to get close to her too. Once someone became an operative, they couldn't live a normal life anymore. It was inevitable that operatives tended to attract each other like magnets...it was really the only way to have a relationship at all.

Of course, there was a whole lot of risk in getting involved with an agent, which Ava knew as well as anybody, she just never thought she'd be gullible enough to fall for it. Which was, of course, her real mistake. Believing she was smarter than Justin...less gullible. Except she'd been the one who got played. She supposed it was inevitable, this instinct to continue assuming she was smarter than him—everyone believed they were smarter than everyone else in the room most of the time. But she wasn't about to underestimate him again.

She would, however, do her damnedest to make sure he thought she'd become a whole lot weaker than she had. Her limp, as she moved slowly, never taking her eyes off Justin, was real, but she might have been exaggerating it...just a little. Maybe more than a little. She swiped at her lip again, reminding Justin of the cut he put there with his clever, clever ways.

"Looks like it hurts," Justin said, a gleam in his eye that Ava decidedly did not like.

It was a little too wild, a little too unhinged.

"It's fine," she said, though she didn't try to sell the point too much.

As she said it, Justin lunged, knife hand out. He was trying to catch her off guard again, trying to make her duck to the left, which would have sent her tumbling over the edge of the loft, but she was too well-trained. Ava didn't even have to try to memorize the details of her surroundings anymore, it happened automatically, and instinct thrust her in the opposite direction.

They continued to circle, Ava watching Justin's eyes, his hands...every twitch of every muscle, her mind working, trying to come up with a plan. She was moving toward the rubble of the vent stack, her gun at the forefront of her mind. She had no doubt Justin had a gun on him somewhere too, but it would likely be hard to get it, and he wouldn't pull it out unless she had one too. He wanted a fair fight. He'd been beaten by Ava before, and his tiny ego wouldn't allow for him to win at a disadvantage. He'd have to win fair and square.

Her feet slid across the floor, the dirt and hay and splintered bits of woods dampening the sound of their footfalls.

She was beginning to form a tiny inkling of a plan. It was a terrible plan, but it was all she had. It was too much to hope she'd happen upon her gun, but if she could get to one of the sharp splinters of wood, one large enough to do a little damage if embedded in the right appendage at the right angle, she could have a chance. Of course, that was a lot of ifs. If she saw an appropriate piece...if she was able to get a hold of it...if she was able to get close enough to Justin to do some damage. But it was what she had. He wasn't going to wait around all day before he made another move.

Justin lunged for her, a flame from one of his fires glinting off the blade, and Ava put her plan into motion. She ducked, rolling along her right shoulder, grabbing as much debris from the floor as her hand would hold as she went. She jumped back to her feet and spun to face him, checking her treasures. There was a single splinter that might do, and as she discarded the rest, she made her own lunge toward Justin, driving the splinter home with all her might, but at the last second, he saw it coming and turned, just enough for the wood to dig into his shoulder instead of closer to his chest where she'd been aiming.

Justin let out an animalistic wail, clearly injured, but also clearly even more pissed off now as his eyes went wild and he came straight for her.

Ava had no time to react as he hit her full-on with his entire weight, sending them both toward the railing of the loft area. The wood railing only crackled for a second before it gave way, sending them into free fall, a sensation Ava had hoped she wouldn't experience again, let alone so soon. Though maybe because she'd already been through this once in the past few minutes, she was less caught off guard than Justin seemed to be. His wild eyes filled with fear. She swung a leg around his body and used the momentum to spin them both, hoping like hell he would be the one to hit the floor first.

Zach lifted his precious cargo down from the attic and set her on the floor. He was as gentle as he could be as he bent down and removed the cloth from around her mouth and cut the rope free from her hands.

Even though she hadn't done it in years, Chloe scurried up and clung onto his neck, not letting go even when he stood, ignoring the slice of pain shooting though his leg. Pain was nothing, not when he finally had his daughter back.

He moved back down the hall carrying his only child,

and tears filled his eyes when Chloe whispered, "I knew you'd come."

He held her close as he continued to stumble toward the door, realizing for the first time he hadn't thought about what he might do when he found Chloe. They had no truck to retreat to, no safe space to go to figure out their next move.

Suddenly, Chloe stiffened. "What's wrong, Dad?"

She pulled back and looked at him, alarm filling her eyes.

"Nothing's wrong anymore, sweetheart," he said, taking another step toward the door.

"Dad," Chloe scolded. "What's wrong with your leg? You shouldn't be carrying me."

"I don't want to let you go," he said, continuing to stumble along.

"Dad!" she said, louder this time. "Stop. Put me down. Please."

Zach didn't want to admit it, but his leg *was* making it a whole lot more difficult to rescue Chloe. He didn't want to be hurt, he didn't want to admit it was hampering the whole "brave, strong dude" thing he had going on, but he wasn't some sort of superhero. He was just a guy who would do anything for his kid.

"It's okay, Chloe," Zach said.

"Dad," Chloe said, her tone more serious than a veteran teacher dealing with the school bully for the fourth time that semester. "Put. Me. Down."

Zach eased Chloe out of his arms as gingerly as he could, trying not to wince. "I want to make sure you're okay."

"Yeah, same," she said, putting her hands on her hips.

A little pang of something—sadness that she was growing up so fast, maybe—shot through him, but he knew this was the real Chloe. The very capable, caring and concerned kid he wasn't quite sure how he raised to be so amazing, and so completely herself.

"I'll be fine," he said, trying not to let his limp betray his words.

Chloe side-eyed him like she knew he was full of it, which he absolutely was. The truth was, his leg hurt like hellfire pokers were twisting around in there, but his job wasn't done yet, so he wasn't about to stop and try to do something about it.

"Come on," he said, leading her toward the door. "We need to figure out what to do next."

"We have to get Ava and get out of here," Chloe said matter-of-factly, as if the whole thing was obvious.

"How did you know Ava was here?"

"*He* kept talking about her," Chloe said, the word coming out like she had a bad taste in her mouth. "It was so annoying. And then he started calling her some dumb bird name." She thought for a moment. "Sparrow, I think. It was so weird. He is *so* weird."

Zach marveled at how even a kidnapping could do little to keep Chloe's feistiness at bay. "That's one word for it, I guess," he said.

Chloe smiled conspiratorially like she knew a few other choice words her dad might prefer to call the guy.

"Okay, you're right. Ava is out here, and I have to find her, but first I need to find someplace safe for you."

"I can come with you—" Chloe started to say, but Zach put up a hand to cut her off.

"There is no way that is happening," he said in the

tone of voice he hated to use, but under the circumstances, it was warranted.

Chloe sighed. "Fine." The word came out with a little pout, but Zach knew she wasn't going to argue.

He hoped to hell that tone was never going to stop working on the poor kid, no matter how much it hurt him to have to use it, since he had no idea what he would do if he didn't have it in his arsenal.

Zach unlocked, then opened the door slowly, peeking out first to make sure the coast was clear. He had an idea in the back of his mind, one that made a lot of sense, but something didn't feel quite right about it. Still, he and Chloe crept out of the house, and after looking in every direction, moved quickly toward the edge of the trees. His instincts screamed at him to run, but something held him back.

They made it to the tree line, and after about eight more feet, Zach stopped.

"What are we doing?" Chloe whispered.

"I don't know," Zach whispered back.

He glanced around again, then headed in the same direction. A few yards more and he stopped. He looked at Chloe.

"What?" she asked, knowing something was up.

He leaned back on a fallen log to give his leg a bit of a rest. As he looked at Chloe, whose eyes were wide with concern and questioning, he decided to be honest.

"I don't know what to do," he said.

"Okay," Chloe replied, as if she had expected as much.

"It's just… I know where there's a place that should be safe, and you'd be sheltered and out of harm's way."

"Okaaaay," Chloe said again, this time dragging the word out as if to say, *spit it out, Dad*.

Zach sighed. "But something doesn't feel right about it."

Chloe shrugged. "So, we don't go there. You always have to trust your instincts, Dad."

The kid was right. Thinking about taking Chloe to the cop car should have been a no-brainer, but visions of his own truck blowing up sent shivers down his spine. If anyone had been even close to the truck when it went... well, he didn't even want to think about that.

He nodded once. "You're right," he said.

He had, after all, always taught Chloe exactly that— trust your gut.

"I don't know where you'll be safe. And I need to know you're safe."

Chloe looked around. "What about right there?" she said, motioning with her hand to exactly where he was sitting.

"With me?" Zach asked, wishing for nothing more than to be able to do exactly that and keep her with him for eternity, but he couldn't leave Ava.

"No," Chloe said, delivering another magnificent eye roll, "under the log you're sitting on."

Zach shifted, looking over his shoulder. The ground was covered in tall fernlike vegetation that would provide almost total cover.

"I can hide in the space under there."

It was pretty brilliant. Still, Zach was hesitant. "What if there are bugs under there?" he asked.

She looked up at him through her lashes, very much

not impressed. "I am not the one who is afraid of bugs," she said, shaking her head the tiniest bit.

Right. Right, it was absolutely him that did not love the creepy-crawlies.

Like, at all.

"What about rain?" he asked.

Chloe squinted up at sky—what little of it she could see through the trees—and stitched a "seriously?" kind of look onto her face. "There aren't even any clouds. And besides, I'll be under a log, the rain isn't going to get me."

"It could seep down under there," Zach said, raising an eyebrow as if daring her to challenge his logic.

"Um, so I guess my butt will get a little wet then," she said, shooting him an "are we done this ridiculous argument yet" look, already starting to crawl under the log.

Zach stood and tested the fallen tree trunk to make sure it was sturdy and wasn't about to fall on her head or anything, but the thing felt like it was stuck there with concrete.

"Fine," he said. "But you need to stay right here."

Chloe nodded.

"I am so serious, Chloe. After everything, can you imagine what would happen if I come back here and you're gone?"

Chloe peeked out from the log. "I'm guessing your head would pop right off."

And the way she said it—so grim—Zach couldn't help but bark out a laugh. "That is exactly correct. My head would pop off and that would be the end of me."

Chloe's face softened but was still serious. "I'm not going anywhere, Dad. I promise."

"Okay," he said, knowing she was telling the truth.

"Just stay here, stay quiet. I don't know, try to sleep or something, and I'll be back as soon as I can."

"Don't worry about me, Dad," she said, as Zach leaned over to plant a kiss on the top of her head. "I'm getting pretty used to entertaining myself."

Zach smiled, but as he stood, a pang of sorrow whooshed through him. The poor kid had been kidnapped and left to essentially fend for herself. Nothing to keep her mind busy, and here she was pretty much taking care of him.

And there he was, leaving her all alone again.

"I will be back soon," he said, turning before she could see the glistening in his eyes.

After everything she'd been through, the last thing Chloe needed was to be worried about him.

Chapter 20

The good news was, the landing had forced the jagged stake all the way through the fleshy part of Justin's shoulder so it poked through to the other side. The not so good news was—as Ava blinked, another round of pain shooting through her body—she noticed her eye was about half an inch from being impaled on said piece of wood.

Unfortunately, Justin noticed too.

He twisted his body, trying to move the stake farther toward Ava's head as her eyes snapped shut and she felt the heavy graze of the wood across her eyelid.

Justin rolled as he twisted, trying to get the upper hand, but with his injured shoulder he was sluggish, and as he moved above her, Ava took advantage of the momentum to maneuver her foot into his torso and kick him away. She scrambled to her feet quickly, at the same time Justin also righted himself.

As they faced off yet again, Ava spoke.

"It doesn't have to be this way, Justin. I'm not in the business anymore. Whoever you were working for—the people who wanted me gone—don't matter anymore. I'm no threat to anybody out here."

Justin plastered on a wild smile. "Sounds exactly like

someone who was trying to pretend they had a nice, quiet life in the boonies would say."

They continued to move slowly, circling again, though they were both moving slower, and with decidedly more effort than before.

Ava sighed. "I'm not working anymore, Justin. If I was, you would have heard about it by now."

"There are plenty of jobs that have been unclaimed or unaccounted for over the past five years. A surprising amount, really. And this place," he said, motioning around him, though Ava knew he meant the entire area of Ambrosia Falls, "is a perfect cover. Remote. No one questioning your comings and goings."

"I live in a small town, Justin," Ava said. "Everyone knows my comings and goings. Believe me, Ambrosia Falls is not a place one can easily keep their business to themselves."

Justin shrugged. "Maybe…maybe not. Either way, my employers are not willing to take that chance." He paused for a moment, as if mulling over whether he should say the next part. Apparently, he decided to go for it. "Besides, I've been waiting way too long for this moment to walk away now."

Ava wasn't surprised. She knew this had long been personal for Justin, even if her emotions over him, other than anger, had ended ages ago.

"I'm sorry to hear that," Ava said in the most impersonal tone she could muster. Nothing frustrated Justin more than not being taken as seriously as he wanted. Sure, the situation was certainly serious, but Ava was going to try damn hard to make Justin think he meant nothing to her. Which, if he hadn't been literally in her face, would be true. "It's going to be tedious having to deal with you."

Justin squinted at her, and Ava knew he was trying to formulate a comeback. She used the moment to lunge for him, aiming toward his bad shoulder. If that piece of wood hurt going in, it was going to burn like the rage of a teen with a bad attitude being pushed back out. She balled her fist and impacted him with the fleshy, outside part of her hand. The wood sliced into her a little, but it was nothing compared to the way it sliced back through Justin, his wail confirming it was not an overly pleasant experience.

Ava desperately needed her gun, but she couldn't be sure Justin hadn't set traps on the ladders, and knowing Justin, if an incendiary of some sort had been set, it wouldn't just be a simple flash-bang to scare someone off. It would do some damage.

She couldn't risk it.

But Justin was already gathering himself, and she needed time to think. She turned and fled down a corridor in the barn, a wall on one side and a row of animal stalls on the other. She considered ducking into one of the stalls, but once inside, she'd be trapped, so she kept running.

"Sparrooow," Justin called, dragging the word out, and it was just like him to be all creepy, as if he were the evil star of his very own horror movie.

What an egotistical ass.

Ava rounded the corner of the passage, making her way back into the main area of the barn, the fires still burning around the room, the heat stifling, an eerie red glow making the whole place seem like it was simmering in a bath of embers.

Ducking and using each firepit as cover, Ava made her way back toward the pile of yard tools she'd found the leaf blower in, and tried to quietly grab something she could use as a weapon. While she successfully managed to get her hands on a simple garden rake, she'd made a god-awful clatter—loud enough to raise the devil himself, which was actually pretty fitting, given her surroundings.

She wheeled around, sure Justin would be right behind her, but he was still a bit of a distance away, just coming around the corner of the passage he followed her through.

Justin smirked in a kind of "aw, isn't that cute" kind of way, looking sadly at her rake.

What a cocky jackass, she thought, and since the rake was all Ava had, she moved toward Justin, wanting nothing more than to end this. But as she made her way across the room, Justin slowly and deliberately reached out his good arm, grabbing hold of a tool of his own that had been conveniently leaning against the wall, hidden behind a few bales of hay. Which, she realized, he'd probably planted there earlier.

A gleaming, and rather sharp-looking pitchfork.

Ava glanced around the massive space, wondering what other items might be conveniently hidden around the place. Not that she had much time to think about it, since she hadn't stopped moving even when Justin pulled out the damn giant fork.

She just needed to be better than him, that was all there was to it. And yeah, maybe she'd let her training lapse a little in the past few years, and yeah, Justin had probably done the opposite, biding his time by honing his skills, but she was still confident. She'd always been better than him. At least that's what she was telling herself, even if a tiny voice somewhere deep in her head was whispering to her consciousness with inklings of doubt.

And maybe it was the doubt that got her. Threw her off her game, because as she neared Justin, something about the glint of the pitchfork distracted her. Or maybe it was the look on Justin's face, like he had so much hatred for her and honestly, Ava didn't know why. Didn't know what she'd ever done to him besides bring him close and make a life with him.

Ava raised her rake. It felt far too flimsy in her hands, far too old and maybe even ready to break, but it was all she had, and she brought it down hard, aiming for Justin's head, sure it wouldn't knock him unconscious, but maybe, if she was lucky, it might do some kind of brief damage. She imagined her follow-through might skim past the nasty gash on his shoulder, but as it turned out, there was no follow-through.

Only two tines of a pitchfork settling neatly and deeply into her forearm as her hands were raised above her head.

The pain was inconceivable. Ava had been hurt before—it had been an inevitability in her past life—but this was breath-stealing, instant agony, the sharp metal piercing straight through her already burned arm. She yanked back in reaction, the tines coming free, but then the blood began to race from her body as if it were being chased from within, pouring to the floor.

Ava tried to run, tried to put pressure on the wounds to staunch the blood and buy some time—it needed to be stopped or, well, Ava didn't want to think about that—but Justin was ready, yanking her back by her hair and throwing her to the ground, straddling himself on top of her.

And then his hands were around her throat. She didn't know how he still possessed so much strength—his injured shoulder should have made it impossible to even move his arm, but he must have been running on pure adrenaline as he squeezed with both hands, the right one doing most of the work.

Ava tried to move beneath him, struggled to bring a leg up and shift him off her, but he was too strong.

Her thoughts became cloudy, and then suddenly the only thing she could focus on was Justin. She didn't want to give him the satisfaction—it was exactly what he wanted—but it was his eyes. Eyes that held so much in them, a wild, possessive rage. A fury fueled by years of failure and obsession and need to destroy…by the embarrassment of having lost once, and a vow it would never happen again.

Then, as the world started to pull in from the edges of her vision, a darkness taking its place, the look changed to something else.

Joy. Pleasure in the fact that he had won.

Ava closed her eyes. She couldn't watch the sick satisfaction washing over his features.

And then, a magnificent, unholy clunk reverberated through the air, and the weight on top of her shifted as her world faded to black.

The shovel felt heavy in his hands. He'd never once wanted to hurt someone like that, but seeing Justin choking Ava, Zach didn't think, he just reacted.

As he shoved the unconscious Justin to the floor, Zach was shocked at how pale Ava looked. Almost lifeless.

He moved quickly to her side, leaning his head close, listening for her breathing.

At first, he heard nothing, but then, the faintest flutter of air moved through her lips, and it was like his whole body exhaled. And that's when he felt it. Something wet soaking into his jeans, and even though the fires were going, the barn was still pretty dim, and he could only see whatever it was, was dark, almost black. He swiped at the stuff and his hands came away red, his stomach clenching.

Instantly, Zach noticed Ava's arm was covered in it too, and he knew he had to move fast—there was so much blood. He pulled his outer shirt off and wrapped it as tightly as he could around Ava's forearm, hoping with everything he had in him that it would be enough. After everything they'd been through, he couldn't lose her now.

He picked her up, the burning in his leg a constant reminder this was not an okay situation, and with one last glance at the lifeless-looking Justin, he hurried out of the barn and into the cool night air, only then realizing he didn't know how he was going to get her out of there. His truck was long gone, and he couldn't trust the police car.

But… Justin must have gotten out into the woods somehow, Zach realized, rushing toward the house, and its attached garage. The main door on the garage was locked, so he headed to the front door of the house. The garage was connected through the front entrance and

Zach made his way there quickly, elated to see a small SUV parked neatly in the center. He flung open the passenger seat and set Ava in as gently as he could, though a small moan wisped past her lips, which was both relieving and a little scary at the same time.

But nothing was more of a relief than a quick glance at the ignition where the keys were dangling. Perhaps Justin was preparing for a quick getaway. He buckled her seat belt and shut Ava's door, running to the driver's side and pushing the button to open the garage door as he slid behind the wheel.

He hit the gas and backed out of the garage fast, simultaneously rolling down the window.

"Chloe!" he yelled, still moving backward, turning the wheel until the headlights hit the edge of the forest. "Chloe, we gotta go!"

Zach was nearly to the edge of the trees, readying to throw the vehicle into park and race back into the woods, but, bless her heart, Chloe was already running out, as if she'd been waiting for this moment all along.

She flung open the back door, scrambled inside, and had the door shut faster than Zach would have thought possible. Her seat belt was on in seconds.

As Zach hit the gas and headed out the winding driveway, he glanced at Chloe in the rearview mirror. "Have you been practicing that or something?"

Chloe shrugged a shoulder. "Maybe a little in my head while I was waiting for you to come back."

Zach shook his head in amazement.

"What? I had a lot of time to think and worry," Chloe said, sounding a little defensive.

It was around that time Chloe noticed Ava was not looking too hot in the passenger seat.

"Dad!" she said, alarmed. "Is she okay?"

Zach glanced back at Chloe again and hated the look he saw on her face—terror mixed with confusion. He wished he still had the innocent confusion of a kid, wondering how something so terrible could happen to a good person.

"I hope so," Zach said.

He wanted so badly to tell Chloe Ava would be fine, but the truth was, he had no idea. He had no medical training, and truthfully, he'd only done what he'd seen people do on TV to wrap her wound. He knew it had to be tight, but beyond that, he had no clue.

"I'm going to be fine," Ava croaked, surprising them both.

She hitched up a little in the seat and turned to face Chloe. "Your dad saved me."

Chloe smiled then. "Me too."

And Zach's whole being burst with an uncomfortable prickle of a thousand emotions coursing through him. Embarrassment. Pride. A sense of not being worthy. Of not feeling like he'd done anything special, and in fact, like he'd done everything all wrong.

But most of all he felt grateful to be sitting there with the two most important people in his world.

"I don't need a hospital," Ava said. "I can deal with all this."

"Of course you need a hospital," Zach said. "You've lost a lot of blood."

Ava shook her head. "I can manage at home," she said, and then she looked at him, the expression on her face serious, like she was trying to tell him something without telling him something.

Something she didn't want to say in front of Chloe.

And then, with his heart breaking in two, and wondering how many times a heart could break in one day, Zach understood. They couldn't go to the hospital. She couldn't be stuck in a hospital with Justin still out there. She'd be a sitting duck.

He cleared his throat. "Yeah, okay," he said. "We'll just head home."

He didn't dare glance back to see what he knew would be an even more confused look on the face of his daughter as the vehicle fell silent for the rest of the drive home.

"I'd like to help you with that," Zach said, pulling into his driveway.

He wondered if it was okay to park the strange SUV right there in plain sight, but it wasn't like Justin didn't know where they both lived anyway, so he wasn't sure what the point would be. Unless, of course, the police came looking...though something told him the car was clear of any connection with Justin or any suspicion of any kind, really.

"Yeah," Ava said, gingerly moving to release her seat belt.

Chloe—the one Zach had been worrying about the longest over the past...how long was it? A day? God, it felt so much longer than that—had already bounded out of the vehicle, as if completely unscathed by the whole ordeal. He didn't have any illusions that she wouldn't have some mental scars, but he was going to do everything in his power to make sure she had help, both professional and his own, in dealing with it all.

His first order of business was to be by Chloe's side as she crawled into bed, exhausted.

"Are you sure you don't want to talk about anything?" he asked, but Chloe shook her head. "I'm fine, Dad," she said, a "just leave it alone" tone to her voice. Clearly, she was not in the mood for some exhaustive rehash of everything right then.

Chloe gently pushed him out of her room so she could change—she was all about the privacy these days—and Ava met him in the hallway.

"You think she'll be okay?" he asked her.

He was the parent. He should have been the one to feel certain about what his daughter was feeling one way or the other, but he honestly had no clue. Why did all the other parents always seem like they knew exactly what they were doing? Were they all faking it too?

"Give yourself a break," Ava said, like she was reading his mind. "She'll be fine, and if she's not, the two of you are going to figure it out together."

Zach nodded, though he was far from convinced.

Chloe opened her door again and they both stepped inside as she crawled into bed.

"Think you'll be able to sleep?" Zach asked.

Chloe nodded. "I can barely keep my eyes open."

"Okay good," Zach said, then did something he hadn't done in years.

Turned on the old baby monitor he used when Chloe was little and hadn't gotten around to putting away yet. Although, truth be told, he'd still used it over the years without Chloe knowing about it. It was a habit he'd only stopped about a year ago, though he wished he hadn't.

Maybe he could have prevented this whole thing before it even started.

"Are you serious, Dad?" Chloe said, giving him a look that said she was not at all impressed.

"Just for tonight, okay?" Zach said. "I just need reassurance for right now."

Chloe sighed. "Fine, but we are not going to make a habit of this, right?" she asked, sounding more like she was the parent.

Zach smiled and stepped back while Ava sat on the bed. "Good night, sweet girl," she said, bending to kiss Chloe on the forehead.

"I'm glad you're okay," Chloe said.

Ava's eyes filled with tears then, and a thrum struck Zach's heart. Ava cared so much for Chloe, and Zach realized he would give anything to have this every night. Minus the abduction/explosions/revenge situation, obviously.

"I'm glad you're okay," Ava managed to whisper, booping Chloe on the nose.

She quickly got up and passed Zach as she left the room. He got the feeling she was trying to hide the extent of her emotions from them, but he wasn't fooled. Ava cared so much more than she would ever let on.

The only thing was, Zach couldn't figure out why she needed to hide anymore.

Ava was almost done rebandaging her arm by the time Zach limped back downstairs, the receiving end of the kid monitor in hand.

She was looking better after some water and clean bandages.

"You did a good job of this," she said, motioning to

her arm and the discarded pile of cloth. "Sorry about your shirt."

"I was worried it might be too tight," he said.

Ava shook her head. "It can never be too tight in a situation like this. More importantly, how's your leg?"

"I have no idea," Zach said, suddenly looking exhausted as he flopped into a chair. "I'm sure I'll live."

"After everything that leg has been through, we should check on the wound closure bandage."

Zach nodded and pulled his pants off, a sheepish look crossing his face. "I kind of hoped it would be different circumstances the first time I took my pants off in front of you," he said.

Ava let the corner of her mouth curl up in a half smile. "Me too."

But she went to work, not wanting to drag out a moment of Zach's pain longer than she had to.

"You should go into town for proper stitches tomorrow," she said, "but for now, this bandage is actually holding."

"Yeah okay," he said.

"And get some sleep," she told him, as she got up from her chair.

"Oh, um…right. Sleep. That's a thing," Zach said, his thoughts jumping all over the place.

He thought…hoped she might stay. It didn't seem right that they would, what? Just go their separate ways after everything? And yeah, maybe things had gotten intense between the two of them, but maybe he was reading too much into everything. Zach suddenly felt like a fool. He realized he'd built up everything in his head to be bigger than it was. They'd really only shared two kisses, after all, and had barely discussed what they even meant.

But she was his best friend, and two passionate kisses had to mean something.

Still, he supposed they could figure it all out tomorrow. He was pretty damn exhausted too.

She headed to the door, and on the porch, she turned back to Zach. "I'll see you tomorrow," she said, kissed him on the cheek and headed toward her house.

Chapter 21

Ava was not going to see Zach tomorrow. She wouldn't see him tomorrow, or on any other day in the near future.

Justin was still out there somewhere, and the only thing she could do now was run. He wouldn't have a way to inform her if he tried to go after Zach or Chloe again, no way to use them as leverage if she could get far enough, fast enough. He would leave them alone and come after her.

But it was going to be the hardest thing she'd ever done. Leaving them.

A tear rolled down her cheek as she climbed the steps to her front door and slipped inside, needing to gather a few things before she left Ambrosia Falls forever.

In less than half an hour, Ava was ready to go.

She took one last look around her house. It had been such a good house, everything she needed in a time where her whole world was imploding, and it had built her back up. Gave her back her life. No, gave her a brand-new life so much better than the one before, and damn it, she was going to miss the place. Which was a new feeling for her. She couldn't remember ever being attached to a place, not even as a kid. But this house, and Ambrosia Falls in general, were special places.

She could only hope the next people to live here would appreciate it as much as she did. She hoped they'd be nice. Zach and Chloe deserved to have great neighbors.

Ava flipped her living room light off for the last time, then turned to head out the door, jolting as she saw the dark figure in the open doorway. At first, it didn't compute. How had someone gotten the door open so quietly? But then she realized she'd left it unlocked. Even with all that was going on, she was slipping. So used to not having to lock her doors in the quiet little town, she'd done the same thing again, purely out of habit.

Cursing herself in her head, she readied to bolt in the other direction, when the figure spoke.

"You're leaving?"

They were just two little words, but they were filled with more emotion than Ava had ever heard in such a short phrase. Anger, confusion, disbelief, but most of all hurt. If a broken heart could stand up and talk, those two words were exactly what it might sound like.

"Zach," Ava whispered, unsure how to answer.

He stepped farther into the house, a stream of moonlight falling onto his face. In one hand he held the little walkie-talkie-like receiver from the baby monitor, which almost made Ava smile, and in the other hand he held...a letter?

Oh no.

"I was about to head to bed when I remembered. I'd been so caught up with Chloe missing and everything, I didn't have a chance to stop and wonder what the heck you were doing at my mailbox."

Ava swallowed, knowing she'd been exposed. That letter was supposed to be for later. For when she was gone.

"But then I was in the shower, and I remembered. You know, the way you always remember things when your mind finally has a chance to slow down and not think for a second, and then everything you missed during the day comes tumbling back at you?"

Ava nodded slowly. Her mind was whirling, panicked, dumbfounded. This wasn't the way things were supposed to go.

"I remembered a little flutter of a thought that something was weird about you standing out by my mailbox. There's nothing out there to see. Nothing to do. Just a mailbox." He held up the letter. "This is you leaving, isn't it?" he said, the crack in his voice giving away more than his face even, in the near darkness.

"I'm sorry," was all Ava could say, the words coming out in a whisper, and tears filled her eyes.

"You don't have to leave, Ava. You can't leave, not after this," he said, the letter shaking a little.

"I have to," Ava said, trying to pull her shoulders back, trying to show she was serious. The only problem was all her body wanted to do was break down into a heap on the floor and sob.

"You don't have to, Ava," Zach said. "You could stay here. We could figure this out together."

She shook her head. "We can't, Zach. It's too dangerous."

And that's when Zach held the letter in both his hands and held it closer to his face to read through the dim light. "'I've been madly, head over heels in love with you for years. Maybe since the moment I first laid eyes on you.'" He looked into her eyes then. "It's like you took the words right out of my head. This is all exactly how

I feel. And now, after everything, I don't know how I could bear to lose my best friend. But I don't know how I could bear to lose the love of my life too."

"I know," Ava managed to say. "But this is the only way. Maybe someday but…"

She picked up the bag she'd packed and tried to push past him, but Zach put his hand out to stop her.

"Let me go, Zach. It's the only way to save the two of you," she said, pulling out of his gentle grip and spinning around toward the door.

And was immediately blocked by a very large, very solid body.

An arm attached to said body reached up, and Ava readied herself for another fight, not knowing how much she had left in her to do so. But the arm kept reaching, not in her direction, but toward…the wall?

The lights flicked on, and Ava was momentarily blinded, blinking, wholly discombobulated. And then her vision adapted, and a familiar face came into view.

Zach didn't know who the hell this guy was, but he swore he would take him out if he laid one finger on Ava. He hadn't known he had it in him, but all the violence of the night seemed to be simmering right on the surface, and Zach was ready to punch the bushy, gray handlebar mustache right off the guy if he had to.

"George?" Ava said, confusion heavy in her eyes.

"Hey guys, am I interrupting something?" the older man said, with an expression on his face that was not at all subtle about the amusement he was getting out of the situation.

"George? What the hell are you doing here?" Ava

asked, looking like she was readying to punch him in the shoulder for scaring her like that.

The man—George—sauntered in without a care in the world and quietly shut the door before he sat on the couch, taking up more space than seemed possible on the large sofa.

"Well," George said, "I wanted to let you know we got him."

"What are you talking about?"

"We got the Crow."

What the hell was that supposed to mean, Zach wondered, but to be frank, George was kind of an intimidating man, and Zach didn't particularly think interrupting him was the best idea.

"What?" Ava asked, as if it were impossible to believe what George was saying. She moved to a chair near George and sat. "How are you even here?" She shook her head a little, as if trying to clear it.

"Well, it's a bit of a long story, and it kind of looks like you were getting ready to leave, so maybe I should leave it for another time."

The guy was starting to remind Zach of his annoying uncle Arthur, who loved the sound of his own voice and dragged his stories out just to get another few seconds of attention.

"George!" Ava said.

And that was all it took. George chuckled a little, but finally started explaining. "I have an old army buddy who's helped me out quite a bit over the years. In fact, he helped me set you up here in this charming little town."

Ava's eyebrows knit together in the most adorable way, as Zach moved to sit. He tried to be discreet about it, but hobbling around mostly on one leg tended to draw attention.

When everyone was settled, George went on. "I think you all may have had a run in or two with him."

Ava's eyes alighted with understanding. "The cop."

George nodded admiringly. "Officer Banyan, to be exact. He and I have kept in touch with one another all these years. In fact, he's been keeping an eye on you." He turned to Ava, his eyes twinkling.

"Is he okay?" Zach interrupted. "The last time I saw him, he looked kind of...dead."

"Luckily, not quite," George said. "When I didn't hear from him when I was supposed to, I got the hell out here and tracked his phone. Lost the signal a little way away from the acreage, but I eventually got to him. He was pretty loopy, but I called the ambulance out to that nice acreage in the forest and they're getting him right as rain. He's at the hospital now."

"Holy shit," Ava said. "And Justin?"

"Told ya," George said. "We got him."

Wait. The Crow is Justin? Realization flooded over Zach. "And you're Sparrow," he said, remembering what Chloe had repeated from her captor.

"Yes," Ava said absently, apparently still trying to wrap her head around everything. "So, it's over?"

"It's over," George said, putting his hand on her knee like a father might. "It's really over this time. They've got Justin in custody. I still don't know who he's working for, and we don't want to risk revealing your real identity, or the fact that Zach here," George continued, turning to acknowledge Zach, "and Chloe are involved, so the state authorities have agreed to work with us to keep all that quiet. But the charges of break and enter out at the acreage, as well as the attempted murder of Officer Banyan, should keep him behind bars for a very long time."

Ava opened her mouth to say something, but nothing came out. She shook her head again as if she still couldn't believe it.

Hope was building inside of Zach, but he was scared to say anything, afraid he might jinx…well, everything.

"Well," George said, clapping his hands together, almost as if washing them clean of the whole ordeal, "I'd better get over to the station. Make sure everything goes smoothly."

George bent down and kissed Ava on the top of the head. "See ya around, kid," he said, then turned to Zach and held his hand out.

Zach stood—after a bit of a struggle—and shook it. "Nice to meet you, sir," he said.

"Likewise," George said, with a nod of his head.

And with that, George sauntered away like he hadn't just delivered the kind of news that changed lives forever.

"What the hell was that?" Zach asked.

Ava blinked. "I think," she began, the words tentative. "I think it was George giving me my life back. Again."

"What do you mean 'again'?"

"He was the one who saved me from Justin the first time. Five years ago. I'd sent him a text, and he got to me, somehow found the strength to pull me out of a burning inferno."

"Jesus," Zach said, shaking his head at the idea Ava might have been through worse than any of them had gone through that day. "I'm sorry."

Ava shrugged. "But in the end, it brought me here."

Zach couldn't hold back any longer from asking the question his mind had been quite distractedly screaming at him for the past ten minutes. "So does this mean you can stay?"

Ava seemed to be thinking about it as he held his breath. He didn't know if he could take another letdown tonight. Or for the next half century or so.

"I think," she said, pausing once more to give it a final mulling. "I think I can," she told him, her eyes widening in delight like a kid at a carnival.

Zach finally saw the thing he now knew he'd been wishing for, for years. An understanding surging between them that the time for questioning was past, and in its place, a realization that they belonged to each other. He went to her, his leg not quite letting him forget he was hurt, but since his entire life had been stolen away and then given back to him in a matter of hours, he was not about to waste even a single second more.

Chapter 22

Zach knelt on his good leg in front of Ava's chair and leaned up for a kiss, and what else could Ava do but meet him halfway, her heart thrumming, her skin humming, and everything inside her tingling.

The kiss was slow, and maybe even a little questioning still, each of them asking, *are you sure?* Of course, neither of them had ever been so sure of anything in their lives.

Ava slipped her hands under the edge of his T-shirt and lifted it over his head, holding his gaze, trying not to wince at the pain zipping through her arm. Concern filled Zach's eyes and Ava hated that she was stopping the moment of intimacy, but his focus only turned to her injured arm, holding it so gently, so lovingly, then softly wisping the lightest of kisses along it.

The carefulness, the tenderness should have brought forth thoughts of sweetness. But knowing that this man, this beautiful, good, courageous man cared for her so wholly—cherished her—made it, oddly, the most seductive moment she'd ever known. Each almost imperceptible brush of his lips triggered sensations that hadn't been roused in years.

Maybe it was relief knowing the moment that had been building for years, maybe even from the first time she saw him that night on her front porch, beer in hand, and each moment after, had finally led them to meaning everything to each other. First as best friends and now to this…to their very own forever. Forever was not a concept Ava had allowed herself to think about, and even now it scared her, but as Zach made his way up her arm with his kisses, over her shoulder and to her neck, thoughts started to retract, becoming far away and unimportant.

Zach found her lips again just as he found the hem of her shirt, pulling it up and pausing for breath as he maneuvered her good arm out of it, then over her head, so careful when he slid it over the bandage on her other arm. He flung the shirt gently to the couch and turned back to her, just looking at her for a moment.

"Hey," he said, his voice husky and ragged.

"Hey," she said back, smiling and wholly content.

Over the years they'd built this thing where they checked in with each other, brought each other back to the moment when things started to get a little too stressful, a little too overwhelming, a little too…well, grumpy on Zach's end. Ava knew this was what they were doing now. Checking in. Coming back to the moment. Connecting.

All this time she'd been so afraid to lose Zach, but she realized it wasn't just Zach the man, it was their relationship. It was the reason they had never gone down this path before, the fear that things would change.

The moment lasted only a second before their lips met again, but it shoved away all the uncertainty and solidified that they were still going to be them—best friends. And now, obviously more, but still them. Ava felt something heavy lift from her.

Suddenly, she was so alive, so hungry for this man she loved more than she'd loved anything in her life, her hands exploring, moving across his skin. His lips drowning her in a desperate kiss before moving downward, kissing his way along as his hand fumbled behind to release her bra, his lips finding her breast, ravenously taking it into his mouth. Every nerve came alive, pulsing, thirsting for more. She couldn't get enough as he moved to the other side, his strong hands tight around her as he grazed, licked, and, in Ava's admittedly biased opinion, unabashedly thrilled his audience of one, her breath coming in gasps.

She fumbled for his button, his zipper, excruciatingly difficult with only one good hand and a need so urgent she thought she might die if she didn't get to him.

"Let me help," Zach said, grinning and regrettably moving away from her, leaning heavy on the arm of the chair as he mostly used only his good leg to stand.

What a pair they were, Ava thought, though she had to admit, she was absolutely going to enjoy this show while it lasted. Once balanced on one leg, Zach gingerly peeled his jeans partway down, the bandage stark white against his skin, though that was decidedly not where her attention landed given the rather impressive arousal situation going on.

He stopped halfway through the removing of his pants and Ava turned her attention back to his face, which was looking a bit more sheepish than you'd expect someone to be in that situation.

"What?" Ava asked, concern rising.

"I, uh, kinda need to sit down for this part," he said, kind of shrugging and hobbling over to the couch, flopping heavily and struggling to free himself of the particularly difficult and maddening jeans.

Ava tilted her head, a smile spreading across her face. "Works for me," she said, standing.

As she stood, she imagined she'd strip in an erotic, seductive way, but with her injured arm, she struggled with her own jeans, the button difficult but not impossible with the use of one good hand, then the actual removal of them being a kind of wriggling, hopping affair.

Sexy it was not, but at least they were both finally free of all obstacles.

"Quite a pair we make," Zach said, with a little chuckle.

Ava moved slowly toward him, gloriously exposed and feeling pretty damn sultry again all of a sudden. She moved close, pausing to allow him a good, long look, his eyes alight with appreciation, before she spoke. "The best pair, in my opinion," she said.

Zach smiled. "One might even say a perfect pair," he said, as he reached up for her, pulling her toward him.

Ava straddled her legs around his, careful of his injury, their lips meeting—urgently now, desperate to achieve their full pairing. As he lifted her and she slid onto him, she cried out in the relief of someone who'd waited and wanted for way too long.

Zach leaned his head back and closed his eyes, releasing a slow breath ending in a low groan like he'd been waiting just as long for this kind of relief. But there was so much more relief to be had as Ava began to move, slowly at first, then quickening as he rose to meet her in a rhythm so natural it was like they were made for each other. Zach found her breast with his mouth again and it was like a string that ran straight through her was pulled taut, the pressure building to unsustainable levels, and then he began to suck, ever so gently. Ava nearly whimpered with need, and as he thrust to meet that need, he sucked harder, the string stretching to the point of no return, and then finally, gloriously breaking as she erupted with a cry that sent Zach reeling over the edge too, surging to his own climax with a sexy, primal roar of a sound as he held her tight—protective, loving, like he was never letting her go.

And she hoped to hell he never would.

Epilogue

They decided a car accident was the best way to explain Zach's limp, Ava's messed-up arm, and the fact that Zach was missing a truck. Officer Banyan had been true to his word, only reporting what was necessary to put Justin in prison and keep him there for a very long while.

Ava and Zach made their debut as a couple two days later by taking a slow walk, hand in hand up Main Street, right through all the people from town who were packing up their booths and tents, the air filled with scents of a crisp fall breeze, some remnants of apple-scented goodies and a touch of sadness that it was all over for another year.

Everyone turned to stare, but not one gaze in the crowd had even the slightest hint of surprise. In fact, as the pair approached, there was more than one murmur of the word *finally* and quite a few knowing glances and approving nods.

When they reached The Other Apple Store, Maureen was waiting for them on the stoop.

"Thank you so much for keeping the place going," Ava said, as she hugged her friend.

"Of course," Maureen said. "We were so worried when you didn't show the other morning, but I figured the least I could do was man the store for a day. When we heard about the accident, I nearly fainted. I'm so sorry I didn't come looking for you or send help or something."

Even though they were bombarded with questions, Ava and Zach kept their answers to the onslaught of questions as vague as possible. Decided to go for a hike. Truck ran off the road. Took them a while to get help and make it back.

Keep it simple and boring, so fewer questions would be asked.

"What you did was exactly what I needed," Ava said, hugging her one more time.

"Well, would you look at that," Barney said, stopping his packing to raise a hand over his eyes to block the sun.

Someone let out a low whistle from a few stalls down and Miss Clara gasped. "Captain Applebottom!" she yelled, as she started running toward her prized chicken. "You've come back to me!"

Sure enough, as Ava gazed up the street, Captain Applebottom was strolling back on into town as if he didn't have a care in the world—safe, sound and pecking at the ground every few steps.

"Guess the little guy wasn't too keen on being the town's damn mascot," Zach said, eyes twinkling with newfound respect. "Now that is one smart bird."

And as Miss Clara scooped Captain Applebottom into her arms, the town resumed its packing.

So many people she'd come to know and love over

the years—Barney, who was already on Miss Clara's case for letting Captain Applebottom get loose in the first place, Donna Mae from the antique store, Jackson packing up his hardware sale, Annie, who was helping some of the others since her knitting had been washed out in the water tower incident, and so many others. People she tried not to let into her heart but who had wriggled their way in anyway.

She felt a warm hand take hers. Zach. The only best friend she'd ever had, and from across the street, Chloe running toward them, clearly with a plan on her mind.

"Can we get one last apple-cinnamon ice cream?" she asked Zach.

"Who? You and me?" Zach asked.

Chloe rolled her eyes. "Obviously not," she said. "Me and Emma. We want something for the walk to the park."

Zach chuckled and dug into his pocket for some money as Ava took a good, long look at her town.

At all the people milling around doing their thing, at Zach, who looked as content as she'd ever seen him, at Chloe rushing back toward Emma, and she realized, for the first time since she'd arrived in Ambrosia Falls, there was absolutely nothing hanging over her head. Nothing stopping her from letting the whole town fill her up. Nothing in the way of enjoying each single mundane, everyday moment. Nothing that could ever force her to leave.

Zach pulled her hand back into his like that was its new home now. "Well, thank goodness that's over," he said, in his signature grumpy way.

For all the quirks of the town and the people in it,

Ava realized with a grin, there was not a single thing she would change.

"Yup," she said, a smile spreading across her face. "And I absolutely can't wait till next year."

* * * * *

Romantic Suspense

Danger. Passion. Drama.

Available Next Month

Colton's Secret Past Kacy Cross
Protector In Disguise Veronica Forand

....

Her Sister's Murder Tara Taylor Quinn
Cameron Mountain Refuge Beth Cornelison

....

LOVE INSPIRED

Tracing A Killer Sharon Dunn
Montana Hidden Deception Amity Steffen

Larger Print

....

LOVE INSPIRED

K-9 Ranch Protection Darlene L. Turner
Guarded By The Marshal Sharee Stover

Larger Print

....

LOVE INSPIRED

Deadly Secrets Cathy McDavid
Texas Revenge Target Jill Elizabeth Nelson

Larger Print

6 brand new stories each month

Romantic Suspense

Danger. Passion. Drama.

MILLS & BOON

Keep reading for an excerpt of a new title
from the Intrigue series,
BOUNTY HUNTED by Barb Han

Chapter One

Crystal Remington repositioned her black Stetson, lowering the rim, after she opened the door of the Dime a Dozen Café off I-45. She scanned the small restaurant for Wade Brewer. At six feet, four inches of solid muscle, the thirty-three-year-old former Army sergeant shouldn't be too difficult to locate against the backdrop of truckers and road-tripping families.

In the back left corner, Mr. Brewer sat with his back against the wall. His position gave him an open view of the room. As a US marshal and someone who was used to memorizing exits, Crystal appreciated the move. At his vantage point, no one would have an opportunity to sneak up on him from the side or behind.

He glanced up and then locked onto her, not bothering to motion for her to come sit down. In fact, he looked downright put out by her presence. What the hell?

Tight chestnut-brown-colored hair clipped close to a near-perfect head and a serious face with hard angles and planes, she didn't need to look at a picture to verify her witness's identity. This was the man she was scheduled to meet. After deciding she wasn't a threat, he leaned forward over the table and nursed a cup of coffee as she walked over to join him.

He picked up a sugar packet and twisted it around his

fingers. "Marshal Remington, I'm guessing." Most would consider him physically intimidating, but she'd grown up around a brother and a pair of cousins similar in size, so it didn't faze her.

"That would make you Wade Brewer." Crystal sat down, then signaled for the waitress before refocusing on Brewer. Even with facial scars from an explosion during his time in the service, the man was still beautiful. "Ready for the check so we can get out of this fishbowl and I can get you to a safe place?"

"Do I look like I need your help?" he shot back with daggers coming from his eyes. She wasn't touching that question. "Remind me why I agreed to this when I'm fully capable of taking care of myself?"

Crystal waved off the smiling waitress who was unaware of the tension at the table. And then she turned all her attention to her witness. "First of all, two of the people I love most in this world are lying in hospital beds fighting for their lives while I'm sitting here with you, so have a little respect."

Brewer didn't flinch. Instead, the most intense pair of steel-gray eyes studied her. The unexplained fear that he might pull something like this had been eating at her since she'd learned about his background. Tough guys like him generally didn't go around asking others for help. They handled life on their own terms and, generally speaking, did a bang-up job of it. She'd dismissed her worry as paranoia. Then there was the fact of her grandparents' serious car accident that had been weighing heavily on her mind. Didn't bad events usually occur in threes? If that was the case and her witness decided to bolt, she had one more to go. Lucky her. "Now that we have that fact out of the way, you are the key to locking away a major criminal who—"

"Is currently in jail," he interrupted without looking away from the rim of his cup.

From here on out, Wade was Brewer to Crystal just like everyone else she referred to. Using last names was a way to keep a distance from people. First names were too personal.

"And has a very long reach on the outside with two lieutenants and more foot soldiers ready to kill on command than you can count on both hands." She needed to get him out of this café and on the road to Dallas if they were going to get there in time to pick up the key to the town house tonight. "Why are we talking about this? I thought this issue had already been decided. It was my understanding that you agreed to enter into my protective custody. Has something changed that I haven't been informed of since six a.m.?"

"I've had time to sit here and think." Brewer took a sip of black coffee, unfazed by the emotions building inside her and emanating from her in palpable waves. "Maybe it's time to change my mind."

"Why is that, Mr. Brewer? What possible thought could you have had that would cause you to do an about-face right now?" If he said the reason had to do with her being a woman, she might scream. She'd come across perps who'd believed they could outrun or outshoot her due to her having two X chromosomes. They'd been wrong. If that was the case with Brewer, she could assure him that she was just as capable as any man to do the job or she wouldn't be here in the first place. Brewer didn't give her an indication this was the issue, but she'd come up against this particular prejudice a few too many times in the past and it always set her off.

To his credit, Brewer didn't look her up and down. Instead, he stared into his cup. "It's simple. I'll be able to stay on the move a lot easier if I'm alone. Being on the move doesn't make me a sitting duck."

"I can offer a stable safe house, Mr. Brewer."

The look he gave said he wasn't buying it. "You have no guarantees." Didn't he really mean to say she wasn't strong enough to cover him if push came to shove?

"Not one witness to date has died while following the guidelines under the protection of a US marshal," she pointed out. "I can't say the same for folks who decided they could do it themselves." She folded her arms across her chest and sat back in her chair. "Our track record speaks for itself."

Brewer didn't seem one bit impressed. The terms *dark* and *brooding* came to mind when describing him.

She needed to take another tack, offer a softer approach. "First of all, I want to thank you for your service to this country." She meant every word. "And I realize your training provides a unique skill set that most who come under my protection don't possess." Pausing for effect would give him a few seconds to process the compliment and, maybe, soften him up a little. "I have no doubt you were very good at your job, Sergeant. But make no mistake about it—my training is suited to this task. And I'm damn good at my job. If you have any doubts, feel free to contact my supervisor or any of the other marshals I've worked with over the years. This isn't my first rodeo."

He dismissed her with a wave of his hand, which infuriated her.

Taking a calming breath, she started again. "If the fact

I'm a woman bothers you, say so upfront and let's get it out of the way."

His face twisted in disgust. "I've served alongside a few of the most talented soldiers in the Army, who happened to wear bras. The fact you do has no bearing on my decision whether or not to strike out on my own."

Embarrassed, heat crawled up her neck, pooling at her cheeks. She cleared her throat, determined not to let this assignment go south. "You have no reason to trust me other than the badge I wear. You don't know me from Adam. I get that. Not to mention your military record is impeccable. If we were at war, you'd be the first person I turned to. This situation is stateside, and you have no authority here."

"I have a right to defend myself," he countered.

"Same as every citizen," she pointed out. No doubt he packed his own weapons, not that he needed a license to carry any longer. Scooting her chair closer to the table, she leaned in and lowered her voice. "Did you take care of your aunt?"

"Yes, ma'am. She has been relocated to a secure location," he said. Taking care of his elderly aunt had been his first priority after Victor Crane had been taken into custody and was the reason they were meeting north of Houston, his home city. "Without your help, by the way."

"Fair enough." Crystal could see she was losing him. Was it time to cut bait? Leave him on his own? The way she saw it, there wasn't much choice. His mind seemed made up. Then again, there was no harm in trying. She'd throw out a Hail Mary anyway and see if it worked. "At least make the drive to Dallas with me. Consider changing your mind about protective custody. What's the worst that can happen?"

He flashed eyes at her.

She put a hand up to stop him from commenting. "How about we get inside my vehicle and you can consider your options on the highway heading north?" she said. "You change your mind, I'll personally drop you off anywhere you request. No questions asked."

Brewer gave her a dressing down with his steel gaze. If he was testing her, she had no intention of backing down.

With the casual effort of a Sunday-morning stroll, he shifted gears, picked up his mug and drained the contents. After reaching into his front pocket and peeling off a twenty, he slapped it onto the table, shouldered his military-issue backpack, then stood. "Let's go."

A celebration was premature. Crystal stood up, turned around, and walked out of the diner, keeping an eye out to make sure no one seemed interested in what they were doing. She didn't like meeting this close to Galveston, Brewer's childhood home, or Houston, where he currently resided. Victor Crane would no doubt have someone on his or her way down to make certain Brewer couldn't testify. With a pair of loyal lieutenants, Crane wouldn't even have to make the call himself if Brewer's name got out as a witness. He'd been Crane's driver, so the odds of that happening were high now that Brewer had disappeared.

He followed her to her government-issue white sedan parked closest to the door without taking up an accessible parking spot. She half expected him to keep walking right on past and was pleasantly surprised when he stopped at the passenger door.

It was too early to be excited. She'd given him the out to change his mind anytime during the ride to Dallas in order to convince him to get into the car.

"I should probably hit the men's room before we continue north," he said, breaking into her small moment of victory like rain on parade day.

"All right." On a sharp sigh, Crystal took the driver's seat, figuring it was a toss-up at this point as to whether or not he would return. She tapped her thumb on the steering wheel after turning on the engine as Brewer headed inside the restaurant. What was he going to do? Sneak out the bathroom window to throw her off the trail for a few minutes? Were negotiations over? His mind made up?

She'd give him five minutes before she gave up and called it in.

BREWER CONTEMPLATED DITCHING the marshal for two seconds in the bathroom. Getting far away from Galveston and Houston was a good idea. Dallas? Was it his best move? He'd only been out of the military for six months now and hadn't come home to a warm welcome in his former hometown other than his aunt despite his service to his country.

In all honesty, he'd brought the town's reaction on himself. He'd barely graduated high school due to the number of fistfights he'd been in. He'd worked two jobs to help provide for his elderly aunt, who was technically his great-aunt, which had tanked his grades. He could have been more focused in school, except that he'd hated every minute of sitting in class. Before he'd shot up in height, he'd been bullied. And then, he'd gotten angry. The football coach, in an attempt to court him, had given Brewer permission to use the weight room before school, which he'd done religiously to bulk up and then use his newfound muscles to punish. By junior year, he'd taken issue with anyone who'd looked sideways at him and had the power to back it up.

And he'd done just that a few too many times for the principal's liking and pretty much everyone else in town whose kid he'd beaten up.

The military had given him a purpose and an outlet for all his anger, not to mention a target to focus on. He'd gone from hating the world and blaming everyone for his hard-luck upbringing to being able to set it all aside and compartmentalize his emotions. His childhood had had all the usual trappings that came with a drunk for a father who apparently couldn't stand the sight of his own child. As for his mother, she'd been a saint to him until she'd up and disappeared. The Houdini act had made Daniel Brewer hate his son even more. The man could rot in hell for all Brewer cared after what he'd ultimately done. As far as his mother went…what kind of person left a five-year-old behind to live with a drunk? Her sainthood had been short-lived as far as he was concerned. It had died along with all his love for her.

Brewer fished his burner cell out of his pocket. He fired off a text to his buddy to say this was him on a new number and to pick up. Then, Brewer put the phone to his left ear and made a call. The burner phone was new since he'd turned his old one over to the US Marshals Service for safekeeping. It was too late to regret the move now.

His buddy picked up on the second ring. "Trent, hey, it's me."

"Dude, I tried to call you." Trent Thomas breathed heavy like he was in the middle of a run. "What happened to your phone?"

"I borrowed this one." He hoped Trent wouldn't ask any more questions. They'd been military buddies early on in Brewer's career, Trent having been the closest thing to a friend in basic training when they'd both had their backsides handed to them.

A disgruntled grunt came through the line. "I had no idea what that bastard was really up to, Brew."

"Figured you didn't," Brewer reassured his buddy. The two had gone to the same middle school, high school, and boot camp. They hadn't really gotten to know each other until the latter. They forked in different directions after basic.

Then Trent had been a godsend when Brewer had medically boarded out of the Army. He'd been the first to make calls to find work for Brewer, work that had given him a reason to keep going after his life-changing injury. And now the job put his life in jeopardy. There was no way Trent could have known Crane wasn't the head of a legitimate company as they'd been told. Brewer's buddy would never do that to him.

"I feel like a real jerk for putting you in that position, dude. Especially after what you've been through and all."

"Don't sweat it," Brewer reassured. "Besides, this'll all be over in two shakes, and I'll be on the hunt for a new job."

"What can I do to help?"

He knew Trent would come through. "I need a place to hide out for a few days until I can figure out my next move. Somewhere off the grid, if you know what I mean."

The line went quiet for a few seconds that felt like minutes as Brewer turned on the spigot to wash his hands.

"I can help with that, Brew. No problem." He rattled off coordinates that Brewer entered into his cell after telling his friend to hold so he could dry his hands.

"I'll owe you big-time for this, Trent."

"Consider it payback for the position I put you in," Trent

said with a voice heavy with remorse. He wasn't normally an emotional guy, so the intensity registered as odd.

After what he'd been through in the past twenty-four hours that had led him to standing in front of a bathroom mirror in a roadside café made him more than ready to get off the grid, where he could catch his meals and cook his own food. Civilization wasn't as civilized as he'd wanted it to be.

"I'll be in touch when I can." He ended the call on the off chance someone was listening. Freedom was near. All he had to do was ditch the marshal sitting in the parking lot and get on the road.

After entering the coordinates into his map feature, he smiled. This place was so remote, all that showed on the screen was a patch of trees. Near the Texas-Louisiana border close to Tyler, he could easily see himself getting lost and finally finding some peace until time to go to trial.

So why was his first thought that he didn't want to disappoint the blue-eyed, ponytail-wearing marshal sitting out front?

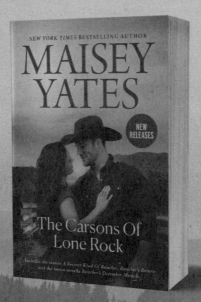

Subscribe and fall in love with a Mills & Boon series today!

You'll be among the first to read stories delivered to your door monthly and enjoy great savings.

WE SIMPLY LOVE ROMANCE

MILLS & BOON